Prima

'Smart, witty writing'

Elle

'Utterly riveting'
Closer

'An emotional – but ultimately uplifting – read'
Woman's Weekly

'A well-drawn story of love, empathy and friendship'
Candis

'An accomplished and gifted writer'
Yorkshire Evening Post

'Heart-warming and inspiring – a great read!'
Katie Fforde

'Warm, well-written, thought-provoking – reminds us
of the power we have to effect change in the world'
Dorothy Koomson

'Heart-rending and packed with emotion –
a thought-provoking read'
Rosanna Ley

'Such a beautiful, careful, thoughtful,
gorgeously observed story'
Louise Beech

'Linda Green gets better and better . . . we're in the hands of an expert'
Jo Spain

'Linda Green is bloody brilliant!'
Amanda Prowse

'A real page turner'
Isabelle Grey

'Authentic, absorbing and unputdownable'
Louise Jensen

'A tale of love, loss and sacrifice'
Milly Johnson

'Enjoyable, original and intriguing'
B. A. Paris

'Inspiring and moving – gets my vote!'
Kate Long

'Heart-warming and original . . . will leave you full of hope'
Vanessa Greene

Linda Green is the bestselling author of ten novels, which have sold more than a million copies between them. Her latest novel, *One Moment*, was a Radio 2 Book Club selection, and her previous novel, *The Last Thing She Told Me*, was a Richard & Judy Book Club pick and a Top 20 *Sunday Times* bestseller. She lives in West Yorkshire with her husband and son.

the marriage mender

LINDA GREEN

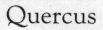

First published in the UK in 2014 by Quercus Editions Ltd
This paperback edition first published in 2021 by

Quercus Editions Ltd
Carmelite House
50 Victoria Embankment
London EC4Y 0DZ

An Hachette UK company

A CIP catalogue record for this book is available
from the British Library

PB ISBN 978 1 52941 672 5
EB ISBN 978 1 78087 526 2

10 9 8 7 6 5 4 3 2 1

Typeset by CC Book Production
Printed and bound in Great Britain by Clays Ltd, Elcograf S.p.A.

For Ian and Rohan

'Mr and Mrs Bentley?'

The woman's voice was regulation soft and soothing. I looked up. She had a sympathetic face too. And comforting strands of grey running through her long brown hair.

'Yes,' I said, standing up.

'I'm Polly. Please do come through.' She gestured towards the open door.

I glanced across at Chris. To a neutral observer his face gave nothing away. But I knew him better than that. Could see the fear in his eyes. Smell it on him, even.

'It'll be OK,' I whispered as I walked past him.

He nodded. Almost imperceptibly.

We went through into a large, airy room with sash windows and beige curtains which were frayed at the edges. Two Ikea-type chairs were positioned facing the windows, an occasional table in between with a strategically placed box of tissues, a jug of water and two glasses.

Polly shut the door behind us and offered her hand and a thin smile. Not thin in a bad way. Just suitably thin for someone who has never met you before and is about to splice you open and perform open-heart surgery.

'Pleased to meet you both,' she said as we shook hands in turn. 'Do take a seat and we can get started.'

I sat down on the chair furthest away. Chris took the other one. He crossed and uncrossed his legs, fiddled with the strap on his watch. The one I'd given him for his fortieth birthday.

Polly launched into the formalities. She spoke calmly and clearly, explaining that this was an initial assessment and we'd then be matched with a counsellor to suit our needs. It was textbook stuff. But I refrained from telling her so.

'Now, let me just have a quick look through these forms,' she said, nodding intermittently as she did so.

'So, you're a photographer,' she said to Chris. 'What sort of pictures do you take?'

'Good ones, hopefully,' he replied, managing a hint of a smile. 'Landscapes when I can, family portraits and other stuff to pay the mortgage.'

'And you have one son from a previous relationship. How old is he?'

Chris looked down at his feet. I saw him swallow hard. No words were forthcoming.

'Sixteen,' I said. 'Josh is sixteen.'

Polly nodded. 'And does he live with you?'

We both hesitated this time. I didn't even dare to look across at Chris.

'Yes,' I said eventually. 'Although not at the moment.'

Polly nodded again and wrote something down. Perhaps sensing that it wouldn't be wise to probe any further at this stage.

'And you've got a daughter together. How old is she?'

'Nine,' I replied. 'Her name's Matilda.'

Polly smiled and nodded. I wanted to say that she was named after the Roald Dahl character. That Chris always called her 'Tilda' but I never did. I didn't say anything, though. In case Chris thought I was getting at him.

Polly turned to my form. It was only a matter of time before she found out now. I waited, watching her face for the sign. To be fair, she didn't even flinch.

'Ah, Alison, I see you're a counsellor yourself. What sort of areas do you cover?'

I hesitated. Aware how utterly ridiculous it was going to sound. I thought of what Matilda always said when people asked what her mother did. She called me a 'marriage mender'. Said I kept people's mummies and daddies together when they were arguing a lot. My stomach tightened as I wondered what on earth she would think if she could see her marriage-mender mummy right now.

'Relationships,' I said to Polly, trying to keep my voice as low and even as possible. 'I'm a relationship counsellor.'

The silence hung heavily in the air. Chris put his head in his hands.

I smiled weakly. 'It is rather ridiculous, isn't it?'

'Not at all,' said Polly. 'I'm divorced. I'd say that's more ridiculous.' She smiled at me.

I smiled back, grateful for her efforts to put me at ease.

'As I'm sure you're aware,' she continued, 'I do need to have some understanding of the situation and why you're here, in order to place you with an appropriate counsellor.

For example, I need to know if there are any sexual problems in your relationship?'

Chris smiled slightly and shook his head. He was thinking of that eighties sitcom – *Dear John*, was it? – the one where the counsellor kept asking if he had any sexual problems.

'No,' I said.

On one level that was a lie. Not having sex for more months than I cared to remember was quite obviously a sexual problem. But it was a symptom of the problem, not the cause. Which meant I could get away with it.

'Fine. And how would you describe the issues which have led you to seek counselling?' asked Polly.

She looked at Chris as she said it but he simply continued fiddling with his watch strap. I shifted in my seat, aware he wasn't doing himself any favours. That if it had been me in Polly's chair, I wouldn't exactly be warming to him. I understood he wasn't being deliberately obstructive. That he was simply unable to engage fully in the process when he was so riddled with hurt.

'We've had some family issues,' I said. 'There's been a lot of change. We've been under a great deal of strain.'

Again, I avoided mentioning her name. I didn't want Polly to think badly of Chris. And she would do if I mentioned another woman. You couldn't help it, even if you were trained not to show it.

'I see,' said Polly. 'And how has the strain affected you both? Has it interfered with communication?'

'Yes,' I replied. 'We haven't really been talking properly.'

'Would you say that's fair, Chris?' Polly asked.

Chris looked up. I worried for a second that he was going to stand up and simply walk out of the room. He looked at me. The first time he'd looked at me properly since we'd arrived.

He ran his fingers through his dark curls. Sighed deeply. 'Yeah,' he replied. 'I would.'

'Good,' said Polly. 'And is either of you able to identify how long ago these problems started? When your relationship started to deteriorate?'

It was my turn to look at my feet. To swallow hard. I heard Chris's voice cut through the silence.

'Saturday, September the 29th, last year,' he said.

Polly raised her eyebrows slightly and turned to look at me.

'Yes,' I said. 'It was.'

PART ONE

1

'When is Josh going to get up? He's already missed loads of his birthday. His presents will be going cold.'

Matilda was sitting talking to us at the kitchen table from her Muppet station halfway up the stairs. She had been barred from going upstairs because I knew she wouldn't be able to resist bursting into Josh's room. And it was still only 10 a.m. on Saturday morning, which, to a teenager, was the early hours.

'Well,' I smiled, 'when it's your sixteenth birthday, you can get up at whatever time you like. But I have a feeling you'll be having a lie-in too.'

'I won't. Lie-ins are for losers.'

She made an 'L' sign and pulled a face as she said it. It was the downside of having an eight-year-old and a teenager: they tended to pick up all the things you'd rather they didn't learn until they were at secondary school.

'Why don't you do something instead of sitting there waiting for him, then?' I said. 'That way the time will go faster.'

'Yeah,' said Matilda, sounding genuinely surprised that her mother might be capable of a good idea. 'I think I will.'

She ran downstairs, rummaged in her toy box in the hallway and went back to her position on the stairs with two sock puppets on her hands, which she proceeded to use in the style of laughing hyenas.

'You have to hand it to her,' said Chris, smiling as he looked up from his mug of coffee. 'She is truly skilled in the art of waking someone without being able to be accused of having woken them on purpose.'

'Josh isn't going to be happy,' I said.

'Oh, he'll be fine. He's slept through worse than that. Besides, he's not going to be grumpy for long on his birthday, is he?'

He was right, of course. He tended to be right when it came to Josh. Probably something to do with bringing him up pretty much single-handedly for the first seven years of his life.

'I still can't get my head around him being sixteen,' I said. 'It seems like only yesterday I was reading *Charlie and the Chocolate Factory* to him.'

'I hope not. I hate to break it to you but he can read by himself now.'

I pulled a face at him. 'You know what I mean. It just kind of creeps up on you. The fact that your child has grown up . . .'

I paused for a second. Even now, after all these years, I still worried sometimes about calling him 'my' child. I knew Chris would laugh if I told him. But it was there, all the same.

'I don't know about grown up. I'm not sure lads really grow up until they leave home. I know I didn't.'

'So does that mean you'll be kicking him out if he's still here when he's twenty-one?'

'What do you mean, twenty-one?' asked Chris. 'I'll be changing the locks on his eighteenth birthday.'

I smiled and kissed him on the top of his head as I stood up. We both knew he didn't mean it.

'Anyway,' said Chris, slipping his arms around my waist, 'it won't really make much difference to the level of noise in this house. Somehow I can't imagine Tilda getting quieter as she gets older.'

At that moment the sock puppets embarked on some kind of roaring competition. A few seconds later, I could hear Josh calling out to keep the noise down. That was all it took. She glanced down at us for a nano-second but didn't even wait for an approving nod before rushing to his bedroom.

'Happy birthday, lazybones,' I heard her call out to him. 'You've missed half your birthday and you've got presents downstairs. One of them's a big one and it's not from me, so it might be something good.'

Chris smiled and shook his head. 'Let's hope he thinks so.'

'He'll love it,' I said. 'So quit worrying.'

Josh emerged from his bedroom, with Matilda prodding him from behind towards the banisters, as if she were herding him to market. He was wearing a purple T-shirt and black boxers. He'd once said that if anyone broke into the house in the night he wanted them to know he was an emo. Personally I thought the black walls in his room (which he'd painted himself) would have given it away, but clearly he didn't want to take any chances.

'Morning!' called Chris. 'Welcome to the house of fun.'

The Madness reference may have been lost on Matilda, but Josh managed a bleary-eyed grin.

'Happy birthday, love,' I said. 'What can I get you for breakfast?'

'Nothing for now, thanks. I'm going to grab a shower first.'

'No, you can't,' insisted Matilda. 'If you don't open your presents right away, I'll open them myself and put any stuff I don't want on eBay.'

Josh rolled his eyes. 'God, you make the people on *The Apprentice* look soft, you do.'

He padded downstairs in his bare feet, Matilda still prodding him from behind, and took a seat at the kitchen table. He ran his hand across his hair – you couldn't really say 'through' because it was cropped short to avoid it going curly like his father's. He had the same pale skin as Chris too. Though fortunately that fitted the emo thing better than the curls.

'Woo,' he said, eyeing up the presents on the table.

'Open the big one first,' Matilda said, looking as if she might wet herself if she had to wait any longer.

Josh looked at Chris and back at the large rectangular parcel on the table. Chris had put it in a box to disguise it. He'd also wisely not told Matilda what it was, despite her constant pestering. Keeping secrets was not her forte.

Josh picked it up and tore at the wrapping paper, his enthusiasm getting the better of his cool demeanour for a moment. There was an audible intake of breath as he opened the box.

'It's a guitar!' screamed Matilda. 'They've got you a guitar. Will I get one when I'm sixteen?'

Chris laughed and shook his head. 'You might not want a guitar when you're sixteen.'

'I will,' she said. 'I'll want the same as Josh. Do they do them in shiny colours as well as black? I think I'd like a silver one.'

Josh looked from Chris to me in turn and back again,

apparently still unable to form words. I noticed the sheen on the surface of his eyes.

'I don't know what to say,' he mumbled as he turned to give Chris and me a hug in turn.

'Say "thank you for my guitar",' said Matilda. 'That way you might get something good next year too.'

'It's not any old guitar,' said Josh. 'It's a Fender Squier.'

'Sorry we couldn't run to the real deal,' said Chris.

'Don't be daft. It's well sick,' said Josh. 'Wait till I show Tom.'

'Well, if the two of you do form a band, just make sure you don't call it something stupid,' said Chris.

'Says the man who was the lead guitarist in Pig Swill,' said Josh with a smirk.

'I still think it was a good name,' said Chris. 'Just a shame about our music.'

'You could call your band No Direction,' said Matilda. 'Then people might get it confused with One Direction and buy your CDs by mistake.'

'Thanks for the vote of confidence,' said Josh. 'Remind me not to make you my agent.'

'Now, if you open the smaller present,' said Chris, 'you'll find something to go with it.'

Josh picked up the box and ripped off the paper, a smile spreading across his face as he saw the amp inside.

'On the strict understanding that you'll use headphones with it after eight o'clock at night,' Chris said.

'I don't mind being woken up,' said Matilda. 'I like noise.'

'Do you?' said Chris with a smile. 'I hadn't noticed.'

Matilda launched into an off-key rendition of something by Jessie J, sung at the top of her voice.

'Open hers next,' I whispered to Josh. 'It might keep her quiet.'

Josh picked up Matilda's present, which she had wrapped herself in tinfoil because the wrapping paper we had in wasn't shiny enough. I sometimes swore she must have been a magpie in a previous life.

'I know, it's a roast turkey,' said Josh.

'No, it's not,' said Matilda. 'I wouldn't get you something to eat. That would be dead boring.'

Josh unravelled the pile of goods beneath. A T-shirt, a hoody and a pair of trainers that had seen better days, all of them black.

'I got them from Oxfam in Hebden Bridge,' she announced merrily. 'Daddy said I could get more things for my pennies there and it helps the starving children.'

'Thank you,' said Josh, bending to give her a hug. 'They're awesome. I mean, really not your usual rubbish at all.'

Matilda appeared chuffed at the compliment. 'The other one is from Grandma. And she's coming round tomorrow, so you're supposed to save it until then unless you really, really can't wait,' she explained.

'I'll contain myself,' said Josh.

Matilda appeared disappointed, shrugged and returned to the sock puppets on the stairs, satisfied that she wasn't going to miss anything.

Josh picked up the guitar somewhat gingerly.

'Go and try it out if you like,' said Chris. 'Take the amp with you.'

'You mean I have permission to make more noise than her?' he asked.

'I doubt you'll manage it, but you can have a go,' replied Chris.

Josh said thank you twice more before he got up to go upstairs.

'How about I bring you up a cup of tea and some toast in a bit?' I said.

He nodded and smiled before leaving the room.

I turned to look at Chris. 'I think we can safely say that was a hit?'

'You can't go wrong with a guitar as a sixteenth-birthday present.'

'Did you get one, then?'

'No. I had to wait until I was eighteen. Saved up all my money from my part-time job when I was at college.'

'Your folks never gave you one?'

'I don't think they could afford it, to be honest. And you know what Dad was like, not one for frivolous things like music.'

'So where is it, your first guitar?'

Chris looked down at his feet. 'Sold it,' he said. 'If I remember rightly, it kept Josh in nappies for a good six months.'

'In that case,' I said, putting my hand on his shoulder, 'I think it only fair that Josh lets you have a turn on his.'

By the time I took the tea and toast up, Josh and Chris were getting stuck into something sounding vaguely like 'Sweet

Child O' Mine'. Josh had the guitar slung across him in true rock-star fashion. And Chris was standing on Josh's bed, presumably demonstrating the finer points of air guitar.

I smiled at them both. 'If Kurt Cobain calls round, shall I send him straight up?' I asked.

Josh smiled and exchanged one of those looks with Chris before turning to me. 'Kurt Cobain topped himself before I was even born.'

'I knew that,' I said. 'I so knew that.'

Josh and Chris did the look again. They were more like brothers sometimes, they really were.

'Says the woman who counts Duran Duran's *Rio* as one of the best albums of all time,' smirked Chris.

He and Josh cracked up laughing.

'Thank you,' I said. 'That's the last cup of tea you're getting this morning.'

'Love you anyway,' Chris called after me as I left the room. 'Despite the dodgy music taste.'

I smiled and went back downstairs. And smiled again as they turned the volume of the amp up a notch or two.

It was lunchtime when Josh finally emerged, showered and dressed, downstairs.

'Well, what's the verdict, then?' I asked.

'Awesome,' said Josh. 'It's got a great tone to it.'

'Well, it did when I played it, anyway,' said Chris.

Matilda, who'd been ploughing through her mental maths homework with a look of utter disdain on her face, immediately put down her pen and buzzed around Josh.

'Can I have a go on your guitar, please? Just a little go.'

'Maybe tomorrow.'

'Why not now?'

Josh looked up, somewhat sheepishly. 'Actually, I was going to ask if it's OK for me to go round to Tom's for a bit?'

'For a bit or a lot?' I asked.

'Well, probably the rest of the day. Only he's desperate to see the guitar and his mum said she'll do us a pizza and we just want to hang out and listen to music and stuff.'

I glanced at Chris. His face had fallen slightly. But I knew he wouldn't say no.

'Yeah. Sure,' he said. 'But family lunch here tomorrow, remember? Grandma's coming, and it would be nice if you weren't stuck in your room all day.'

'No probs,' Josh said.

'And if Tom's mum asks you to turn the amp down, you turn it down, OK?' I added.

Josh nodded.

Chris rolled his eyes and did the sign of the cross in front of him. 'Watch out,' he said. 'The noise police, otherwise known as mums, are on the march.'

'You're worse than he is,' I said.

'Reliving my youth.' Chris smiled, putting his arms around me. 'Guitars do that to men in their forties.'

'Right. I'd better get going,' said Josh, displaying the first sign of urgency we'd seen from him that day as he went back to his room to get the amp and the guitar.

Chris kissed me, then nodded at Matilda who was sitting at

the table swinging her legs and staring mournfully at Josh's empty chair.

'Listen, love,' I said, putting an arm around her shoulders. 'You have to remember it's Josh's birthday and it's only fair that he should get to hang out with his best friend, if that's what he wants to do.'

'But I want to do stuff with him.'

'I know, but teenagers like to do their own thing. You probably will, one day.'

Matilda pulled a face. 'I won't. I'll want to be with all of you on my birthday.'

I smiled, deciding not to argue or point out that Josh probably wouldn't be around by then, anyway. 'Well, we're going to have a nice birthday meal together when Grandma's here tomorrow. And in the meantime, it's jacket potatoes for lunch.'

Matilda looked at me intently. 'Josh is having pizza,' she said.

I looked at her and shook my head. Sir Alan Sugar really had missed a trick not doing a primary-school version of *The Apprentice*.

'Well, we'll have pizza for tea, then,' I said.

A smile flickered onto Matilda's face.

'And after lunch,' said Chris, scooping her up from the chair and hoisting her up onto his shoulders, 'I am going to thrash you at Mouse Trap.'

'Yay!' shouted Matilda as they galloped around the kitchen table.

'Hall, please, if you're horse racing.' I smiled. 'I've got hot potatoes about to come out of the Aga.'

'You heard your mother,' said Chris, galloping into the hall, Matilda clinging on to his neck and grinning.

Josh came back downstairs, loaded up and looking somewhat like a roadie. 'Right,' he said, 'I'll see you later.'

'You're gonna miss Mouse Trap,' Matilda shouted out from Chris's back.

'I'll get over it.'

Matilda poked her tongue out at him.

'If you need me to give you another lesson, just call,' Chris said to Josh.

'No chance. You are so playing Mouse Trap all afternoon,' Josh called out before pulling the door shut behind him.

Of course, the thing with Mouse Trap is it takes so long to set up that by the time you're ready, you've lost the will to live – let alone play a board game.

We'd been at it for about half an hour when there was a knock on the door. Usually, Matilda would leap up and dash for it before Chris and I even moved. But she was at the particularly delicate stage of replacing the mouse trap, and when I said it would probably be the window cleaner coming back for his money, she decided she was staying put. I got up from my cushion on the floor, being careful not to jog the board, and stopped to pick up a ten-pound note from the pot in the hall, at the same time making a mental note to check before I went back to the game that I had enough icing sugar in the cupboard to finish decorating Josh's cake for tomorrow.

I opened the door, ten-pound note in hand. A dark-haired woman stared back at me, her smoke-coloured eyes rimmed with kohl. She was wearing skinny jeans and a black top and holding a large present wrapped in black and silver paper. I noticed her hands were shaking. I knew who she was straight away, even though it had been years since I'd looked at her photo, which had been taken years previously. You don't forget cheekbones like that. And besides, I was reminded of them every time I looked at Josh.

I watched her look me up and down. The corners of her mouth turned up slightly, whether in an attempt at friendliness or simply satisfaction that she was still the brightest star in the sky, it was hard to say.

'Hi, is Josh in?' she asked.

'Er, no, he's not.'

'Oh, is there a time I can call back to see him? Only I'd like to give him this myself.'

I was taken aback by her gall. She still hadn't even introduced herself. I might not have had any idea who she was. She didn't know who I was, for that matter, although she could probably guess. I wasn't sure what to say. I couldn't send her packing without consulting Chris first. And I couldn't accept the present without checking with him either. She was back. And whichever way you looked at it, Chris needed to know.

'Chris!' I called from the hallway. I tried to do it in a casual tone so as not to bring Matilda running out with him. But at the same time I couldn't help thinking I should have tried to warn him in some way. No one should be flung from an innocent game of Mouse Trap unwittingly into the jaws of their ex. It wasn't right.

She flinched as I said his name. The corners of her mouth

returned to neutral, her eyes narrowed slightly. I thought for a second that she might simply dump the present and make a run for it. Fight or flight. She stood her ground, though, until he appeared behind me in the hallway. His footsteps faltered as he caught sight of her. He stopped dead behind me. I felt his breath fast and shallow on the back of my neck before he spoke.

'Lydia.'

She smiled at him. Not at her full wattage, I was sure, more of a seductive glow.

'Look, I know I should have called or something.'

Chris was in front of me now. On the edge of the doorstep, his face doing a good impression of a question mark. Many question marks, to be honest.

'What . . . ? Why . . . ? I don't understand.'

'I wanted to give him his present,' she said.

'Well, you can't. He's not here.'

'I know. She's already said.' Lydia nodded in my direction but didn't bother to remove her gaze from Chris's face.

'You can't just turn up like this,' said Chris. 'What if Josh had been here?'

'Then I could have given him the present.'

'And what would you have said?'

'The truth,' she said. 'It's usually the best thing to start with.'

'Jesus,' said Chris, shaking his head.

They paused for a second. It was long enough for my mediation training to get the better of the lurching feeling in my stomach.

'Look,' I said, 'I don't think this is the time or the place for this conversation. We've all had a bit of a shock. How about we take the present for Josh and let him decide what he wants to do?'

'OK,' she said with a shrug. 'There's a note inside the card. Could you give it to him, please? Make sure he reads it. It's got my contact details on.'

For a second I thought Chris was going to tell her where to stick her present and card. Maybe he would have. But at that moment Matilda came out into the hall.

'Oohh, that's a big present,' she said. 'Is it for Josh?'

I saw Lydia look at her and straight away back to me. Presumably spotting the maternal resemblance but perhaps seeing Chris's eyes too. Because for the first time that afternoon she appeared to have been rendered speechless.

'Yes, it is,' I said, filling the silence. 'The lady's just leaving it for him.' I took the present from Lydia, my look warning her not to say anything, give any clue as to who she was.

The box was heavy. Whatever it was, I suspected it wasn't cheap.

'Thank you,' I said. 'We'll be in touch.'

Lydia looked at Chris and then back to me and nodded, turned and walked out of the garden. She stopped just outside the gate and lit a cigarette with shaking hands before carrying on down the lane.

I shut the door, needing to feel safe inside my own home. I wasn't any more, though. None of us were. That much was clear. I only had myself to blame. Chris had offered to move when we got married, but I'd said no because I hadn't wanted to uproot Josh. It was a big enough deal acquiring a step-mother without being kicked out of the only home you'd ever known as well. I hadn't wanted to be one of those stepmothers out of fairy tales. I'd wanted to break the mould. Yet in doing that I'd left myself open to attack.

I turned to smile at Matilda, knowing we had to pretend that everything was fine for her sake.

'Right,' I said, 'I do believe I was in the process of beating you at Mouse Trap.'

'What do you think it is?' asked Matilda, ignoring my taunt and nodding towards the present.

'I don't know, love,' I said, putting the box in the tall hallway cupboard in the hope that it would be a case of out of sight, out of mind.

'Who was that lady? Why haven't I seen her before?'

I hesitated, unsure whether to let Chris answer. He remained silent.

'Someone Daddy and Josh knew years ago,' I said. 'Now, let's get on with that game.'

Matilda nodded and ran back into the lounge. I turned to look at Chris. His face was ashen, his eyes burning fiercely.

'She has no right to see him,' he said. 'No right whatsoever.'

'Listen,' I whispered, taking hold of his hand and squeezing hard, 'try not to worry. We'll work out what to do. We'll talk later, when Matilda's gone to bed, OK?'

He nodded and tried his best to smile. I followed him back into the lounge, realising I still had the ten-pound note for the window cleaner in my hand.

*

It was gone eight before Matilda finally went to bed. As soon as I came down after reading to her, I went out the back door. I knew exactly where Chris would be. The wooden bench in the back garden faced west, allowing huge vistas of the sunsets over our beautiful part of the Pennines. The sun had set more than an hour ago but Chris was still sitting there, soaking up the faintest trace of colours left in the sky. Staring out into the darkness beyond.

I sat down next to him. Put my hand on his thigh. Wanting to let him know I was there, but not attempting to wrench him out of wherever he was right now. It was bad enough for me, coming face to face with the woman who'd come before me. Who, for all I knew, had sat on this very bench with him, sharing this view. But what it must be like for him to have the mother of his son turn up after all these years. The maelstrom which it must have unleashed inside him, I couldn't begin to imagine. I sat with him a while longer before I finally spoke.

'She's never been in touch? Not until today?'

He shook his head. Closed his eyes for a second. 'I did what she asked,' he said. 'I never came after her or tried to find her. And now she decides she wants to bloody see him.'

We sat silently for a minute or two. Each immersed in our own thoughts.

'What do you want to do?' I asked eventually. 'About the present, I mean.'

'Personally I'd chuck it off the edge of the crags, but I guess that's not one of the options.'

I smiled at him and stroked his leg again. 'If she's come here once, she'll presumably come again if she doesn't hear anything. We can't just stick our heads in the sand. Josh could be here next time.'

'I don't want her anywhere near him.'

I took hold of his hand. 'Maybe Josh won't want to see her, anyway. The key thing is that we ask him. Give him the present so that he can make his own mind up. Can you imagine what he'd say if he found out she'd turned up and we hadn't told him?'

Chris looked at me. 'I know,' he said. 'It's difficult, that's all. What if he wants to see her?'

'Would that be such a bad thing?'

He gave me one of his 'What do you think?' looks.

'Maybe she's changed,' I said. 'People do.'

Chris made a '*pppfffft*' sound and shook his head.

'Well, let's wait and see, shall we? We don't even know where she's living. It might be a flying visit, and she'll be off again.'

Chris sat for a while, staring up at the sky. It was getting cool now. I pulled my cardigan further across me.

'OK,' he said. 'But if you don't mind, could you talk to Josh? I'm not sure I'd say the right things. Not sure I'd be capable of saying anything, really. I'm pretty numb with it all.'

'Sure,' I said, rubbing his arm. 'Tonight, when he comes home?'

Chris shook his head. 'No, I'm not having anything spoiling his birthday. Tomorrow. After Mum's been and Matilda's gone to bed.'

'OK,' I said, standing up. 'You coming in?'

'In a bit,' he replied.

I nodded, kissed him on the lips and walked slowly back indoors.

From the Counselling Room

I know this is going to sound stupid, but we were at this Handmade Parade workshop thing they do in Hebden Bridge every year. I was helping our daughter with her costume – it was a mythical creature theme and she wanted to be some kind of goblin – and I asked him if he could make me some horns to wear, because I hadn't had time to make my own costume.

Anyway, he comes back five minutes later with these pathetic-looking brown bits of corrugated card he'd scrunched into a bendy shape and said, 'Will these do?'

And at exactly the same moment a woman next to us put on the horns that her husband had made for her, and they were these huge things, made from wire, with papier mâché around them, painted purple and silver, and she looked so chuffed and I thought to myself: that's what I want. Not her horns but a husband who could be bothered to make something special for me.

So I turned to him and said, 'No, they won't do. They won't do at all.'

2

I should have realised that Matilda would say something. She lulled me into a false sense of security by chatting away about a random selection of innocuous subjects on Sunday morning without so much as a passing reference to the present.

But as soon as Josh appeared in the kitchen she chirped up, 'A lady came to the house yesterday with a massive present for you.'

Chris put his mug down heavily on the table.

Josh looked at him. 'What lady?' he asked.

'The pretty lady with long dark hair,' said Matilda.

'Oh yeah, I know loads of those,' replied Josh.

'You do know her. Mummy said you and Daddy knew her years ago.'

Josh turned to look at me. There was no way we were going to hold this conversation back until the evening.

'Right, Matilda,' I said, deciding a diversionary tactic was needed, 'hadn't you better go and get ready?'

'Ready for what?'

'Swimming. Daddy's taking you to the family fun session.'

'Yay!' said Matilda, throwing her arms around Chris.

He looked up at me, no doubt ruing the loss of his

Sunday-paper-reading time but also realising what I was trying to do.

'Yep,' he said, taking a last slurp of coffee, 'and if you get a move on, we might even have time to go to the scooter park beforehand.'

Matilda disappeared to her bedroom and returned with her swimming bag and scooter helmet in record time.

'Right, then,' said Chris, bending to give me a kiss, 'I'll see you later.'

I could hear the tightness in his voice as he said it. He looked at Josh – a slow, regretful look – and patted him on the shoulder before he left. A forlorn gesture, but a gesture all the same.

Quiet descended on the house.

Josh sat down at the table. 'So who's the woman?'

I sat down next to him.

He knew about his mother. Chris had answered the inevitable questions when he was growing up. He had photos of her somewhere that Chris had given him when he was younger, feeling the need to make her tangible, so she wasn't up there with Father Christmas and the Tooth Fairy as someone you couldn't be one hundred per cent certain existed, because no one had ever actually seen them.

I had no idea if he still looked at the photographs. If he thought about her, wondered about trying to find her one day. I'd done my best to fill the gap but I'd never tried to replace her. I'd always been Alison to him, not 'Mum'. And here I was, about to bring the past crashing rudely and unrequested into his present.

'It was your mum.'

I said it as gently as possible, but sometimes words weigh so heavily that it doesn't matter if you breathe them out, the impact is still the same.

Josh stared at me, his mouth gaping open. 'My mum? She came here? Why?'

'To see you, Josh. She wanted to give you a present.'

'But she hasn't wanted to see me for, like, virtually my entire life. Why is she bothered now?'

The hurt was seeping out of him. Collecting in a pool under his chair. I wanted to hug him to me, as I had done when he was younger, but I wasn't sure if I could do that any more.

I squeezed his arm instead. 'It doesn't mean she wasn't bothered, Josh. Maybe she had problems to sort out.'

'Must have been bloody big problems to take nearly sixteen years to sort . . .' He sat quietly for a bit before curiosity got the better of him. 'What did she say? Did you see her?'

'Yeah, I answered the door. She seemed fine. A bit nervous, but that's hardly surprising. She said there's a note inside the card with the present. She asked that you read it.'

He said nothing for a few moments. His brow was furrowed, his hands clenched. 'Where is it? The present, I mean.'

'It's in the hall cupboard. Would you like me to get it for you?'

He nodded. Like Edmund being offered Turkish delight by the White Witch and knowing he shouldn't take it, but being unable to resist.

I brought the present in and laid it on the kitchen table. Josh didn't open it first, though. He took the envelope off the front and tore across the top. The card had an arty, graffiti-style 'Happy Birthday' on the front. He opened it; the letter fell out onto his lap.

He sat there for a minute looking at it, picked it up and put it down again before passing it to me. 'Can you read it, please?' he asked.

'Are you sure?'

He nodded. I opened the pieces of paper. I was struck instantly by the writing. She wrote in what appeared to be a black fountain pen. The letters were tall and beautifully formed with flourishes on the loops. It looked like a work of art, not a hastily scrawled note.

'"Dear Josh,"' I began, '"you probably hate me – if you know I even exist, that is. I understand that. I wish I could explain why I did what I did, but I'm not sure I can. I'm not going to try to justify it and I don't want to make excuses. All I'll say is that I wasn't thinking straight at the time. I was pretty messed up. And the trouble with being messed up is that you do things you should never have done and then afterwards, when you're not so messed up, you wish you could take them back. But you can't, and nor can you explain to the person you hurt why you did it."'

I glanced over at Josh. He was sitting staring at his hands. He nodded for me to continue.

'"What I want you to know is that I didn't get in touch because I thought it would be best for you, not because I didn't want to. I'd already screwed up big time and I was worried that, if I came back, I'd do the same thing again. And I knew that your dad would be doing a brilliant job of looking after you.

'"But I don't want you to think that I didn't get in touch because I wasn't thinking about you. I've thought about you every single day since I left. That's why I wanted to give you this present now, on your sixteenth birthday. Because I always vowed that I would and that it might help you to see that I was thinking about you all the time, even when I wasn't there.

'"If you'd like to meet up, or speak on the phone, that would be fantastic. But don't feel you have to. I understand if you don't want to see me, but always know that I am thinking of you and that I love you."'

My voice caught as I read the last line. I'd never hated her. How could I, when I hadn't known her? I'd hated what she'd done. Hadn't been able to understand how she could have done it. But at that moment I simply felt sorry for the woman who had poured her heart out to the son she had never known. Although not as sorry as I felt for the son who was sitting before me, crumpled and contorted with emotion.

'Come here,' I said, pulling him to me. Stroking his hair, kissing him gently on the top of his head as his shoulders shook beneath me.

'She's not my mum,' he sobbed. 'I mean, how could she do that to a baby? It's not right. Not right at all.'

'Sometimes, love, people do the most awful things. Things you can't begin to get your head around. I hear about them all the time. People who come to see me who've behaved in such a bad way to the very people they say they love the most.'

'And do the people they say they love hate them?'

'Sometimes they do,' I said. 'But often they love them too. There's a thin line, as they say.'

'Chrissie Hynde from the Pretenders,' said Josh.

I managed a smile. 'I wasn't sure if you'd know that one. My era, really.'

'She's class,' said Josh.

'You know what?' I said. 'Your mum looks a bit like her. Dark hair and eyes, dead slim.'

Josh nodded. I let go of him.

He sat and thought for a bit. 'Dad doesn't want me to see her, does he? That's why he got you to talk to me.'

'Your father wants what's best for you. He's a bit shaken up, that's all. He wasn't expecting her to turn up like that.'

'And what about you?' asked Josh. 'What do you think?'

'I think it should be up to you. And I'll understand if you do want to see her and I'll understand if you don't. Whatever you decide, I'll support you. We both will.'

Josh put his head down and sighed. 'I don't know,' he said. 'All these years it's been like she never really existed. It's so weird to think I could get to know her. I'm not sure if I want to, though.'

'Take some time, then. You don't have to make your mind up straight away. See how you feel in a few days.'

Josh nodded.

I got up to put the kettle on. 'Are you going to open it, then?' I asked.

'Oh,' he said, turning back to the present on the table. 'Yeah, I guess so.'

He picked it up and unpicked the tape from one end, sliding the paper off the large cardboard box beneath. It was a wide-screen television box. For a moment I thought that's what she'd got him. I was wondering where the hell we were going to put it. And then he opened the box and took something out and I saw that it wasn't a TV at all. It was a red guitar. An electric one. Like the one we'd got him, only better.

'Jeez,' said Josh. 'Look at this.'

He pointed to a scrawled signature in black marker pen on the front. Above it, I could just make out 'To Josh, London's Calling!' followed by a signature.

'It's Joe Strummer's guitar,' said Josh, his mouth gaping open. 'She's given me Joe Strummer's fucking Fender Telecaster.'

For once I ignored the language. In the circumstances it was probably justified. She'd managed to give him the one thing which would now make it very hard for Josh not to want to meet her.

'I don't get it,' he said, shaking his head. 'How could she have got this?'

'Your dad said she used to work in music promotion. One of the big record labels, I think.'

I could almost hear the cogs going round in Josh's head.

'She got him to sign it for me,' he said. 'Even though she hadn't seen me since she left. She still got him to sign it for me.'

I nodded and smiled. Realising at that point that Josh was lost to her. And there was nothing we could do about it.

Josh was upstairs in his room playing the guitar when Chris and Matilda came home. Tom was up there with him. Josh must have texted him. He'd come round pretty sharpish.

It was Matilda who realised first. She never missed a thing. Her brow furrowed as she looked at Josh's guitar from us, which was lying on the sofa.

Her head spun round, the ends of her still-wet hair flicking water as she did so. 'What's he playing?' she asked. 'That's not his guitar.'

'No. It's a different one. He's playing it with Tom.'

'So did Tom bring it? Has he got one too?'

I hesitated. Chris looked at me. He twigged before I said anything. I could see it in the way his eyes darkened.

'Er, no. It's his. It was the present the lady brought round yesterday.'

'So he's got two guitars? Can I have one, then? Or just borrow his when he's playing the new one?'

'Maybe ask him nicely, later, if you can have a quick turn.'

'I want to ask him now.'

'No,' I said. 'Grandma's coming round soon. Why don't you put on a DVD while I finish cooking?'

She ran over to the TV without another word. Chris followed me into the kitchen, shutting the door behind us.

'Great,' he said, shaking his head. 'I suppose she thinks giving him a guitar will make everything OK.'

'Look, I need to tell you something,' I said. 'It's not just any guitar. It's signed by Joe Strummer.'

He stared at me as if he thought I was having him on for a moment. His jaw set with the realization that I wasn't.

'It's signed "To Josh",' I continued, sitting down at the kitchen table.

He frowned again. It clearly didn't fit with the scenario he had in his head.

'It must have been within a few years of her leaving, then,' he said. 'He's been dead a good ten years or so.'

'She wrote a letter,' I said. 'It was in with the card. Josh asked me to read it to him.'

'What did it say?'

'That she never stopped thinking about him. That she screwed up and wants the chance to put things right but that she'd understand if it's too late.'

Chris blew out and sat down next to me. 'Has he said what he wants to do?'

'He's pretty mixed up. I suggested he take a few days to think about it. I suspect the guitar's probably swung it, mind.'

Chris nodded. Put his head in his hands.

'They might only meet up once,' I said, rubbing his shoulder. 'Maybe she simply needs to get it out of her system.'

'No,' said Chris, 'that's not Lydia's style. All or nothing. That's how it is with her.'

'I still don't think we can say no,' I said. 'He's sixteen. We couldn't stop him. And I'd rather not try if it's going to push him away. We need to be here for him. Need to let him deal with it in his own way.'

'It's easy for you to say.'

I looked down at my hands. He was right, of course. I'd never met the woman until yesterday. I hadn't been the one she walked out on. The one who'd brought Josh up single-handedly. Who'd made so many sacrifices that I didn't know where to start.

'No one's taking him away from you,' I said. 'She can never compete with what you did for him. But at the end of the day she's his mother. It's natural that he'd want to meet her, even if it's just out of curiosity.'

Chris shut his eyes and bowed his head. I put my arms around him. Pulled him in to me.

'OK. I guess we've got no choice,' he said eventually.

'Thanks,' I said, knowing that although he was doing his best to sound reasonable and rational, inside he must be feeling anything but. 'Right. Well, I'd better get on with dinner,' I said, squeezing his shoulder.

'I'll give Mum a ring,' said Chris. 'See what time she wants picking up.'

'She said she'd come by bus.'

'I know. But it's started to rain. You know how slippery the cobbles get.'

By the time Chris arrived back with Barbara, Tom had gone home but Josh was still up in his room. Matilda had built some kind of set for *The Muppets* movie in the hallway and was busy perfecting her Miss Piggy voice.

'Grandma!' Matilda yelled as soon as she heard the key in the door.

I hurried out from the kitchen as she leapt at Barbara, almost knocking her off her feet.

'Steady, please,' I said, wiping my hands on my apron before taking my turn to give Barbara a hug.

Her cheeks were soft and downy. She looked like a grand-mother should. She smelt like a grandmother should. She was everything a grandmother should be, to be honest. I wished I'd had one like her. Or a mother like her, for that matter.

'Hello, love. Summat smells good. Just what I need to warm me up, turned a bit nippy out there, it has. Autumn's proper on its way. I always say it starts on Josh's birthday. We've hardly ever had his party in the garden. Once when he were a wee lad, I think. One of those Indian summers we don't get any more.'

'Well, the kitchen's nice and toasty. You come and warm yourself up. Matilda, will you pop and tell Josh Grandma's here, please?'

Barbara slipped off her sensible lace-ups and went through. I glanced at Chris. The darkness hung heavily over his eyes. I realised he still hadn't seen Josh since he'd been told.

'It's OK,' I whispered. 'Remember, nothing's changed. Not really.'

He nodded, although he didn't appear convinced.

I followed Barbara into the kitchen. She was warming her bottom against the Aga. She had a jumper and a cardigan on. In the summer she swapped the jumper for a blouse but she never went without the cardigan.

'Chris was quiet on way over,' she said.

I busied myself stirring the gravy while I worked out how to reply. Barbara wouldn't eat anything without gravy on it.

'It's a big thing, your son turning sixteen. A whole new set of stuff to worry about.'

'There's no need to worry about Josh, though, is there? He's a good lad.'

I smiled at her and nodded. I heard Josh come down the

stairs two at a time and run into a Kermit and Miss Piggy ambush. Chris was now hovering in the doorway, seemingly unsure which side was safer.

'Let me see the birthday boy, then,' called out Barbara.

Josh came through, squeezing past Chris without making eye contact, and gave Barbara a hug.

'Eeh, you definitely look older. It's downhill from here, you know. You'll have wrinkles like mine before you know it.'

Josh kissed her on the cheek.

'Happy birthday anyway, love,' she said, her eyes sparkling as they always did in his presence. 'And I'm told you haven't opened my present yet. Must be getting old, then, if you can contain yourself.'

Josh smiled.

'It's in the other room,' Matilda piped up. 'I'll go and get it.'

'It's OK,' I said. 'We'll all come through. Just for a few minutes, and then lunch will be ready.'

We followed Matilda through to the lounge. The present was on the coffee table. I knew exactly what it was, because we'd bought it. Barbara always gave us the money and asked us to get something Josh really wanted.

He peeled off the wrapping paper. His face lit up.

'It's a new iPad!' squealed Matilda.

'I have no idea what you do with it but I were told your old one was broken,' said Barbara.

Josh gave her a big hug. 'I did. Thank you. It's like a portable mini-computer. You can do everything on it. I'll show you, if you like.'

'It'll have to be after lunch now,' I said.

'Right you are,' said Barbara.

'And this is the guitar Josh got from Mummy and Daddy,' said Matilda, pointing to the sofa. 'Only he's got another one now, so he doesn't really need it.'

I glanced at Chris. He looked like he had been kicked in the stomach.

'Oh,' said Barbara. 'Who were other one from, then?'

Josh looked at me for help.

'Just someone who wanted to pass it on to him,' I said.

'It was the pretty lady who came to the door yesterday,' chipped in Matilda. 'Mummy hid it in the cupboard.'

Barbara looked at me.

'Lunch,' I said. 'Lunch will be ready. I'd better go and get the roast out.'

They followed me through and sat down at the kitchen table.

Matilda could always be relied upon to fill any awkward silences with her chatter. Barbara suspected something. I was pretty sure of it. She might have been in her seventies but she was sharp. Pin sharp. She glanced at Chris and Josh intermittently throughout the meal. Tried to engage them in conversation. Josh at least responded to the inquiries about how his GCSE revision was going and whether he'd had any more thoughts about where to do his 'A' levels (he was trying to find a sixth form or college which offered music technology, art and history). But Chris remained pretty monosyllabic. There were none of his characteristic wisecracks, no egging Matilda on with her jokes. He didn't even finish all of his lunch, and roast chicken was his favourite. Always had been.

'Not hungry?' inquired Barbara as I took Chris's plate.

'Oh, I'm saving some room for pudding,' said Chris.

'What's for pudding?' asked Matilda.

'Well, it's a birthday meal, isn't it?' I said.

'Cake. Has Josh got a birthday cake? Has it got Smarties or sprinkles on it?'

'He's got a cake but no sprinkles or Smarties. Plenty of chocolate, mind.'

Josh smiled at me. You were never too old for chocolate, after all.

I beckoned Matilda to follow me to the larder, where I unveiled the triple chocolate cake I'd made, meticulously following the recipe I'd found online. We had plenty of cookery books with cake recipes in but they all had pictures with them, and I hated making something which I knew wouldn't look anything like the picture.

'Wow!' said Matilda, who thankfully tended to be impressed by pure size rather than aesthetic appeal. 'That looks yummy.'

'Well, hopefully it will taste yummy as well,' I said.

We carried the cake over to the table between us. Matilda started singing 'Happy Birthday', and Barbara joined in, despite Josh looking a tad embarrassed. Chris opened and closed his mouth the best he could, but I could barely hear any words coming out. I'd put a number sixteen candle in the middle of the cake. It seemed a bit more grown-up than having sixteen candles.

'Don't forget to make a wish,' said Barbara as Josh took a deep breath.

He closed his eyes as he blew, as if he was still a little kid. I had no idea what he wished for. But I did know that it wasn't the same as whatever Chris was wishing for at that moment.

Barbara waited until the others had gone into the lounge to say something. She stayed in the kitchen on the pretext of giving me a hand with the teas. But I knew from the look on her face that there was something far more important on her agenda.

'What's bothering him, Alison?' she asked.

She might have been a silver-haired grandmother, but there was no mistaking the steel beneath the surface. I wasn't going to lie to her. I wasn't even going to be economical with the truth, as I had been earlier. I figured she was bound to find out sooner or later, and I'd rather it came from me.

'Lydia came to the house yesterday,' I said quietly. 'She bought Josh the guitar. The other one. The one upstairs.'

The colour drained from Barbara's cheeks. It took her a few moments to compose herself enough to be able to speak. When she did so, her voice was shaky.

'Did she see Josh?'

'No. He was at a friend's house.'

'Chris saw her, though?'

I nodded.

Barbara shook her head. 'She's got a nerve.'

There was a tone in Barbara's voice that I didn't recognise. She never usually had a bad word to say about anyone.

'She left a letter for Josh,' I went on. 'It was in with his card. She apologised for what she did and said she'd like to meet up with him.'

'Chris isn't going to let him, surely?'

'He's sixteen, Barbara. It's not a matter of letting him.'

'He's still living under your roof. You can still say no to him. He has no idea what she's like.'

'But that's just it. He doesn't know what she's like. That's why he's curious to meet her.'

'Well, I can tell him exactly what she's like. Save him a lot of time and heartbreak.'

Barbara's permanent smile had disappeared from her face. I noticed her hands were shaking.

'He might not even meet her. He's still making his mind up about what he wants to do.'

'Don't be taken in by her, Alison. She can be very charming when she wants to be. But you weren't there. You didn't see what she did to Chris. To leave a baby the way she did. No mother worth an ounce of anyone's sympathy would do that. So don't you start feeling sorry for her.'

I was taken aback by her tone of voice. The undeniable strength of feeling.

'I just think it's important that this is Josh's decision,' I said. 'And that we all support him along the way.'

'What about Matilda?'

'She doesn't know who the woman was.'

'But she saw her?'

I nodded.

'She ruined Chris's life once,' Barbara said. 'Don't let her do it again. No good will ever come of that woman. No good at all.'

She picked two mugs of tea up, her hands still shaking, and took them silently out of the kitchen.

From the Counselling Room

I have no idea why he said it, but we were in the middle of having sex – that means about three minutes into it, in his case – and I was going through the motions, as usual. I mean, he has no idea I fake it. I've watched that restaurant scene in When Harry Met Sally *enough times to know how to do it well.*

Anyway, he suddenly put on the voice of that old-fashioned motor-racing commentator in Chitty Chitty Bang Bang *and said, 'She's here, she's here. She's coming, she's coming.'*

And the worst part about it was that he actually thought it was funny. Roared with laughter afterwards. And I just knew that I would never even be able to fake it with him again.

3

'Where's Daddy?' asked Matilda as she sat down at the kitchen table.

'He had to go to work early.'

'Ohhh . . . I wanted to play with him.'

'I'm sure he'll play with you later, when he comes home.'

'Will you play with us too?' she asked Josh.

'Depends what you're playing,' he said, before taking a bite of his toast.

'What do you want to play?' asked Matilda.

'My guitar.'

'OK. You play that, then,' she said. 'And I'll play the one Mummy and Daddy got you. We can pretend we're in a band. Daddy can be the singer.'

Josh smiled at her. They might only have been half-siblings but it was hard sometimes to imagine them being any closer. Matilda knew that Josh had a different mum, of course. Knew that he couldn't remember her and that she'd had to go away and no one knew where she was. She could handle that. But Lydia turning up and being a real person, a real mum who wasn't her mum, someone who could come between her and Josh, that was another matter entirely.

If I had to tell her, I would. But not until Josh had made up his mind. And when I did tell her, I wanted to do it in the right way. Not five minutes before she left for school on a Monday morning.

'Are you OK?' I asked Josh when Matilda ran upstairs a little later to get her uniform on.

'Yeah. Why shouldn't I be?'

'Just checking, that's all. It's been a pretty big weekend.'

Josh shrugged.

'Well, if you need to talk about anything –'

'Yeah, I know. You're a registered counsellor.'

I smiled at him. 'Just remember that, unlike my clients, you don't need an appointment.'

Josh shook his head, took a last gulp of tea and stood up. 'See you later, then,' he said on the way out of the kitchen.

'Give your sister a shout for me, please.'

'Tilda, the house is on fire!'

'Thank you, Josh,' I called after him, before he slammed the front door behind him.

Had the house really been on fire, it appeared Matilda would have been content to be fried alive rather than curtail the impromptu puppet show she was staging on the landing. I had to go upstairs and physically remove the puppets from her hands before she reluctantly came downstairs. Her school polo shirt was a bit crumpled, and her skirt was skew-whiff, but as there was nothing new about either of these scenarios I decided to let them go.

When she got to the hall, I pulled the brush through her long brown hair half a dozen times, popped her headband in

(I had long ago informed her that, as neither I nor her father were capable of plaits and I still had nightmares about the religiously straight fringe I'd had as a child, headbands were the only option in the hair-styling department) and we were ready to go.

It was a fifteen-minute walk to the village school in Midgley, along country lanes and footpaths. There was only one road to cross outside the school, which had a lollipop man called George in attendance. No doubt it wouldn't be long before Matilda wanted to do the walk on her own but, for now, it was a precious part of our day. A chance to talk and enjoy the outdoors together. Or a chance to be talked at, at least, while she rather brutally picked the heads off dandelions.

'When will I get an iPad?' Matilda asked, as she swung her book bag in the air.

'I don't know. Maybe when you're eleven, so you've got one when you start at secondary school.'

'How old were you when you had one?'

I laughed. 'Er, I still haven't got one, actually. Hadn't you noticed?'

Matilda looked at me aghast. 'Shall I get you one for Christmas? I can start saving up my pocket money.'

'Thank you, love, but there's no need.'

'Oh. Is it because you're old?' asked Matilda.

'Charming.' I laughed. 'Daddy's older than me, and he's got one.'

'So you just don't want one?'

'I can think of things I'd rather have.'

'Like what?'

'Oh, I don't know. There are lots of books I'd like, for a start.'

'OK,' she said. 'I'll get you a book instead.' And with that she skipped off ahead of me, picking up two yellow leaves which had fallen and immediately turning them into hand puppets.

Life was good for Matilda. Life was straightforward. The way it should be when you are eight years old.

'So did Josh have a good birthday?' asked Debbie when the playground melee had finally dispersed and I found myself standing next to her among the other mums at the school gates.

'Sort of.'

'You don't sound too sure.'

'It wasn't quite as we'd planned,' I said.

'Why?' asked Debbie.

I beckoned to her to start walking back with me. I'd never been one to discuss the ins and outs of my private life at the school gates. That was one thing I'd learnt quickly about living in a village. Debbie was different from the rest of the mums, though. I'd known her since Matilda and Debbie's daughter Sophie had been tiny. I knew I could trust her.

'Chris's ex turned up,' I said. 'Josh's mum.'

Debbie stared at me. 'I thought she was long gone.'

'She was. Until Saturday, at least.'

'So did she see him?'

'No, fortunately he was at his friend's when she called. She left a letter and a present for him. An electric guitar.'

'But isn't that what you were getting him?'

I nodded. 'Yeah. Only this one was better.'

'Jesus. I bet Chris was happy.'

'He's been very quiet since.'

'I'm not surprised. Must have been a hell of a shock. What did she look like? Is she older than you?'

'Yeah, a few years, I think. Not that you could tell. She's stunning, to be honest.'

Debbie stopped and looked at me. 'You don't think she wants to get back with him?'

I laughed.

'What's so funny?'

'Well, even if she does, Chris hates her. I mean, really hates her. He didn't even want us to give Josh the present.'

'But you did?'

'Yeah. Of course.'

'And does Josh want to see her?'

'I don't know. He's pretty mixed up about it, but I think the guitar swung it.'

'I wouldn't let her anywhere near him.'

I looked across at Debbie. 'Why do you say that?'

'She's your husband's ex, she's Josh's mum and she's stunning. It's a no-brainer.'

'And what about Josh?' I asked. 'Hasn't he got a right to see her?'

She looked straight at me. 'You're his mum,' she said. 'Maybe not biologically but in every way that matters. He doesn't need her. He's done pretty well for sixteen years without her, and that's down to Chris and you.'

'But doesn't she have the right to see him?'

'She lost that right the day she walked out on him. Get

shot of her, Ali. Or get Chris to do it, if you're too bloody nice to.'

The new couple walked into my room. Awkward didn't begin to go anywhere near. Sometimes it was actually painful to watch people. They wore their anguish on their faces, in the tortured movement of their limbs. Some would seemingly rather walk across hot coals in bare feet than be entering my room, about to bare their souls.

It was a close call but, of the two of them, he looked more apprehensive. It didn't surprise me. He was of a certain age. One thing you learnt pretty quickly was that men over sixty were probably the least comfortable discussing their emotions. And yet the expression on her face suggested she hadn't dragged him here against his will either. She was trying hard to smile through the pain, but there was no doubt that was what it was.

I smiled at them. My comforting, reassuring 'It's OK, I'm not going to eat you' smile. I pushed a strand of loose hair back behind my ear and extended my hand to each of them in turn.

'Mr and Mrs Crossley, pleased to meet you. I'm Alison Bentley. Is it OK if I call you by your first names?'

They both nodded. I gestured to them to take a seat. Bob let her sit down first, then pulled his grey slacks up slightly as he lowered himself into the easy chair.

'Now, I've had a look through the notes my colleague passed on, so I know a bit about the background to this. But I'd like to go through it with you, to make sure you're happy with everything and we're all agreed about how things stand.'

I looked up. Neither of them said anything. I carried on.

'Right. So you've been married thirty-six years and have one daughter, Cassie, who's thirty-three.'

I glanced up and saw Jayne swallow. Bob nodded, so I continued.

'You've both recently retired – Bob from your job as a sales rep and Jayne from yours as a part-time hotel receptionist. You say the problems in your relationship mainly stem from your daughter's decision to emigrate to Australia.'

Jayne started crying. Small tears that rolled delicately down her cheeks and plopped onto her pleated skirt. Bob shifted in his seat for a moment, took a tissue from the box on the table between them and leant forward to pass it to her. Jayne took it, removed her glasses and dabbed at the corners of her eyes.

'I'm sorry,' she said.

'Please, don't apologise for crying in here. I'm used to it. It's why the tissues are there. I understand that this is really difficult for you. Take all the time you need.'

She sniffed, a small, delicate sniff, and dabbed at her eyes some more. I glanced at Bob. He was looking down at his hands, his shoulders hunched. I waited a while longer.

'Are you OK for me to go on?'

Jayne nodded and put her glasses back on.

I turned to Bob. 'When did Cassie announce she was going to emigrate?'

He cleared his throat before speaking. 'Two months ago. She met a chappie from Sydney, see. Through work, it were. Always been a bit of a career girl, our Cassie. Never thought she'd want to settle down. Never thought she'd go off to another country either, but there you go.'

'And understandably you've both found that really hard,' I said. 'Have you been able to talk to each other about how you feel?'

Bob opened his mouth to say something and then looked down at his hands again.

'It's not Bob's fault. It's me who can't talk about it,' said Jayne. 'It's me who's finding it difficult. That's why we're here.'

'Right,' I said. 'Are you able to explain how it's made you feel?'

She looked down at the tissue, which was scrunched up in her hands. 'Empty,' she said. 'Bereft, really.'

I nodded. 'Thank you, Jayne. And Bob, no doubt you've found this tough too.'

'I've done everything I can,' he said. 'It doesn't seem to be enough, though. I'm at a loss to know what to do.' He shrugged.

Jayne started crying again.

Sometimes people came to me and they behaved so badly towards each other that, if they were characters in books, I really wouldn't have cared if they stayed together or not. I still helped them, of course, I was always professional. But, if I was brutally honest, I didn't have too much invested in it. And other times couples came to see me and I knew, during that very first appointment, that I would move heaven and earth to try to help them sort things out.

'It's OK,' I said. 'We'll find a way through this together. It might take time, but we'll get there.'

Bob nodded solemnly. Jayne took another tissue from the box.

Debbie was picking Matilda up after school. We'd arranged the play date – or rather, Matilda and Sophie had arranged it – the previous week. As it happened, it couldn't have been better timing. I wanted to be there when Josh came home from school. To grab that small window of time before Chris came home from work to be able to talk to him alone.

I hadn't spoken to Chris all day. I'd sent him a text telling him I loved him. I'd got one straight back saying the same thing. It was from his outbox. Number three on the scroll-down menu after 'I'll pick Tilda up from school' and 'Have we got anything planned for Saturday?'

He didn't do weddings if he could help it. He'd never advertised himself as a wedding photographer. But word got around, people passed on numbers and, if he took a family portrait they liked, people assumed that he'd be up for doing weddings. And sometimes he did. If he was having a quiet month, and if they asked nicely, and particularly if they agreed to his suggestion to shoot it reportage-style in black and white. Anyone who asked for stiff, formal, bride's-side-of-the-family group shots was told that, unfortunately, he was unavailable that weekend. Even if we had nothing on at all.

It was four thirty before I heard Josh's key in the door. Maybe he'd gone to Tom's house. Perhaps they'd gone down to Hebden to hang out for a bit. Or maybe he'd just needed some time alone.

I heard him throw his rucksack down in the hall. He came straight through to the kitchen.

'I'm going to meet her,' he said.

'OK,' I said, drying my hands on the towel and turning to face him.

'If I don't like her, I won't see her again.'

'Fine, you call the shots on this one.'

'Is Dad going to be mad at me?'

I shook my head. 'No, but he's going to find it hard. We need to give him some space and time to get his head around it all.'

'Where shall I meet her?'

'Well, probably not best to ask her here. Somewhere neutral where you'll both feel comfortable. The Milk Bar in Hebden, maybe?'

Josh shrugged. No doubt he considered himself too old for it now, but he was at that awkward age which was also too young for pubs.

'I guess so,' he said.

'Do you want someone to come with you?'

'I'm not a kid.'

'I know. But it might be a bit awkward, and I expect you'll both be feeling a little nervous. And sometimes it's just better to have someone else with you to help break the ice.'

He thought for a moment. 'Not Dad,' he said.

I breathed a silent sigh of relief that I wasn't going to have to ask him.

'You can come. Just the first time, though. If I decide to see her again, I'll be fine by myself.'

'OK. How soon do you want to arrange it?'

'Soon.'

'What about the weekend? Saturday afternoon, maybe. Dad's not working, so he could have Matilda.'

'Are you going to tell her?'

'I don't know. I think I probably should do. I don't want to have to lie to her about where we're going.'

'She'll want to come too.'

'I'll explain to her that she can't.'

'OK. Saturday afternoon, then. I'll text her. I don't want to speak to her. Not before I've actually met her. I think it's better that way.'

I nodded. 'Sure. Just let me know when you've got a time sorted.'

'Will you tell Dad?'

I nodded again.

'And are you sure he won't be mad at me?'

'He won't. I promise.'

He nodded and walked out of the kitchen.

A few seconds later, I heard him going upstairs, his footsteps seemingly lighter than they had been the day before.

I waited until we were lying in bed at night to tell Chris. I felt his body tense next to mine. He said nothing. I took his hand. It felt colder than usual.

'He might only see her the once,' I said.

'And then again, he might not.'

'We don't know how long she'll be around. Or if she'll want to see him again. She might find it too upsetting.'

I knew even before the last word had fully left my mouth that I'd said the wrong thing.

'What's she got to be upset about?' said Chris, turning to look at me with a frown.

'What I meant to say is, it's not going to be easy for her, seeing him after all this time.'

'It was her choice to leave, remember.'

'Yes, but we all do things we regret, don't we?'

'Name one of yours.'

I thought for a minute. The only thing I could think of was wasting too many years with Matthew when I should have realised the relationship wasn't going anywhere. But I wasn't going to say that. One ex was enough in this conversation.

'OK, so maybe I haven't got anything as big as that, but you know what I mean. Let's just leave it and see how the first meeting goes.'

Chris said nothing. He let go of a small sigh. 'This is doing my head in,' he whispered.

I slipped my arm around him, kissed him gently on the shoulder. 'I'm not surprised. It's a massive thing. It's doing Josh's head in as well, mind.'

'I don't know what to say to him.'

'Well, just say something. He thinks you're mad at him for wanting to see her.'

'Did he say that?'

I nodded.

'OK. I'll talk to him tomorrow. I thought I'd had all the awkward conversations with him when he was a kid. I didn't think we'd ever have to go through all this again. It's going to be on a whole new level now.'

'He needs you, though, love. You're the one constant thing

in his life. Just let him know you understand that he wants to see her.'

Chris turned and stared up at the ceiling. 'I do,' he said. 'I understand completely. I'm scared, that's all.'

'Of what?'

'That she'll take him away from me.'

'Of course she won't. She couldn't. Nobody could break what you two have.'

'Nobody except a mother.'

'He doesn't know her. He can't remember a thing about her. You're the one who's been there for him every step of the way. You're the one he relies on. He's not going to forget that simply because she's finally putting in an appearance, is he?'

'I guess not,' he said.

'I know not,' I replied, putting my arms around him.

Chris gave a tentative smile. Kissed me on the lips. 'I don't know what I'd do without you,' he whispered.

'Well, that's the one thing you don't have to worry about,' I said.

He kissed me again. Harder this time. And with the type of intensity which was fuelled by insecurity. It didn't matter what sparked it, though. What mattered was the connection. And what kept it burning. He moved his hand down between my legs. I arched my back and bit the pillow to stop myself moaning too loudly. I was lost to him. I always had been, right from the beginning.

Soon he would be inside me. And the connection would be strengthened again.

From the Counselling Room

I actually stay up watching crap TV at night, just to avoid going to bed at the same time as him. Because I can't bear for him to touch me or to breathe over me or even to speak to me. He makes my skin crawl.

And that's ridiculous, isn't it? I mean, who'd want to live like that?

And I think I've just woken up to the fact that I don't have to live like that because, yes, I might spend the rest of my life on my own and die a sad and lonely old woman. But at least I'll be able to go to bed when I want to.

4

I waited until the following Saturday morning to have 'the conversation' with Matilda, venturing into her room while she was playing. She hadn't reached the age yet where she wanted a lock on her door or even when you had to knock to enter. She welcomed any visitors. The only danger was of being talked to death.

'I'm doing Sooty and Sweep,' she said from behind her puppet theatre. 'You can do Soo, if you like.'

I blamed Chris for our retro child. And the fact that there were far too many clips of classic seventies children's shows available on YouTube.

'Actually, love, I wanted to have a chat with you about something.'

'Yeah?' she said, still inside the puppet theatre.

I sat down on her bed and patted the duvet next to me. 'Come and sit here.'

She did as she was asked. Still with Sooty and Sweep on her hands, mind. It was like one of those softly, softly police interviews with children where they get them to talk about difficult things with the aid of puppets.

'I'm taking Josh to meet someone this afternoon,' I said, desperately trying to locate a casual, by-the-by tone.

'Who?' asked Matilda.

'Remember that lady who came to the house with Josh's present?'

Matilda nodded.

'Her.'

'Why are you seeing her again? Has she got another present for Josh?'

'No, love. We're seeing her because she's actually an important person in Josh's life. Someone from a long time ago.'

Matilda stared at me blankly. I was going to have to spell it out.

'You know that I'm not Josh's mummy? That he had a different mummy, but he doesn't remember her because she left when he was a baby?'

She nodded again. I took hold of her hand – or Sweep, to be more precise.

'Well, that lady who came to the door is his real mummy. Her name is Lydia.'

Matilda stared at me for a moment, a slight frown creasing her forehead. 'Is she going to be his real mummy again? Is Josh going to go and live with her?'

'No, love,' I said, giving her hand a squeeze. 'She just wants to meet him. And Josh has decided that he'd like to meet her too.'

She remained staring at me. I could almost hear the cogs turning.

'Why did she go away when he was little?'

'It's complicated. I don't really know for sure. She must have had some kind of problem.'

'But why couldn't Daddy help her?'

'It doesn't always work like that, love,' I said, stroking her hair.

'You don't know, do you?'

'No.' I smiled. 'That's why we're going to meet her. Josh has got lots of questions for her too.'

'Can I come?'

'I'm sorry, love. It's important that Josh gets a chance to talk to her on his own.'

'But you're going.'

'Just to make sure he's OK.'

'Is she a stranger danger?'

I sighed and cursed whatever it was they talked about in circle time at school. 'No, love. I just want to be there for Josh. It's a big deal for him.'

'So who's going to look after me?'

'Daddy. He's going to take you to the cinema. What was that film you wanted to see?'

A huge smile spread across her face. '*Paranorman*. Really, am I going to see *Paranorman*?'

I nodded.

'Can I go now?'

'In half an hour or so,' I said.

'Woo hoo!'

She danced around the room with Sooty and Sweep. I waited a moment in case there were any more questions.

'Can I make a zombie puppet when I get back?' she asked.

I smiled and nodded. Clearly, there were more pressing things on her mind.

I was about to leave when I caught sight of myself in the mirror. 'Mumsy' was the word which sprang to mind. Well-worn cardigan, tunic (to hide the fact that I had never regained my waist after Matilda), coupled with jeans which were just jeans, not any particular type of jeans. It wouldn't usually have bothered me but I still had the image of Lydia in my head from our front doorstep. It wasn't that I wanted to outdo her. She was clearly in an entirely different league to me. It was simply that I wanted to be able to sit at the same table as her without feeling that I was a member of an entirely different species.

I ran back upstairs and riffled through my wardrobe. I opted for leggings instead of jeans. I wasn't sure they made much difference so I put on a different tunic as well. And when that didn't help much, I removed the cardigan. I would wear a jacket instead. A jacket would help.

I went downstairs. Josh was waiting in the hallway. He was wearing jeans, a T-shirt and a hoody and was effortlessly hip with it. I tried to recall whether I'd been the slightest bit hip at his age. If I had, it certainly hadn't been effortless.

He glanced up at me. 'Where's your cardigan?' he asked.

He didn't mean it nastily, I knew that. I also knew that Chris would have cracked up laughing, had he heard it.

'I'm wearing a jacket,' I replied, hooking one off the coat stand.

He shrugged and opened the door. He looked even paler than usual.

'Are you OK?' I asked.

'Yeah,' he said. He didn't sound too sure, though.

'Remember what Dad said. He's OK with you seeing her.'

'I know. It still feels wrong, though. Like I'm consorting with the enemy.'

'She's not the enemy.'

Josh looked up at me. 'Then why have I been hating her all these years?'

Lydia was already there when we arrived. I saw her through the glass as we approached the Milk Bar. Sitting on a high stool near the window, like some strategically placed mannequin designed to bring the punters in. There was something of the sixties about her. The long, straight limbs and the eyeliner. Her posture, even. I had no doubt that, pre-smoking ban, she would have been puffing away on a cigarette. She used to chain-smoke. Chris had told me that once. He'd blamed her for getting him started. And been cross with her for starting up again after Josh was born, though he'd managed to kick the habit for good by then.

I glanced at Josh as we entered; his eyes were already on her. He was like a kid seeing an object of beauty for the first time. His mouth gaping slightly, his movements awkward and uncertain. We walked over to her. She was engrossed in the review section of the *Guardian*. And she had the air of someone who knew she didn't need to look out for anyone, because she would be spotted first.

'Hi,' I said.

She looked up, and her gaze passed straight over me to Josh. I saw the tears rush to her eyes, saw her swallow hard and look as if she might collapse for a moment. She didn't, though.

She slid down from her stool and smiled at him. 'Hi,' she said. 'Thanks for coming.'

A second later she had her arms around him. Not a big, embarrassing mother-bear-of-a-hug but a seemingly casual good-to-see-you embrace.

Josh stepped back and glanced at me, as if to check that physical contact with his own mother was acceptable. I smiled at him, keen to reassure him that it was all right.

'Can I get you a drink?' I asked Lydia.

'No, I'm fine, thanks,' she said, pointing to a half-drunk cup of black coffee in front of her.

'What would you like, Josh?'

'A Coke, please,' he replied.

I nodded and went up to order. I glanced back over at them a couple of times. Josh had climbed up on the stool next to Lydia. They appeared to be talking to each other. I wondered if anyone looking at them would think they were mother and son. Probably not. She looked too hip to be anyone's mother.

I walked back to them, put my tea and Josh's Coke down and wriggled up onto the stool in what I hoped was a not too embarrassing fashion. Lydia looked across at me as if seeing me for the first time. I wondered what she made of me. Whether she was wondering how the hell Chris had ended up with someone like me.

'Thanks for letting Josh come,' she said. 'And I'm sorry for turning up out of the blue like that.'

'It's OK,' I said. 'It was just a bit of a shock, that's all.'

'Well, please pass on my apologies to Chris. I didn't mean to freak him out.'

'Sure,' I replied, trying to ignore the fact that the way she said Chris's name made my stomach twist inside.

'Your daughter's beautiful,' she said. 'Her eyes are gorgeous.'

I smiled, aware that any compliment on Matilda's eyes would also apply to Chris's. 'Thanks,' I said.

'She's crazy, actually,' said Josh. 'And incredibly loud and nosey.'

Lydia smiled. 'Bet you love her really.'

'Course I do,' he said. 'She's my sister.'

His words hung in the air for a moment. Lydia took a sip of coffee.

'Thanks for Josh's present,' I said.

'That's OK, he's already thanked me.'

'He gave it to her when she worked for Mercury Records, in London,' said Josh. 'She got to hang out with him for a bit. How awesome is that?'

'Fantastic,' I said.

'I knew I'd give it to him one day, you see,' Lydia explained. 'I was just waiting for the time to be right.'

I nodded. Avoiding the temptation to ask why the time was right now.

'So have you moved back to the area?' I asked.

'Yeah. Only last week. I'm renting a little flat in Hebden, nothing special. It's good to be back, though. This valley's still the place I consider to be home.'

I nodded. Did my best to smile. Any thoughts of this being a fleeting reappearance had just disappeared. I realised I didn't even know where she was from originally. Her accent was definitely a northern one but it had a London drawl mixed in which made it hard to pin down.

'So you actually used to live at our house?' asked Josh.

'Yeah,' she said. 'For about four years. Which is your bedroom now? Still the wonky one at the back?'

'Yeah,' he replied.

'I always liked that room,' she said. 'Such a beautiful view too.'

'Must have been weird,' said Josh. 'Seeing the house again after so long.'

'It was. It felt like I was in some kind of time warp where a place has stayed exactly the same but all the people have moved on and changed.'

She glanced at me as she finished the sentence. Maybe she hadn't figured on a new woman being there. Maybe she thought Chris would have been a single parent all these years. Living there alone with Josh. She clearly hadn't expected to see another child there.

I wanted to ask her so much. To try to get answers to all the questions which were hammering away inside my head. I didn't feel I could, though. Not in front of Josh.

'So how did you meet Chris?' Lydia asked me.

I stared at her. I hadn't been expecting anything quite so direct. But then I hadn't stopped to think that she would have questions too. That she would want to fill in all the gaps of the people she had left behind.

'Through Josh, really. Chris used to bring him to the library where I worked.'

'She did these really cool kids' events,' said Josh. 'Like a *Charlie and the Chocolate Factory* day where we got to make Violet Beauregarde paper chains and eat Willy Wonka chocolates that she made.'

I found myself blushing unexpectedly. Warmed by Josh's memories and my own memories of meeting Chris for the first time.

'So you're a librarian,' said Lydia.

She didn't say it patronisingly. It was just how the word always came out.

'Not any more,' I said. 'I'm a counsellor now.'

'Right. What made you switch to that?'

I was unnerved by her questions. I'd only just met the woman, and I certainly wasn't about to go into details about my parents' marriage.

'Just something I'd always fancied doing,' I said.

'And is your dad still a photographer?' she asked Josh, as if sensing that she'd get more information from him.

'Yeah. He's got a studio in town. Does portraits and that.'

'Oh, so he's given up the newspapers, then?'

For the first time that afternoon I felt riled on Chris's behalf. 'Yeah,' I said. 'Deadlines and a baby didn't really mix.'

She nodded. Maybe she squirmed a bit. Or perhaps it was my imagination.

'So what about you?' I asked, deciding not to let her ask all the questions. 'Are you still working in the music industry?'

'Yeah, off and on,' she said. 'Only on a freelance basis these days.'

'Who have you met?' asked Josh.

Lydia smiled and flicked back her hair. 'Loads of people you've probably never heard of.'

I looked at Josh's face. It was the first time she'd said something that hadn't gone down well.

'I knew who Joe Strummer was,' he said. 'I know loads of stuff from the seventies and eighties. Dad's still got all his LPs.'

Lydia bit her lip, looked out of the window for a moment. 'Of course,' she said, turning back to Josh. 'I should have realised. Will Keith Richards do you for starters?'

Josh grinned. He had that childlike expression on his face again. She had redeemed herself and she was now going to regale him with tales of music legends she had once lent a cigarette lighter to.

He was hers now. She might as well have offered him Turkish delight.

'What was your mum like?' asked Matilda when we got back home later.

Josh glanced up at Chris before answering. 'All right,' he said. 'She knows a lot about music stuff.'

'Is she going to come here?' asked Matilda.

Josh didn't answer.

'Probably not, love,' I said. 'At least, not for now.'

'Why? Don't you like her?'

'These things take time,' I said. 'Josh still doesn't really know her. Now, why don't you go and get your reading book out and I'll be up to listen to you in a few minutes.'

Matilda groaned, simply because that was Josh's reaction

to homework, not because she actually disliked it, and disappeared upstairs.

'So it went all right, then?' Chris asked Josh.

'I think so.'

'Do you think you're going to see her again?'

'Yeah. She's invited me around to her flat to see her record collection.'

'Good. Well, I mean, if that's what you want.'

'Sounds like she's got some really good stuff. Not that you haven't, like.'

Chris nodded. 'Sure. I understand.'

'OK. Sorted,' said Josh, before going up to his room.

'Thanks,' I said to Chris. I went to give him a hug.

He pulled away sharply.

'What?' I asked.

'Sorry,' he said. 'It's just I can smell her. I can actually smell her on you.'

From the Counselling Room

She got to the point where she just said 'like' about everything, as if her entire life was played out on Facebook. So if she saw a pair of shoes she wanted in a shop, she'd say 'like' and she'd even do a little thumbs-up in the air.

And half the time at home she didn't talk to me, she'd only communicate through Facebook. So if I said something funny, she wouldn't laugh, she'd share it on Facebook with an LOL next to it. Even if I was sitting bloody next to her on the sofa.

Once, when we were supposed to be going out for a meal, she was late because she couldn't decide what to wear. She'd shared photos of three outfits on Facebook and was waiting for her 'friends' to decide. By the time they'd decided I'd ordered myself a takeaway instead. When she asked why I hadn't ordered her one, I told her that I didn't know what her friends on Facebook would think she should have. She nodded, like that was a fair point, and went back on to her laptop.

5

Josh bounded downstairs and into the kitchen. He was still in his dressing gown but had the customary cables leading to his ears. Sometimes, I was sure he actually slept with them in. It made me think that one day, in an evolutionary move, babies would actually be born with earphones, ready to be plugged into any device.

'Morning, all,' he said as he sat down at the table and started buttering a piece of toast.

I raised my eyebrows at Chris before we both bid him a good morning.

'What you listening to?' asked Chris.

'The Velvet Underground,' said Josh.

'I didn't know you had any of their stuff on your iPhone.'

'I didn't. Mum got it for me.'

The word 'Mum' hung heavily in the air. It wasn't the first time he'd used it in the past two weeks, but it still had the ability to throw us. Chris particularly.

'I could have downloaded it for you,' Chris said.

'No, it's some rare session they did. She got it through someone she knows in the industry.'

Chris said nothing. I poured him another cup of tea.

'It must be good to have two mums,' piped up Matilda. 'It means you get more stuff.'

Josh glanced at me before taking another mouthful of toast.

'When is she going to come here?' asked Matilda.

'Like I said, love. It's still early days.'

'Oh, is it because you don't like her?'

'No, love. Not at all.'

'So doesn't Daddy like her?' Matilda looked up at Chris as she said it.

Josh looked at him too.

'It's not that I don't like her.'

'Do you love her, then? You must have loved her when she was Josh's mummy that lived here.'

Nobody said anything.

Josh stood up, walked over and put the radio on. Sometimes he was very much older than his sixteen years.

We met Debbie and Sophie at the end of the lane. Or rather, Matilda charged into them, and she and Sophie ran off in front, doing their scrunchy leaf stomp along the verge.

'How's things?' asked Debbie. Her nose was already red and her hands were thrust deep into her pockets against the cold.

'Oh, much the same,' I said. 'Still treading on eggshells around the breakfast table.'

'Did Josh see her again at the weekend?'

'Yeah, seems to be a regular Saturday afternoon fixture.'

'And how does Chris feel about that?'

'I think the thing that's really getting to him is how happy Josh is. Not that he was miserable before, or anything, but he's buzzing with it all. It's like he's got a new girlfriend or something. Except it's not a girlfriend, it's his mum.'

'And what about you?' asked Debbie.

'What about me?'

'Well, it can't be easy. To all intents and purposes you've been Josh's mother for the past nine years.'

'Yeah, but she's not like a mother to him. She's more like a really cool older sister. I think that's how Josh sees her, anyway.'

'So basically she gets to do all the fun things with him and you get to wash his socks and cook him tea.'

'Yeah, something like that,' I said.

'See. I told you to get shot of her.'

'She's Josh's mother, Deb. It's his choice. It's not up to me.'

'And Chris agrees with that, does he?'

'Chris is doing his best. It's difficult for him.'

'Why did she leave in the first place?'

'I don't know. Chris has never gone into it. And I don't think now is a good time to ask.'

'It's the perfect time to ask. She's back on the scene, and it's only fair that you know what you're dealing with.'

I shrugged.

She was right, of course. I just didn't want to admit it. Not even to myself.

The first thing which struck me about Catherine and Nathan wasn't how beautiful they were (although they were undoubtedly beautiful) but what a very impressive front they were putting on. Usually, by the time people get to see me, they have given up pretending that everything is OK or, if they haven't, the facade cracks within a few seconds of entering my room.

Nathan strolled in, shook me firmly by the hand and said it was good to meet me, as if I were a business associate. Catherine stretched out a long and elegant hand to shake mine. She smiled at me, a genuine smile which exuded warmth. They sat down. Both of them were dressed immaculately, he in a well-cut suit and she in a long-sleeved purple shift dress with a silk scarf and tall grey boots.

Nathan poured two glasses of water and handed one to Catherine. They both looked at me, bright and attentive, as if they had wandered in here by accident, thinking I was the small business adviser next door.

'Thank you both for coming,' I said. 'I do understand what a difficult process this can be. If you need to take a break at any time, just ask.'

They both nodded. Nathan crossed his legs. Catherine took a sip of water. I noticed her hand was shaking. Our eyes met for a second and she put the glass back down.

'Right, well, at the first session I usually go through the notes from your initial assessment. If there's anything which you feel isn't accurate, or there's anything missing which you believe is important, please let me know.'

They nodded again. Nathan glanced at his watch.

'So you've been together twelve years, since meeting at university in Manchester. You've no children and you both work full-time. Nathan, it says you run your own web design company.'

'That's right, if you ever need a website setting up pronto –' He took a business card from his pocket and put it on the table.

I thought I saw Catherine cringe, but I couldn't be sure.

'And Catherine, you co-own an art gallery in Hebden Bridge and work as a part-time arts promotions officer.'

'Yes,' she said, before looking down at her hands.

I noticed for the first time that the nail varnish was chipped.

'And as far as the problems you've been experiencing go, you both say there are issues regarding whether to start a family or not, which have led to lots of arguments.' I looked up.

Catherine was still staring at her hands. The smile had disappeared from her face. Nathan, however, remained decidedly upbeat.

'That about sums it up,' he said.

I looked at Catherine. 'So how do you feel about starting a family?'

She looked down as she spoke. 'I don't want children, but I don't want that to be an issue between us. I don't see why it needs to be.'

'The thing is,' said Nathan, 'people don't always know what they want, do they? Until it's too late, that is. And I don't want Catherine to regret this in later life. I think she'd make a great mum. I thought coming here and talking about it might make her see that.'

I scribbled some notes.

When I glanced up, Catherine was gazing out of the window behind me, her eyes moist with tears.

*

I don't think Josh meant for me to see him. True, he didn't usually leave his bedroom door open. But Matilda had gone to bed, so the main reason to shut it had disappeared.

I'd only nipped upstairs to get a cardigan. For some reason I happened to glance in as I walked past his doorway. Josh was sitting on the end of his bed, his cheeks wet with tears, gazing down at what appeared to be a shoebox on his lap.

'Hey,' I said, stepping inside the room, 'what's the matter?'

'It's OK,' he said, wiping his nose with the back of his hand and managing a watery smile. 'Nothing's happened, I just got out the box and I think it all kind of caught up with me.'

I sat down on the bed next to him and put my arm around his shoulders. The box on his lap was open. On the top of a small pile of things inside was a black and white photograph of a young, dark-haired woman clutching a newborn baby to her chest. Her eyeliner was smudged, her hair lank with sweat, but the look on her face was one of immense pride.

'She seems so happy,' said Josh.

'I know,' I said. 'I'm sure she was.'

'There are others,' he went on. 'Quite a few of them.'

He flicked through the wallet of photos underneath. Pictures of him and Lydia snuggled together on a rug on the floor, wrapped up together in a bath towel, both sporting Santa hats on what would have been his first Christmas. Lydia's expression was one of unwavering devotion. She smiled less as Josh got older, though. In the ones where he was sitting up, she was hardly smiling at all.

'I've never seen these before,' I said.

'Dad gave me the box when I was a kid, a year or so

after I started school, I think. We were doing something on families and they asked us to bring in photos of us as babies. I remember Dad saying he wanted me to know what my mum looked like and that she'd really loved me but she'd had to go away.'

I nodded and squeezed his shoulder.

'When I got a bit older, and started to get angry about it all, I put the box away inside another one in the back of the wardrobe. I guess that's why you've never seen it. I only just remembered it and got it out. I can't believe how similar she looks. She's hardly changed at all, has she?'

I shook my head.

He opened another wallet underneath. There was a photo of baby Josh sitting on Barbara's knee with Lydia sitting next to them. Barbara was beaming down at him. Lydia holding one outstretched hand.

'It's weird, isn't it?' said Josh. 'I hadn't even thought about her knowing Grandma. Stupid, really, cos the only people she didn't know are you and Tilda. And look, this one was taken in the garden, see how small the apple tree is.'

I nodded and swallowed hard. Lydia in our house, in our garden, with our family. Long before I knew any of them. Her imprint was here. I had always felt it but had tried so hard to ignore it. She had cast a shadow over this house when she'd left. But for Josh, at least, her reappearance had been like someone throwing open the shutters to let the light in.

I squeezed his shoulder again. 'It means a lot to you, doesn't it? To have her back, I mean.'

Josh nodded. 'It was like, for years, I hated her but I realise now I didn't really hate her, I just hated that she wasn't around. Hated that I didn't have a mum when other kids did.' He looked up sharply. 'Sorry,' he said.

'No. I understand. I'm not your mum. I've never pretended to be. I just love you like a son, that's all.'

He smiled across at me. 'Some kids at school think you are my mum,' he said. 'The kids who I only met at high school, who didn't know me before you were around. I've never bothered to tell them.'

'You don't mind them thinking your mum is some uncool woman with a nice line in cardigans and Ugg boots, then?'

Josh dug me in the ribs with his elbow. 'You're not that bad.'

'I'll take that as a compliment.'

'It's weird, really. I mean, she's my mum and yet she doesn't know me at all, not really, not all the little things about me. And you're not my mum but you know me miles better than her. I couldn't talk to her like I can to you.'

'No, but you can talk to her about other things – music, and stuff I know nothing about.'

'Yeah. Yeah, I guess so.'

A floorboard creaked on the landing.

I looked up to see Chris standing there. He looked at me, at Josh and at the box.

Then he turned and walked away without saying anything.

From the Counselling Room

I took her to see Fatal Attraction *and she leant over in the cinema, put her hand on my crotch and whispered into my ear, 'I boil bunnies, you know.'*
    End of.

6

'But why can't we all go together?' asked Matilda at breakfast.

I opened my mouth to say something but Chris shook his head slightly at me, indicating that he was going to take the question.

'We didn't all go together last year, or the year before that. Josh went with Tom, if you remember.'

'Yes, but that's different,' said Matilda. 'That was because you said he was old enough to go with his friends. He isn't going with his friends this time, he's going with his mum, and that's family so we should all go together.'

I had to admit that for an eight-year-old, her logic was pretty impressive. Unfortunately, on this particular point, it was not appreciated. Josh came into the kitchen before either of us had had a chance to formulate an answer.

He looked at Matilda's expectant face and both of us. 'What's up?' he asked.

'Nothing,' Chris said.

'Yes, it is,' said Matilda. 'I want to know why we can't all go to the fireworks as a family. I don't see why you have to go with your mum and me with my mum and we can't all go together like we should.'

Matilda's evident fury took me back a little. I could tell Chris was trying very hard not to react.

Josh looked down at the floor. 'Sorry,' he said.

'Don't be silly,' I said. 'It's not a problem.'

'Well, it obviously is for her,' he replied, gesturing towards Matilda.

'It's just going to take time to adjust,' I said. 'For all of us.'

Josh hesitated. 'Look, I'll go with you guys if it makes things easier. I'll text Mum and let her know.'

'No,' I said. 'You don't have to do that.'

Chris looked up at me sharply.

'He's made arrangements,' I said. 'It's not fair to mess people around at such short notice.'

I could see Chris itching to reply, could hear the words formulating in his head, fighting to escape through his mouth. He took a swig of tea, maybe to stop them, before turning to Matilda.

'Tilda, you heard what your mum said. It's too late to change things this year. But how about I let you have an extra turn on the hook-a-duck at the fair? How does that sound?'

Matilda considered the offer. For a moment I wondered if she was going to try to negotiate two extra turns, but I think even she sensed that Chris was not in the mood.

'OK,' she said. 'As long as you don't complain if I pick two big fluffy things.'

'Deal,' said Chris, managing a smile as she high-fived him before skipping upstairs.

'Take it out of my pocket money,' said Josh.

'What?' asked Chris.

'The money for her extra turn.'

'Don't be a daft bugger,' said Chris. 'It was my decision to offer her that.'

'You mean bribe her?' smiled Josh.

'Yeah, well, whatever. It's not your fault, OK? None of this is your fault.'

Josh nodded and went to pour himself some cereal.

'Thanks,' I whispered, stroking Chris's arm.

He shrugged and squeezed my hand. It was a long time before he let go.

Kelly didn't look old enough to be married, let alone be on the verge of a divorce. She was what Barbara would have called 'a slip of a girl', fair hair scraped off her face and tied back with a scrunchie, dimples when she smiled. Only a fleeting smile, mind. Though that was understandable under the circumstances.

Luke's frame was massive next to hers. Broad shoulders and tall with it, his fair hair cropped short around his freckled face. His jaw set firm. He had the expression of someone who has been told they have to choose between cutting off their right leg or their left. Things were clearly not good.

I introduced myself and sat them down, told them how the sessions worked, asked if they had any questions before we began.

'Do you mind if I keep my mobile on?' asked Kelly. 'Only Luke's mam's got the kids, and they are a bit of a handful. And in case there's an emergency or whatever.'

'That's fine. I understand,' I said.

'Thanks,' said Kelly.

She shuffled uncomfortably. She looked like someone about to sit a GCSE maths exam.

'Just remember, there are no right or wrong answers,' I said. 'We're here to talk about how you're both feeling, why you're feeling that way and how we can work together to make things better.'

Luke stared resolutely out of the window behind me.

'OK, so perhaps we can start by talking about how you got together? Because I gather from my colleague's notes that there are a few issues which have stemmed from that.'

Kelly looked at Luke. He said nothing.

She fiddled with a strand of loose hair before starting to talk. 'Well, I were only, like, thirteen when we started seeing each other. He were in year eleven at school and I were in year nine. We didn't tell anyone until the summer when Luke left school and started working on the building site. And then me mam flipped her lid.'

'She didn't approve?'

'No. Cos of age difference, which were daft because her and me dad have got a bigger age difference than us. But she reckoned that were different cos she'd been seventeen when they'd started going out.'

'And what about your family, Luke?' I asked. 'What was their reaction?'

'It's only me mam, like, because me dad buggered off when I were a kid. But she didn't have a problem with it. She thought it would be good for me to settle down young. And she liked Kelly, she still does.'

'And you got married when you were eighteen, Kelly.'

'Yeah, day of my eighteenth birthday. We would have done it earlier, but me mam and dad wouldn't give permission.'

'And why did you want to get married rather than just live together?'

Kelly glanced at Luke before answering. 'He'd been ribbed by the lads at work saying he were a paedo and that. And I'd had two years of people saying it were only a schoolgirl crush. We wanted to show people that it were, like, forever.'

Her voice caught as she said it. She looked down and started fiddling with her wedding ring. Luke shifted in his seat. I gave them both a moment.

'And so I take it you got no support from your family after you were married, Kelly?'

She shook her head. 'No, they practically disowned me. Which is daft, innit? I mean, I weren't taking drugs and I weren't up the duff or nothing. They disowned me for getting married. *Duh.*'

She pulled a face as she said it. I was reminded again of how young she still was.

'But you were happy?'

'Yeah. We were dead happy,' said Kelly. 'And when I found out I were pregnant, we were chuffed about it.'

'And then you had the baby and wondered what the hell had hit you,' I said.

Kelly and Luke both stared at me as if I must have had some inside information.

'It happens to everyone,' I said. 'I was thirty-two when I had my daughter, and I already had a stepson, but I found it incredibly tough.'

'Really,' said Kelly. 'You're not just saying that?'

'No. I had no idea what I was doing, I worried all the time that I was doing the wrong thing. It changes your relationship with your partner too, doesn't it?' I looked at Luke as I said this.

'To be honest,' he said, 'it were like someone had kidnapped Kelly and put someone else back in her place. She were always so bright and sparky before, always having a laugh. She never used to moan about owt.'

'I get right arsey when I haven't had any sleep,' Kelly said.

'I weren't getting at you,' said Luke. 'It were just hard, that's all. Not like we thought it would be.'

'And Callum were a right whingey baby,' added Kelly. 'So being the eejits we are, we thought we'd have another one, just to see if it were any better.'

She laughed as she said it, but I could tell she was trying to put on a brave face.

'Only "it" was twins,' I said.

'Yeah, we weren't expecting that,' said Luke. 'Me mam were made up at the time but she's said to me since that it were probably worst thing that could have happened to us, like.'

'Did she?' asked Kelly. 'You never said.'

'She didn't mean it in a bad way,' said Luke. 'She loves Liam and Ava to bits. She just meant that it were too much to cope with. It was her that suggested coming here,' he said, turning to me. 'Said she'd pay for it, like.'

'We do have the discretion to reduce fees to suit ability to pay. Has that all been explained to you?'

'Oh yeah, but we ain't accepting charity, like,' said Luke. 'We've always paid our way.'

I nodded. I'd had people earning twice as much ask if they could pay less. Although the difference was that they didn't appear to love each other half as much as Kelly and Luke did.

To the untrained eye, Matilda might have appeared to be fizzing like a firework herself at the prospect of the Bonfire Night out. But I was well aware that she had reached nothing like her usual excitement level. I glanced at Chris. He was obviously aware of it too.

'Why can't Josh come with us for the children's fireworks and then go with his mum for the grown-up ones?' asked Matilda.

I looked at Chris. It was a good compromise and no doubt he, like me, was wishing one of us had come up with it earlier. It was too late now, though. We were due to leave in ten minutes. I was also aware that it would feel a little like those arrangements children of divorced parents have on Christmas Day. And having hated it myself as a teenager, I didn't want to put Josh through the same thing.

'Good idea, love. Maybe next year we can do that, eh?'

Matilda sighed.

I was praying she wouldn't take the protest any further; I suspected from the look on his face that Chris was approaching breaking point.

'We might see them while we're there,' she said, her face brightening for a second. 'We'll probably be standing right near them.'

'I doubt it, love,' I said, stroking her hair. 'Remember how busy it is? There are thousands of people there. We probably won't see them.'

'We will if I ask Josh to wear something bright. I could lend him my flashing Santa hat, then we could easily spot him.'

I smiled at her, though the thought of Chris having to make small talk to Lydia in front of Matilda and Josh was actually making me feel rather queasy inside. 'Look, I'm afraid it's just not going to happen, love. Now, let's get our coats on and wrap up warm, it's nearly time to go.'

'She's spoiling it,' said Matilda, her voice an octave higher and considerably louder than previously. 'I don't want Josh to have another mum. I want it to be like it was before. I want her to go away again.'

I could see the whites of Chris's knuckles. Hear him choking back the words which were, no doubt, fighting to come out. I hurried Matilda into the hallway, desperate to get her out of the house as quickly as possible. It was only then I saw Josh on the landing.

'It's OK,' he said, 'I'm coming with you.'

'No, love,' I said, 'you don't have to do that. We can handle it.'

'No, Mum texted. She can't make it.'

It was as if the light from Josh's face had somehow been drained and fed directly into Matilda's.

'Yay! Josh is coming with us,' she said. 'We're all going to the fireworks together.'

'Did she say why?' I asked Josh.

'Something about a guy she'd met at the Trades Club last night.'

I caught Chris's eye. He appeared to be torn between being mad at Lydia and relieved that Josh was coming with us.

He pulled on his jacket. 'Right,' he said. 'Last one down the hill is the boring Catherine wheel of the firework box.'

'I like Catherine wheels,' said Matilda.

'Then the last one can be a Roman candle.'

'I like them too.'

'Well,' said Chris, giving her a squeeze, 'it doesn't matter if you're last, then, does it?'

They went out of the door, laughing and poking each other. I put my scarf on and pulled my hat down over my ears.

'I'm sorry, love,' I said to Josh. 'I know you were looking forward to seeing her.'

'It doesn't matter,' he said as he took his coat from the peg.

It did, though. It clearly mattered very much.

From the Counselling Room

And then one day he hit Millie.

And all the times he'd hit me went flashing through my mind. Only instead of seeing me, I saw him hitting Millie, heard her screaming, saw her arms and her legs turn black and blue and saw his footprint on her belly, and I knew I couldn't stay there a second longer.

I just scooped her up off the floor and walked out of the door.

7

'Is it OK if I go out tonight, to a club?'

Josh's voice was the brightest it had been for a week, which made it very difficult to say no. I glanced at Chris. He shrugged and nodded.

'I guess so,' I said. 'But I thought you and Tom were watching a film at his place?'

'I'm not going with Tom,' Josh said.

I knew instantly what that meant. Chris must have too.

He snapped down the lid of his laptop. 'So who are you going with?' he asked.

Josh looked down at his feet before answering. 'With Mum. She's got a spare ticket for some band she reckons are really good.'

'And how does Tom feel about being blown out?' asked Chris.

'He's cool about it. Really.'

I looked at Chris.

He sighed, aware he was cornered. 'OK. But don't make a habit of letting down your best mate.'

'Thanks,' said Josh. 'I'll let you know if the band are any good. Mum reckons you'd like them.'

My skin bristled. She still claimed to know him. To know him in the way that you only do if you live with someone, if you're their soulmate. I imagined them lying together listening to music. Lying in what was now our bedroom. I wondered if she used to make him compilation tapes. Whether she'd done dance ones. And ones to have sex to.

Chris leant back in the chair and ran his fingers through his hair as Josh left the room and bounded back upstairs.

'She doesn't make it easy, does she?' I said.

'No. She never did.'

I stared out of the window, hating the way she was doing this. Leaving silent footprints all around us.

'I tell you what,' I said, leaning over and kissing him on his forehead. 'We should go out tonight.'

'Why?'

'Because we never do.'

'Fair point. I could ask Mum to babysit.'

'You're sure she won't mind?'

'What, spending a few hours of quality time with her only granddaughter?'

'It might stop Matilda complaining about everyone else going out,' I said. 'And she'll like having your mum all to herself.'

'Good. That's sorted.'

'I'll book a table, then,' I said, smiling at him. I wasn't going to let her do this. Let her memory come between us.

'You off already?' I asked Josh later. 'I thought you might see Grandma before you go.'

'Sorry, we're going somewhere to eat first. Nelson's, I think.'

'Is she vegetarian?'

'Yeah, didn't you know?'

I shook my head, wondering what else I didn't know about her. 'Do you need some money, then?'

'No, it's OK, thanks, Mum's paying.'

I'd heard him say the word enough times that I should have been used to it. I wasn't, though.

'Have you got your emergency money?' I asked.

'Yeah and the monkey chaff, Mrs Potato Head,' said Josh, grinning.

I could still remember watching *Toy Story 2* with him when he was a kid. I think Chris had started calling me it first. But Josh was the one who'd carried it on every time I started listing items he may need.

'Thank you for the cheek,' I replied. 'Home before midnight, please.'

'Or I'll turn into a pumpkin.'

'How are you getting home? Has she got a car?'

'No. She said she'd get me a cab.'

'Well, have some more money, just in case,' I said, reaching for my purse.

'I'm fine,' he replied. 'Stop being such a mum.'

It must have shown on my face. Even though I tried hard to stop it.

'Sorry,' he said. 'I didn't mean –'

'No, it's OK,' I said. 'It's fine.' I smiled at him. Put the ten-pound note back in my purse. 'Have a good time, then,' I said.

'Thanks. And you.'

He closed the front door quietly behind him. I sat down for a second on the bottom of the stairs. Conscious that Lydia had once been a proper mum to him. In this very house. Had fed him, winded him, changed his nappy, things that I had never done. So I had no right, really. No right to feel the way I was feeling. She had been here first. I was the newcomer. I was the one who couldn't complain that a mother had come to reclaim her child.

As long as that was all she was trying to reclaim.

I sighed and looked at the clock. Chris and Matilda wouldn't be back from picking up Barbara for a good half an hour yet. I decided to go and have a bath.

I took a long while doing my make-up afterwards. It was like being a teenager again, having the luxury of taking your time to get ready for a night out.

I tried to remember the last time Chris and I had been out for a meal. It was probably my fortieth. Too long, really. Like dating someone every eight months, except sillier than that, because the person in question happened to be my husband. I, of all people, ought to have known not to let that happen. But somehow it had. It was time to put a stop to it.

I took the lipliner and drew a careful outline before filling in with lipstick. It was my colour. Something called 'damson rose'. It had taken me until I was forty to find it, but sometimes the important things in life did take time.

I caught sight of the photo on the dressing table. The black and white one of me cradling a newborn Matilda in my arms, my cheeks red and my eyes moist with tears. I hadn't realised until that moment how similar it was to the one of Lydia with Josh which he'd shown me. It wasn't surprising, of course. The same photographer had taken it. The only difference was that mine hadn't been put away in a box, out of sight and out of mind.

'Well, you scrubbed up pretty well.'

I gave a start as I heard Chris's voice behind me. 'I'll take that as a compliment.' I smiled.

'I only came in to change my shirt. I suppose you want me to make more of an effort now.'

'Well, maybe just this once. It's not often we get the chance, is it?'

'Where are we going?'

'Somewhere nice.'

'It wouldn't be first date territory, would it?' he asked.

'Might be,' I said, trying to hide my disappointment that he'd guessed.

'Decent shirt and trousers, then,' he said. 'But I draw the line at a tie.' He squeezed past me to get to the wardrobe. 'Wow, you smell good too.' He stooped to kiss me on the neck.

And I was momentarily transported back to a time when this was happening for the first time. And I was breathing him in, unable to believe that someone like him was doing this with someone like me.

'If I kiss you properly, I'm going to get lipstick all over me, aren't I?' asked Chris.

I nodded.

'Oh well, I guess it'll just have to wait for later.'

I heard voices downstairs through the open doorway. A male voice particularly. One which shouldn't have been there.

'That's Josh,' I said.

We both hurried downstairs. He was standing in the hall looking forlorn. Barbara was next to him, using her best soothing tones.

'Hey, what's happened?' I asked.

'Mum didn't show,' he said, his voice an uncertain mixture of anger and defensiveness.

'Have you tried ringing her?' I asked.

'Yeah. Just goes to her voicemail. I've left a message and I've texted her but she hasn't got back.'

'That's bang out of order,' said Chris from behind me. 'I'm not having her mess you around like this.'

I realised Matilda was standing in the doorway, and whispered to Barbara to take her back into the lounge and put a DVD on. Chris waited until she'd shut the door behind her.

'Maybe something came up,' said Josh.

'Yeah. Something's come up all right.'

'Chris,' I said.

'Well, it's pretty damn obvious.'

'Why don't you call Tom?' I said to Josh. 'See if he's still around.'

'I already have. He's gone round to his cousin's.'

'Well, we can stay in, if you like,' I offered.

'No, there's no need. You go.'

'Are you sure?' I asked.

'Yeah.'

'Thanks,' I said, rubbing his shoulder.

Though I suspected the evening had been ruined already.

*

Chris didn't speak until we were in the car. Until I'd pulled out of the lane and was heading down the hill.

'You know what's happened, don't you?' he said. 'She was blown out by that guy she's seeing. Offered the ticket to Josh and told her boyfriend she was going with someone else to try to get back at him. Then when he's come running back, she's ditched Josh. She's just using him.'

'If I didn't know you better –' I began.

'What?' he broke in.

'It doesn't matter.'

'Yes, it does. You think I'm jealous, don't you?'

'You seem very het up about it, that's all.'

'Yeah. Because she's messing Josh around.'

'And that's all it is?'

'Jesus, what do you take me for?'

'Well, what am I supposed to think? Ever since she came back you've been on edge, and you refuse to talk about her.'

'Because there's nothing to say.'

'Of course there is. You lived with her for nearly five years, Chris. You had a child with her. You obviously –' I stopped short of saying the words.

He was quiet for a minute or two, until we pulled up at the traffic lights at the junction with the main road.

'Look, it doesn't matter what I felt for her back then. The day she walked out on us everything changed for ever.'

I heard the catch in his voice. Noticed his clenched hands in his lap. I knew that I had to tread very carefully.

'She looked happy,' I said. 'In the photos with Josh, when he'd just been born.'

'Yeah. She was.'

'Was he a planned baby?' I asked.

'No. Not really. He was very much loved, though. By both of us.'

'So what happened?' I asked.

'She scared me,' he said. 'That's what happened. And that's all you need to know.'

I drove on in silence. To a meal I no longer had an appetite for.

Barbara was sitting in the lounge reading when we got home. Chris went upstairs to check on Matilda. He always did it when we'd been out. He even put his head round Josh's door as well. Old habits die hard.

'How was your meal?' asked Barbara.

'Fine, thanks,' I said. 'The food was good, anyway.'

Barbara nodded. She understood what I meant. 'Don't let her spoil things,' she said. 'She's not worth it.'

'Were they happy together?' I asked.

'Yes,' she said.

'So what happened?'

'She abused his trust,' said Barbara. 'And when she got found out, she knew exactly how to hurt him.'

From the Counselling Room

He'd always been into the Carpenters. I mean, I didn't mind them, I was never keen on that 'Jambalaya' one but the rest of their stuff was perfectly OK to listen to. If anyone ever asked him who his favourite singer was, he'd say, 'Karen Carpenter – voice like velvet,' and give a little sigh afterwards. There was always a Carpenters CD on in the car, I don't think he had anything else in there, and I never even complained about that.

And then, one day, I came home early from the shops, when he wasn't expecting me, like. He obviously didn't hear me because he had 'Close to You' on at full volume, and I walked into the front room and there he was, stark naked in front of the gas fire apart from his socks, pleasuring himself, like, while he looked at a picture of her, of Karen Carpenter.

I told him that night. I said he had to choose, me or Karen. And he, well, he chose her.

8

It was snowing the next morning. And even though we'd had a carpet of snow for much of the previous winter, the arrival of the first of this season's offering was still enough to elicit squeals of delight from Matilda when I pulled back her bedroom curtains.

'Can I go out and play in it?' she asked.

'After breakfast, yes.'

'Will Josh come with me?'

'Probably not, he's still in bed. So keep the noise down, please, missy.'

'Why didn't his mum tell him she wasn't coming?'

'We don't know, love.'

'I don't think she's a very nice mummy, is she?'

'We can't say that, love. There could be a good reason.'

'Can I build a snowman?'

'I don't think there's enough for that yet.'

'But if there is after breakfast, can I?'

'Of course you can.' I smiled.

I went back downstairs while she got dressed. Chris was gathering his camera gear. He'd hardly said a word to me since we'd come home the previous night. I was annoyed with myself for letting Lydia get the better of me. I wanted to make amends.

'You off out?' I asked.

'Yeah. You don't mind, do you? Only the light's perfect right now. I won't be long.'

'Of course not,' I said. 'As long as you take a turn with the sledging this afternoon.'

'Is she up for it?'

'Has she ever not been up for it?'

'Fair point. I'll see you later.'

I nodded. He gave me a peck on the cheek before he left. I watched him walk across the field behind our house and start to climb the hill beyond. He thought nothing of lugging all the camera gear with him. He used to go up on the tops taking photos with Josh in a backpack, when he was little. He'd told me about it. I imagined watching them there sometimes. A tiny Josh tight against his back. Safe with his father. And Chris happy because he had everything he needed. Everything he loved. And no one could take that away from him.

'Where's Daddy?' asked Matilda as soon as she came down.

'He's working. He's gone up on the tops to take some photos.'

'Ohhh. I wanted to go too.'

'You'd be bored, love. He wouldn't have time to play. He's going to get the sledge out for you when he comes back.'

'Yay!' Matilda grinned and sat down for her breakfast.

She ate her cereal in record time, ran to put her wellies and coat on and scrabbled at the back door like a mad puppy desperate to be let out.

'It's OK,' I said, putting her hat on and digging out her scarf. 'It's not going to melt. It's freezing out there.'

'Are you coming too?' she asked.

'Later,' I said. 'I'm going to cook some breakfast for Daddy and Josh first.'

She played happily in the snow for about fifteen minutes. I glanced out to check on her every now and again. She was utterly engrossed in creating some kind of snow monster by the look of it. She opened the back door as I was turning the sausages over.

'I've run out of snow,' she said. 'Can I go out the front to get some more in my bucket?'

'OK, but go carefully. It'll be slippery on the paving stones.'

She nodded and disappeared round the side of the house. We only had a small front garden but the snow tended to drift against the house in a certain wind.

There were still no sounds from upstairs. I wasn't going to wake Josh, although I was still tempted to have a chat with him before Chris came back, try to smooth things over in advance.

I heard a shout from outside. I wasn't sure at first, but then I heard it again.

It was Matilda calling 'Mummy!'

I knew from the tone of her voice and the volume of the shout that something was wrong. I took the pan off the hot-plate and ran straight out the front, still in my slippers and dressing gown.

Lydia was standing in the garden, entirely inappropriately dressed for the weather in a short black skirt, crop top and bare legs. She had a cigarette in one hand and a morning-after-the-night-before look about her.

Matilda ran full pelt at me, throwing her arms around my waist and burying her face in my tummy.

'Are you OK, love?' I asked.

'She made me jump. And she shouted at me.'

'I didn't mean to scare her,' Lydia said, slurring slightly as she spoke.

'Why did you shout at her?'

'I asked her if Josh was in and she didn't fucking reply.'

'Go inside, love,' I said to Matilda. 'Pop a DVD on. I'll be with you in a minute.'

Matilda scowled at Lydia and ran inside.

'Will you watch your language in front of her, please.'

'I need to see Josh.'

'You were supposed to see him last night.'

She walked a few steps closer to me. I could smell the alcohol on her breath from ten paces.

'I know. I came to say I'm sorry. He's turned his phone off.'

'Well, it'll have to wait. You're drunk. Josh is still asleep. I'll tell him you came. And if he wants to call you, he will.'

'He's my son, you know, not yours,' she said, her face close enough to mine that I could smell the cigarette smoke in her hair.

'I know,' I said. 'But he lives in my house.'

'It's not yours,' she said. 'It's Chris's. And I lived in it long before you.'

She took a puff on her cigarette and blew the smoke out in

my face, before turning on her heels and tottering off, making stiletto prints in the snow as she left.

'Please don't come here again without asking first,' I called after her.

I stood shaking in the garden for a second before hurrying back indoors. Josh was on the landing.

'That was Mum, wasn't it?' he asked.

I nodded.

'What was all the shouting about?'

'She was drunk. She scared Matilda.'

'Is Tilda OK?'

'Yeah, she's fine. I'm going to check on her now.'

'Sorry.'

'You don't have to apologise for her, Josh.'

'She's my mum, isn't she?'

'She's not your responsibility, though. She's old enough to know better.'

'Dad's going to go ape, isn't he?'

'Yeah,' I said, 'he probably will.'

Josh sighed and disappeared back to his room. I went into the lounge. Matilda was sitting on the sofa. She still had her coat on. I sat down next to her and put my arms around her. Kissed her softly on the forehead.

'Are you OK, sweetheart?' I asked.

She nodded, not taking her eyes off the television where *Scooby-Doo* was on. 'I don't like her. She shouldn't have come here.'

'No, love, she shouldn't. And I've told her not to come back without asking first.'

'Why wasn't she dressed properly?'

'I don't think she was really thinking straight.'

'And she was smoking and she said a bad word.'

'I know. I'm sorry.'

She looked up at me, her big brown eyes unusually serious. 'I want it to go back to how it was before.'

'I know, love. But it can't do. Not now.'

She started to cry.

I hugged her in to me, stroking her hair. 'It'll be OK, love,' I said. 'Everything will be OK.'

I heard Chris's key in the door. Before I could stop her, Matilda pulled away and ran out to him.

'Josh's mum was in the garden and she made me jump and she said a bad word and Mummy got cross with her and made her go away.'

I heard the words tumble out of her mouth and got to the hallway in time to see Chris's eyes darken, his jaw tense.

'Is this true?' he asked.

'Yes. Matilda's fine. Lydia didn't touch her. She just scared her.'

'Did she see Josh?'

'No, he was still in bed. He heard some of it and he knows what happened.'

'Right. Well, he'll understand that it stops there, then.'

I gestured down at Matilda. I wasn't going to have this conversation in front of her.

'Can you manage a second breakfast, love?' I asked.

She nodded.

'Take your coat off and pop and wash your hands, then. I think we all need warming up.'

'Shall I get Josh?' she asked.

'Yeah, you can do. But if he says he's not hungry, that's OK.'

I watched her go up the stairs. Chris waited until she was out of earshot.

'What the hell was she doing here?'

'She said she'd come to apologise to Josh.'

'Oh yeah, turning up drunk and scaring his little sister, that's a great way of apologising.'

'Just don't say anything to Josh if he does come down for breakfast. He looked pretty cut up about it. You know how he hates anyone upsetting his sister.'

Chris sighed. Shook his head. 'Are you OK?' he asked.

'Yeah, bit shaken, that's all.'

'I'm sorry.'

'Don't you start apologising as well.'

'No. I've been thinking. She's my ex. You shouldn't have to put up with any of this.'

'It's not that easy, though, is it? We can't just make her go away.'

Matilda came back downstairs with Josh trailing behind her. We sat down together in the kitchen, Josh seemingly unable to look anyone in the eye. I dished up what was left of the cooked breakfasts. We sat in silence. Josh prodded the sausage around on his plate for a bit, then pushed back his chair and stood up.

'Sorry,' he said. 'I'm not really hungry.'

When I went into Matilda's room the next morning she was curled tightly in her duvet, her back facing me. I sat down on the edge of the bed and reached out to stroke her head.

The sheet next to her was damp. Very damp. I raised my hand towards my nose. The smell was unmistakable.

I shut my eyes and bit my lower lip. I could barely remember the last time she'd wet the bed. Not for years. Maybe once, when she was about five, and she was poorly.

I stroked her cheek with the back of my hand. It was a moment or two before she came round. She opened her eyes. Within seconds there was a frown on her face.

'I'm all sticky,' she said.

'I know, love. You've had a little accident. It doesn't matter. We'll soon get you cleaned up.'

Her face crumpled. The tears came.

And I wished to God that Lydia hadn't come back.

From the Counselling Room

He texted me and asked if I'd like to come and watch him play badminton.

I just texted back 'No, not really'.

9

The text messages started that evening. Maybe it had taken her that long to sober up. Maybe Josh hadn't turned his phone back on until then either, as some sort of mark of respect to the rest of the family or simply because he didn't know how to handle it.

At first I thought it was Josh and Tom just texting back and forth but one look at Josh's face at the dinner table when his phone beeped from upstairs gave it away. I glanced at Chris. If he did realise, he was doing a very good job of keeping his expression neutral.

I said nothing at the time. Waited until after tea. Until the dishwasher had been loaded and Chris was reading Matilda a bedtime story. I knocked on the door of Josh's room.

'Yeah,' he called.

I went in, taking it as teenage for 'enter'. The darkness of the decor always looked worse in winter. At least in the summer the sunlight crashed through his sash windows and his blinds could offer little in the way of defence. In winter it was as if the darkness outside somehow reflected back the darkness from within. The one condition we had laid down was that, if we ever put the house up for sale, he'd have to paint the walls magnolia (black not featuring highly on those 'How to sell your property' lists).

Josh was lying on his bed, his earphones in, something sounding conspicuously like 'Back to Black' coming out of them.

'Didn't know you were into Amy Winehouse,' I said.

He took out his earphones, somewhat defensively. 'Mum got me into her,' he said.

I imagined Lydia listening to her. Sharing in the anguish. Spitting out the words. Mourning her death. I sat down on the corner of Josh's bed.

'Have you spoken to her?' I asked.

He shook his head. 'No, just texted.'

'What's she saying?'

'That she's sorry. She screwed up and she wants us to start again.'

I nodded. 'And what do you reckon to that?'

He shrugged. 'I dunno. It's hard. I can forgive her for mucking me about but coming here and shouting at you and Tilda –'

His voice broke off as he shook his head.

'Has she said why she behaved like that?'

'Just that she was mad at herself for letting me down and mad at her boyfriend too. That's why she started drinking.'

'She obviously didn't know when to stop, either. Does she drink when she's with you?'

'No. Never. Smokes a lot, mind.'

'So, basically, you've just found the mum you've never known, she's messed you about and screwed up, and you can't work out what the hell you're supposed to do about it.'

'You're good at your job, aren't you?' said Josh, with a half-smile.

'I get a lot of people with problems where there are no easy answers.'

'The thing is, it doesn't really matter what I think. Because Dad's not going to let me see her again after this, is he?'

'You've got to understand that he just wants to protect you.'

'I don't need protecting. I'm not a kid.'

'You're his kid. You always will be.'

'But I'm old enough to make my own mistakes. And if I want to give her another chance and it all goes pear-shaped, then I'll deal with it.'

I wanted to explain that it wasn't that simple. That it would still be us who had to pick up the pieces of whatever mess she left behind. I knew it was pointless, though. And that what I really needed to do was to make him feel listened to.

'Look, if you decide you do want to see her again, I'll talk to your dad,' I said. 'I can't promise I'll change his mind but I'll talk to him.'

'Why would you do that?' asked Josh. 'You must hate her. She's Dad's ex, after all.'

'I don't hate her,' I said. 'And even if I did, love is always more powerful. I want you to remember that.'

'As stepmums go,' said Josh, 'you're really not that bad.'

I smiled at him. 'Thanks. I'll take that as a compliment.'

The knock on the door came early the following morning. Chris was in the shower so I scrambled out of bed, pulled on my dressing gown and hurried downstairs.

I could hear whistling. It was the postman. He always whistled. I guessed he liked conforming to stereotype.

I didn't even look at the name on the box he handed me until I got it inside. Written on it in thick black marker pen was 'Matilda Bentley'. I racked my brains, trying to think of any competitions or giveaways Matilda had entered, although I knew sometimes these things took ages to be sent out.

I put the box on Matilda's place mat and went back upstairs to grab a shower while Chris got dressed.

'Morning, sleepyhead,' I called as I went into Matilda's room afterwards and drew back the curtains. 'There's post for you downstairs. A box with your name on it.'

That was all it took. She was up and out of bed in record time. I followed her downstairs. Chris was already in the kitchen making breakfast.

'Morning, Daddy,' Matilda said, before picking up the box and shaking it. 'I don't know what it is.'

'The normal practice,' said Chris, 'is to open it and find out.'

Matilda picked at the tape without success.

'Here you are,' said Chris, fetching some scissors and scoring along the tape.

Matilda opened the box. Her gasp made me turn round sharply. She lifted up a large puppet of a girl with long brown hair, a smiley face and wearing a stripy top and jeans.

'It's me,' squealed Matilda. 'It's like a puppet of me.'

'Wow, that's great,' said Chris. 'Who's sent you that?'

I knew straight away. I'd barely met the woman but I somehow knew it was the sort of thing she'd do. I walked over to the table and looked inside the box. There was a card at the bottom. It said, 'Sorry, hope we can still be friends. Lydia.'

I handed it to Chris. He read it, shut his eyes for a second and shook his head.

'What is it?' asked Matilda, reaching up to see the card.

'It's from Josh's mum,' I said to her.

She took the card from my hand, examining the writing, tracing Lydia's name with her finger as if to make absolutely certain. All the time I was watching her face, seeing her weigh it up in her head: how much she loved the puppet against how she felt about Lydia. For a moment I thought it might be in the balance, she might be about to throw the puppet back in the box and say she didn't want it. It was only a moment, though. And then she took another look at the puppet, put her arm inside and walked the cloth legs along the floor. Her face lightened. She had made her decision. Although, really, what she didn't know was that the decision had been made by the person who sent it.

'I love it,' she breathed. 'I absolutely love it. I'm going to call her Amy.'

Josh came into the kitchen. 'Hey, cool puppet,' he said.

Matilda rushed over to him. 'It's from your mum,' she shrieked. 'She sent it to me to say sorry. I'm calling her Amy.'

Josh looked from me to Chris and back to Matilda.

'Did you tell her to do that?' asked Chris.

'No. I told her I was mad at her for upsetting Tilda. That was all.'

'Then how did she know Tilda likes puppets?'

'I probably mentioned it at some point, I don't know.'

'I haven't got to send it back, have I?' asked Matilda, a frown creasing her brow.

'No, love,' I said. 'Of course you haven't. It was a present. We'll write a thank-you note for it later.'

'But how will we give it to her?' asked Matilda.

I looked at Chris. He looked away.

'We'll sort it out. Don't worry,' I said.

Matilda gazed again at her puppet and started dancing it around the kitchen.

'Come on,' I said, knowing Chris's pressure valve would be close to bursting. 'Let's put it away for now. You don't want it getting spoilt over breakfast.'

The flowers came when the others were all out. It was probably just as well. I didn't think Chris could take much more. They were yellow and orange gerberas. I wondered if she'd asked Josh about my favourite colours, or whether it was just a lucky guess.

I took them from the florist, said 'Thank you' to her, shut the front door and put them down on the hall table. The stems were in one of those cellophane water holders so they stood up by themselves. I stared at them for a long time before I opened the card which came with them.

'I'm so sorry. Please forgive my behaviour. Lydia,' it said.

I could throw the card away now, try and pretend they were from one of my grateful clients. I wouldn't do it out of spite, I'd do it to try to make things easier for everyone. But the truth was, this wasn't going to go away.

Lydia wasn't going to go away.

And somehow or other we were going to have to find a way to try to live with it.

Josh guessed straight away when he came home.

'They're from Mum too, aren't they?' he said, looking at the flowers.

'Yeah. Will you thank her for me, please? In a text or whatever.'

'Sure ...' he said. He hesitated for a moment. 'Where's Tilda?'

'In her room. Playing with the puppet.'

He stared some more at the flowers before saying, 'I want to give her another chance.'

My stomach clenched. I looked at Josh and nodded. 'OK. So you'd like me to talk to Dad?'

'Yeah. If you don't mind.'

'Like I said, I can't promise.'

'I know. Just tell him that she really is sorry. She's been beating herself up about it.'

I nodded. Not sure if I believed her.

Chris didn't even mention the flowers. I knew he'd seen them. I'd left them on the table in the hall, having sensed that bringing them into any of the rooms would be the wrong thing to do. He would have walked past them on his way in from work and, unlike some men, he was far too observant to have missed them. He hadn't asked who they were from but he knew. He had the air of a man who was trying hard not to make a bad situation worse.

And I was very aware as I sat down next to him in the lounge, after Josh and Matilda had gone to bed, that what I was about to say was indeed going to make things worse.

'Josh wants to give Lydia another chance,' I said.

He nodded slowly and said nothing. It was worse than him blowing a fuse.

'He says she's genuinely sorry. That she won't do it again.'

Chris rolled his eyes and looked at the ceiling.

'He's really been cut up about this, love. He's given it a lot of thought.'

'Well, surely you don't want him to see her again?'

'No. In an ideal world I wouldn't want him to have anything more to do with her. But it's not an ideal world, is it? And I still think this should ultimately be Josh's decision.'

'Believe me,' said Chris, 'I hate seeing him cut up like this as much as you do, but I don't trust her not to screw up again.'

'OK,' I said. 'Let's say we go down your route. We ban him from seeing her, for his own good, of course. How do you think he'll be? Will he be happy? Will he confide in us about anything in the future?'

Chris shut his eyes and sighed. 'I know what you're saying, and you're probably right. But it's like letting him lie down on a train track when you know there's a train coming.'

'But at some point we've got to let go. Let him make his own mistakes. The important thing is that what he doesn't regret later on are the mistakes we made on his behalf.'

'Is that what your clients say?' asked Chris. 'The old "They fuck you up, your mum and dad" routine.'

'Yeah,' I said. 'Because, for a lot of them, it's true. And I don't want Josh going to see some shrink in twenty years' time and telling them he's screwed up because we stopped him from seeing his own mother. From seeing if he might have been able to have some kind of relationship with her as an adult.'

Chris shut his eyes. He sat for a long time without saying anything.

'OK,' he said. 'But this is the last chance. If she messes up again, we take the decision out of his hands.'

I smiled at him. Only a small smile, because it wasn't necessarily what I wanted either. But I did believe it was the right thing for Josh.

I'd hoped that Jayne and Bob would look slightly less anguished the next time they came to see me. To be honest, if anything, they looked worse. Bob's face was grey and drawn. Jayne's hands were clenched tightly in her lap, the expression on her face one of resignation.

'So how have things been since I last saw you?' I asked.

'Fine, thank you,' said Jayne.

Bob looked down at his feet.

'This isn't like one of those social occasions when you have to pretend everything's OK,' I said. 'I'm well aware that things weren't fine the last time I saw you, so I wasn't expecting them to have got better already. I may like to think I'm good at my job but I'm not that good.' I smiled at them.

Jayne's face softened a little. 'Things haven't been very good at all,' she said.

'Bob, would you agree with that?'

He nodded. 'It's like I'm treading on eggshells. I have to avoid mentioning Cassie at all. Only place I can relax is on the golf course.'

'And do you go there a lot?' I asked.

'More than I used to.'

'What about you, Jayne?' I asked. 'Do you have hobbies and interests of your own?'

'Oh, I've got plenty going on. I'm active in the WI and I make handmade cards and do a bit of painting with water-colours, though I'm not very good.'

'Great,' I said. 'And what things do you do together, as a couple?'

My question was greeted with blank looks and silence.

'Do you go out for meals at all?' I prompted.

'Occasionally,' said Jayne. 'I like Thai and Mexican, but Bob's not one for foreign food or anything spicy. Sometimes we'll go to the Italian, though. They do a very plain sauce for him there.'

'Right. And what about holidays? When did you last go on holiday?'

'In June,' said Bob. 'There's a nice place in Brittany we've been to a few times. We get ferry over.'

'Bob doesn't like flying, you see,' said Jayne.

'OK. So obviously that will be an issue with Cassie going to Australia.'

'He won't step on a plane,' said Jayne. 'If I go, it'll be on my own.'

Bob shrugged. They both looked down at their hands.

'Where's Cassie living at the moment?' I asked.

'She's down in London,' said Jayne. 'She's in event management.'

'And do you see a lot of her?'

'Well, no,' said Jayne. 'She's very busy with work. She comes up at Christmas and for Mother's Day and my birthday. And in summer we always go down to London for a long weekend.'

'Right, but would it be fair to say that if you went over to Australia and stayed with her for a fortnight, you'd probably be spending more time with her in a year than you do here?'

Jayne frowned. 'Yes, but it's not the same, is it? Come January she'll be on the other side of the world. I'm losing her. I'm losing my baby girl.'

Chris made sure he was out when Josh left on Saturday afternoon. He volunteered to take Matilda to the cinema, even though the film she wanted to see was only on at the new multiplex in Halifax and he had vowed never to set foot in it.

It turned out that the one good thing about the place was that it wasn't in Hebden Bridge. That was clearly the one place Chris didn't want to be this afternoon.

Josh came downstairs a good half an hour before I knew he was due to meet Lydia. He had Matilda's thank-you letter in an envelope in his hand.

'All set?' I asked.

He nodded. Although he didn't seem too sure about it himself.

'Are you going to her flat?'

'Yeah.'

'I'll run you down there, if you like.'

'No, thanks, I'm OK. I'll get the bus.'

'Any problems, just give us a call.'

'There won't be,' he said.

I watched him go.

His gait was not quite as confident as usual. Sometimes venturing back into familiar territory is far more worrying than striking out for undiscovered lands.

From the Counselling Room

We went out for a meal on her birthday. It was the first time we'd been out without the kids for a year. I'd asked the restaurant to put a vase of red roses on the table. The first thing she did was get her mobile out, take a photo of it and tweet it. She spent the entire meal tweeting about what people on other tables looked like, or what she'd overheard.

Princess Di said her relationship was a bit crowded with three in it. Mine's got her and 1,072 followers.

10

'So what are you going to do about Christmas?' asked Debbie.

We were walking down to school together to pick up the girls. We often took it in turns to do the afternoon run, depending on how Debbie's shifts at the hospital worked out and whether any of my sessions overran. But it was nice when we did go down together. It gave us the chance to talk properly without having to worry about being overheard.

'I don't know. I haven't talked to Chris about it yet.'

'Surely he's realised that she'll invite Josh?'

'I'm not sure he's even registered that it's December tomorrow, let alone thought about Christmas Day.'

'Well, at least when you magically produce an Advent calendar for Matilda in the morning, it might ring a bell somewhere.'

'Oh hell,' I groaned.

'You've forgotten the Advent calendar, haven't you?'

I nodded.

'Just as well I've got two, then. My mum always sends one for Ben too, but he's decided he's officially too old for it now he's at high school. Especially as she doesn't send ones with chocolates in. I'll drop it round for you later this evening.'

'Thanks, you're a lifesaver.'

'I know. Which is why you should listen to me. And now it seems the ex from hell is here to stay, I want to know what you're going to do about it.'

'What can I do?'

'Find out if she really is seeing this guy, for a start.'

'What do you mean?' I asked, pulling my scarf tighter against the cold.

'Well, it's a classic, isn't it? Pretending you've got a boy-friend to make your ex jealous.'

'Chris says he isn't jealous.'

'You've been worried enough to ask him, then.'

'I had a little wobble.'

'You're a better woman than me, then, Ali. I'd have had a bloody enormous one by now.'

'Whatever they had together is in the past.'

'Yeah, but they've got history. And you can never discount that completely.'

Her words stung. Not because they were meant to, but because they were true.

'I know, but she wrote it off the day she walked out on Josh. She knows that too. She's come back for Josh, not for Chris. I'm pretty certain of that now.'

'And you'd happily have her over for Christmas drinks, would you? Leave them sharing a bottle of wine together while you went and stuffed your hand up a turkey's arse.'

'Thank you for the delightful picture.' I smiled.

'Listen, when you've been a midwife for sixteen years, a turkey's arse makes a welcome change, I can tell you.'

'Sometimes,' I said as we stopped at the edge of the road outside school, 'I give thanks that I didn't meet you until after Matilda was born.'

'How's the revision going?' asked Chris, when Josh finally emerged from his room for a late breakfast the following morning. He might as well have thrown a lighted touchpaper into his room.

'Fine,' said Josh.

'Fine as in "I think it'll be eights and nines all round" or fine as in "It would probably be fine if I'd actually done any"?'

'The latter, I guess,' said Josh as he poured himself some cereal.

'And have you got any idea yet when you might actually start revising for your mocks which, if I'm not mistaken, start in a little over a month's time?'

'That's next year. I'll start after Christmas,' said Josh.

'Some parents,' continued Chris, undeterred, 'tell their children they're not allowed out to play until they've done their homework.'

'Bit of luck mine aren't like that, then, isn't it?' replied Josh with a smile.

Chris sighed and shook his head.

'I think what your father is suggesting,' I said, passing Josh the milk jug from the fridge, 'is that you put a couple of hours' work in before you go out later.'

'I might do,' said Josh.

'Only might?' I asked.

'Jeez, I don't need you both getting heavy on me. Some kids crack up under exam pressure, you know.'

'Somehow,' said Chris, 'I don't think there's any danger of that with you.'

'Anyway,' said Josh, 'you flunked your "O" levels, you've told me that enough times.'

'Yeah, and look where it got me,' said Chris. 'Anyway, I had a valid excuse.'

'And what was that?'

'I had a girlfriend. She led me astray.'

Josh smirked. 'That'll have to be Tom's excuse too. He's seeing a hell of a lot more of Alicia than he is of his history textbooks.'

'I didn't know he was going out with her,' I said. 'The tall girl who plays piano so beautifully?'

'Yeah, she's well fit. Can't understand what she's doing with him, to tell you the truth.'

'Sometimes, a shared musical passion can impress a girl a lot more than a six-pack,' said Chris.

'Speaking from experience, are you?' asked Josh.

Chris opened his mouth to say something, then stopped himself. Josh glanced up at me, his cheeks flushed. I didn't want to hear it. Whatever the attraction had been on Lydia's part, I didn't want to hear about it or think about it. Because if I allowed myself to imagine them together, for even a second, I would see them everywhere. Every time I entered a room I would hear their laughter, smell their happiness. And I was trying very hard to block that past from my mind.

'Anyway,' said Chris, standing up and busying himself by stacking the breakfast things, 'I'd better go and see what Tilda's up to.'

*

Nathan strode purposefully into my room as if he was about to chair a business meeting.

'Right, let's get down to work,' he said, rubbing his hands, sitting down and crossing one ankle up onto his knee.

Catherine followed behind, altogether more uncertain, and perched on the edge of the chair.

'So, welcome back,' I said. 'How have you both been?'

'OK,' said Nathan, 'though I don't think we've really made any progress since the last session.'

'Right,' I said. 'And what makes you say that?'

'We obviously did ... er ... talk about things afterwards, and Catherine still hasn't changed her mind about starting a family.'

I looked at Catherine. She was staring intently at the floor.

'Well,' I said, 'that doesn't mean there hasn't been progress, and certainly my aim isn't to get either of you to change your mind about an important issue like that. It's to help you find a way forward together, and that will undoubtedly mean some compromises on both sides.'

'Yeah, well, starting a family isn't really something you can compromise on, is it? I mean, you either do it or you don't. Someone wins, someone backs down.'

Catherine's gaze still hadn't moved from the knot in the wood on the floor. I noticed her hair was different. She was wearing it loose and swept over one side of her face.

'It is important that you don't see this as a battle of wills, Nathan. I'm not asking anyone to back down. What I'd like to do today is find out a bit about your family backgrounds, to help me understand who you are and how best to help you.'

Nathan let out something which sounded suspiciously like a sigh. 'The thing is,' he said, 'we know who we are and, no offence, but we're both busy people and we really haven't got time to sit around navel-gazing. Time is money and all that, eh?'

I hesitated before speaking. Partly to allow time to compose myself and partly to see whether Catherine would step in to fill the silence. She didn't.

'What I need you both to understand,' I said, 'is that very often when we look at people's family backgrounds and early life, patterns of behaviour and learnt beliefs begin to emerge. And that helps you both to understand each other's current position and helps me to see how best I might help you to move forward.'

'OK,' said Nathan, 'though I really don't think there's much to tell, certainly not on my part. Born and brought up in Salford. Youngest of four children. Worked hard, first in my family to go to university, blah, blah, blah. Set up my own company, now employ three people. Coming from a large family, I always wanted a family of my own, children to pass the company on to when I take early retirement and all that.'

'OK,' I said. 'And what about your parents' relationship? Was it a good one?'

'Yeah, they're still together, if that's what you mean.'

'So it was a loving relationship, one where there was plenty of give and take.'

'Oh yeah, my dad used to take the housekeeping down the bookie's at the weekend.'

He laughed as he said it and turned to look at Catherine.

He appeared noticeably riled when she didn't crack even the faintest smile.

'So when you met Catherine,' I said, deciding to ignore the comment, 'what were you looking for in a relationship? What qualities did you see which attracted you?'

'Well, we were just going out together at first. I was only young, you don't really think about being with someone for life at that age.'

'I understand, but once the relationship became more established, I mean. A lot of couples break up when they leave university. Why did you two stick together?'

'We were both having a good time. There was no reason to split up. I wasn't interested in anyone else. Not when I had Catherine. I mean, look at her.'

Catherine shifted in her chair. She didn't smile at him or appear at all flattered by the comment. I was aware that she hadn't said anything yet.

'And what about you, Catherine? How would you describe your childhood?'

'Fine. Normal, really. I was the older of two sisters. We lived in a nice house. I always had lots going on, piano lessons, horse riding, that sort of thing.'

'And your parents, what was their relationship like?'

'OK, I think. They led pretty separate lives, but that was just how they were. They didn't like being in each other's pockets.'

'And are they still together now?'

'No, they ... er ... split up when I was nineteen.'

'I'm sorry,' I said. 'That must have been a difficult time.'

'It was,' said Nathan. 'But I helped her through it the best I could.'

Catherine glanced at Nathan and back to me. 'Yeah,' she said, 'he did.'

'I think you'd better tell her about the other stuff,' said Nathan.

Catherine stared firmly at the floor again.

'I mean, if we're talking about our early lives and that, she needs to know what was going on.'

'I really don't think that's necessary, Nathan.'

I tried not to show my surprise at hearing Catherine snap like that.

'It is necessary, because it still affects you now,' said Nathan. 'She can't help us properly unless she knows about it, sweetheart.'

Catherine stared up at the ceiling and blinked hard.

'Please do understand that I need you both to feel comfortable with whatever we're discussing,' I said. 'And remember that whatever is said in this room remains entirely confidential, unless I feel either of you is at risk.'

Catherine stared straight ahead. 'I used to have an eating disorder,' she said, her voice soft but clear. 'Anorexia. When I was a teenager.'

'Thank you for telling me,' I said. 'Did you receive treatment for it at all?'

She shook her head. 'It started when I was about fourteen. My parents were in denial about it, I think. But I kind of grew out of it by my twenties.'

'Not completely, though,' said Nathan, his voice quieter than before. 'Catherine still finds it difficult to eat in front of people. Don't you, sweetheart?'

Catherine said nothing for a moment. Then whispered, 'Yes, yes, I do.'

'OK, so how do you cope with that?'

'I usually have my evening meal before Nathan gets home,' she said. 'It just makes things easier.'

'And she doesn't like going out for meals,' said Nathan. 'Which is a problem for me as it's something I enjoy. And sometimes it's important for business things too.'

'So what do you do, if you do go to a restaurant?' I asked.

'Just have a drink, usually,' said Catherine. 'I might pick at a salad a bit, that's all.'

I nodded, trying to look at Catherine without making it too obvious.

She was thin. Although, in an age when a size 12 was considered on the large side, it hadn't particularly struck me until then. She also wore long sleeves, and scarves around her neck, which tended to hide the points where it would have been most obvious.

'And do you see it as a problem, Catherine? Now, I mean.'

She shook her head. 'People simply think I'm on a diet. It's not a problem. Not for me, anyway.'

I turned to Nathan. 'And what about for you?'

'Well, I worry about her, obviously. I tried to support her through uni, when it was worse than it is now, but I'd still like her to get help for it. It would be nice to be able to eat out together like other couples. And I worry, of course. About whether that's why she doesn't want children. The whole gaining weight thing.'

Catherine shook her head vehemently. 'No,' she said, 'that's got nothing to do with it. Nothing at all.'

'Thank you for making that clear,' I said. 'Nathan, I hope that eases your concerns a little.'

He shrugged. 'I still don't understand it. Because when I met Catherine she said she wanted children. We talked about it, how I wanted a large family, and she was fine with that.'

I turned to look at Catherine. Struggling to work out which one of them was being economical with the truth.

'I changed my mind,' she said, looking down at her hands. 'That's all.'

I saw Nathan's jaw set, his finger tapping on the table.

'OK,' I said, 'I think over the next couple of sessions it might be useful if I see you individually so we can explore these issues in more detail. How do you feel about that?'

Nathan nodded. 'Whatever you think,' he said.

I looked at Catherine. She nodded her head ever so slightly.

I was late getting home that afternoon. Debbie picked Matilda up from school for me. She texted to say she'd taken her back home and would feed her cheese on toast if she stopped talking for long enough.

I hung my coat up, slipped off my boots and padded into the kitchen to warm myself in front of the Aga. I didn't see Josh sitting at the table until I turned round and gave a start.

'God, you made me jump,' I said. 'I didn't even realise you were back.'

'Sorry. I thought the coat hanging up in the hall might be a clue.'

'Probably would have been, if I'd had my head together.' I smiled.

'Work stuff?'

'Yeah. One of my clients I'm a bit worried about.'

Josh nodded. Bit his lower lip for a second before speaking. 'Mum's invited me to her place for Christmas dinner,' he said.

From the Counselling Room

When Nelson Mandela died, she came into the room and said, 'Mandela's dead and I'm a Celebrity's on in a minute, if you fancy it.'

I mean, I was a member of the Anti-Apartheid Movement, for fuck's sake.

11

'Right,' I said to Josh, attempting to appear calm about it. 'And would you like to go?'

'Well, yeah,' he replied. 'Kind of. I mean, it's not that I don't want to be here. You and Dad do a really mean Christmas lunch, it's just that, well, I've never had the chance to spend Christmas with my mum before. Not since I was a baby, anyway.'

I nodded in what I hoped was an understanding fashion, all the time trying to steel myself inside and ensure that, when I did speak, my voice sounded reasonable and measured.

'You don't have to apologise, love. I know what it's like. I had to spend a Christmas Day half at my mum's and half at my dad's after they split up.'

'Did it lead to loads of rows?'

'It did the first year. Then, next year, Mum had to work at the hospital on Christmas Day so I stayed at Dad's. And by the following year she'd moved to Portsmouth and I was living full-time with my dad by then, anyway.'

'Why didn't she keep in touch after she moved away? I mean, it's not like Portsmouth's a different country.'

I hesitated before replying. 'Some people just aren't cut out for motherhood, and I guess she was one of them.'

'Would you give her another chance now, though? If she got in touch and said she wanted to meet up?'

'I don't know,' I said. 'She didn't come to our wedding or to Grandad's funeral. And she's never sent either of you so much as a birthday card. Sometimes you just have to accept someone's not interested. There's only so many chances you can give them.'

Josh sighed. 'If I do go, Tilda's going to be well upset, isn't she?'

'She'll come round. Especially if you get her a nice Christmas pressie.'

'That's if Dad lets me go.'

'Maybe it's time you two talk about it. I mean, if your mum's going to be around from now on, we ought to have a chat about how that will all work.'

Josh looked doubtful. 'Only if you'll be there too, so we don't end up rowing.'

'You two used to be the best of friends.'

'Yeah, and then Mum came back. And he can't handle it.'

'He needs time, that's all.'

'You've been saying that for months now.' There was a catch in his throat as he said it.

I sat down next to him at the table. 'Your dad's always been there for you, always protected you. If he is a bit over-protective sometimes, it's only because he loves you so much.'

Josh sat and thought for a while.

'Tonight, then,' he said, 'when Tilda's gone to bed. I'll ask him about Christmas tonight.'

*

I may have been physically present during the evening meal but mentally I was elsewhere. Looking down on the proceedings from above, as if I was having some kind of out-of-body experience.

I saw a little girl who really wasn't so little any more. A girl who sparkled with aliveness, whose many voices and animated expressions rendered everything she said and did a performance.

I saw a young man still trying to find his place in the world. Quieter than his sister, but who sat and watched and listened and saw and heard everything, even words that went unsaid. A young man who was so like his father in so many ways, and who was trying desperately to bridge the gap which had opened up between them.

And a man, a man who wasn't like any other man I knew. Who ached with love for his children. Who made them tea and made them laugh and made them want to be like him.

And hovering over all of them was this dirty great cloud. The one that I was sitting on. The one which was about to throw down its contents with no regard for the dampener it was about to put on everything. Because it wasn't just about one day, though it was a very special day. It was about trust and love and letting go.

And I was the outsider. Because I was the only one who wasn't related to all of them.

They were linked, the gang of three. Held tight in a triangle. And sometimes I joined in and made it a square, but it never felt as tight, as strong, as when it was just the three of them. And somewhere out there – performing the rain dance, perhaps – was Lydia, who had the power to break that tightness. To loosen the bonds. And what I didn't know was whether one person could weaken the structure of our family so much that it might never be as strong again.

Because, if so, it might be better to invite her in, to build a new, different-shaped family in the hope that it would be stronger that way.

I didn't forewarn Chris. Josh was trying to be grown-up about this. It was my job to be there to support him. Not to do his job for him.

Josh came into the lounge about half an hour after Matilda had gone to bed. Chris was looking at something on his laptop. I put the newspaper down and nodded at Josh when he looked at me.

'Dad, I need to talk to you,' he said. 'It's about Christmas.'

'You mean, you've found out that Santa doesn't exist?' said Chris, before looking up and seeing Josh's deadpan face. He slowly closed the lid of his laptop.

'Mum's invited me to her place for Christmas lunch,' said Josh.

Chris sighed. 'She has, has she?'

'Yeah.'

'And I suppose you want to go?'

'Yeah, but only if it's OK by you.'

'Of course it's fine by me. You go and spend Christmas Day with the mother who hasn't sent you so much as a card for the last fifteen years.'

'Chris,' I said. 'That's not fair.'

'Why not? It's the truth.'

'It's not Josh's fault. He's in a difficult situation, and he's trying to do the right thing.'

'It's OK,' said Josh, turning to me. 'I knew he'd be like this.'

'Like what?' asked Chris.

'Flying off the handle. Being unreasonable.'

'And she always behaves reasonably, does she?'

'Oh, forget it,' said Josh, the colour rising in his cheeks. 'If it's going to cause this much grief, forget it. Forget the whole fucking thing.' He turned on his heel and left the room.

I heard his feet running up the stairs. There was no slamming door, though. He always thought of Matilda, even when he was having a strop.

I looked at Chris. He was sitting with his head stretched back on the sofa and his eyes shut. Normally, I would have gone straight to put my arms around him. I didn't, though. Not on this occasion.

'Oh God,' he groaned. 'I handled that well, didn't I?'

'He was really making an effort, you know. He cares so much about what you think.'

'I'm sorry. It's just . . . I can't bear it.'

'What?'

'Losing him.' His voice cracked as he said it.

I got up and went to sit next to him. 'You're not losing him.'

'Well, that's how it feels. First Christmas Day . . . what's next, family holidays?'

'I said last year it would probably be the last one we had all together.'

'Yeah, but that was because you thought Josh and Tom

would want to go off somewhere next summer, not because his mother would turn up and whisk him away.'

'She hasn't put a foot wrong since that incident, you know. Maybe it was a one-off. Maybe it'll be a positive thing for Josh to have her in his life.'

'You don't know her.'

'So you keep saying.'

'What do you mean by that?'

'I've been thinking, maybe it's time I did. Maybe it's time we all got to know her. Not the Lydia who left but the one who's come back.'

'You're scaring me now,' said Chris.

'Look, you want to spend Christmas Day with Josh, right? To have all of the family together. We could still do that. All we need to do is invite Lydia here.'

Chris looked at me and started laughing. 'You are joking?'

'No,' I said, 'I'm deadly serious. It's the only way I can think of to keep everyone happy.'

'Well, I won't be happy.'

'Why not? It'll be a damn sight better than not seeing your son for most of the day.'

Chris looked at me and shook his head. 'Even if I agreed to it,' he said, 'what would we do about Mum?'

'What do you mean?'

'She won't be in the same room as Lydia.'

'Of course she will, if we explain that we're doing this for Josh.'

'No,' said Chris. 'Really. You've got no idea.'

I tried to imagine Barbara putting her foot down, refusing

to do something Chris was asking of her. I simply couldn't see it.

'Why don't you talk to her, then? Explain the situation. I'm sure you can talk her round.'

Chris hesitated. 'I'm still not sure it's a good idea.'

'Neither am I. But I can't think of a better one.'

I knew as soon as I popped my head round the waiting-room door that all was not well. Kelly and Luke were sitting with a spare chair between them. Luke, with his legs splayed wide, was staring up at the ceiling. Kelly, with her hands clenched tight, was looking down at her feet.

I smiled and gestured to them to come in. They entered silently and sat down, taking up the very same positions on the chairs. This time they had the table between them. Though I suspected the Berlin Wall would have made them feel more comfortable.

Before I'd even said anything, Kelly started crying, wiping the tears away with the back of her hand.

Luke looked as though he'd rather have all his teeth pulled without anaesthetic than be in the room at that moment.

'Kelly, if you need to take some time on your own, or if you're not up to it today, please just let me know, it's not a problem.'

'No. I'm fine,' she said, in the way people do when they are very clearly not fine. 'Please start, I'll be OK.'

I nodded but paused for a moment, trying to give her time to compose herself. It was Luke who broke the silence.

'Sorry,' he said, 'it's my fault. I've been staying at me mam's.'

His words were greeted with fresh tears from Kelly. 'He's left us,' she said.

'I haven't moved out. I need some space, that's all –'

'OK,' I said, cutting in. 'Let's go through exactly what's happened. Luke, when did you move into your mum's?'

'Four days ago,' he said, his forearms resting on his thighs as he clasped his hands together.

'And was there a particular incident which prompted that, or was it a general build-up of things?'

'I dunno. I got home from work that day and the place was covered with kiddy things all over the floor, as usual. And then I saw that Callum had broken my tablet. He should never really have been playing with it, of course. But when I said that to Kelly, she went off on one about how she hasn't got eyes in the back of her head and it shouldn't have been left somewhere where he could get hold of it. And the twins started crying and Kelly had to go to work, because she starts at Lidl at five, and I stood there in the middle of all that and I couldn't even hear myself think . . .'

He paused, finally. It was as if he'd been punctured and the air had come rushing out.

'And did you talk to Kelly later about how you felt?' I asked.

'No. Because I never got the chance. When she got home, she said she wanted an early night cos she were dead knackered.'

'I were knackered,' Kelly said. 'I am most nights.'

'And have you had the chance to talk since?' I asked.

They both looked at me blankly. Luke shrugged. Kelly fiddled with her wedding ring.

'Do you want to move back home, Luke?' I asked.

'Yeah, but not like it is now. It's doing my head in.'

'And what about your relationship with Kelly? How important is that to you?'

He swallowed hard before answering. 'She means every-thing, like. Her and the kids.'

Kelly started crying again. 'That's what's so stupid,' she said. 'He still loves me. I still love him. We both love the kids. And yet we're not living together. And I can't bear to think about waking up on Christmas Day and him not being there.' The tears fell heavily now, full-blown sobs.

I waited and watched Luke. He didn't know where to look. He went to stand up, then seemed to stop. I caught his eye and nodded. He finally got to his feet, walked over to Kelly, sank down onto his knees and gathered her sobbing body up in his arms. His broad back shaking too.

I got up quietly and went to stand outside the room for a few minutes. Sensing they needed some privacy. And feeling that, whatever the problems at home, our Christmas wasn't going to be so bad after all.

From the Counselling Room

I feel utterly trapped. I'm only staying with him for the sake of the kids and because I couldn't afford anywhere decent for them to live if I was on my own. And I'm not going to scrounge off the state. I would never do that. He knows it too, so he doesn't bother making any kind of effort. He comes home in the evening and just eats, watches telly, grunts at me and goes to bed.

And this is all I've got to look forward to for the next ten years or so. I have that Colonel Abrams song 'Trapped' going round in my head, it's like the anthem to my life, and I never even liked it in the first place.

12

'How long till she gets here?' asked Matilda for what seemed like the 324th time. She had spent most of Christmas Eve asking, 'How long till he gets here?' (At various points in the year she had voiced her doubts about Santa's existence, but by the time December the 24th came around she had clearly decided that it paid to be a believer.) And no sooner had she opened all his presents than she had turned her attention to Lydia's arrival.

'I told you, half past twelve. Look at the clock, you can work it out for yourself,' I said.

'Fifteen minutes,' said Matilda.

'Well done. Now sometimes people are early and sometimes people are late, especially when they haven't got a car. It's not always easy to judge these things. So please be patient.'

I still hadn't worked out whether Matilda was excited or apprehensive about Lydia's visit, but I suspected a bit of both. She wasn't the only one. Josh had been on edge all morning. The closer we got to her arrival, the more he seemed to be doubting the wisdom of it. Him and me both.

I was well aware that I'd taken a huge risk in inviting her.

And now here we were. About to try to play happy families. And the one thing I realised I hadn't even considered, while trying to keep everyone else happy, was how I would feel about it. Having Lydia in our home. Her old home. The one she'd made with Chris.

Maybe she'd chosen it. Brought him here to see it and begged him to say yes. Or maybe he'd found it, picked something out that he'd known she would love. Whichever it had been, their shared history was here. As much a part of the house as the stone and the slate. And yet I'd invited her back here. Inviting that shared history, and all the emotions mixed up in it, to reignite. Debbie had said I was barking, when I'd told her. I'd insisted, at the time, that it was the best of a bad set of options. But now I wasn't quite so sure.

There was a knock at the door. Matilda jumped up but I managed to catch hold of her.

'Let your brother go,' I said. 'It's his mum, remember.'

Josh clambered up from the floor, where he'd been playing a game with Matilda, his face uncertain.

'Go on,' I whispered. 'It'll be fine.'

Chris was standing by the fireplace, staring into the flames, the colours warming his otherwise icy face. Barbara was sitting rigidly on the sofa. Her face set to neutral. Clearly the best she could do in the circumstances.

I heard the door shut. There were hushed voices in the hallway and then, a minute or two later, Lydia was standing in our lounge, resplendent in a swirling black skirt and a black and red V-necked top, the splash of colour presumably her concession to the festive season.

She smiled, somewhat uncertainly. Josh hovered next to her in the doorway. Neither Chris nor Barbara said a word.

'Happy Christmas,' I said. 'Come in and warm up.'

I took a couple of steps towards her. Enough to be able to smell her perfume. I wasn't sure whether to kiss her on the cheek or not.

'And happy Christmas to all of you,' she said, looking around the room.

Chris nodded at her and mumbled something, which may or may not have been 'Happy Christmas'.

Barbara stared straight at her without saying a word, then looked away again.

Lydia appeared unperturbed. She was studying the room in detail. Her gaze settled on our wedding photo on the mantelpiece. I wondered what she was thinking. Whether she would make some comment about how slim I was in the photo. I sucked my stomach in a little. She said nothing.

'Oh, these are for you,' Lydia said, handing me the bottle of red wine she was carrying and a bag containing presents.

'Thank you,' I said. 'Really, you didn't have to.'

She shrugged. 'I wanted to.'

I nodded, glad I'd got a present for her too. Only Josh knew. I'd asked his advice before buying it. His own present to Lydia was also under the tree. I hadn't even got around to asking him what it was.

'There you are,' I said, passing the bag on to Matilda. 'A job for Santa's helper, I think.'

Matilda looked inside the bag. 'Oooh, presents,' she said. 'Is there one for me?'

'Matilda,' I said, 'that's not very polite.'

'It's OK,' said Lydia. 'And yes, there is something for you.'

She smiled at Matilda, who dutifully ran off to arrange the presents under the tree, giving each one a squeeze as she did so. The rest of us stood there.

I glanced at Chris, hoping he'd say something, maybe offer Lydia a drink, but he appeared to be incapable of speech. He also appeared to be avoiding any eye contact with Lydia. I noticed her left hand shaking. The other one was fiddling with a loose bit of cotton on her skirt.

'Can I get you something to drink?' I asked.

'Yeah, thanks. Whatever everyone else is having.'

'Barbara?' I asked.

'Tea, please, love,' she said.

'Chris?'

'Same for me, please.'

I looked back at Lydia, suspecting she'd wanted something stronger. Though I also suspected she may well have already had some before coming here.

'Tea's fine,' she said.

Matilda returned from present duty. 'Would you like to see what Santa gave me?' she asked Lydia.

'I'd love to,' she said and followed her to the corner of the room where Matilda had carefully arranged her presents.

Josh hesitated, seemingly unsure which side of the room to be on. He sat down on the sofa next to Barbara. She smiled and patted his leg.

'Right,' I said, smiling at everyone, 'I'll go and put the kettle on and check on lunch.'

Normally, I found making Christmas dinner quite stressful. All that pressure not to screw up on the big day. But today I was grateful to escape to the kitchen. I checked on the turkey. I'd rather have had chicken myself, but Barbara was a great one for tradition. I'd made a nut roast as well. Josh had said vegetarians didn't really eat nut roasts any more, it was something out of the seventies, but I'd figured that if we were going to be traditional, Lydia may as well be too.

I could have asked Chris, I suppose. If she'd been veggie when they were together, he could have told me what she used to have for Christmas dinner. He may even have cooked it for her. I hadn't asked him, though. I kidded myself it was because I hadn't wanted to upset him. When really it was more because I hadn't wanted to hear about their shared Christmases.

I lifted the tray of roast potatoes out of the Aga, putting it down quickly on the trivet as the heat pierced through the oven gloves which had seen better days. I didn't even know what you were supposed to serve with nut roast. We were having roast potatoes, Yorkshire pudding, honey-glazed carrots and parsnips. Maybe they wouldn't really go with a mushroom nut roast. Anyway, it was too late to do anything different now. It would have to do.

I flicked the radio on. They were playing 'A Spaceman Came Travelling'. Even BBC 6 Music couldn't resist it on Christmas Day. I boiled the kettle. I didn't even hear Chris come in until he was standing right next to me.

'Are you OK?' I asked.

'Yeah. Just needed a minute to myself.'

I nodded and poured the water into the mugs. 'I do appreciate this, love,' I said. 'I know it must be really hard for you.'

'It's messing with my head,' he said, pacing up and down. 'Her being in the house. It doesn't seem right. Like some kind of dream where people from different parts of your life are all mixed up together.'

'Please try to talk to her, though. At least over lunch. It'll be hard for Josh if you and Barbara don't talk to her.'

'I know. I'm working up to it. I'm not sure Barbara will say anything to her, mind.'

'Did she never like her?' I asked. 'Even before she left, I mean?'

Chris shook his head. 'She thought she was a bad influence on me. I never smoked till I met her, you see.'

I nodded. Though I suspected it was a lot more than the smoking. Lydia was not the sort of woman you'd want your young son to hook up with. She was sex and drugs and rock 'n' roll. Not future daughter-in-law material. And certainly not the bearer of your first grandchild.

'At least she's making an effort,' I said. 'I mean, she's been the perfect house guest so far.'

'I've never said she couldn't be charming,' said Chris.

'When she's sober, you mean?'

'She's not sober,' said Chris. 'That's her after two or three drinks.'

'She was probably nervous about coming here,' I said.

'Yeah,' he replied. 'Something like that.'

I fished the tea bags out of the mugs and started pouring the milk in.

Chris stopped me on the fourth one. 'No,' he said, his hand on my arm. 'She has it black.'

I put the milk down slowly, feeling a clawing sensation deep inside. 'Right,' I said. 'Thank you.'

We sat down at the kitchen table at one o'clock. The seating arrangements had been thought out meticulously so that Lydia was not next to either Chris or Barbara, nor within 'Can you pass the gravy, please?' distance of them. Everyone sat in their appointed places. Chris and I were at either end of the table, which was dressed with a vintage table runner, holly and berries from the garden and antique candlesticks which I'd picked up at various shops over the years.

'The table looks beautiful, as ever, Alison,' said Barbara.

'I helped decorate it,' said Matilda. 'I put the crackers out.'

'Smells good too,' said Chris, rubbing his hands. 'Do I get my usual job?'

I nodded and handed him the carving knife. 'Maybe do it over there on the counter,' I said.

'Why, what's wrong with the table?'

I nodded my head towards Lydia. 'I just thought . . .'

'Oh, no honestly, it's fine by me,' said Lydia. 'Chris always used to carve it in front of me, didn't you?'

'Yeah,' said Chris, still avoiding eye contact.

He got the turkey out of the oven, put it at his end of the table and started to carve. I took the nut roast out. I wasn't altogether sure what it was supposed to look like, but it seemed done to me. I turned it onto a plate and put it on the table next to the cranberry sauce.

'Please help yourself,' I said, handing Lydia a metal slice to use. 'I hope it's OK.'

'It looks great,' said Lydia. 'Thanks.'

'Why isn't she having the same as us?' asked Matilda.

'Her name's Lydia,' I reminded Matilda. 'And she's vegetarian. She doesn't eat meat.'

'Why don't you eat meat?' Matilda asked her.

'Um, because of the animal thing, really,' said Lydia, flicking her hair back from her face.

'What about the animals?'

'Well, eating them isn't exactly being nice to them, is it?' said Josh.

I gave him a suitable look and passed Matilda's plate up to Chris.

When it came back with a couple of slices of turkey on, Matilda looked at it, poked it a bit with her finger and said, 'Can I have what Lydia's having?'

'It's nut roast, love,' I said. 'It's got nuts and mushrooms in. I don't think you'd like it.'

'I'd still like to try some,' she said. 'You always say to try new things.'

I picked the plate up, cut a small slice of the nut roast and popped it onto Matilda's plate. Chris went to take Josh's plate.

'It's OK, thanks,' said Josh. 'I'm having the nut roast.'

'You always have turkey,' said Chris.

'I know. I fancy a change.'

Lydia looked down. She was fiddling with the handle of her fork.

'Anyone else?' I asked, when Josh passed the nut roast back. Chris shook his head.

'No, thank you, love,' said Barbara. 'I'll have some of your gravy, though.'

I passed it down to her and started dishing up the roast potatoes.

'I have to say, Barbara, you're looking incredibly well,' said Lydia. 'Are you still doing a lot of walking?'

A silence hung over the table for a moment. It could go one of two ways.

Josh put his fork down and looked at Barbara. I think it was that which swung it.

'Yes, still rambling, thank you.'

The table breathed again. Josh's face visibly relaxed. Maybe it was going to be OK, after all.

'Right, I'll pour the wine, then,' said Chris.

Lydia's bottle of red was already uncorked on the table. Chris got the white from the fridge. He started with Barbara, just half a glass of white, then me, rather a large glass of white. He walked round to Lydia's place and poured her a glass of red. He didn't ask which she'd prefer. Clearly he didn't need to.

'Thank you,' she said, looking up at him.

It came out like a purr. She probably didn't intend it to. Or maybe it was simply my ears that heard it that way. He made eye contact with her, the first time since she'd arrived. He said nothing. Just continued round the table, back to his seat.

'Hello, am I invisible?' asked Josh as Chris walked past him.

'No, but you're under-age,' replied Chris.

'Mum lets me have some,' said Josh.

The table fell silent again.

'Only a little bit, like,' he added quickly.

'It's what they do in Europe, isn't it?' said Lydia. 'Let them have a taste of wine at family meals rather than go off binge drinking on their eighteenth birthday.'

'They do a lot of things in Europe,' said Barbara. 'Doesn't mean we have to do them.'

'I thought we lived in Europe,' said Matilda. 'Mrs Eddington at school said so.'

'We do, love,' I said. 'It's complicated.'

Chris was still standing next to Josh, a bottle in each hand.

'Maybe just a taste,' I said. 'As it's Christmas.'

Chris looked at me. For a moment I thought he was going to argue the toss. He didn't, though.

'Red or white, sir?' he asked.

'Red, please,' said Josh.

Chris poured a very small amount of red into his glass. Josh opened his mouth to say something, caught me looking at him and obviously thought better of it.

'Crackers,' said Matilda, as Chris poured his own glass of red, put the bottles in the centre of the table and sat down. 'We haven't done crackers yet.'

She picked up the cracker in front of her, held it out to me and whooped as the hat, gift and joke flew out of her end. She pulled crackers with Barbara and me in turn.

'Come on, the rest of you,' said Matilda.

Josh picked up his cracker and turned, holding it out to Lydia. I watched as they did it, Josh's eyes smiling, Lydia laughing at her inability to pull it open. When it finally banged, Lydia and Chris both offered Josh their crackers at the same time. He sat there, seemingly unsure whose to take.

'Pull both of them at once,' said Matilda. 'Go on, I bet you can't do it.'

Josh had never been one to turn down a dare. He grabbed hold of both crackers. Chris had no choice. He had to pull. He was connected, albeit via Josh, to Lydia. They all pulled. Lydia almost fell off her chair at one point. Chris's cracker was the first to bang, seconds before Lydia's. He held his fist aloft in triumph. Lydia laughed. Josh did too.

And I sat there imagining them on that first Christmas with Josh. Here, in this very room. Maybe they got him to sleep while they had Christmas dinner. Maybe he sat propped up on Lydia's lap. I wouldn't know. I wasn't part of that family. I was suddenly acutely aware of that fact.

Matilda, whose purple paper hat kept slipping down her silky hair and over her eyes, instructed everyone else to wear theirs. Josh put his on upside down, Chris's sat awkwardly on top of his wavy hair, Lydia wore hers (which just happened to match her top) at a jaunty angle and somehow managed to look cool, Barbara played it straight with hers and I popped mine on, knowing it made me look like a photo captioned 'The British Being Naff at Christmas'.

'Right,' I said, picking up my glass, 'we need a toast.' I looked at Chris as I said it, hoping he'd be able to think of something suitable.

'Here's to Christmases, past, present and future,' he said. I stared at him, trying to work out why he'd said it when the Ghost of Christmas Past was sitting at our table.

Everyone raised their glasses, even Matilda with her Ribena. We all clinked together at our end of the table before stretching our arms out to the other end. Lydia reached out her glass to Chris and Barbara. There was a wordless, gentle clink.

It was only seconds later that Lydia's phone beeped with a text message. 'I'm sorry,' she said, fumbling in her bag which was hanging over the corner of the chair, 'I should have turned it off.'

She got out her phone. I watched the lightness fade from her face as she read the message. Her eyes became dark and heavy. Her fingers jabbed at the keys under the table. She sent the message, turned her phone off and thrust it back into her bag.

'And a Merry Christmas to you too,' she muttered, raising her glass and taking several big gulps before putting it back down on the table.

I glanced at Chris. He was eyeing Lydia warily. I had a pretty good idea who the message had been from. And a pretty good idea that it had not been welcome news.

'So, what have you got in store for us tomorrow?' Chris asked Barbara.

'I thought we'd walk down to Jerusalem Farm,' said Barbara, 'and maybe come back over Midgley Moor.'

'Ohhh, that's miles,' said Matilda. 'My legs won't go that far.'

'Barbara always likes to come up with a family walk for us on Boxing Day,' I said to Lydia.

'Yeah. I remember. Although I used to be able to get Chris out of it sometimes, didn't I?' she said, turning to smile at Chris. 'If we had something more pressing to attend to.'

Chris put his knife down on the edge of his plate and looked at her sharply. Barbara pursed her lips.

'Roast potatoes are lovely, Alison,' she said. 'And turkey's very tender, i'n't it?'

'Thanks,' I said. 'Help yourself to cranberry sauce, everyone.'

Lydia took another large swig of wine. My stomach tightened. I was willing everyone to eat more quickly.

'Can I have some, please?' asked Matilda.

I passed it to her and watched her smother the nut roast with it so she could actually eat it and pretend she liked it. She still hadn't touched her turkey.

'That Aga's always cooked good roast potatoes,' said Lydia. 'I'm hopeless at cooking but they always tasted good out of there, didn't they, Chris?'

Chris stared at her and nodded slowly.

'Do you still have that same man come to service it? The little beardy weirdy guy with the odd laugh . . . what was his name?'

'Malcolm,' said Chris.

'Oh God, yeah, Malcolm. He was a blast. You'll have to send him my regards next time he comes.'

'Which was your bedroom?' asked Matilda. 'When you lived here, I mean.'

It was as if she'd been programmed to ask the most inappropriate questions.

'The same one your dad has now, I expect,' said Lydia. 'With the lovely cast-iron fireplace and the big sash window looking out across the back.'

'That's it,' said Matilda. 'That's Mummy and Daddy's room.'

'Is it still black and white?' asked Lydia.

'No, it's a sort of beige colour. "Coffee and cream" Mummy calls it. Do you want to come and have a look?'

'Not now, Matilda,' I said. 'We're having Christmas lunch.'

'Afterwards, then,' said Matilda. 'I'll show her it afterwards, while you're clearing away, and she can tell me what it used to be like.'

I remembered my less than pristine dressing gown hanging up behind the door. My pyjamas, which I'd flung on the bed in the mad rush to get dressed and downstairs in time to see Matilda open her presents. It was freezing in our bedroom, you needed pyjamas at this time of year. Although I couldn't imagine Lydia ever wore them. I decided to change the subject in the hope that Matilda would forget all about the guided tour. I also knew that Lydia had plans later, as Josh had told me. Although I didn't know if that was still the case after the text message.

'So, Josh, what film have you got lined up for us?' I asked.

It was our family tradition. One that Lydia wouldn't know about. We took it in turns to choose the film to watch on Christmas evening every year. Last year, Matilda had made us sit through *Santa Paws*. I suspected Josh was about to get his own back.

'I'm between three at the moment,' he said.

'So are you going to tell us what they are?'

'Nope. I'll make you sweat on it.'

'And you're sticking to the criteria, are you?' asked Chris.

The criteria were that it had to be a U or PG certificate, something which wouldn't give Matilda nightmares. And ideally something that wouldn't make the rest of us, apart from Matilda, want to throw up.

'Yep,' said Josh. 'It'll be something dark and satanic and scary as hell.'

'Thank you,' said Chris.

'Just be aware that it's my turn next year,' I said. 'So I can always get my own back.'

'I know what you're going to choose already,' said Matilda, tugging my sleeve. 'You said about it last year. *It's a Wonderful Wife.*'

There was laughter from all corners of the table.

'What?' said Matilda.

'I think you'll find it's called *It's A Wonderful Life*,' said Josh.

'And it's a classic,' I said. 'I think you'd both like it.'

'It is pretty good, actually,' said Josh.

'When have you seen it?' I asked.

'At Mum's, last Saturday,' he said, in a tone which implied this should have been obvious.

'We used to watch it every Christmas Eve, didn't we, Chris?' said Lydia.

He nodded and looked down at the table. Lydia drained her glass and poured herself another one. I was tempted to have some red myself. Anything to limit the amount she had at her disposal.

'Curled up on the sofa, in front of the fire,' she went on. 'With Josh feeding on me that first Christmas we had him. We used to have our family traditions too, you see.' She spat the words out, looking at me as she said them.

Josh shifted in his seat. His face was pleading with her to

stop, but she wasn't looking at him. I tried to make eye contact with Chris but he avoided it. His jaw had tightened. I suspected he was trying very hard not to say something.

'Was Josh a good baby?' asked Matilda.

Normally I'd have been pleased at her interest and conversational skills. But right at that moment I wished she would keep quiet.

'Not really,' said Lydia, already halfway through her next glass. 'He cried a lot. Never liked going to sleep, you see. You were a bit of a night owl, like your mother, weren't you?'

She leant over towards Josh and put her arm around his shoulders. Josh smiled awkwardly.

'He was a very good baby, actually,' said Chris quietly.

'I'm sorry?' said Lydia.

'Just saying.'

'More potatoes, anyone?' I asked, holding out the dish. I suspected it was futile. I was right.

'So I don't know my own son, is that what you're saying?' asked Lydia, her face hardening, her words starting to slur.

'Well, it's hardly surprising, is it?' said Chris.

'Leave it, love,' I said.

'No, I'd like to hear what he has to say,' said Lydia.

'Of course you don't know him. Until a couple of months ago, you hadn't seen him since he was a few months old.'

'Six months,' said Lydia.

'You know what I mean.'

'Why don't you fill me in, then?' said Lydia. 'Tell me what I missed.'

'OK, we'll start with the night you left, shall we?' said Chris, his tone falsely jolly. 'He cried because he couldn't feed on you, and he couldn't understand why, because there is no way to make a baby understand that his mother has run off and left him. I had to drive down to the petrol station with a screaming baby to get some formula. That was fun, I can tell you.'

'What did you want me to do?' screamed Lydia. 'Take him with me? You wouldn't have liked that, either, would you?'

'Stop it, both of you,' said Josh. His voice was breaking, and he swallowed hard.

Chris looked down at his plate.

Matilda got up and came to sit on my lap. 'I don't like it, Mummy,' she said. 'Why is everyone being cross?'

Lydia drained her glass and went to pour a refill.

'I think you've had enough,' I said, moving the bottle out of the way.

'Oh, you do, do you?' said Lydia. 'And of course, you know everything, don't you? You know what's best for everyone. At least, you think you do.'

'Leave Ali out of it,' said Chris.

'Ahhh, touching, isn't it? Sticking up for your little wifey here. Only she's not Josh's mother, is she? She's got no right to stick her nose in where it's not wanted.'

'She's been more of a mother to him than you ever were. Who do you think was there when he got picked on at school? When he fell off his bike and knocked his tooth out? It wasn't you, was it? You obviously had better things to do. Like you had better things to do on Bonfire Night, when Josh was sitting waiting for you in a cafe. I hope he was worth it, that's all I can say.'

'Shut up!' screamed Lydia. 'You have no fucking idea.'

Josh's eyes were screwed tight shut. I knew I had to do something before this escalated any further.

'Barbara, can you take Matilda up to her room for me, please?' I asked.

Barbara nodded, wiped the gravy from her mouth with her napkin and stood up. Matilda ran to her, burying her head against her chest.

'That's right,' said Lydia. 'Run to Grandma. Good old Barbara. Never good enough for your son, was I? Thought I was corrupting him. That butter wouldn't melt in his mouth. And all the time he was smoking dope while he was shagging my arse off.'

Matilda started crying. Barbara tried to lead her towards the stairs, but she refused to move.

'That's enough,' shouted Chris, getting to his feet and jabbing his finger in the air towards Lydia. 'Get out. Now.'

Lydia picked up her glass.

'Mum. No!' shouted Josh.

But it was too late. She threw it. Chris ducked. It narrowly missed Matilda and smashed against the wall behind her, fragments flying everywhere. Matilda screamed and covered her eyes. I ran over to her. There were bits of glass in her hair, splashes of red on the collar of her dress. Chris bent down next to her, prized her hands away from her eyes, eased the paper hat up over her forehead.

'It's OK,' he said. 'Her face is fine. I think the red's just wine.'

Barbara strode over to Lydia, who had scrambled unsteadily to her feet.

'You have done enough damage to my family to last a

lifetime,' she said, her voice an unrecognisable steely rasp. 'Don't you ever come anywhere near them again. Do you understand me?'

Lydia picked up her bag and headed for the hall. She walked straight past Josh, who was still sitting at the table, his eyes small and scared, his face pale.

A few moments later, the door slammed behind her.

I breathed. For what seemed like the first time in minutes. And all I could think, as I looked around at my family, was how ridiculous it was that we were all still wearing our paper hats.

From the Counselling Room

So I came downstairs and he had Page Three open on the breakfast table and he drew a circle in green felt tip around the girl's tummy at the top of the thong and said, 'She needs to get rid of that, she's got a bit of an overhang there.'

I looked at it. I mean, there was nothing there. Her belly looked perfectly flat to me. And then I looked at him, all sixteen stone of him, most of it hanging over the top of his trousers.

13

'Is Tilda OK?' asked Josh, the first to break the silence.

I nodded, feeling her little chest heaving against me, and picked out the bits of glass I could see in her hair.

'I'm sorry,' he said, his voice small and shaky. 'I'm really sorry.' He pushed his chair back, got up and walked out of the kitchen.

I listened to his footsteps on the stairs. To his bedroom door shutting behind him. To the hurt that seeped out under it. Matilda was still clinging to me.

'Do you think I've got it all out?' I asked Chris, handing him the three shards of glass I'd found.

'I don't know,' he said. 'I'll get a comb. We'll go through it.'

I nodded. Barbara was already on her way back from the kitchen with a dustpan and brush. We were doing that thing British people did in crises. Coping stoically without a mention of what had gone on before.

Barbara swept all the big pieces of glass on the floor into the dustpan while I sat holding Matilda. Stroking her back. Making soothing noises. Chris returned with the comb and a piece of card. He ran the comb gently through Matilda's hair.

Once or twice there was a tiny sound as a fragment dropped out onto the card which he held underneath.

Still Matilda said nothing. She didn't even complain when the comb pulled on her tangles. Just gulped for air and clung on tight to me.

Barbara brought the vacuum cleaner in. 'I'm going to go over floor,' she said. 'Make sure I've got it all up.'

Chris continued working on the other side of Matilda's hair. He didn't make eye contact with me once, but stayed entirely focused on the task in hand. Eventually he stepped back. 'That's everything I can find. Might be a good idea to wash her hair, though, just to be on the safe side.'

I nodded. 'Let's go upstairs,' I said to Matilda. 'We'll get you all clean and changed. You'll feel better then.'

Matilda peeled her damp face off my jumper. 'We haven't even had our Christmas pudding yet,' she said.

I nodded and stroked her hair, surveying the remnants of the Christmas dinner on the table. Half-eaten potatoes and prostrate parsnips littered the dinner plates like casualties of war on a battlefield.

'Tell you what,' I said. 'After we've got you sorted, why don't we come down and eat Christmas pudding?'

Matilda nodded, her face brightening a fraction. 'All of us?' she asked. 'Will we all eat it together?'

'Nearly all of us,' I said. 'I don't think Josh will be hungry.'

'He's never really liked Christmas pudding, has he?' said Matilda.

'No, love. Not really.'

I didn't say anything to her about what had happened until I'd washed her hair in the shower and she was in the bath, enveloped womb-like in warm water, with a few drops of lavender oil thrown in for good measure.

'I'm really sorry, love,' I said, kneeling next to the bath, 'about what happened just now. You shouldn't have had to see or hear any of that.'

'Why did she change?' Matilda asked. 'She was really nice at first.'

'I think she had a text message which upset her, love. And she had too much to drink. Unfortunately, adults can get very upset and angry when they've had too much alcohol.'

'Had Daddy had too much to drink?'

'No, love.'

'So why did he get angry?'

I sighed. 'Because he's very protective of you and Josh. Of all of us, really. He didn't like her saying bad things.'

'So why did you let her come here? She spoilt Christmas dinner for everyone.'

'I know, love. But Josh wanted to be with her on Christmas Day, and I thought it would be nicer if she came here than if Josh went to her house. Only, sometimes, adults get things wrong.'

'She won't be coming next year, will she?'

'No.'

'Is Josh ever going to see her again?'

'I don't know.'

Matilda sat for a moment staring at the tiles opposite. The troubled look on her face remained.

I wondered if I should say anything more. It was hard to know how much she had understood of what had been said down there.

'Are there things you're still not sure about?' I asked.

She nodded her head.

'You can ask me anything, you know that.'

'Can I still open my present from her?'

'Yes, love,' I said, managing a faint smile. 'Of course you can.'

When we got back downstairs, Barbara had cleared away the debris of lunch.

'I've saved what I can, love,' she whispered to me. 'We can always have turkey sandwiches for tea.'

I nodded and squeezed her hand. 'Where's Chris?' I asked.

'In the lounge. He's not said a word since.'

'Has he been up to see Josh?'

Barbara shook her head.

'Matilda, why don't you pop and play with your presents for a bit, while we get the pudding ready?'

'OK,' she said and went through to the lounge.

If anyone could get Chris out of the place he was in right now, it was Matilda.

'Can you warm up the pudding for me, please?' I asked Barbara. 'I'm just going to pop upstairs.'

I knocked on Josh's bedroom door.

'I don't want anything else to eat,' he called out.

'I know,' I said. 'I wanted to check you were OK.'

I waited to be told where to go. He said nothing. I pushed open the door. Josh was lying on his bed, staring up at the ceiling, his eyes red and puffy, the sound of something loud and thrashy coming from his earphones.

I sat down on the end of the bed. 'Matilda's fine, love,' I said. 'I think it was the shock more than anything.'

Josh turned his music off. 'She didn't have any scratches?'

I shook my head. 'I'm sorry,' I said. 'It was a bad idea to invite your mum here.'

'So why did you suggest it?' His tone was hurt rather than angry.

I sighed and shut my eyes for a second. 'I was trying to keep everyone happy. Obviously it didn't work.'

'It wasn't your fault,' said Josh after a while.

'Well, I'm really sorry, anyway. It should never have happened.'

'Dad shouldn't have started on her either. Not when she was in that state.'

'I know. It was hard for him, though. I should have realised how hard it would be.'

Josh lay for a while, staring at the ceiling. 'They hate each other, don't they?'

I put my hand on his shin, rubbed it a little. 'I don't think it's really hate. Just leftover hurt. And that comes from loving someone. What you've got to remember is that they did love each other once, when they had you.'

'Whatever, it doesn't matter. I'm not going to be allowed to see her now, am I?'

'Do you want to see her?'

'I don't know. Not right at this moment, I don't. Not after what she's done. But she's still my mum.'

'I understand that.'

'I've never seen her like that before. I don't ever want to drink, if that's what it does to you.'

'It doesn't do that to everyone. It's only if you don't know when to stop. Or if you use it to try to blot out your problems.'

'You think she's got problems?'

'I think most people have.'

Josh sighed and propped himself up on his elbows. 'The text was from her boyfriend, wasn't it?'

'I imagine so. Though he doesn't seem much of a boyfriend.'

'I don't know why people bother with relationships, if it makes them that unhappy.'

'I'll remind you of that one day,' I said.

'It's true. It only ever seems to lead to rows.'

'Not for everyone. Tom seems very happy with Alicia.'

'Yeah, but they've only been going out for a bit. And they're still at that sick-making lovey-dovey stage. Wait till they have some big fallout and I have to put up with Tom being a miserable git for weeks.'

I smiled at him, wanting to say the 'Better to have loved and lost' line but deciding I'd sound way too much like a relationship counsellor if I did.

'Are you sure you won't come down for some Christmas pudding?' I asked.

Josh shook his head. 'No, thanks. I'm really not hungry.'

'You'll come down later, though? For the film. Matilda will complain like mad if you're not there, and she'll end up making us all watch *Santa Paws* again.'

'OK,' said Josh.

When I got back downstairs the pudding was ready, and Barbara was about to dish up.

'Is Josh not joining us?' she asked.

I shook my head.

'She should never have been allowed anywhere near him,' Barbara said.

'I'm sorry. I had no idea it would turn out like this.'

'The trouble with nice people like you,' said Barbara, taking my hand and patting it, 'is you don't seem to realise how horrible other people can be.'

'She's his mother, Barbara. She deserved a chance.'

'No,' said Barbara, her eyes stern, the corners of her mouth for once neutral. 'You're more of a mother than she ever was. Blood means nothing in the end, you know. Not compared to love.'

Matilda came running through to the kitchen with a princess glove puppet on her hand.

'Look,' said Matilda. 'She got me another puppet.'

Chris was standing behind her in the doorway. I could practically hear his skin bristling.

'That's nice, love,' I said.

'When are you going to open yours?' she asked.

'I don't know. Let's not worry about that now, eh? Pop that down and come and have some Christmas pudding.'

Josh came down for tea later. I told him we'd have turkey sandwiches while watching the film. Anything to avoid sitting around the kitchen table again and pretending everything was OK.

He chose *Finding Nemo*. It had been his favourite film when he was a kid. I think he'd related to the fact that Nemo, like him, didn't have a mum.

I remembered watching it with him and Chris at the cinema not long after we'd got married. Wondering where the hell I was going to fit into a family with a father and son relationship as tight as the one we were watching on screen. And knowing at the point where Marlin and Nemo had been reunited, and I'd turned to see Chris sitting with tears rolling down his cheeks, that whatever he felt for me, it was nothing compared to the love he felt for his son.

Chris took a deep breath as Josh loaded the DVD. I wasn't sure he'd be up to watching it either, but I knew we couldn't say anything. It met all the criteria. Matilda loved it too.

And I sensed that Josh had chosen it specially. It was his cinematic equivalent of daubing everyone with antiseptic.

Matilda cuddled up between me and Josh on the sofa. The curtains were drawn. The door firmly shut. Our family was safe now.

'Can you fast-forward the bit at the beginning?' she asked.

I knew which bit she meant, of course. The bit where the barracuda came along and ate Coral and all the eggs, bar Nemo.

Josh nodded and hit the fast-forward button.

It was as if Coral had never existed. And I wished like hell you could do that in real life.

'I'm sorry,' I said when Chris returned from dropping Barbara back home later that night.

He said nothing, simply took his boots off, hung up his jacket and walked through to the kitchen. I followed him, shutting the door behind me in case anyone upstairs was still awake.

'I mean it. I'm really sorry. I didn't think –'

'No,' said Chris, turning to face me, 'because you wouldn't listen to me.'

'I did listen.'

'Well, you didn't take any notice of what I said.'

'I was trying to make the best of a bad hand. I didn't want you and Matilda to be upset if Josh went to hers for lunch.'

'But we were only in that situation to start with because you wanted to give Lydia a second chance.'

'For Josh's sake, yes.'

'And Josh is happy now, is he? This has all worked out for the best?'

I sighed. 'I said I'm sorry. What more do you want me to do?'

'To stop doing it.'

'What?'

'Trying to mend people. Couples, families, whatever. Not everyone can be mended, you know.'

'So what, I'm supposed to let people carry on hating each other?'

'Yes, if that's what they want to do.'

'But what about Josh? He didn't hate his mother. Not really. It was simply that he'd never had the chance to get to know her.'

'Because she ran off and left him. Shit happens, Ali. And sometimes you just have to leave it alone.'

He walked over to the sink, staring out of the mullioned windows into the darkness beyond. I sat down at the kitchen table and held my head in my hands. I tried very hard not to cry. But I'd already been trying very hard not to cry for most of the day. Chris came over to me and rubbed my shoulders. Kissed me on the top of my head.

'Sorry,' he said. 'I shouldn't have had a go at you. Only this whole thing has done my head in.'

'No, you're right,' I said. 'I guess I do like to try to fix things.'

'The thing is,' said Chris, 'you had no idea what you were dealing with.'

'How could I? You won't talk about her. There's so much I don't know. So many gaps that need filling in.'

'No,' said Chris. 'They don't. It's the past, and you have to leave it there. I drew a line under it when I married you, and I don't want to go raking it all back up again. You're my family now. You and Josh and Matilda, and that's all that matters. And when I said I didn't want Josh to have anything to do with her, it was because I knew he'd end up getting hurt again. And as it turned out, it wasn't just him but Matilda too.'

'I know, and I feel awful about that. But it was a no-win situation.'

'Well, at least we haven't got to worry about him seeing her again now he knows exactly what she's capable of.'

'I think it's too early to say that.'

'What do you mean?'

'He's pretty mad at her right now, but I'm not sure he's ready to say goodbye to her either.'

'He hasn't got any choice. Mum was right. She's not coming

anywhere near our family again. And none of our family are going anywhere near her.'

'That's easier said than done. He's sixteen, Chris. He goes out on his own. He's got a mobile, he goes online. We can't do some Big Brother thing on him.'

'No, but he can be told very clearly that he's not to have any contact with her. And we can explain what the consequences will be if he doesn't go along with that.'

I shook my head.

'What?'

'I just don't think that's the approach to take with Josh. We've got to support him through this, not ban him from seeing her. It will turn him against us, if we do.'

'There you go again,' said Chris, throwing his hands up into the air. 'Assuming we can do this with some kind of softly, softly approach. Look where that got us, Ali. She's already ruined Christmas. I'm not having her spoil another single day in any of our lives.'

He walked past me, his eyes burning dark, his breath hot. I heard him go upstairs. The bathroom door clicked shut. He was going to bed. Without me. On Christmas night. That was where we were at. I could have gone after him. Tried to reason. Tried to smooth things over. But I knew Chris well enough to know that it was pointless. I had to let him burn himself out. I would try again tomorrow, when the embers might just be cool enough to touch.

I got up and wandered into the lounge. All was dark apart from the lights on the Christmas tree, it being completely oblivious of the fact this was far from a twinkly house tonight.

The unopened presents lay under it. Ours to Lydia. Lydia's to the rest of us, apart from Matilda, of course.

I knelt down next to the tree and found the present with my name on the gift tag. It was soft, very light. I peeled off the tape at one end and pulled out the contents, opening the layer of tissue paper. It was a scarf. One of those delicate alpaca wool ones from the designer shop in town. They were expensive. I knew that. It was why I'd never asked for one, though I'd often admired them through the window. And Lydia, of all people, had bought one for me. I held it up to my face, the softness of the wool immediately soothing. I had no idea what I was going to do with it. I didn't see how I could wear it, not with Chris knowing where it had come from. I slipped it back into the wrapping paper and resealed the tape.

I was about to go when I noticed Chris's name on the gift tag attached to the present next to it. I picked it up. The one downside about LPs was that you could never really disguise them when wrapping one as a present. I held it in my hands for a moment, knowing I shouldn't. But also knowing that, come the morning, Chris would probably put it straight in a bag for Oxfam. He certainly wouldn't open it.

I peeled the tape back and slid the LP out. It was *The Division Bell* by Pink Floyd. He already had it, I was pretty sure of that. But I also had a vague recollection of him saying it was a replacement for one he'd lost. I opened up the gatefold sleeve and carefully slid out the record. It was made of marbled blue vinyl. I didn't know much about these things but I knew enough to know it was likely to be pretty rare. It was only as I went to put it back in the wrapping paper that I noticed the note inside. Written on a sheet of spiral-bound notepaper was the message – 'Returned to its rightful owner – with apologies for the long loan!'

I slid it back inside the wrapping paper and hastily sealed the tape. It was a fragment of history. Of their shared history.

She was trying to put right wrongs from the past. Or, at least, she had been. Until the present had got in the way.

I woke early the next morning, before Matilda's usual alarm call, anyway. Chris was still asleep next to me. It took me a moment to realise it had been a sound which had woken me. A sound from downstairs.

I got up, grabbed my dressing gown and crept out of the room, pushing the door gently to behind me. I poked my head round Matilda's door. She was asleep, curled up tight in a ball hedgehog-style. Josh's door was shut tight. I didn't want to risk opening it in case I woke him.

I heard the noise again. A whining, almost whimpering sound. I went to the edge of the banisters and peered down into the gloom. I saw the figure immediately. Sitting on the front-door mat, legs bent in front of him, forehead on his knees, his body shaking as he sobbed.

It was Josh.

I ran downstairs, knelt down next to him and pulled him to me. He was cold. He'd been outside. He still had his parka on.

'What's happened?' I asked.

'She's gone,' he mumbled.

'Who's gone?'

'Mum.'

'Gone where?'

'I don't know,' he said, looking up, his eyes red and puffy. 'I went to her flat. I wanted to give her my Christmas present. I never got a chance yesterday. I knocked loads of times but there was no answer. The guy below her came out. Said she'd left yesterday evening. That she'd been carrying a suitcase.'

'Did she tell him where she was going?'

'No. I've been texting her all the way back, but there's no reply. She's left me. She's done it again.' He broke into a fresh round of sobs.

I held him tighter to me. It was only then I realised he was clutching something.

'What's this?' I asked.

He handed it to me. A heavy pewter photo frame, and in it a photograph of Lydia and Josh together. His arm draped casually around her shoulders. Both of them beaming.

'It was her present to me. She took it on her mobile,' he said. 'And it's all I've got of her now.' He threw his arms around me and clung on tight.

He was a little boy again. Throwing his arms around me for the very first time. And I felt the same combination of intense love and fear. Fear that this person expected so much of me. And that I might not be able to live up to those expectations.

Chris came to the top of the stairs, obviously woken by the noise. 'What's happened?' he called out.

'It's OK,' I said. 'Lydia's gone. She's left her flat.'

Chris came downstairs. 'You've been round?' he asked Josh.

'Yeah.'

'Jesus Christ.'

'Leave it,' I said to Chris. 'He's upset enough.'

'Yeah. Because of her. Because it wasn't enough for her to hurt him once.' He took hold of Josh's shoulders. 'It ends here, OK?' he said. 'We forget the whole thing. And we get back to how we were before.'

There was another cry. This time from upstairs.

'Mummy!' Matilda called. 'I've wet the bed.'

I jumped up and ran upstairs. Knowing that how we were before was going to be a very hard place to get to.

From the Counselling Room

I went into our bedroom and she was on her laptop looking at this video of Daniel Radcliffe – you know, him from the Harry Potter films – doing some photo shoot. He was wearing a vest top and sweatpants, and there was this lingering close-up shot of him smoking and blowing it out. All seductive, like. She was moving the cursor back to the beginning and starting again.

I have no idea how many times she'd done it. When she saw me, she went bright red and snapped the lid down.

It would have been easier if I'd found her watching porn or something. Not fucking Harry Potter.

PART TWO

14

My eyelids opened before either the alarm clock's intrusion into my slumber or Matilda's noisy entrance into our bedroom. They'd been doing that a lot lately. Pretty much since the start of the year. It was as if I was still on edge. Still expecting a crisis to erupt at any moment. Still listening out for the sound of my family imploding.

The house was quiet, though. All was peaceful, except for the sound of the clock on the bedroom wall ticking. Marking the passage of time: seconds, minutes, hours – and now days and weeks – since she'd gone.

I was relieved. I'd have been lying if I'd said anything different. We were all relieved. All of us apart from Josh, anyway. But none of us could show our relief for fear of adding to his hurt. And he was hurting. Not in an obvious, anguished-cries-from-the-bedroom kind of way, but in an achy, hollow, empty way.

I couldn't talk about it to Chris, of course. Because he was still hurting too. And even the mere acknowledgement that Josh was mourning the loss of his mother would have been enough to intensify that. So it wasn't mentioned. She wasn't mentioned. She had been airbrushed from our lives.

But the person who had done the airbrushing had missed

some vital clues. Some obvious ones: the photo of Josh and Lydia on his bedside table; the puppets, which Matilda still played with on a regular basis; the Pink Floyd LP, which had been restored to Chris's album collection silently by me and which, if it had been noticed, had not been removed; the alpaca scarf wrapped in tissue paper in my top drawer, which couldn't be seen, although I knew it was there. Other clues were not so obvious because, although the marks she had left were indelible, they were not all visible with the naked eye.

I turned to look at Chris, lying next to me, head on one side. He even looked more peaceful in his sleep since she'd gone. I was glad of that, of course. But also sad that Lydia had simply been shoved back in the filing cabinet marked 'the past'. She was too important, what had happened was too important, never to be revisited again.

I sighed, sat up and swung my legs out of the bed, immediately reaching for my dressing gown and pulling it around my shoulders. I padded across the floorboards to the window and peered through the gap in the curtains. January stared back at me. Cold and mean and hard. I wondered where Lydia had gone. Whether she was looking out on a very similar January landscape or whether her view was now of somewhere else. Somewhere urban. London, maybe.

And most of all I wondered if she'd gone for good. Or whether this was simply a lull before a further storm.

Josh was the first one to arrive downstairs for breakfast. That never used to happen much either. I suspected that he too found a deep sleep harder to come by these days.

'Morning, love,' I said. 'Is it a beans on toast kind of morning?'

He nodded, a half-smile on his face. That was it, really. It was as if he was on a permanent dimmer switch.

Chris arrived in the kitchen, his hair still wet from the shower. 'Morning,' he said, his lips fleetingly brushing mine as I walked past him with a saucepan of beans.

'Art mock today, isn't it?' he asked Josh.

'Yep.'

'Should be a good one for you, then.'

Josh shrugged. 'Yeah. I guess so.'

Chris poured himself some coffee and cereal and sat down.

'Do you want some toast?' I asked.

'No, thanks. I'm fine.'

I nodded.

We had turned into one of those families who talked but didn't really say anything.

'She seems more her old self,' Debbie said as we walked down the lane, Matilda regaling Sophie with the details of her latest puppet show as they dawdled behind us.

'Yeah, she's getting there. At least the bed wetting's stopped now.'

'How about Josh?'

'Still not good,' I said.

'Does he talk about her?'

'He can't, really. Not when Chris or Matilda are around. I've tried a few times, when it's been just the two of us. Asked if he's heard anything from her. All he does is shake his head and change the subject.'

'Maybe that's fine, maybe he wants to put it behind him.'

'It's hard, though, because I know he's hurting and he won't let me in. He used to be so close to Chris too, and yet this whole thing has driven a real wedge between them. Neither of them will admit that anything's changed. But it has.'

'And what about with you two?'

I shrugged, trying to compose myself before I answered. 'We're OK.'

'You used to be a hell of a lot better than OK.'

'I know. That's what makes it so hard.'

'Can't you talk to him? Tell him how you feel.'

'He won't let me. It's like he wants to pretend the whole thing never happened. Only it did, and it's not going to go away. Sometimes I think he . . .' My voice trailed off as I swallowed hard.

'He what?' asked Debbie.

'Doesn't love me any more,' I whispered.

Debbie reached out her hand and squeezed my arm. 'Don't be a daft bugger. He adores you.'

'Those things he said on Christmas Day.'

'Heat of the moment stuff. People come out with all sorts in traumatic situations. You should hear what some women call their blokes when they're giving birth.'

'Yeah, but I bet they take it all back afterwards. At no point has he said that he didn't mean it. The things he said about me meddling in other people's business have been left there, hanging in the air. Hanging over us.'

We walked on in silence for a bit.

'When did you last go away together?' asked Debbie. 'You

know, just the two of you, actually away for a night or two.'

I thought for a moment. 'I can't even remember,' I said. 'Probably not since Matilda was born.'

Debbie stared at me and shook her head. 'What would you say to a couple who came to see you at work and told you that?'

'Yeah, I know. But it's different when it's you.'

'Well, it shouldn't be. Practise what you preach and all that. Book a weekend away. I'll have Matilda to stay. There'll be no excuse not to go, then.'

'Are you sure?'

'Yeah, I wouldn't say it otherwise. It'll do you both the power of good. You deserve a break after the past few months.'

'Well, it is Chris's birthday in a couple of weeks, though he doesn't normally bother with birthdays.'

'And I do believe it's Valentine's Day too,' said Debbie.

'Yeah, although as you know, he's not really one for that either.'

'It doesn't matter. Just do it anyway. He's not going to complain about being whisked away for the weekend, is he?'

'No, you're right,' I said, giving Debbie a hug.

'Why did you do that?' asked Matilda, catching up with us.

'Because that's what you do to friends, isn't it?' I smiled at her.

Matilda nodded and gave Sophie a huge hug.

'Just don't complain when she keeps Sophie up all night talking and attacks you with a sock puppet in bed at seven in the morning, will you?' I whispered to Debbie.

*

Jayne had lost weight. I could see it in her face as she walked into my room behind Bob. She was wearing a sober navy two-piece. Bob was in a jacket and tie. They were of the last generation who would be concerned with looking smart when going to see a counsellor.

'Good to see you both,' I said. 'Come and sit yourselves down.'

Bob still wore the expression of a man who was at a loss to understand what had happened to them. Jayne, as ever, appeared to be on the verge of tears, even before we began.

'So,' I said, as they settled into their seats, 'how did it go over Christmas?'

'It was fine, thanks,' said Bob.

I was aware that, in the spirit of fairness and solidarity, I should probably confess to them that however bad their Christmas had been, it wouldn't have been as much of a disaster as mine. I didn't, though. Somehow I thought it would undermine my credibility.

'Now, tell me really, what was it like?' I asked.

Bob looked down at his hands. 'It were lovely to see Cassie. To have her staying with us and that. But very difficult too, you know. Because of what's about to happen.'

I turned to Jayne.

Her bottom lip was already trembling.

'And how did you feel about it, Jayne?' I asked.

'It were like Bob said. Bitter-sweet, I suppose you'd call it.'

'And were you able to support each other through it? To keep talking about how you were feeling?'

It was Jayne's turn to look down at her hands.

'Jayne finds it difficult,' said Bob.

I looked at him and nodded. Wanting him to know that his chivalry was not lost on me.

'Jayne, is there anything more Bob could do to help you feel able to talk to him?'

She shook her head. 'Bob's done nothing wrong. I just don't really see any point in talking about it. It's not going to change owt, is it?'

'No, but it might make you feel better. It might make Bob feel better too, to know that you're able to share your feelings with him.'

She shook her head again. 'Some things are best kept inside,' she said. 'I'd only upset myself and him.'

I nodded, unsure where to go from here. I wanted to take a tin-opener to her. But even if she'd let me, I still wasn't exactly sure what I'd find inside.

'And how long is it until Cassie goes now?' I asked.

'Three days,' said Bob.

'And did you talk about when you'll next see her?' I asked.

'She's going to try to get over in the summer. If her and Nigel's work allow it, like.'

'And you still don't think you'll be able to go and see her? Because of the flying thing.'

Bob shook his head.

'Have you ever sought help with it?' I asked.

'No,' he said. 'It's just not for everyone, is it? Being cooped up in a metal box in sky like that.'

Jayne said nothing. She appeared to be biting her lip very hard.

'OK,' I said, 'so what plans have the two of you got for the next six months?'

'Well, Bob'll be out on golf course when weather allows it,' said Jayne. 'And I'll be busy with WI.'

'And what about together?' I asked. 'What things will you be doing together?'

They both looked at me blankly. Jayne fiddled with her bracelet.

I made a mental note to get that weekend away booked.

'What's for tea?' Josh asked, bounding into the kitchen that evening and pinging Matilda's headband.

Matilda laughed rather than complained. I suspected that, like me, she was simply pleased, and more than a little surprised, to see him in such a good mood.

'Macaroni cheese,' I replied.

'Yay!' said Matilda, who would have quite happily lived on the stuff.

'How did art go?' Chris asked as Josh sat down at the table.

'Yeah, pretty good, I think.'

'You're on the home straight, now then. Just history and music to go.'

'Yep. Shame they're not the real things, mind. Then I wouldn't have to go through it all again in May.'

'You'll be fine,' I said.

'I'll be brain dead by then.'

'You'll have a massive long summer holiday to get over it, though,' said Chris.

'I might get a summer job.'

'You can give me a hand at the studio, if you like,' offered Chris.

'What, and you pay me the minimum wage for being your lackey?'

'Less of the cheek, please,' said Chris.

He was smiling, though. As I was. He glanced across at me. I shrugged. Whatever had prompted the dimmer switch to be turned up a little, I wasn't going to complain.

'You could give it a try-out on Saturday, if you like,' Chris continued. 'I've got two family portraits in and lots of stuff to edit on the Mac.'

'Sorry,' said Josh, 'I've got plans.'

My stomach tightened a little. Josh hadn't had plans on a Saturday afternoon since Lydia left. Not now Tom was seeing Alicia all the time.

'Oh,' I said. 'Anything interesting?'

'Might be,' he replied. The colour rose in his cheeks.

That was when I realised. It wasn't Lydia. It was a girl.

'Anyone I know?'

'Not really.'

'Maybe someone I'd like to meet, though?'

'God, what is it with you?' said Josh.

He didn't mind, though. I could tell that by the expression on his face. He wouldn't have mentioned that he had plans if he'd minded us knowing what they were.

'What's her name?' I asked.

Josh rolled his eyes at me. 'Caitlin, if you must know.'

'Who's Caitlin?' asked Matilda.

'Josh's girlfriend,' replied Chris.

'She's not my girlfriend,' said Josh. 'She's a friend.'

'Who happens to be a girl,' said Chris.

'Have you kissed her?' asked Matilda.

'No,' laughed Josh.

'Well, she isn't your girlfriend, then. She's only your girl-friend if you kiss her and hold her hand and it makes the birds sing and stuff.'

I shook my head. Disney princesses had a lot to answer for.

'Is she in your year?' I asked.

'No, she goes to Crossley's.'

It was the grammar school in Halifax. The one Josh hadn't wanted to do the entrance exam for.

'Oh. So how do you know her, then?'

'She's a friend of Alicia's. She plays violin in the Calderdale Youth Orchestra. She's dead good.'

'Cool,' said Chris.

'And don't ask me what her parents do and all that stuff. Cos I don't know, and I don't care,' said Josh.

'That's fine,' I said. 'So where are you going Saturday?'

'To the cinema. The new one in Halifax. She wants to see *Les Misérables*.'

I glanced at Chris. His face had much the same expression as mine. Josh had gone for someone with a bit of culture. We must have done something right, after all.

'Good first date material,' said Chris.

'It's not a date.'

'Of course not,' said Chris with a wink. 'Just a friend, eh?'

'Unless you kiss her in the cinema,' said Matilda. 'And if you do that, you'll have to marry her.'

Josh rolled his eyes and tucked into his macaroni cheese. I caught Chris's eye and smiled. He smiled back.

From the Counselling Room

I lay there in bed one night and I tried to remember the last time he'd said something to make me laugh, or smile even. The last time he'd done something which had made me feel a bit special, a tiny bit warm inside.

I couldn't think of anything. Not since we were married. And that isn't very good, is it?

Not very good at all.

15

Bob was early. He was also on his own. As he was my first client of the morning I showed him in straight away. His face was pale and his eyebrows heavy.

'Is everything OK?' I asked as he sat down.

He shook his head. 'Jayne's taken a turn for worse.'

'What do you mean?'

'She's in floods of tears. She's shut herself in bathroom and said she's not coming today. That she's not coming back here at all. Says she doesn't think it'll do any good and we're wasting our money.'

'Is this because Cassie's gone?'

'I don't know. To be honest, I were going to tell you that she dealt with Cassie going better than I thought. She went out for lunch with her WI friends, managed to keep herself busy with this and that. Didn't speak about it all the whole day.'

'And how's she been since?'

'Quiet. She's not been as chatty as she usually is. But she's not been upset like this, like she is today.'

'And there's nothing you can think of that's set it off?'

'No. She spoke to Cassie on phone last weekend, but she seemed fine afterwards. Bit subdued, but that were all. And then I woke up this morning and the bed were empty, like. Went to see where she were, and that's when I heard her crying in bathroom.'

'Did you ask her what was wrong?'

'Of course. She just said she hadn't had much sleep and were feeling a bit emotional. That were it.'

'You didn't, er, forget Valentine's Day, did you?'

'Oh, it's not that,' he said. 'She doesn't do that. Hates it actually. She's always made me promise not to buy her a card, right from the start.'

'I understand. My husband's the same. Not one for all that commercial nonsense. Well, anyway, I'm happy to see you on your own today. Just so long as you're OK to do that. If you want to get back to Jayne, I totally understand.'

'No,' said Bob. 'You're all right. Jayne said she wanted to be on her own. I may as well stay now that I'm here. Not sure what else I can tell you that will help, mind.'

'Don't worry about that,' I said. 'It will all help me build up a picture of what's been going on. We'll talk about your family and your upbringing, and maybe you can tell me a little bit about Jayne's.'

'There's nothing to tell there,' he said.

'What do you mean?'

'She hasn't got a family.'

'What, no one left alive?'

'She lost touch with them years ago, before she even met me. Some big fallout it were. She says she wanted nowt more to do with them. Simple as that.'

'And she's had no contact with them since?'

'Not that I know of. I don't think they even know where she lives.'

'And does that bother her?'

'She says not. Reckons it's best that way. It can't be nice, though, can it? Not having your family around you. Not having any sense of your roots.'

'No,' I said, scribbling some notes on Jayne's file. 'It can't.'

I felt an odd churning sensation inside me as I packed our case for York. It was wrong to feel like that when you were preparing to go away for the weekend with your husband. But then again, it was so long since I had been away with my husband that maybe it wasn't surprising.

Chris didn't even know yet. I'd asked him not to work on his birthday, but he was probably expecting a family meal or something. Not a weekend away for two. There was also something faintly sleazy about even the sound of it. The element of nudge, nudge, wink, wink, we know what you'll be up to. Which maybe explained why I was feeling so unsure about it all. At home you could blame work and the children and being tired for not having sex. A weekend away left you no room for manoeuvre.

It wasn't that I didn't want to. Simply that I had to believe that he wanted to as well.

And still it refused to go away. This image of him and Lydia together; the hunger in his eyes, the undoubted spark between them. Whereas with us it had been Josh who had brought us together. There had never been just the two of us. The job description had changed by then. I'd fitted it, obviously. Although I still wasn't sure I'd have fitted the original one.

I opened my nice lingerie drawer. It was a long time since I'd worn some of this stuff. I was lucky if I got out of the house in the morning wearing matching underwear, let alone having time to put stockings on. I dug out a Rigby & Peller ensemble from the back of the drawer. Debbie had got it for me for my fortieth birthday the previous year. I hadn't had the heart to tell her that the thing about big knickers from M&S was that they were safe and comfortable and could hide all sorts of misdemeanours.

She hadn't forgotten, though. It was the last thing she'd said to me when I'd dropped Matilda off at her house earlier. 'Don't you dare leave the posh knickers at home, OK?'

I popped them in the case, alongside the camisole that it was always too cold to wear at home and a couple of pairs of Chris's boxer shorts. It was so much bloody easier for men.

'Where is everyone?' asked Chris when he got home, dumping his photographic bags in the hall.

'Matilda's at Sophie's. She's sleeping over.'

'Oh, I didn't know.'

'And Josh is at Tom's. He's staying over too.'

Chris raised his eyebrows. 'Don't tell me they've blown their girlfriends out on Valentine's Day?'

'Nope. They're going out as a foursome, apparently. Some rom-com at the cinema and then Pizza Express because they've got an offer on giving out free roses to the ladies.'

'Now there are a couple of lads who have got it sorted,' said Chris.

'I know. All very grown-up and civilised. Then Caitlin's mum's dropping the boys off at Tom's and taking the girls back to their place.'

'Right,' said Chris.

It was only at that point that he glanced down and saw the suitcase in the hall.

'So whose is this?' he asked. I hestitated for a second, still unsure how he'd respond.

'Ours,' I said. 'We're going away for the weekend, for your birthday. Just me and you.'

'Are we?'

'Yeah. I thought it would, you know, do us good.'

He nodded again. Neither of us was going to mention her by name, but he clearly understood.

'Where are we going, then?'

'You'll find out when we get there.'

'Do I need my passport?'

'Don't worry.' I smiled. 'We're not even leaving Yorkshire.'

The hotel was one of those boutique places: beautiful building, contemporary touches and rooms that were classy without being pretentious. It was quiet in the foyer. I was conscious of my heels clicking on the dark, wooden boards as we walked in.

'Hello,' I said to the woman in her fifties behind the desk. 'We've got a double room booked, it's Bentley.'

'Ah, yes,' she smiled, checking on her computer screen before handing me a key card. 'First floor on the right. It's a lovely room, plenty of space for you to spread out.' For a second, I wanted to grab hold of her hand and squeeze it.

Have her see us up to the room and give me a 'You'll be fine, dear' pat on the hand, as if I was some virginal newly-wed, about to be carried over the threshold. I wasn't, though. I was a forty-year-old mother and stepmother who'd been married nearly ten years. It was simply that the man standing next to me, the one who was looking particularly dapper in his overcoat, felt more like a stranger at that moment than my husband.

I thanked her. Chris picked up the case. He took the stairs and I followed him, my footsteps silent now on the patterned runner on the wooden staircase. Chris put the case down and opened the door. It was a big room, twice the size of the box-like ones you get in the big chains. There were two large sash windows to the front. I suspected we'd be able to see the top of York Minster through them in the morning. An antique brass bed dominated the room. That was the thing about hotel rooms. There was no getting away from the bed.

'Do you like it?' I asked.

'Yeah,' said Chris, slipping off his coat and walking round to the far side to run his fingers along the marble mantelpiece. 'It's great. Thanks. I really wasn't expecting this.'

'I know. You don't mind, though?'

'Of course I don't mind. I could get quite used to this, actually,' he said, sitting down on the bed and lying back, his hands behind his head.

'Don't get too used to it,' I said. 'Back to reality on Sunday, I'm afraid.'

'Were the kids OK about it? Didn't complain or anything?'

'No. Although I made sure I told Matilda she was having a

sleepover at Sophie's first. So I'm not sure she even registered the part about us going away, she was that excited.'

'It's weird, isn't it?' said Chris. 'Not having her around.'

'It's certainly quieter.'

'Not for Debbie and Dean, it isn't,' he said.

'Don't feel too bad. I told Debbie we'd return the favour sometime.'

'Oh,' he said. 'Remind me of how nice this was when that happens, will you?'

I smiled. He patted the bed next to him. I walked round to his side of the bed, slipped off my shoes and lay down next to him, the two of us staring up at the ceiling.

'Lovely clear sky. Isn't that the Plough over there,?' said Chris, pointing at the light fitting.

I laughed. 'Remind me to get a room with a retractable roof next time,' I said.

'So there's going to be a next time?'

'I hope so. Depends how this goes, I suppose.'

'It'll be fine,' he said, turning to face me. 'Better than fine, even.'

I'd booked a table at a restaurant a couple of roads away, somewhere Chris had once remarked looked nice when we'd walked past it with Josh in tow, on our way to indulge his Viking fascination at the Jorvik Centre.

Chris leant over to me as we waited to be seated. 'I think I forgot to say how great you look,' he whispered.

I smiled at him and looked down. I'd worried the dress was a bit too 'autumn berries in a blender'. Apparently not. They suited me, plums and dark reds. Which was a bit of luck as I was one of those rare women who didn't look good in black.

A waiter showed us to our table and gave us the menus. Chris opened his and started reading.

'I think there's been a mistake,' he said after a few moments.

'What?'

'This is grown-up food. And nobody's whining that they don't do pizzas.'

I laughed. 'And we won't have to spend the entire meal reminding her not to talk with her mouth full.'

'No one will end up nicking most of my pudding either.'

'I wouldn't bet on it,' I said.

Chris smiled. 'You're right. We should do this more often. Make it happen. It's what other people do.'

'Well, it's getting easier now Josh is older. We'll be able to leave him on his own soon.'

'I'm not so sure. Not now he's got a hot girlfriend.'

'How do you know she's hot?'

'What, a violin-playing grammar school girl? I can picture her now, one of those willowy blonde sixteen-year-olds the *Daily Telegraph* always puts on the front page the day after GCSE results.'

'She's got brown hair, actually.'

'How do you know?'

'Josh told me.'

'As in he volunteered the information or you winkled it out of him with the use of Guantánamo Bay interrogation techniques?'

'It came up while we were watching the news. He said people say Caitlin looks a bit like Kate Middleton.'

'Well, at least the boy's got taste.'

'I thought you were a Republican?'

'I mean, to go for a brunette rather than a blonde.'

He appeared to realise almost as soon as he said it. He at least had the good grace not to dig himself any further into the hole by saying something complimentary about women with mousey-coloured hair with highlights.

The wine waiter arrived at our table during the silence which followed. Chris ordered a bottle of white before I could say anything.

'You should have ordered a red,' I said. 'It's your birthday.'

'Not till tomorrow,' said Chris. 'It's fine, honestly.'

'Thank you,' I said. The waiter came back and poured. Another came over to take our order. I wished there was some background music on. The sound of conversation from other tables always seems louder when yours is quiet.

'Anyway,' I said, 'I think Caitlin's the best thing that could have happened to Josh. It's so good to see him smiling again.'

'I know,' said Chris. 'Let's hope it lasts a while before they split up.'

I shook my head. 'I know where he gets it from now,' I said. 'He told me not so long ago that all relationships are doomed to failure.'

'Well, at least his expectations are realistic.'

'Come on, give them a chance.'

'Look, it might last a year or so at best. Then she'll go off to uni and meet someone else and he'll be gutted.'

'When did you become such a cynic?' I asked.

Chris raised his eyebrows. I looked down at the table, wishing I'd engaged my brain before opening my mouth. Our starters arrived. They looked great. But I couldn't help wondering if the spectre of Lydia would hang over us all the way to the bitter-chocolate torte.

Chris held my hand as we walked back to the hotel. He was trying. I really appreciated that. I was trying too. And yes, we'd still managed to talk about the children for pretty much the entire meal. But lots of parents did that. It wasn't that we had nothing else to talk about, simply that they were the most important things to talk about. I didn't have a problem with that.

What concerned me more was what we hadn't talked about. Not because I desperately wanted to spend our weekend away discussing my husband's ex but because I couldn't see how we could move on until we did. Lydia was the elephant in the room. A skinny one, maybe, but an elephant none the less.

'Do you want a drink?' Chris asked when we got back to the hotel.

'I think I've had enough, actually,' I said. 'Haven't got the tolerance levels I used to.'

'You would at least be able to have a hangover in peace tomorrow morning,' said Chris.

'Thanks,' I said with a smile, 'but I'll still pass on it.'

'Another coffee?'

'No, thanks.'

'We'll just go up, then, shall we?'

I nodded.

Neither of us said anything on the way up the stairs. Chris fumbled in his pockets trying to locate the key card. I waited without saying a word. I couldn't help thinking this was all wrong, we should be falling about giggling or trying to rip each other's clothes off. It all felt a bit Monday morning at the office rather than Friday night at the hotel.

'Got it!' said Chris, holding up the key card.

I nodded and smiled. He let us in. The bed loomed large in front of us, reminding me of student days, inviting a male friend back to your bedsit and wishing you hadn't because the bed made it look like such a blatant come-on.

Chris hung his coat up on the back of the door. He stepped behind me and helped ease my jacket off, his hands brushing my bare shoulders as he did so. The knot inside me twisted tighter. He hung the jacket up and turned back to me. His eyes locked on to mine, his lips turning up slightly at the edges.

I wanted him. I wanted him really badly, but still she was there. I could feel her presence in the room. I wanted to check behind me, in case it was her he was smiling at. I kissed him hard on the mouth. Hoping it would get rid of her. Send her fleeing from the room and free me in the process.

He kissed me back, pulled me in closer to him. His hand was cold on the back of my neck, the other hand already pulling at the zip of my dress. He wanted me. He wanted me, not her. And still she smiled. And still she laughed. And still she dug the knife in.

Our lips parted for a second. I pulled back and took a breath, fighting to control the feelings inside. It was no good, though. She had the better of me, and she knew it. She laughed in my face and the moment was gone. My hands dropped to my sides.

'What is it?' Chris asked, the hunger still visible on his face.

'I'm sorry,' I said. 'It's just, I can't, you know.'

'I thought you wanted –'

'Yes,' I said. 'I did. I do.' I shut my eyes and tugged my fingers through my hair.

'So what's the problem?'

I sighed and looked up at the ceiling. 'It's her.'

He stared at me, his brow furrowed. 'I don't understand.'

I sat down on the edge of the bed. 'Lydia. The whole thing. It . . . it just won't go away.'

'But she's gone.'

'Not for me, she hasn't. She's left her mark on everyone. Nothing's the same, and yet you're acting as if everything's fine now. And it isn't.'

Chris blew out and sat down heavily on the bed next to me. 'She's gone. End of story.'

'It's not for me. Your ex turns up, tears our family apart, goes away again, you blame me. And yet we're not supposed to talk about it.'

'I don't blame you.'

'Well, it sounded like it on Christmas night.'

'I was angry because you kept giving her chances when I knew she was going to screw up again.'

'What was I supposed to do? Our family was being torn apart, and you wouldn't see anyone else's point of view. I was trying to hold things together and I messed up. I'm sorry, OK?'

I turned my head so he wouldn't see the tears forcing their way out of my eyes and down my face.

Chris put his arm around me, pulled me towards him and held me. Held me like he hadn't done for a long time. Stroked my hair. Gave me tiny delicate kisses on my eyelids until they were soothed enough to open again.

'I'm sorry,' he said.

'What for?'

'Having an ex from hell, for a start.'

'I don't think she's from hell. She's just got issues.'

Chris smiled and shook his head. 'It's a bit of luck you don't work in TV,' he said.

'What do you mean?'

'Well, all those reality TV shows would be called things like *The Neighbours Who Need a Facilitator to Improve Relations*, or *The Divorced Couples Who Might Like to Consider Mediation*.'

I managed a weak smile. 'Am I that bad?'

'No,' he said. 'You're not bad at all. You're lovely. You're the nicest person I know. Maybe that's why I want to protect you from all the shit out there.'

'I don't want protecting,' I said. 'I want us to be in this together. If you're upset, I want to know about it. If I'm upset, I want to be able to talk to you.'

'OK,' he said. 'I didn't mean to shut you out, but when she came back I sort of shut down. It was the only way I could cope.'

'You never really dealt with her walking out on you, did you?'

'Probably not. I was too busy looking after Josh.'

'It's not too late to get help, you know.'

Chris looked at me and smiled.

'I've gone into relationship counsellor mode, haven't I?' I said.

He nodded. 'I really don't want to trawl back through the whole thing. I just want to get on with my life. And my life is with you and Josh and Tilda.'

'You don't think she's coming back?'

He shook his head. 'No.'

'She's still Josh's mum. That's one hell of a pull.'

'But if she really cares for him, like she says, she'll stay away.'

'And what if she doesn't?'

Chris shrugged. 'Well, Josh has got Caitlin now. She ought to prove enough of a distraction.'

I wasn't so sure but I didn't want to push the point any further. I looked up and caught sight of myself in the dressing-table mirror. Half of my hair, which had been tied up, was now straggling down my face. My mascara was smudged. My dress was still half unzipped at the back. The phrase 'hedge backwards' sprang to mind.

'Look at the state of me,' I groaned.

Chris kissed me on the forehead. 'I don't care about all that,' he said. 'I'm here with you, and that's all that matters.'

'Good,' I said.

'Now, how about we start this whole thing again? I do believe I was fumbling with the zip of your dress.'

He leant over and kissed my neck, one hand reaching for the zip. All was quiet this time. I couldn't hear her. See her. Feel her presence. It was just me and Chris.

'Here,' I said, standing up, undoing the zip and slipping the dress down over my hips, 'does this help?'

'Oh yes,' said Chris, smiling as he stepped towards me. 'That helps a great deal.'

'So,' said Debbie, when I called to pick up Matilda on Sunday evening, 'good weekend?'

'Yes, thank you,' I said, smiling and feeling like a teenager who had stayed over at her boyfriend's for the first time. 'York was lovely, as ever.'

'Well, I hope you didn't see too much of it,' said Debbie. 'Or have time to send me a postcard.'

'No worries there,' I said. 'How's Matilda been?'

'Oh, you know. Ransacking the house, all-night parties, the police have been round to serve an ASBO.'

'They've had a good time, then?'

'Yep, I'm surprised they haven't talked each other to death. But they appear to have survived on five hours' sleep and midnight snacks of marshmallows and strawberries dipped in chocolate.'

'Jesus, can I come next time?'

'Only if you promise to let me have her for the weekend again. Ideally at some point before she's sixteen.'

'OK,' I said, 'it's a deal.'

'Mummy!' screamed Matilda, appearing at the top of the stairs. She ran down, gave me an enormous hug and ran straight back up again.

'Come on,' said Debbie. 'I think we've got time for a cuppa. And I want all the gory details.'

From the Counselling Room

Last Christmas she gave me a Thermos. I mean, George Michael would never write a song about that, would he?

I wouldn't mind but I'm not even forty yet. What would it be next year, a bed-pan? I'm not going to hang around to find out.

16

I'd asked Catherine to come alone. I'd already seen Nathan. To be honest, we hadn't really made much progress. He still seemed to have the idea in his head that my role was to make Catherine change her mind about starting a family. My attempts to get him to look at areas where he might be willing to compromise had been met with a polite but firm refusal.

Catherine sat down opposite me. She crossed her legs. Her hands were still clasped tightly in her lap but her shoulders were not as hunched as usual.

'Thanks for coming,' I said. 'I know it's been a good few weeks since I saw you. How have things been?'

'OK, I guess,' she said.

'And what does OK mean for you?'

She hesitated. 'It means things haven't got any worse.'

'Right. And how bad would you say they were? To start with, I mean. Say on a scale of one to ten, with one being fantastic and ten being unbearable.'

The pause lasted a lot longer this time. 'About nine,' she said softly.

I nodded, made a note on her file while I gathered my

thoughts. 'Nathan clearly doesn't think things are that bad,' I said.

'You won't tell him, will you?' she asked.

'No. But I am concerned about the difference in your perceptions of the situation. Whose suggestion was it that you came for counselling in the first place?'

'Nathan's,' she said.

'And yet he doesn't seem to think it's that serious. He only scored it a four.'

She didn't say anything.

'Why do you think that is?' I asked.

She shrugged. 'I guess he sees things differently.'

I didn't buy it for a second. The way she looked down at her hands suggested she knew that too.

'Why did he say he wanted to go for counselling?'

'To get the baby thing sorted. He said it would make me come to my senses.'

'And how did you feel about that?'

'I knew it wouldn't change my mind.'

'But you went along with it all the same.'

'Yeah,' she said. 'It was easier that way.' She took a sip of water. Her hand was shaking a little.

Part of me felt it was wrong to chip away like this. But sometimes it was the only way.

'So why didn't you suggest coming to counselling yourself?' I asked. 'If you say things are as bad as a nine.'

Catherine looked down at her hands. The nail varnish was chipped on at least three fingers today.

'I didn't think it would help.'

'Why not?'

'The situation was beyond that. Talking about it doesn't help everything, you know.'

It was the first time she had been curt with me. I knew I shouldn't take it personally. She was clearly under a lot of strain. It was simply unfortunate that it had hit a rather raw nerve.

'Why was it beyond that, Catherine? What had been happening between you?' I had to steel myself to carry on, even though I could see it was making her uncomfortable.

'He can be very controlling.' Her voice cracked slightly as she said it.

I nodded. Trying to give her every encouragement to carry on. 'In what ways?'

'Not liking me to go out on my own. Always needing to know where I am. Who I'm with. He doesn't like the fact that my co-owner at the gallery is a man. He gets very jealous.'

'And have you reassured Nathan that he has no grounds for this?'

'Yeah. My business partner's gay for a start. I've told Nathan that, but he doesn't buy it. Not even in Hebden Bridge.' She almost spat out the last sentence. The previously buttoned-up exterior was in the process of unravelling.

'And what happens, if you do go out on your own or stay late at work? If he doesn't know where you are or who you're with?'

Her hands were trembling. It was not only her hands, but pretty much her whole body. Her eyes were focused intently on a spot on the floor in front of me. She opened her mouth, then shut it again.

'It's OK,' I said. 'Take as much time as you need.'

She tried again but with no success. I could see the whites of her knuckles growing ever clearer. She stood up, still staring at the floor. Took off her cardigan. The bruises reached all the way from her shoulders down to her elbows. They varied in colour from yellow to a dark mauve. A timeline tapestry of pain, of hate, of suffering. She took her boots off and peeled off her tights. If anything, the bruises on her legs were worse. And finally, she rolled down the top of her skirt so I could see her belly. It may have been a knee, or a foot, it was hard to tell. The mark was fresh, though. Maybe only twenty-four hours old.

'This,' she whispered, finally looking up from the floor. 'This is what happens. And this is why there is no way on earth I am getting pregnant.'

We weren't supposed to touch our clients. It wasn't considered professional. But I wasn't a professional at that moment, and she wasn't a client. She was a woman, reaching out to another woman. And I was damned if I was going to let her stand there alone.

I took her in my arms and held her. Her body was still shaking. Not shivering, shaking. I held her until the shakes turned to sobs and she sank down on her knees to the floor. I picked her cardigan up and put it over her shoulders.

'It's OK,' I said. 'It's done now. You're not on your own any more.'

I was still thinking about Catherine on Mother's Day morning. She wasn't a mother. And maybe she never would be. But she was still nurturing, still protecting. Albeit towards a foetus which didn't even exist. You didn't have to be an actual mother to be worthy of a thought on Mother's Day.

She hadn't wanted to call the police or a women's refuge. She wouldn't even take the numbers in case Nathan found them. She'd gone home to him. That was the hardest part for me to understand. Having come that far and given so much of herself, she had somehow rolled all the hurt back inside. It was the emotional equivalent of one of those hold-it-all-in garments from M&S. Her pain might not have been visible from the outside, but somewhere along the line it would need to find an outlet. It was simply a matter of pushing it deep inside for now and hoping it wouldn't pop out at an inconvenient time and place.

She was completely and utterly dependent on Nathan. Because of her eating disorder. Because he had genuinely helped her with it when they'd first met. So she'd let him gradually take control of her life to the point where it wasn't hers any more. All because she had it in her head that he was the only thing which stood between her and it coming back again. And instead he was eating away at her, sapping her confidence, pummelling her into submission.

I had at least persuaded her to make another appointment to see me. She was going to tell Nathan that we were working on her issues. And he'd swallow that whole, of course, because he clearly didn't think he had any issues that needed sorting.

Chris stirred next to me, rolling over and draping an arm across my body. I couldn't imagine it, sleeping in a bed with a man who hit you, who abused you. And yet somewhere that was what Catherine was doing. I hoped that one day she'd think herself worthy of more than that. And in the meantime, I owed it to her to appreciate everything I had in my life which she didn't.

'Happy Mother's Day!' Matilda barged into the room in her pyjamas and leapt onto the bed brandishing a card which, even in the dim morning light, practically glowed, it had that much yellow paint on.

'Thank you, sweetheart,' I said, propping myself up on one elbow while I opened it.

'I'll turn the light on so you can see it properly,' said Matilda.

Chris groaned and screwed up his eyes as she flicked the main light on.

'It's beautiful,' I said, squinting.

'It's got a poem inside. I wrote it myself.'

'As opposed to commissioning Carol Ann Duffy,' whispered Chris.

I dug him in the ribs, opened the card up and read it out loud.

'"My mummy is a busy bee / She's very good at nagging me / She goes to M&S for my tea / And washes my hair so I don't have fleas."'

Chris stuffed a corner of the pillow into his mouth to stop himself laughing out loud.

'It's lovely, sweetheart, thank you,' I said, giving her a kiss.

There was a picture of me underneath. I had a large oval body and something flappy on my arms.

'Are they wings?' I asked.

'No, it's your cardigan,' she said.

I nodded. Clearly, I was that kind of mum.

'Come on,' Matilda hissed, jumping on top of Chris. 'We've got to get to work.'

She dragged Chris out of bed, allowing him enough time only to pull on a dressing gown, before marching him out of the room.

I allowed myself a smile as I heard the bash of a pan downstairs. It would be blueberry and banana pancakes for breakfast. I turned over, not that I actually expected to get back to sleep.

The knock on the bedroom door a few minutes later was a faint one. I looked up to see Josh's face poking round it.

'I didn't think you'd be asleep,' he said with a smile.

'No,' I said. 'I shall look forward to a Mother's Day lie-in when she's your age.'

'You'll probably miss it, actually,' he said.

I smiled at him. 'Do you know? I expect you're right.'

'Anyway,' he said, 'as you're awake, I may as well give you this.'

He held out an envelope and a small thin box wrapped in tissue paper.

'Thank you,' I said. 'You know I always say you don't have to.'

'Yeah, and I always tell you I want to.'

I smiled at him and opened the envelope. It was one of those 'For someone who's like a mother to me' cards. Chris had started getting them for him after we got married. And at some point Josh had decided to carry on doing it himself. Inside he had written 'Thank you for being there'. I blinked hard and picked up the present. I peeled the tape off one end, slid out the box and opened it. It was a bracelet of plum and purple stones.

'Oh, Josh, it's beautiful.'

'Caitlin helped me choose it.'

'You told her the colours, though,' I smiled.

'Yeah.'

'You really shouldn't go to this expense, though. Your pocket money's supposed to be for you.'

'I wanted to. After all the, you know, stuff . . .'

He looked down at his feet. For a second he didn't look anywhere near sixteen.

'Come here,' I said.

I hugged him to me. Sometimes, just occasionally, he was still my little boy. I let go but, surprisingly, he held on a bit longer.

'Are you OK?' I asked.

'Yeah.'

'I know it's going to be really difficult for you today.'

'I'll be fine.'

'I'm glad Caitlin's coming.'

'Me too.'

'You've told her not to worry about it, haven't you?' I asked. 'The whole meeting-the-folks thing.'

'Yeah. She knows you don't bite and all that stuff.'

I smiled. 'I remember being so nervous when I met my first boyfriend's family. I spilt peas all over the floor and used the wrong cutlery and everything.'

'What was his name?' asked Josh.

'Patrick McDowell. He had red hair, but I was past caring because I was the last one of my friends to have a boyfriend.'

Josh smiled. 'You mean, you were desperate.'

'Yeah, I guess I was. Probably why it didn't last long.'

'How long?'

'About eight weeks, I think. He dumped me for someone called Vanessa in the sixth form. I wasn't that gutted, to be honest. I played "Is She Really Going Out with Him?" by Joe Jackson a couple of times and I was pretty much OK.'

Josh smiled again.

'You really like Caitlin, don't you?'

He nodded.

'I can't wait to meet her.'

'Just so long as you don't do all that "Welcome to the family" stuff.'

'Did her parents do that?'

'No, they were pretty chilled, actually. Much better than Alicia's, anyway. Tom said her dad sat down and had "the talk" with him.'

'What, about whether his intentions were honourable?'

'Something like that. He basically wanted to know if he was going to knock up his daughter.'

'I take it he said he wasn't.'

'Yeah, cos he wanted to get out of there alive.'

I nodded, aware we hadn't had a similar conversation with Josh yet.

'But was that the honest answer too?'

'Course it was. He's not an idiot, you know.'

I wasn't sure if that meant Tom wasn't having sex with her. Or simply wasn't stupid enough to do it without condoms.

'And I take it Caitlin's dad didn't ask you anything like that?'

'No, just wanted to know what "A" levels I was planning to do.'

'Should he have asked, though?'

Josh looked down at the floor. 'No. She wants to wait.'

'Good for her. I know girls get a lot of pressure these days.'

'Not from me, she doesn't.'

'No, I know. But from society, the media, all that stuff. It's really important that you support her.'

'Is this the bit where you turn into the embarrassing agony aunt type?'

'Possibly,' I said.

'I think I'd better go, then,' smiled Josh.

'Your sister will be wanting you to help with the pancakes.'

'I know. I'm on my way,' he said, getting up off the bed.

'Josh.'

He turned back to me.

'I think Caitlin's a very lucky girl.'

The colour rose in his cheeks a little. 'Let's hope you lot don't scare her off, then,' he said.

So the family was gathering in our house for a special occasion and we were preparing to welcome Josh's special guest into our midst. The parallels with Christmas were obvious, and yet no one mentioned them, which only served to make it even worse.

It was Matilda who cracked in the end. She wandered into the kitchen, unusually quiet, and came and stood next to me.

'People won't end up shouting again, will they?' she asked.

I crouched down and pulled her to me. 'No, love,' I said. 'This is going to be a lovely Mother's Day tea.'

'What if Lydia comes?'

'She won't.'

'Why not? She's Josh's mother.'

I could see her logic, and I also shared a tiny bit of her concern. I wasn't going to show that, though.

'She won't come because she's not invited.'

'Because of what happened at Christmas?'

'Yes.'

'Why is Caitlin coming?'

'Because she's been invited.'

'But you're not her mother.'

'No. But we thought it would be nice to invite her because she's very special to Josh, and we want her to know that she's therefore special to us too.'

Matilda weighed this up for a moment and obviously decided it was an acceptable answer. 'OK,' she said, and skipped back out of the kitchen.

Chris arrived back with Barbara first.

'Thank you for the flowers, love,' she said as I stooped to kiss her. 'They're beautiful.'

'You're very welcome.'

Chris always got them, actually. I was fortunate enough to have got one of those rare men who didn't stop buying their own Mother's Day presents as soon as they had a wife to do it for them.

Matilda ran out and threw herself at Barbara. 'Grandma, you're just in time to do the Grandma puppet in *Little Red Riding Hood*.'

'Give your grandma a chance to get in the door,' I said.

'It's OK,' said Barbara. 'I'm ready for action, just so long as wolf's not too scary.'

'He's really scary,' said Matilda. 'But it's OK because, after he eats you, we'll cut him open and get you out again.'

Barbara laughed and allowed herself to be dragged off into the lounge by Matilda.

'It could be worse,' said Chris. 'She could be doing Hansel and Gretel, in which case Mum would be about to be burnt to death in an oven.'

I smiled at him. 'You OK?' I asked.

'Yeah,' he said, putting his arms around me. 'I'm good, thanks.'

We'd offered to pick Caitlin up but Josh had insisted he was going to walk her up from the bus stop. I suspected it was cover for some kind of briefing which would be going on, warning her of all our various foibles.

It was gone four when I heard Josh's key in the door. I had vowed not to go running out there, embarrassing the poor girl, but the fact that Matilda jumped up and dashed out gave me an excuse to go after her.

Caitlin was standing in the hallway dressed in a dark red Puffa jacket, short black skirt, opaque tights and boots. Her long brown hair curled over her shoulders. It did look a bit like Kate Middleton's, but her face was younger and refreshingly devoid of make-up. She didn't need it, anyway. She was absolutely gorgeous.

'Hi, Caitlin,' I said. 'I'm Alison, it's lovely to meet you at last.'

I went over and kissed her on the cheek. It felt the right thing to do. She didn't appear too embarrassed.

'You too,' she said, revealing a couple of dimples as she smiled and handing me a bunch of gerberas.

'Thank you,' I said, 'they're lovely.'

I smiled at her and Josh in turn, suspecting he had tipped her off in the favourite flowers department. Matilda was bouncing up and down next to me. Josh ruffled her hair.

'And this is my sister, Tilda,' he said.

'Hi,' said Caitlin, giving her a little wave.

'Are you his girlfriend now?' piped up Matilda. 'Only you're holding hands.'

They looked at each other and laughed. Neither of them let go, though.

'Thank you, missy,' I said, guiding Matilda back towards the lounge before turning back to them. 'Here, let me take your jacket.'

Caitlin slipped it off and handed it to me. She started to take her boots off.

'You don't have to worry about those,' I said.

'It's OK, I have to do it at home. My mum hates shoes in the house.'

I smiled at her. Caitlin and Josh followed me into the lounge.

Chris was sitting with Barbara on the sofa. He stood up as soon as we came in, walked over to Caitlin and offered his hand.

'Hi, I'm Chris, Josh's dad. Good to meet you.'

I could see Josh cringing behind her, but Caitlin appeared undaunted and shook his hand.

'And you,' she replied.

Barbara got up from the sofa, came up to Caitlin, patted her on the hand and said, 'Hello, lovey, so you're the one who's put a sparkle in our Josh's eyes.'

Caitlin smiled and looked down at her feet.

'And this is my grandma, who's very good at embarrassing me,' said Josh, giving her a hug.

He was a good six inches taller than her now. Caitlin wasn't far behind him, mind you.

'What do they feed you girls nowadays?' asked Barbara. 'You're all so long and stringy.'

'My whole family are tall,' said Caitlin. 'My brother's over six foot.'

'How old is he?' I asked.

'If you say ten, we're going to worry,' added Chris.

'No, he's nineteen,' she laughed. 'He's away at uni.'

'Which one?' I asked.

'The London School of Economics. He's doing a social policy degree.'

Chris looked suitably impressed. Her family might be well off but they still had a social conscience.

'Anyway,' I said, seeing Josh's stop-asking-her-questions face, 'come and sit down. Can I get you something to drink?'

'A cup of tea would be great, but only if you're making one.'

'Oh, she drinks tea,' said Barbara. 'She must be all right.'

I smiled at Caitlin. 'We're always making one in this house,' I said.

They sat next to each other at the tea table. It was probably the first time they'd stopped holding hands. But there were still constant glances at each other, and I wouldn't have been surprised if there was some foot contact going on under the table. They were plainly smitten, the pair of them, which thrilled me and scared me in equal measure.

'So how long have you been playing the violin, Caitlin?' I asked.

'Since I was about six. My family had to put up with a lot of screeching in those days.'

'It's paid off from the sound of it, though,' I said. 'Josh says you're very good.'

She looked at Josh and smiled. 'Thanks, I'm getting there,' she said.

'Can you teach me?' asked Matilda. 'Josh lets me play his guitar sometimes. Not the one his real mum got him, the other one.'

Chris and Josh remained silent, both looking down at their plates. I felt the familiar twisting sensation inside.

'Yeah, I'd love to,' replied Caitlin. 'As long as that's OK.' She looked across at me as she said it.

'That would be lovely,' I said. 'Thank you.'

'Just let me know in plenty of time when the first lesson is,' said Chris. 'I may have some work on that day.'

'Yeah, and I think I'll be busy revising at Tom's,' added Josh.

They were both smiling. It was OK. We'd moved on. In every sense.

Chris took Caitlin home later that evening. Josh insisted on going with her – presumably to spare her any further embarrassing dad moments – and Barbara was in Matilda's room, reading her a bedtime story.

I remembered that Josh needed a shirt ironing for school the next day, so I quickly pressed one from the laundry basket and took it into his room. Lydia's guitar was on his bed. I assumed it was where he'd left it after showing it to Caitlin earlier. He'd played a bit too. We'd heard him from downstairs, where the rest of us had been having a conversation about how nice she was.

I hung the shirt up in his wardrobe. As I closed the door, his mobile beeped with a message. He'd left it on top of his chest of drawers. I glanced down as I walked past. I saw 'Mum' first, in bold type, as the sender. And then after it, the message: 'Thanks, love. I'll be in touch.'

From the Counselling Room

I caught her watching Mr Bloom's Nursery *on catch up one night, long after our little girl had gone to bed. I mean, the woman in* Nina and the Neurons *is quite cute. But you still wouldn't catch me watching CBeebies after nine o'clock at night.*

17

Lydia hadn't said when. That was the trouble. This week, this month, this year. It was like being told you had cancer but the doctor neglecting to mention the prognosis.

And because of that I didn't tell anyone. The last thing on earth I wanted to do was get Chris in a state again for no good reason. It might never happen. All I knew for certain was that there'd been one text exchange between them. It could have been the first, it was quite possible. Mother's Day would have been an understandable day for Josh to have contacted her. And she hadn't said she was going to see him, only that she'd be in touch.

So what if they texted each other? Was that really going to cause a problem? Only if I turned it into one.

I could have talked to Josh, but that would have meant admitting I'd read his text message. I knew I hadn't been snooping. But I was well aware that was how it would look from his point of view. And really, was it so bad that he'd sent a Mother's Day greeting to his own mum? Would I have wanted to have brought up a boy who didn't do that?

The questions swirled around in my head. Sometimes things clouded over, I couldn't see clearly at all. Other times

I was convinced the only sensible course of action was the one I was taking. Everything was fine at home. Better than fine. The best it had been since last September. I'd had a lovely birthday, we'd been out for a meal together. Just the four of us. No unwanted guests. No nasty surprises. Everyone was happy. And I wasn't going to jeopardise that for something which, at the moment, was nothing more than a solitary text message.

I woke up with a start early on Friday morning. I lay there for a second, unsure whether it really had been the doorbell which had woken me or whether I had merely imagined it, in the way I used to wake up thinking I'd heard Matilda crying for a feed when she was a baby long after she'd stopped doing it.

The doorbell rang again. I hadn't imagined it. I jumped out of bed, leaving Chris (who used to sleep through Matilda crying as well) slumbering next to me, pulled on my dressing gown and hurried downstairs.

It was in my head straight away, the idea that it could be Lydia. Probably it had been in my head that it was her even while I was asleep. I had no idea what I was going to do if it was her. All I knew was that I wanted to get to the door before anyone else. I pulled my dressing gown across my chest, fumbled with the lock and opened the door.

It was the postman. Delivering some trainers I'd ordered for Josh online.

I thanked him and shut the door, sat down on the bottom step of the stairs, closed my eyes and let out a long, loud breath.

'What's stopping you going home, Luke?'

I'd hoped that Christmas would have been the turning point

for Kelly and Luke. That not seeing his three young children excitedly discovering what Santa had brought them would have been enough of a jolt for him to want to move back home. It hadn't been. And three months on, he was still living at his mum's. Still going to the house every afternoon to look after the kids while Kelly went to work, and still returning to his mum's at night. I was worried they'd reached a kind of impasse. They were both maintaining their positions but nobody seemed to want to make a move.

'Nothing's changed, has it?' he said. 'It would still be exactly the same, if I moved back in.'

'You could give it a try and find out if that's the case.'

'There's no point. I don't want to muck the kids around, move back in and move out again a few days later. At least this way everyone knows where they stand.'

I thought for a minute about what he'd said. Wondered if Lydia would stay away from Josh because of a similar rationale.

'And what about you, Kelly?' I asked. 'Where do you think you stand?'

She hesitated before replying. 'I think he's left us,' she said, looking down at her hands. 'I don't think he's ever coming back, he's just doing it gradually because he feels bad about it and at some point it will become permanent.'

Luke shook his head. 'No. It's not like that.'

'I think it is,' said Kelly. 'You've got it too easy, having your mam fussing over you. It must be like living in a bloody hotel.'

'Yeah, but I'm not with my family, am I? Not where I want to be.'

Luke looked down at his feet. Kelly bit her bottom lip hard. There were occasions in my job when the desire to bang people's heads together was almost too much to bear.

'So what would you like to happen now?' I asked, looking at Kelly.

She fiddled with her nails before answering. 'I want him to come home,' she said. 'The kids think he's left them for good.'

'Why? What have you told them?' asked Luke.

'I haven't told them anything,' said Kelly. 'It's because you haven't lived with us since before Christmas. That's for ever, as far as they're concerned. Callum talks about Daddy's new home at Grandma's. What am I supposed to say?'

'You can tell them it's only temporary.'

'Well, it doesn't feel temporary to them or to me,' said Kelly, her voice on the edge of cracking.

'What about you, Luke?' I asked. 'What do you want to happen now?'

'I want to move back home. But I don't want it to be like it was before.'

'OK,' I said, sensing it was time to intervene. 'How about we put together a plan for moving back in? A proper timeline, setting out what needs to be achieved before that happens, but agreeing an actual date for it, if everything goes to plan. I'll see you both individually, we'll work on what changes you're both willing and able to make, and then we'll get back together and go through them all, see if we can come to some kind of agreement. What do you say to that?'

Kelly looked up at me and nodded, her ponytail bobbing up

and down as she did so. Luke shrugged. But I thought I saw a glimmer of hope in his eyes.

It was enough to go on. At least for now.

It was the flash of red which caught my eye. I'd left Chris and Matilda in the park and was hurrying to the Co-op to pick up some bits and pieces for tea, when my attention was drawn to the other side of the road. It was the Puffa jacket I recognised, rather than its occupant, at first. But as my gaze lifted to the face of the person wearing it, I remembered where I knew it from. It was Caitlin. She was with a friend, a friend I recognised as Alicia.

I stopped in the street, pretending to browse in the book-shop window while discreetly looking across the road. It wasn't that I wanted to spy on Caitlin, that I didn't trust her. Not in the slightest. It was because Josh had told me he was spending the afternoon with her.

Caitlin and Alicia appeared to be deep in conversation. Their faces were serious, none of the giggling and overly ani-mated expressions often favoured by teenage girls. My eyes scanned up and down the road. Maybe Josh had got waylaid in the music shop, or was loitering by the cafe somewhere with Tom, waiting for them to arrive. There was no sign, though.

The twisting and contorting inside me started again. There was only one reason why Josh would have lied to me. Her name was Lydia.

Caitlin and Alicia disappeared round the corner. And with them went any hopes I had of being able to kid myself that the text had been nothing to worry about. Lydia was back.

Josh was with her right now. And I had no idea what I was going to do about it.

I negotiated the aisles in the Co-op on automatic pilot and somehow found myself at the checkout with a basketful of items from which I could manage to throw a meal together.

I walked back to the park, trying to compose myself, to morph back into the bright and breezy person who had left there half an hour ago. It was difficult, though. The best-case scenario was that this was their first meeting. But even if it was, I suspected it wouldn't be the last.

It started to rain. I saw other children hurriedly leaving the playground, mums and dads gathering up belongings and making a dash for it. Matilda was sheltering under the big slide.

'Mummy!' she called. 'We've been waiting for ages.'

'I know, I'm sorry, love,' I said, crouching down to give her a hug. 'There was a long queue.'

I smiled at Chris. One of those overly enthusiastic smiles people do when they're trying hard to pretend that everything's OK.

'Right,' I said. 'Shall we make a move, then?'

He nodded.

We made a dash for the car. And with every step the knot in my stomach got a little tighter.

We were having tea when Josh got home. He'd texted earlier to let me know not to bother doing anything for him as he'd already eaten. He had always been good like that. Very considerate. Only, of course, this time I didn't feel inclined to tell him so.

'Hi,' he said, strolling into the kitchen and pinching a pasta tube from Matilda's bowl.

'Hey,' she said, 'that was mine.'

'You should have eaten it quicker, then. Instead of talking so much.'

He said it with a smile on his face and an accompanying jovial nudge with the elbow. Matilda pulled a face at him, but essentially he'd got away with it.

'Are you sure you don't want anything to eat?' I asked.

'I don't know. What are you having for pudding?'

Normally I would have laughed at his cheek. But at that moment I couldn't find it within myself.

'Banana and blueberry pancakes,' shouted Matilda.

'Wow! What's the special occasion?'

'I've just got a lot of eggs to use up,' I said.

'Maybe just a small one, then,' he replied.

'How's Caitlin?' asked Chris.

'Yeah, good,' said Josh.

He said it without hesitation. Without blinking, even. I'd always thought he was a rubbish liar. Maybe he was improving with practice.

'When is she going to teach me the violin?' asked Matilda.

'After her exams, like I explained,' I said. 'Caitlin and Josh are both going to be very busy until then.'

'They're not too busy to go out together,' said Matilda.

She was sharp, way too sharp for an eight-year-old, really. I dreaded to think what she'd be like by the time she was thirteen.

'No, and it's important that they have some time off. But Caitlin's got her violin practice and her revision to do too.'

'Don't worry, she hasn't forgotten you,' said Josh. 'Weirdly, she's looking forward to it. You're going to be her first pupil.'

Matilda's face flushed with pride.

'Just make sure you don't split up with her in the meantime,' said Chris. 'Violin lessons cost a fortune.'

Josh gave him a look.

'Aren't you going to pay her?' asked Matilda.

'Daddy was joking,' I said. 'Of course we'll pay her.'

'She won't accept it,' said Josh, who was warming himself with his back to the Aga.

'Well, we can at least offer,' I said. 'And if she turns it down, we'll find some other way to say thank you. Maybe your dad could take a portrait of her.'

Josh turned his nose up.

'What?' said Chris.

'Bit weird, my dad taking photos of my girlfriend.'

'Jeez, what do you take me for?' asked Chris.

'Just saying. The whole "Would you like to come to my photographic studio?" thing sounds a bit suspect.'

'Says he who hasn't set foot in it for as long as I can remember.'

'Why would I want to hang out there?'

'I told you, there's a Saturday job going, if you fancy it.'

'No, thanks.'

'Why not? It's good money. I'm sure it would come in handy.'

'Saturday's not a good day for me,' said Josh. 'I've got stuff on.'

'You mean Caitlin?'

I glanced up at Josh, wondering if he did mean Caitlin. Or whether it was more Lydia who was on his mind.

'Yeah.'

The colour in his cheeks had deepened a fraction. And I suspected it wasn't from standing in front of the Aga.

'She'll still be around at five o'clock, won't she?'

'That's not really the point.'

'So what is the point?'

'I don't fancy it, that's all.'

'Didn't you say Tom's got a Saturday job?'

'Yeah, collecting glasses.'

'There you go, then. You'll be complaining you haven't got as much money as him soon.'

Josh shrugged. 'Whatever.'

'When are we going to have pancakes?' sighed Matilda.

I hadn't even noticed she'd finished. 'Now,' I said. 'Let's get them started.'

Josh moved out of the way of the Aga. I caught his eye as he did so. He hated lying. He always had.

I used the sound of the running bath taps as cover. It was one of the downsides about an old house, the pipes were so narrow that filling the bath was a project you had to plan ahead for, not something you did on a whim.

I crept past Matilda's room and hesitated before I knocked on Josh's door. The ostrich position, while not universally acclaimed, was at least a safe one.

I was about to throw a hand grenade into Josh's room. I wasn't entirely sure what the fallout would be. Whether our relationship could survive unscathed or would forever bear the scars.

I knocked.

'Yeah?'

I went in. He was sitting on the bed, his legs out, his back propped up against the wall. I think he knew straight away. There was something about his demeanour which said 'rumbled'. There was no point in doing anything but coming straight out with it.

'I saw Caitlin in town today.'

Josh looked up at the ceiling. 'Oh,' he said.

'I'm not going to have a go at you for lying to us. But I do expect you to have the decency to tell me what's going on without us having to play any silly games.'

He nodded slowly, still averting his gaze from mine. 'Mum's back in Hebden,' he said.

'Right. And I take it you've been seeing her?'

'Only today. It was the first time. We've just texted and that before. She's really sorry about what happened. She wants us to start over again.'

I nodded.

Josh had the expression of someone who'd been waiting for a bomb to go off and was surprised that it hadn't detonated.

'Why didn't you tell us?'

'Why d'you think?'

'You could have told me. We could have discussed it together.'

'Yeah, but you'd have told Dad.'

'I keep things confidential for a living, remember. If it's what the person involved wants.'

'I wanted to do things my way this time,' said Josh. 'And I figured it was better that none of you knew.'

'And what if she messes you about again?'

'I can handle it, Ali. I can deal with her. Anyway, she's better now.'

'What do you mean, better?'

'She hasn't had a drink since Christmas Day.'

'And you believe that, do you?'

'Yeah. I do, actually.'

I nodded. It was so hard. I didn't want to cast doubt on his mother's honesty, but at the same time I wanted to protect him.

'The thing is, Josh,' I said, 'people can be on the wagon for a long time but that doesn't mean they're not going to fall off at some point. If she has got an alcohol problem, she may well need professional help.'

'Are you saying my mum's an alcoholic?'

'I'm suggesting you keep a close eye on her. And talk to me if you think she's started drinking again.'

Josh looked down at his hands. 'Are you going to tell Dad?' he asked.

'I don't know. I probably should do.'

'But it's not a problem. I'm not going to bring her here. I don't expect any of you to have anything to do with her. I'm keeping it all separate from home.'

'I know, love, and I appreciate that you've obviously put a lot of thought into how to handle this. But you're still part of this family. And if she hurts you, she therefore hurts all of us.'

'What's the worst she can do?' asked Josh. 'Disappear again?

If it happens again, I'll deal with it. I'm giving her one last chance. I figure she deserves that.' His voice was shaking as he finished.

'How often are you planning to see her?' I asked.

'I don't know. We're going to take it slowly, see how things go.'

'What does Caitlin think?' I asked.

'She's cool about me seeing her. Family's important to her too. She gets it.'

'And have you told her the background. About what happened?'

'Yeah,' said Josh. 'She knows Mum left when I was little, and that there was a big scene at Christmas after she came back.'

'That's good,' I said. 'I'm glad you can talk to her about stuff like that. Difficult stuff.'

'I'm not going to let anything spoil what I've got with Caitlin, if that's what you're worried about.'

'Good,' I said. 'Because I think she's really special.'

Josh smiled. 'So do I. And the thing is,' he continued, 'if you tell Dad now, it'll all blow up into a massive thing again, and I don't need that. I'm supposed to be revising for my GCSEs. I just want to be allowed to get on with my life the way I want to. That's all I'm asking.'

I sighed. You couldn't fail to be impressed by his maturity. And he had a point. Everything was good, everything was fine. Did I really want to be the one who upset all of that at such a critical point in his life?

'I tell you what,' I said. 'There are going to be two conditions. One is that you don't lie to me about what's going on.

If there's a problem, I want to know about it. If the whole situation feels like it's getting out of hand, or if Lydia starts drinking or messing you around again, you tell me straight away.'

Josh nodded.

'And I want you to agree that, if Lydia's still around after your exams and you still want to carry on seeing her, you talk to Dad about it then. I'm not at all comfortable about keeping this from him, and I'm only going to do it until that point.'

Josh nodded again, a broad smile on his face. 'Thanks, Ali,' he said, 'for not kicking off, like.'

I smiled. 'Right. Well, I'd better check on my bath. But remember what I said. Keep talking to me, OK?'

'Sure,' he said. 'I won't let you down.'

I'd never for a minute thought that he would do. It was Lydia I wasn't so sure about.

From the Counselling Room

He found me self-harming. I told him I did it because I was so unhappy, because he made me feel like a piece of shit on the bottom of his shoe, because it was the only way to get him to see my pain.

He just shrugged and walked out of the room.

18

'So are you just going to your mum's flat this evening?' I asked.

We were in the kitchen together. Matilda had gone round to Sophie's for tea after school. And the one good thing about the agreement I had with Josh was that I was back in the loop. He would tell me when he was due to see Lydia, where they were going (sometimes her flat, sometimes the cinema or a cafe in town) and occasionally, when he got back, he told me a bit about what they'd done, what she'd said, even a joke they had shared.

It had been strange, getting to know Lydia again, this time solely through Josh's eyes. The picture he painted was of an entirely different woman to the one who'd fled in disgrace on Christmas Day. She was back to being the Lydia of that first meeting: cool, relaxed and seemingly relishing the opportunity to build a relationship with her son.

'Well, that's what I was supposed to be doing,' he replied with a sigh.

'What do you mean?' I asked, concerned that Lydia had blown him out again.

'This party thing's come up.'

'What party thing?'

'This friend of Caitlin's is having a party tonight. I wasn't going to go but Caitlin really wants me to. Because of what's happened.'

I put down my mug of tea. 'And what has happened?'

Josh stopped pacing about the kitchen and turned to face me. 'Alicia's broken up with Tom.'

'Oh no. Poor Tom.'

'Yeah, he reckons it's no big deal. But I think he's pretty gutted, actually.'

'I thought you said she was besotted with him?'

'She was. Still is, apparently. Caitlin said it was Alicia's parents who made her call it off because they were worried she was going to screw up her GCSEs. Only now Alicia's in bits.'

I shook my head. No doubt they had thought they were doing the right thing too. That was the trouble with parenting. What seemed right in your head didn't always work out in practice.

'So I take it Tom's not going to the party?'

'No. He's working, anyway.'

'Right. But Caitlin is going, and she wants you there?'

'Yeah, because she's trying to persuade Alicia to go and reckons she might need me to lend a bit of support and tell her that Tom doesn't hate her for dumping him.'

I nodded, still trying to process it all in my head. 'Well, what do you want to do?' I asked.

'I want to go. I mean, Caitlin's asked me to but I don't want to let Mum down either.'

'Do you know what?' I said. 'I think she'd understand. It's not as if you make a habit of it, is it?'

I looked at Josh. I was trying to avoid saying that Lydia could hardly complain after the number of times she'd let him down.

'I guess not,' he said, still not sounding convinced.

'Why don't you give your mum a ring? Tell her what's happened. I'm sure she wouldn't mind. You could always fix something up for next weekend.'

'Yeah,' said Josh, nodding. 'You're probably right. It's just . . .'

'Just what?'

'I don't want her to, you know, take it the wrong way.'

'It's not such a big deal, is it? There'll be plenty of other times to see her, love. She knows that. It sounds like Caitlin could really do with you being around tonight.'

'You're right,' said Josh. 'Even if it will just be girly-crisis-in-the-loo stuff.'

I smiled at him. 'She'll thank you for it,' I said. 'That girly-crisis stuff's really important when you're sixteen.'

'You'd better stand by your phone,' he said. 'I'll give Caitlin your number, if it gets really heavy.'

He walked out of the kitchen, a smile on his face and a newfound air of maturity about him.

'So where's this party he's gone to?' asked Chris later, when Matilda was in bed and we were sitting on the sofa.

'It's in Warley. I've got the address. I said I'd pick them all up and run Caitlin and Alicia home. Josh is going to text me when they're ready.'

'I'll go, if you like, love,' Chris said. 'It'll probably be late.'

'It's OK, thanks, I don't mind. Anyway, I don't suppose you fancy dealing with teenage girls blubbing in your car.'

Chris looked at me, a slight frown on his face. 'Why will they be blubbing?'

'Big crisis. Alicia has dumped Tom. Or rather, her parents made her break it off so she could concentrate on her revision.'

'Jeez,' said Chris. 'Big stuff, indeed. Are we the bad parents, then? For letting Josh carry on seeing Caitlin?'

'Not from where I'm standing,' I said.

'You think they went in too heavy?'

'She's not going to be able to concentrate on her exams if she's as miserable as sin, is she?'

'No, but it will probably all blow over in a week or two.'

'Not at that age. It's a massive deal. He was her first proper boyfriend.'

'And we've got all this to look forward to.'

'No, we haven't. Not if Josh behaves himself and we don't try to meddle where we're not wanted.'

'They have been seeing a lot of each other lately.'

I was about to take issue with that. Then I remembered that, as far as Chris was aware, they'd been seeing a whole lot more of each other than they actually had.

'Good. I think she's a great influence on him.'

Chris shrugged. 'You won't be saying that if she ends up pregnant.'

'She's got far too much sense for that.'

'How do you know?'

'Josh told me. Said she wanted to wait.'

'How come he tells you stuff like that?'

'I had my counsellor face on at the time.'

'Well, I hope she sticks to her guns, for everyone's sake.'

'You just want to avoid having "the talk" with him, don't you?'

'Oh no,' said Chris, smiling. 'That is firmly your department.'

'I don't know what it's like to be a sixteen-year-old lad, do I?'

'Imagine raging hormones and a one-track mind and multiply that several times. Then you'll be about halfway there.'

'Sounds lovely.'

'And that'll be exactly why Alicia's parents are very relieved tonight.'

'What, you think they were worried that she'd get into trouble?'

'I bet that was part of it.'

'It's still tough on them both, whatever the reasons.'

'They'll get over it.'

'Still fancy doing the taxi run later, then, do you?' I asked, a smile nudging the corners of my mouth.

'Like you said, maybe she'll need a sympathetic ear. Female solidarity and all that.'

'Thank you,' I said. 'And in return I'll let you get up with Matilda in the morning.'

I waited outside the house for what seemed like an age. Fortunately for them, the meter wasn't running. When they did finally emerge, I could tell by the body language and the lack of noise as they approached the car that it was a rather subdued end to the night.

Josh got in the front passenger seat. Caitlin and Alicia climbed into the back. I could see Alicia's puffy red eyes in the rear-view mirror. I wanted to give her an enormous hug, though I barely knew the girl.

'Hi,' said Josh.

It was pointless asking them if the party was good. I sensed it was more of a case of surviving the night.

'Everything OK?' I asked.

He nodded.

'Thanks for this,' said Caitlin, as she put her seat belt on. 'Sorry it's so late.'

'No problem at all,' I said.

I set off for Alicia's house. I put the radio on, more to hide the awkward silence than anything else. It only took five minutes to get there.

Alicia took her seat belt off. 'Thanks very much,' she said, in a voice which vibrated with emotion.

'You're very welcome,' I said, turning round. 'You take care, OK?'

She nodded. Her bottom lip wobbled, and she got out. Caitlin got out with her and they stood hugging on the pavement for a minute. I could hear the sound of Alicia's sobs. It wasn't long before I was wiping my own tears away.

'Don't you start as well,' said Josh. 'I'm in danger of being waterlogged.'

Caitlin got back in the car after a few minutes. 'Sorry,' she said.

'Don't be daft,' I replied. 'I wanted to give her a hug myself. 'I'm glad she's got friends like you around to support her.'

We waited while Alicia walked up her garden path and opened the door. A light flicked on in an upstairs room. I suspected her mum hadn't even got to sleep. Probably lying there wondering if she'd done the right thing and, even if she had, whether she'd lost her daughter in the process.

'I can't believe they've done this to her,' said Caitlin, shaking her head.

'Maybe she and Tom can survive it,' I said. 'Get back together again when the exams are over. Persuade her parents to give them another chance.'

'It's not *Romeo and Juliet*, you know,' said Josh. 'Tom's already changed his Facebook status to single.'

I sighed and pulled away, feeling sad that everything moved on so quickly these days. No one seemed to have time to reflect on things, to reconsider. To try to make wrongs right.

'Thanks again,' said Caitlin, when I pulled up outside her house.

'No problem, love. See you soon.'

Josh got out of the car with her. I tried very hard not to glance over my shoulder as they embraced on the pavement. It was a good few minutes before Josh got back in again.

'Is she OK?' I asked.

'Yeah, a bit paranoid that the same thing's going to happen to us, that's all.'

'Her parents aren't worried about her seeing you, are they?'

'It's hard to tell. They haven't really talked to her much about it.'

'But she knows how you feel about her?'

'I haven't spouted poetry to her while she's on the balcony, like, but I think she's got the picture.'

I smiled at him as I pulled away. He reminded me of Chris

when he did that. Only he was even worse at hiding his true feelings.

Josh's phone beeped as we turned off the main road. He got it out of his pocket and read the message.

'Eejit,' he said, shaking his head.

'Who?'

'Tom. Reckons he's pulled some fit woman in the bar. Says he's going back to her place. Sounds like he's wasted.'

I raised my eyebrows. Trying hard to put the knowledge that Tom was the same age as Josh out of my mind.

'That's not exactly going to help the situation, is it?'

'Nope. So much for star-crossed lovers, eh?'

'And is this going to get back to Alicia?'

'Dunno,' he said. 'But it won't be from me, if it does. I don't want to be the one to push her over the edge.'

I nodded, relieved. There was only so much a girl her age could take.

Chris did let me sleep in the next morning. When I got downstairs, there was a note on the kitchen table saying he was taking Matilda for a bike ride because she had way too much energy for a Saturday morning. I smiled to myself and flicked the kettle on. Giving thanks that I had a good few years yet before I needed to start worrying about Matilda being more interested in boys than bikes.

I poured some muesli. I only had it at weekends, the rest of the week there never seemed to be time to chew properly. At some point I heard Josh's mobile beep. It was another ten minutes or so before he emerged in the kitchen. He had a

T-shirt, jogging bottoms and a hoody on. He clearly hadn't been in the shower yet, although the need was obvious.

He sat down. He didn't look at all with it.

'You OK?' I asked.

'I dunno. I just had a text from Tom. He said he was sorry. Really, really sorry.'

'What for?'

'I don't know. I tried texting and calling him, but his phone's turned off.'

'Maybe he means about last night. He's probably worried you'll tell Caitlin and it will get back to Alicia.'

'Yeah. I guess so.'

The banging on the front door made us both jump. I thought for a moment it was Matilda, back from her bike ride. But Chris wouldn't have let her carry on hammering away, I knew that.

I got up. Hurried through to the hall. Whoever it was clearly wasn't going to go away until the door was opened. The smell of alcohol hit me first, even before it registered that it was Lydia standing on the step, barely able to hold herself upright.

'I need to see Josh,' she said.

'I don't think so,' I replied. 'Not in that state.'

'You're not his fucking mother!' she screamed at me. 'So don't tell me I can't see my own son.'

Before I could compose myself enough to answer, Josh was at the door.

'What are you doing here?' he asked, staring at her dishevelled appearance.

'I need to talk to you.'

'I told you not to come here.'

'I need to talk to you. Alone.' She looked at me as she said the last bit.

'Anything you need to say to Josh will have to be said in front of me,' I said. 'I'm not going anywhere.'

She snarled at me, took another swig from the bottle in her left hand and turned to face Josh.

'I'm sorry,' she said.

'Why does everyone keep apologising to me?' asked Josh.

'Have you spoken to Tom?' she asked.

'No. He texted me.'

'Well, I didn't know,' she said. 'I had no fucking idea, and don't let him try to tell you otherwise.'

'I don't know what you're on about,' said Josh. 'Will you please tell me what's going on?'

'I slept with him!' shouted Lydia. 'I slept with your best mate. I didn't mean to but I did, OK?'

Josh stared at her. Disbelief clouding his eyes.

'Come on,' I said, taking his arm. 'Let's go in. You don't have to listen to another word of this.'

'Tom?' Josh said, not moving an inch. 'You slept with Tom?'

'Yeah, I did. We were both pissed. And for what it's worth, he was a crap shag and I wish to God I hadn't.'

'But you knew what he looked like. I've shown you a photo of him.'

'Jesus, Josh, I can hardly remember every person I've ever seen a photo of, can I?'

'So how do you know it was him?'

'Because he saw your photo on the bedside cabinet

afterwards and had a fucking fit on me. Crying like a baby, he was.'

I stared at Lydia, struggling to take it in. 'He's sixteen years old,' I said.

'Yeah, well, I didn't know that, did I? He's a big lad for his age. And he was working in a bar. Anyway, he was still legal.'

'You disgust me,' Josh said.

'Maybe if you hadn't been so busy shagging your little girl-friend you wouldn't have blown me out, and it would never have happened,' she shouted.

'Is that what this is about?' I asked. 'Are you jealous of her?'

'What, some prissy little schoolgirl?'

Josh lurched towards Lydia. I managed to grab hold of him. 'Leave it,' I said. 'Caitlin's worth a hundred of her.'

'Very touching, you sticking up for her,' said Lydia. 'You hate the fact that she's had a relationship with Josh for longer than you've ever managed to, don't you?'

Lydia rushed at me. It was only the combination of her drunk state and Josh's intervention that stopped her pushing me to the ground.

As I regained my balance, I saw two cycle helmets bobbing in and out between the bushes. I tried to gesture at Chris to carry on down the lane, but if he did see me, he was too distracted by Lydia to take any notice. He jumped off his bike, checked that Matilda was safely on the pavement and came marching up the path.

'What the hell are you doing here?'

'She was just leaving,' I said.

Lydia turned to Chris and smiled, went to put her arm

around his shoulders. He pushed her away and she staggered backwards a few steps. Matilda had got off her bike and was standing at the front gate, looking between me and Lydia and back again, seemingly unable to move. I ran into the garden, grabbed her hand and hurried her into the hall with an instruction to go and put a DVD on.

'That's right,' said Lydia. 'Protect that precious little daughter of yours. We wouldn't want her hearing anything untoward, would we now?'

'Get out of here,' said Chris. 'I told you not to come anywhere near my family.'

'I know, but my son wanted to see me, didn't he? And I didn't want to let him down.'

Chris spun round to face Josh. 'Is this true?' he said.

Josh nodded, swallowing hard.

'Jesus Christ,' said Chris.

'I thought it would be OK. I thought she'd changed.'

'You never learn, do you? You wouldn't listen to me.'

Josh looked down at his feet. 'I'm sorry,' he said.

'How long has this been going on?' asked Chris.

Josh glanced at me. I was complicit in this. There was blood on my hands. It was simply that Chris couldn't see it.

'About a month,' said Josh. 'She's been fine. She hasn't been anywhere near the house. Until today.'

Chris turned to Lydia. 'Why are you here?' he asked.

'I came to explain a little misunderstanding.'

'She slept with Tom,' said Josh, his voice cold and hard.

Chris looked at Lydia, then at me.

I nodded.

He turned back to Lydia. 'And I thought you couldn't sink any lower.'

'I didn't know who he was.'

'You have a son the same age, for fuck's sake.'

'That's it, play the dutiful father,' she said.

'Well, it's a bit of luck one of us takes our responsibilities seriously, isn't it?'

'Shame he's not yours to be responsible for,' snapped Lydia.

'What do you mean by that?'

'Oh, forget it,' she said, starting to walk away.

Chris grabbed her arm. 'No, I won't forget it. Why did you say that?'

'You want to know?' asked Lydia. 'You really want me to tell you, in front of him?'

'Tell me what?'

'He's not even your fucking son, Chris.'

The words circled around my head, trying desperately to find a way in. I wouldn't let them, though. Nor would anyone else. They hung heavily in the air in front of us all. The colour had drained from Josh's face. His mouth was slightly open.

'You're lying,' said Chris.

'Why would I lie about it?'

'Because you're drunk and you've lost your son and you're lashing out at everyone around you.'

'Fine, then. Don't believe me, if you don't want to.' She started to walk away.

'It's not true,' said Josh. 'Say it isn't true.'

'I wish I could,' Lydia said.

'You're saying he's not my father?'

She nodded.

'So who is?'

She looked down. If it was possible to appear embarrassed in such an inebriated state, Lydia gave a very good impression of what that would look like.

'He was a drummer in a band. Not a famous band. Just one that was doing some gigs in local clubs.'

'What was his name?' asked Josh.

She kept looking down. 'I can't remember. It was just a . . . you know . . . a one-night thing.'

'You're lying,' Chris said again.

She shook her head.

'So why have you never once said that before?' he asked. 'Why did you walk out and leave your baby with some guy who wasn't even his father?'

'Because I knew you'd be a bloody good father,' said Lydia. 'A much better father than I would ever have been a mother.'

The words were seeping in now. Not only into my head but into everyone else's. I could almost see them flowing through Josh's body like some radioactive dye. I looked at Josh's face and back to Chris's, searching for the similarities which I had always thought were there.

Chris saw me do it. Realised that if I was doubting, Josh must be doubting too.

'Tell me it's not true,' said Josh, his voice shaking.

Lydia shook her head. 'I'm sorry,' she said.

Josh screwed his eyes up but he couldn't stop the tears from bursting through.

'Go!' Chris shouted at Lydia. 'Get out of here and take your pathetic lies with you.'

'Fine,' said Lydia. 'Believe what you want to believe. I don't care.' She turned and staggered down the path.

I put my arm around Josh. 'Don't take any notice of her,' I said. 'She's drunk. She had no idea what she was saying.'

'Yes, she did,' said Josh, gulping down air between the sobs. 'She told me she'd slept with my best mate, and that *he* is not my dad.' He was pointing at Chris as he said it.

He may as well have been aiming a gun; the words hurt far more than any bullet could.

'Come on,' I said. 'Let's go inside and we can sit down and talk about this.'

'There's nothing to talk about, is there?' said Josh. 'She's said it all. And now I haven't got a mother, or a father, or a best mate.'

'It's not true,' I said. 'You heard what your dad said. She's telling lies.'

'Yeah, well, I don't know who to believe any more,' said Josh. 'My whole life is a fucking mess.'

He pulled away from me and ran up the stairs, slamming his bedroom door behind him. Chris was standing next to me, his face ashen, the shock still reverberating in his eyes. And I turned round to see Matilda standing in the doorway of the lounge, tears streaming down her face. Still with her bloody cycle helmet on.

My family was imploding. I had to choose to go to one of them first.

I chose Matilda. I ran to her, unclipped the chin strap of

her helmet, tossed it onto the floor and hugged her, letting her empty her tears into me.

'Why is everyone shouting again?' she wailed.

'It's OK,' I said. 'Josh's mum said a lot of bad things, but it's OK, she's gone now.'

'Josh was shouting too.'

'I know. She upset him.'

'Is she coming back?'

'No.'

'You said that before. You said you wouldn't invite her again.'

'She wasn't invited, love. She just came.'

Matilda clung on harder to me. I wasn't sure what she'd heard. What she'd understood. What she hadn't understood.

'You mustn't take any notice of what she said. She'd been drinking. She said a lot of things which weren't true.'

I held her tight, stroked her hair. Waited for the sobs to subside a little.

'Now, what DVD were you watching?' I asked.

'*Brave*.'

'Right, well, that's exactly what I want you to be. Let's go and sit down.'

I took her back into the lounge, sat her on the sofa and pressed 'play' on the remote. It was before the bit where her mother turns into a bear, which I was glad of. I'd never understood why they'd done that, anyway.

'Now, you start watching it. And when I've checked on Josh, I'll come back and watch it with you, OK?'

She gave a little nod. I hated having to leave her so soon, but there were other wounded soldiers in the field hospital.

I found Chris in the kitchen. He was sitting at the table with his head in his hands.

'Come here,' I said, putting my arm around him.

He didn't move. His body remained rigid. 'What if she wasn't lying?' he asked.

'She was.'

'You're sure about that, are you?'

'Chris, he's your son. He's more like you than you are sometimes.'

'He doesn't look like me, though. Not really.'

'You don't look much like your mum.'

He stared at me. His body shook. He banged the table with his fist. 'She had no right. She had no fucking right to do this.'

'Why don't you go and talk to Josh?'

He shook his head. 'He won't speak to me right now.'

'I'll go and talk to him,' I said. 'We'll get this sorted out.'

Chris said nothing.

'Can you go and sit with Matilda?' I asked. 'I don't want to leave her on her own.'

Chris nodded. Wiped at the corners of his eyes with the back of his hand. 'I'll go through in a minute,' he said.

I went upstairs and knocked on Josh's door. There was no answer but I decided to go in, anyway. He was lying face down on his bed. The photo of him and Lydia was lying on the floor. The picture of him and Tom, taken when they were about thirteen, had been torn from the front of the wardrobe.

'Who are you angry at the most?' I asked, hovering at the side of the bed.

There was no answer.

'Because your dad had no idea about this. And Tom clearly didn't either. There's no way he'd have done that, if he'd known.'

'Yeah, well, he should have known, shouldn't he? He's seen photos of her too.'

'He was drunk. He was also upset. I expect all he was trying to do was put Alicia out of his mind. Pretty stupid way of doing it, I know, but people do stupid things when they're upset.'

He said nothing.

I stood there for a long time, not wanting to say the other thing I needed to but eventually succumbing. 'He is your dad. You know that, don't you, Josh?'

'I don't know anything any more.'

'Well, I do.'

'You can't. You weren't there, were you? The only person who was there was her. And she says he's not.'

'She said a lot of things today. I wouldn't put too much store by them. You saw the state she was in.'

'She didn't lie, though, did she? She could have lied about what happened with her and Tom. She didn't, though. She told the truth.'

'And you heard how jealous she was of Caitlin, of anyone who is close to you. She knew that you'd be mad at her for what she'd done and she had to find a way to distract you from that.'

'No. It didn't sound like that to me. It sounded like something she just blurted out. Those things are usually true.'

'We'll have blood tests done,' I said. 'Whatever it takes to put your mind at rest.'

'And what if they say he's not my dad?'

'They won't. But if they did, we'd cope with it.'

'What, the fact that my whole life's a sham? That none of the people I live with are my own family. My mother walked out on me as a baby and left me with someone who wasn't even my dad. And just when she came back, and everything seemed to be working out, she shags my fucking best mate. Oh yeah, we'll cope with that. No problem.'

I shut my eyes. Hating to see him like this. I took a step towards him, but the squeaky floorboard gave me away.

'Go, please, Ali. I want to be on my own.'

I nodded, even though he couldn't see me.

'OK,' I said. 'I'll be downstairs, if you need me. Maybe talk to Caitlin. That might help.'

'Yeah, I'll probably find out she's shagging my real father, whoever that is.'

He was in too much pain for me to comfort him right now. I was going to have to leave him until it subsided a little before he'd listen to anything I said. Which was a shame. Because the one thing I would have liked to have told him was that even the way he behaved when he was hurt reminded me of Chris.

I went downstairs. Matilda was curled up on the sofa with Chris. Her eyes were still red from crying. His face was still rigid with doubt, his eyes glassy and faraway.

Somehow, some way, I was going to have to try to put my family back together again.

From the Counselling Room

Twenty-four years and three hundred and sixty-four days we'd been married. And in all that time he'd not once said he loved me or said thank you for pretty much single-handedly bringing up his two sons or for all the cooking and cleaning and washing and shopping and darning his bloody socks I'd done.

So when I woke up on the morning of our silver wedding anniversary and found he hadn't even remembered, I decided I was not going to waste one more single day of my life with him.

19

I woke up. The first thing I felt was the coldness of the bed next to me. Chris wasn't there. And he hadn't been there for some time.

I got up. My mind was instantly awake and my body was going to have to follow its example.

I pulled back the curtain. I had expected to see him sitting on the garden bench. It was usually where he went when he had a lot on his mind. The bench was empty, though. Save for a sparrow perched on the end, perusing the ground below for options for breakfast.

The bathroom was empty. I went downstairs. He wasn't in the kitchen either. The cold kettle suggested he hadn't had his morning cup of tea yet. I checked the lounge and the study before hurrying back upstairs. Only then did I notice that Matilda's bedroom door was open a little further than usual. I walked up to it and stuck my head round the door.

Chris was sitting on the floor, leaning against the wall, his legs outstretched in front of him, staring at Matilda as she slept.

'Are you OK?' I whispered.

He shrugged.

'What are you doing?'

'Watching my daughter sleep.'

I nodded. The pain he was feeling was so sharp it could have drawn blood from five yards away.

'I'll grab a shower first, then, shall I?' I asked. He didn't reply.

By the time I emerged from the bathroom, Matilda was awake. So awake that she had rigged up a puppet theatre across her bedroom door and had persuaded Chris to lie flat on the floor as a sort of human puppet stand.

I smiled at her. Maybe she was only putting on a brave face but at that moment, I was very glad she was.

'Morning, love,' I said. 'Just keep the noise down a bit so you don't wake your brother.'

'OK,' she whispered, before immediately returning to her normal volume.

We had breakfast in the kitchen. Just the three of us. Josh never made it down in time on a Sunday morning. Chris barely said a word, although fortunately Matilda filled in all the potentially awkward silences.

He believed Lydia. Or if he didn't believe her, he doubted himself enough to consider the possibility that she might be telling the truth. Either way he was effectively paralysed by it. Unable to function in any real sense of the word.

Matilda finished her toast and ran off into the lounge to play with her toys. Chris cleared the breakfast things, seemingly on automatic pilot, before turning to me.

'Is it OK if I go out for a walk?'

'Of course,' I said, moving closer to him so I could stroke his arm. 'Take however long you need.'

He nodded. A tiny movement of his head, barely noticeable.

'When you get back,' I said, 'I think we need to talk. Me, you and Josh. We can't let this tear us apart. We have to find a way through it. Together.'

Chris said nothing. Simply walked through to the hall and sat down on the bottom step of the stairs to put on his boots.

My words would be wasted now, I knew that. I needed to let him go. To walk high and far across the moors. To have the wind blow through his hair, the rain beat down on him, to be surrounded by nothing but the elements. It was his equivalent of one of those video-recorder head cleaners you used to get. And only when all the noise had been erased would I have any hope of being heard.

'Love you,' I said as he opened the door. And again after he shut it behind him.

I stood there for a moment, trying to get myself together enough to be able to put a smile on my face for Matilda. But somewhere, something registered in my head as not being right. It took a few seconds for me to work out what it was.

The coat peg Chris had taken his jacket from was empty. He shared it with Josh. I looked down at the mat. There was the usual jumble of shoes and boots. Matilda's purple wellies on the top of the pile. I moved them aside. Sorted through the rest of them. They weren't there. Josh's boots weren't there. I turned and ran up the stairs. I didn't even stop to knock on his door, just pushed it open.

It was empty. His bed was empty.

The duvet was turned back. You could almost see the imprint of his body on the memory-foam mattress beneath it.

But Josh was not there.

The lurching feeling returned.

I told myself it was fine. He would have gone to Caitlin's. That was all. But I still couldn't stop myself opening his wardrobe. Half of his clothes had gone. There weren't that many in the wash. His rucksack was gone too. I tried to breathe. To open my mouth. Blow out through my nose. The blood rushed around my body, seemingly in the wrong direction. I started to feel dizzy. I sat down on the bed. I looked around for his phone. It was gone too, of course. I ran through to our bedroom, grabbed the home phone and dialled his number. It went straight to voicemail. I hung up, dialled it again and managed to form a few words.

'Josh, it's Ali. Please call me when you get this. Or text me. Just let me know you're OK.'

I hoped we'd be able to laugh about it later. Me being paranoid and leaving some frantic message on his phone. It didn't feel funny right now, though. It didn't feel funny at all.

I should call Caitlin. He would have talked to Caitlin, surely. I didn't have a number for her, though. Everything was in Josh's phone, and Josh had his phone with him. I longed for the days of address books and everybody being listed in the phone book. Social media was only OK if you were connected to everyone in the first place.

It was only as I stood up that I saw the piece of paper on top of the chest of drawers. I knew what it was straight away. In the old days it would have been in an envelope. I doubted if Josh even possessed an envelope. I supposed I was lucky it hadn't been posted on Facebook. I picked up the piece of paper, torn out of an A4 pad, and tried to steady my hands enough to unfold it. I heard Josh's voice as I read the words. Saw his pain etched into each letter.

I can't deal with this right now. I need to be on my own so I can work out who I really am. Please don't come looking for me.

Tell Caitlin I'm sorry, but she's way too good for me. And please don't worry. Especially you, Ali.

Josh.

P.S. Can you tell Tilda I've gone backpacking or something? I don't want her upset.

I read it through over and over again in the hope that the words would change. That they weren't written in ink in front of me but were merely in my head. The contents of my worst nightmare. I looked down at the piece of paper. The words were still there. Arranged in the same order.

It was true. Josh had gone. And I had no idea when, or if, he'd be back.

I sat down heavily on his bed. Took a gulp of air. Told myself repeatedly to hold myself together. That this was a time to be strong, not to fall apart.

I folded the piece of paper back up and put it in my jeans pocket. I would go and see Caitlin. I did at least know where she lived. If he'd seen anyone, if he'd rung anyone, it would be her.

I hurried back into our bedroom, picked up my mobile and called Chris. It went straight to voicemail. There was no point leaving a message, I knew I couldn't compose myself enough to do it. I would leave a note on the mat asking him to ring me, in case he got home before I did.

I rang Debbie, hoping it wasn't her turn for a lie-in. She picked up the phone. I could hear Sophie and Ben arguing in the background.

I opened my mouth to say something but all that came out was a high-pitched whimper.

'Ali?' said Debbie. 'Ali, are you OK?'

'Sorry,' I said, my voice wobbling all over the place. 'I was wondering if you could have Matilda for a bit. Josh has run away. He left a note. Lydia came here yesterday. She'd slept with his best friend and said that Chris isn't his real father.'

'Oh Christ. The poor kid. I'll come straight round.'

'Don't say anything in front of Matilda. She doesn't know yet.'

'Sure. I'll see you in a bit.'

I put the phone down and sat there for a moment, waiting for my body, my brain or ideally both of them to go into that autopilot mode you hear people talking about when there's a real crisis. It didn't happen, though. I simply felt empty inside. Empty from the knowledge that this was all my fault. And that somehow I had to explain that to Chris.

I went into the bathroom and splashed some water on my eyes before quickly applying enough make-up to conceal what remained of the redness. There was still a chance that Josh could be back before the end of the day. I didn't want to alert Matilda to the fact that anything was wrong before I absolutely had to. As I went downstairs I counted each step out loud, in the hope that the numbers would calm me, ground me somehow.

Matilda had got virtually everything out of her largest toy box, including things she hadn't played with for years. Normally I'd have asked her to tidy up before going anywhere, but today was not normal.

'Debbie's invited you over to play with Sophie.'

Matilda looked up. 'Yay! When?'

'Now. Debbie's on her way over.'

'What are you going to do while I'm gone?'

She always had this idea that the rest of us couldn't possibly manage to entertain ourselves without her.

'Nothing much,' I said. 'The usual chores, I expect.'

'Where's Daddy?' she asked.

'He's gone for a walk.'

'What about Josh?'

'You're not missing out on anything, OK?'

The smile was meant to reassure her. And the comment to avoid having to lie to her. If he wasn't back by night-time, I'd tell her. I'd have to. But I really couldn't bring myself to tell her now.

There was a knock at the door.

'Right, you nip to the loo and I'll go and let Debbie in.'

She nodded and skipped out of the room. Which made it even worse.

I opened the door. Debbie checked to see that the coast was clear and flung her arms around me.

'How long's he been gone?' she asked.

'I don't know. I only just realised his jacket was missing. I didn't hear a thing. None of us did, obviously.'

'He's not gone to Lydia's?'

'I don't think so. He was pretty mad at her yesterday. I'm going to go to Caitlin's, in case she's heard anything.'

'Where's Chris?'

'Up there somewhere,' I said, gesturing towards the moor. 'He doesn't even know Josh has gone yet.'

'Look, I'll have Matilda as long as you need me to. And if there's anything else I can do –'

'Thanks,' I said.

Matilda came running out. 'How long can I stay for?' she asked Debbie.

'Definitely for lunch. If you help me with the Yorkshire puddings, that is. And we'll see about tea later.'

Matilda grinned at her.

I kissed her on the top of the head as I put her jacket on. 'Best behaviour now, remember.'

I waved as she skipped off holding Debbie's hand. Thinking how rude it was of the daffodils to look so bloody cheerful at a time like this.

Caitlin's mum answered the door. I'd only met her briefly a couple of times, when I'd dropped Caitlin off or collected her, but she'd seemed very nice. Her husband too. I wondered if she was going to think the same thing about our family by the end of the day.

'Hello, Sandra. I'm ever so sorry to bother you. I wondered if Caitlin was in. If I could see her for minute, please?'

'Yes, of course. Is everything OK?' she asked.

'I hope so,' I replied.

She called Caitlin. I heard footsteps on the stairs before she appeared round the corner.

She stared at me, a frown creasing her forehead. 'Is Josh OK?' she asked.

I wondered if she'd been trying to phone him. If he hadn't answered her calls.

'Yeah,' I replied. 'But I wondered if I could have a quick word.'

She nodded.

'Come in,' said Sandra. 'Can I get you a coffee?'

'No, thanks. I'm fine.'

'Do you want to come up?' asked Caitlin.

'Thanks,' I said, stepping inside and taking my boots off.

'Oh, you don't have to worry,' said Sandra.

I glanced at Caitlin, remembering what she'd once said, and smiled. 'It's OK,' I replied. 'We do it in our house too.'

I followed Caitlin across the parquet-floored hall and up the wooden staircase. Her room was tidy and tastefully furnished, a cast-iron bed in the corner, white-painted walls. My gaze rested on the photo of Josh she had on her bedside cabinet. I swallowed hard.

'He's dumped me, hasn't he?' she said, her voice barely more than a whisper.

'No, love,' I said, 'he'd never do that. He has gone, though. He wasn't in his room this morning.'

Caitlin stared at me. She clearly hadn't been in on it. She was struggling to form words in the same way I had been doing a short while ago. I walked over to her, put my arm around her shoulders and gently sat her down on the bed.

'He left this,' I said, taking the note out of my pocket and handing it to her. I watched her eyes following the words until they got to her own name, when they shut for a second and reopened with a liquid coating.

'I don't want anyone else,' she said. 'I only want him.'

'I know,' I said, sitting down next to her and squeezing her hand. 'And I'm sure deep down he knows that too. But he's hurting very badly right now.'

'He called me last night,' she said, wiping the tears away from the corners of her eyes. 'He told me about Tom and his mum. I'm not surprised he couldn't get his head around it.'

'I know. Did he tell you what she said . . . about Chris?'

She nodded and looked down.

'She was lying,' I said. 'I'm as sure of it as I can be. But I think it pushed him over the edge.'

Fresh tears fell from Caitlin's eyes. I squeezed her shoulder.

'I wanted to come round last night,' she said. 'But he wouldn't let me. Said he needed to be on his own. I shouldn't have taken any notice. I should have come anyway.'

I shook my head. 'Don't blame yourself, Caitlin. You're the last person who should do that, believe me.'

'I tried his phone this morning,' she went on. 'It was switched off. I've left a message. Lots of them.'

'Me too,' I said. 'Let's keep doing that. Hopefully, when he realises how much people care about him, he'll come back.'

'Do you think he's gone far?' she asked.

'I've got no idea, to be honest. I was going to ask if you could think of anywhere he might go. Anywhere he talked about.'

She shook her head. 'Not really. Have you tried his mum?'

'I haven't got a number for her,' I said. 'Or an address even. He never took you there, I suppose?'

'No. He said he wanted to keep her separate from other stuff. Anyway,' she went on, 'as far as I'm concerned, you're his mum.'

I smiled at her. 'I don't think he'd have gone there, anyway,' I said. 'Not after what she said.'

'He said last night he never wanted to see her again in his life.'

I nodded, grateful for the information. 'Let's swap numbers,' I said. 'I'll let you know if I hear anything. With any luck he'll be back by tonight.'

She got out her mobile and keyed in my number. 'Shall I tell your mum on the way out?' I asked as she sent me a text. 'Can you talk to her about stuff like this?'

'A bit, maybe.'

'Good. Only I want to make sure there's someone here to support you. I'd better be getting back. Just in case, you know . . .'

She nodded. 'Does Matilda know yet?'

'No,' I said. 'Chris doesn't even know. I came straight here.'

'Thank you,' she said, her voice quivering.

I gave her another hug. 'He'll come back,' I said. 'Because of you. I know he will.'

She nodded, because she wanted to believe it. Like I did.

The house was empty when I got home. Empty was different to nobody being in. I went back outside and sat on the bench in the garden. It was better like that. I felt closer to Josh, wherever he was. Scenarios started flashing through my mind: I saw him on a train, leaning his head against a window; on a coach, squashed up against a fat man with a carrier bag full of lager; walking along a road somewhere trying to hitch a lift. The one thing I didn't see in my head was Josh coming home.

I shivered, not wanting to think about the night ahead, about where he might spend it. I sat and stared out into the distance, watching and waiting until finally the figure of a man could be seen striding towards me in the distance. The weight of responsibility, of guilt, weighed heavily on me. I was going to stand up and do what was right, though. Take whatever was thrown at me. Knowing the punishment would still nowhere near fit the crime.

The figure was nearer now, much nearer. I saw him looking, straining his neck, no doubt wondering what on earth I was doing sitting out there on my own. I pulled my jacket further around me as the sun dipped behind a cloud. I waited until he rounded the corner, came up the path and was standing in front of me before I looked up at his face. When I did so, all I could think was what a shame it was. The walk had done him a power of good; the pain was still there, but he wasn't smothered by it. He had managed to shake a little off, to allow the tiniest chinks of light, of hope, to show through. And now I was going to snuff them out again. And this time no amount of walking would put them back.

'Josh has gone,' I said, my voice steadier now that I had already said it a couple of times.

'What do you mean "gone"?'

'He wasn't in his room this morning. He'd taken his ruck-sack and a lot of his clothes. He left this note.'

I handed the by now crumpled piece of paper to him. I wished Josh could see it, watch the faces of the people who loved him as they read it, feel their fingers tense on the paper, see the fear gather in their eyes.

Chris looked at me. 'I didn't hear a thing.'

'No, I know,' I said. 'Nor did I.'

'Where's Matilda?' he asked.

'At Debbie's. She doesn't know. I managed to get her out of the house without realising.'

'Who have you tried?'

'I went to see Caitlin. She knows nothing. He's not answering her calls either. She's got my number in case he contacts her.'

'What about Tom?'

'I've left a message with his mum. She's pretty sure he hasn't heard from him. Although she clearly doesn't know what happened.'

'Lydia?'

I shrugged. 'I haven't got a number for her. Or an address. And given the state he was in, I don't suppose Tom will be able to remember where he went on Friday night. I don't think Josh would have gone there, though. Caitlin doesn't either. According to her, he said he never wanted to see her again.'

Chris sat down heavily on the bench next to me. 'So what do we do now?'

'I don't know. I suppose we could ring the police.'

Chris shook his head. 'Not yet. It's not as if he's disap-peared or anything. He left a note. And he's over sixteen. They probably wouldn't be bothered. Especially when we tell them why he's gone.'

'What's that got to do with it?'

'Well, if Lydia's telling the truth, Josh isn't related to either of us.'

'She's not, though.'

'How can you be so sure?'

'Because I've known him since he was six years old. I've seen him grow more like you every day.'

'Yeah. Because he lives with me. It could be nurture, not nature.'

I shook my head. 'He's got your lips, for goodness' sake.'

'They're not particularly unusual lips. Half the population has got lips like this.'

I sighed. Decided to try a different tack. 'Have you ever had any reason to doubt that he was your son before?'

'No.'

'There was nothing suspicious going on at the time?'

He shook his head.

'The dates on her pregnancy added up and everything?'

'Yeah, I guess so. Although I don't even remember thinking about it at the time.'

'Then why on earth should we believe her?'

'Because of the way she said it. The way she blurted it out, like she didn't really mean to.'

'No,' I said. 'I don't buy that. The only reason she came up with it was because she had to distract Josh from the fact that she had slept with his best friend.'

Chris sat there staring out at the hills. 'The thing I don't get,' he said eventually, 'is what the hell she was doing sleeping with Tom in the first place.'

'She was pissed off with Josh,' I said. 'Because he stood her up to go to the party with Caitlin.'

'How do you know that?'

I shut my eyes. I was going to have to tell him. I couldn't live with myself if I didn't. But I was astute enough to know that his reaction was not going to be pretty. Or quiet.

'We'd better go inside,' I said.

I stood up and headed towards the door. Chris followed me through to the kitchen without a word. I turned to face him. It seemed the decent thing to do under the circumstances.

'Josh was supposed to be seeing Lydia on Friday night but he wanted to go to the party with Caitlin instead. I told him to call his mum and explain, I said she'd understand. I'm sorry. I should have realised she'd take it badly.'

Chris was staring at me. 'You knew he was seeing her again?'

I sighed and tugged at my hair with my fingers. 'I saw Caitlin in Hebden one afternoon when he was supposed to be out with her. I made him tell me where he'd been. He begged me not to tell you. Said there'd be a massive row and it would mess up his revision. I agreed on the condition that he told you as soon as his exams were over and that, in the meantime, he kept me informed of exactly when he was seeing Lydia.'

My words felt like they had run out of fuel. It was hard to believe now that they had always sounded so sensible in my head.

Chris was still staring at me. 'I don't believe I'm hearing this,' he said.

'I'm sorry,' I said again. 'I'm really, really sorry.'

'You knew. You knew he was seeing Lydia behind my back.'

I nodded.

'How long for?'

'Almost a month.'

'Fucking hell.' He shook his head over and over again as he paced about the kitchen.

'I wanted to tell you, I really did. But everything was going so well and Josh was happy and you were happy. And the last thing I wanted to do was spoil all of that.'

'So, basically, you thought you knew best.'

'I didn't say that.'

'No, but that's what you meant. You made a judgement that I didn't have the right to know what my son, or the boy who I thought was my son, was up to.'

'That's not how it was at all.'

'Well, that's what it sounds like to me, Ali.'

'It was only temporary. Until his exams were out of the way. I didn't want him to end up as miserable as Alicia. And I made him promise to tell me if Lydia started drinking again or messed him around.'

'Yeah, and that worked, didn't it? That really worked.'

'I had no idea it was going to end up like this. If I had done, I would never have agreed to it.'

'So how did you think it would end up? That we'd all go for a cosy little summer holiday together?'

'No, of course not.'

'You knew what she was like, Ali. You were there on Christmas Day. You saw how quickly she can change. How destructive she can be.'

'And I also saw how gutted Josh was afterwards, to have lost her when he'd only just found her again. He got in touch with her. It was his choice. I was trying to let him make grown-up decisions for himself.'

'Except he's not grown-up, is he? He's sixteen years old. And now he's out there somewhere, on his own, and we haven't got a clue where. All because you thought you knew best.'

Every word stung. My flesh was already raw and his words ate further into it. And what made it worse was that he was right. I had brought this whole thing down on top of us.

'Believe me, if I could turn back the clock –'

'Yeah, well, you can't, can you? That's the one thing you can't do.'

He walked towards the window. He had his back to me but I could see his body shaking. I wanted to go to him. To soothe the pain away. But I couldn't. Because I was the one who had inflicted it.

'Look, I know I screwed up. I screwed up really, really badly. And I don't think I'll ever be able to explain to you exactly how bad I feel about it. But please, we need to get through this together.'

He turned to face me. 'Oh, we're together now, are we? Together as in trusting each other, having no secrets? It's a bit late for that, isn't it?' He spat the words out as he walked past me.

A few moments later, I heard the front door bang shut behind him and watched as he retraced his steps. Away from me. Away from home. Away from the wreck of what had once been a family.

From the Counselling Room

I've met someone else. I didn't mean to. In fact, I tried really hard not to. I went out of my way to avoid meeting single, middle-aged men. Because I knew I was so desperate, you see, so desperate for any scrap of affection which might be thrown my way.

But the person I met was the postman. I could hardly avoid him, could I?

You can't stop people sending you things through the post, and we've got a really tiny letter box which is hard to open. And it's not my fault if he's never fixed it, is it? I've asked him enough times. Anyway, I started ordering things on the internet, just so he'd have to knock.

It wasn't as bad as it sounds. I didn't answer the door in my underwear or invite him to get up to any funny business. We just talked. And sometimes I talked and he just listened. And I realised that my husband never did that. He never listened to me. Not once. Not like the postman does, anyway.

20

'Is Josh home?' asked Matilda.

I shook my head.

'But it's a school day.'

'I know, love.'

'You wouldn't let me go off on an adventure if it was a school day.'

She had a point. I'd come out with the adventure line the previous night. Wanting to follow Josh's request, as if it was a last will and testament he'd left, not a leaving note.

'Teenagers sometimes take what they call a gap year between school and college.'

'But he hasn't finished school yet, he's got exams, important exams. The ones he hasn't been revising for very much.'

She was too shrewd to lie to, really. You couldn't get anything past her. And quite how we were going to keep up the pretence of being OK with the fact that Josh had gone off on an adventure, I had no idea. I suppose I had gone along with it in the hope that it was a short-term lie. That we wouldn't have to keep it up for very long at all. But, of course, we didn't know if that was going to be the case. Twenty-four hours in, we still had absolutely no idea where he was and when, or if, he would be coming home.

'Yeah, well, you know what Josh is like. He doesn't always do exactly what he's supposed to do, does he? And on this occasion he decided he wanted to go off travelling straight away, he didn't want to wait. Even though we told him to.'

'I still don't get why he didn't say goodbye, though.'

'No, love, I know. I'm cross he didn't say goodbye too.'

'Has he gone with Lydia?' she asked.

'No,' I said.

'Caitlin?'

'No, sweetie. He's gone on his own.'

'But what about Caitlin? She's his girlfriend. You're not supposed to go off and leave your girlfriend, are you?'

'Not really, love, no.'

'Is she mad at him?'

'A bit.'

'Is she still going to give me violin lessons?'

'I don't know, love. We're going to have to wait and see.'

She looked up at me, her brown eyes riddled with doubt and disappointment. I had failed spectacularly in the reassuring-your-child department. I couldn't even lie effectively when required to.

She chose to say nothing more. Which only served to make me feel worse. We went downstairs. Chris had already left for work. He hadn't said a word to me. Not this morning or the previous night, when we'd lain awake in the same bed, both worrying, imagining, fearing the worst but unable, or unwilling, to share our concerns.

The kitchen seemed quiet. Too quiet. Even Matilda's cereal pouring into the bowl tinkled unreasonably loudly in the absence of the usual background chatter. I put the radio on. We sat and ate, pretty much in silence.

Matilda went upstairs to get dressed for school without me even having to tell her. She emerged several minutes later in her uniform and descended the stairs. I thought for a moment that something was missing but realised just in time that it was only the smile on her face.

There was a knock at the door. I'd asked Debbie to call for us. Thought it would make it easier for Matilda that way.

'It's no trouble to take her on my own, you know,' said Debbie as Matilda ran out to Sophie.

'Thanks, but I want to come too. I need to speak to Mrs Eddington, for a start. Let her know what's happened, in case Matilda gets upset.'

Debbie nodded and gave me her best understanding face.

I pulled the door shut behind me. It was a glorious morning. And, more importantly, it had been a dry night. The thought of Josh sleeping somewhere in the wet was almost too much to bear.

'I take it you've heard nothing, then?' asked Debbie.

I shook my head.

'He'll be back, Ali. He'll get his head sorted and he'll come back.'

'When, though?' I said. 'And what the hell is he going to do in the meantime?'

'Has he got much money with him?'

I shrugged. 'I'm not sure. I think he had some Christmas

money left. About forty quid, maybe. He was saving for something for his guitar. It can't have been much more, though. Certainly not enough to live on for more than a day or two.'

'He'll get a job, then.'

'What, with no qualifications or references?'

'He'll find something. He's a bright lad, your Josh.'

We walked on a bit further. Sophie had at least got Matilda smiling again. They were pulling faces at each other and doing weird things with their hair.

'Keep into the side of the road,' I called after them.

'How's Chris taken it?' asked Debbie.

'Not good. We had a massive row yesterday.'

'It's not your fault he's gone.'

'It is, actually.'

'Why?'

I hesitated before I said anything. When your husband wasn't talking to you, there was a natural resistance to losing your best friend too.

'I knew Josh was seeing Lydia. I found out by accident. He begged me not to tell Chris.'

'Jesus, Ali.'

'Yeah. I know.'

'What were you thinking of?'

'Keeping everyone happy. I made a pig's ear of that, didn't I?'

'I take it you've apologised?'

'Yep. Countless times. He won't forgive me for this one, though. I've messed up big time.'

'Oh, Ali,' said Debbie, stopping to give me a hug.

'Don't,' I said. 'You'll set me off. And I need to hold myself together for Mrs Eddington.'

She nodded. We walked on together, Debbie telling me about some woman who'd given birth to twins over the weekend. It could have been triplets, actually. I wasn't really listening.

I was trying to work out how far you could travel on forty quid on a young person's railcard.

As soon as I got home, I rang Josh's school. It's not something you expect to have to do as a parent, phone school to let them know that your child has run away. They had a dedicated line to report absences. I didn't think that was appropriate, though. Not in this case. I got through to the office and asked to speak to the Head Teacher.

'Can I ask what it's regarding?' said the secretary

'It's about my stepson, Josh Bentley. I need to report that he's left home.'

'You mean he's left for school?'

'No. No, I mean he's run away from home.'

Even as I said it, I knew it didn't sound right. Josh would never have used that term. He'd say he'd gone off travelling. Although, unlike Matilda, I didn't think the Head would buy that.

There was a pause on the other end of the line and I was put through. The Head answered in a suitably sympathetic voice; the message had obviously been passed on to her.

'Hello, Mrs Bentley. I understand it's about Josh.'

She was going to make me say it again. To spell it out. Just in case the secretary had got it wrong.

'Yes, I'm afraid he ran away yesterday morning. He left a note and took some of his clothes with him.'

'I see. I'm . . . er . . . very sorry to hear that. Were there any problems at school? Anything we should know about?'

'Not at school, no. Everything was fine at school.'

I imagined the relief on the other end of the line. Nothing had happened on her watch. She wasn't going to have to answer any awkward questions.

'I take it you've informed the police?'

'No. Not yet. I wanted to ring you first. To let you know he wasn't going to be in.'

'Right. Well, I would suggest you call them straight away. Bearing in mind the seriousness of the situation. I'll advise the Local Education Authority and I expect one of their welfare officers will give you a call.'

She had clearly gone into officious mode, now she knew she was off the hook.

'Thank you,' I said.

'If there's anything further the school can do to help, please do let me know. And in the meantime, let's hope Josh comes home very soon.'

I thanked her again and hung up. I knew she was right, I should ring the police. I wasn't going to do it myself, though. It needed to be Chris's decision. And I wasn't even going to attempt to have this conversation over the phone.

I got into the car and drove straight to his studio. It looked a bit old-fashioned from the outside. Definitely not one of those shiny glass-fronted designer places which had sprung up in city centres in recent years. *In Focus*, the plain black sign above the shop said. Chris had never been one for anything flashy. He got by on word of mouth because his photographs were bloody good. Though I suspected one of those high street shopping gurus would have had plenty to say about how much more successful he could be if he put his mind to it.

I opened the door. The bell rang and I heard hurried footsteps on the stairs before Chris appeared at the back of the shop. His face was searching mine. Maybe thinking I'd heard something. And that it might not be good.

'I haven't heard anything,' I said straight away. 'I rang his school. Told the Head. She advised us to call the police straight away.'

Chris shut his eyes for a second. 'What does she know?' he said. 'She probably doesn't even know what he looks like.'

'It's been over twenty-four hours,' I said. 'And he's never done anything like this before. Maybe they could put a description out. Someone in another force might pick him up.'

'He told us he was going. He wouldn't want us to call the police.'

'Well, if we get him back, I'll tell him it was my idea to call them. That you asked me not to do it.'

'So then he'll hate both of us.'

I looked at Chris, wondering for a second if he'd said it with a half-smile on his face. He hadn't.

'You were right, though,' I said. 'Being a parent isn't about being popular, it's about doing the right thing.'

'And I take it you know the right thing to do?'

'I'm trying to put things right, Chris. Make up for the mess

I made. I think we should tell the police. I think we might get him back earlier than if we don't.'

Chris shrugged.

'Do I take that as a yes?' I asked.

'I guess so.'

'So are you going to call them, or shall I?'

'You do it,' said Chris. 'You're better at those sorts of things.'

'OK. If I haven't heard anything by this afternoon, I'll phone them. Have you spoken to your mum?'

Chris shook his head.

'I think she should know. I don't want her finding out from anyone apart from us.'

'Fine.'

'I could go round and see her after work,' I said. 'Unless you want to go.'

'Like I said, you're better at those sorts of things.'

'Will you be done in time to get Matilda from school?'

'Yeah. Can be.'

'Thanks.'

We stood there wordlessly, more like a couple in the awkward stages of getting divorced than the supposedly happily married parents of two.

'Right, well. I'll let you know if there's any news. Is it OK if I give the police your number?'

'Why? I'm not his father.'

In different circumstances it would have been laughable: I was going to work to help other people with their problems in order to avoid having to deal with my own. As it was, there was nothing remotely amusing about it. I had considered not going in, wondering if I should stay at home instead. But waiting in for someone who wasn't going to call was never a good idea. Besides, my first client of the day was Catherine and there was no way I was going to let her down.

She'd told Nathan that I'd asked to see her again on her own. That I was trying to get to the bottom of her eating disorder. I wasn't going to do that at all, of course. But we both knew Nathan was so sure of himself, he would buy it.

When Catherine entered the room, she moved more easily than the last time I had seen her. Maybe it was simply the fact that she wasn't harbouring a secret any longer but she greeted me with a warm smile and sat down in the chair, ready to start. It was difficult to know where to begin after what had happened last time. But I didn't have to worry about that, because she did it for me.

'I'm going to leave him,' she said.

I smiled at her and nodded, unable to say anything for a moment.

'You were right,' she went on. 'That isn't love. And no one deserves to be treated like that. Not even me.'

'Especially not you,' I said. 'But I do need to know that you've thought this through. That this is what you want. My job is to support you in your decisions, not to tell you what to do.'

'I understand that,' she said. 'But it is my decision. I went home last time and realised that it had taken a lot of strength to do what I did in front of you. Strength that I didn't know I had. I bared my soul, not just my knickers.'

I smiled at her.

She managed a smile back. 'I guess it made me see that I had sunk to a point where I was either going to drown or I had to start kicking and screaming to save myself.'

I looked at her and nodded. Her strength made me want to roar.

'Well, if you're quite certain, I can give you the phone numbers of organisations who will support you both practically and emotionally. I also need to ask you to think about your safety. Do you know where you're going to go?'

'My business partner Simon has got a spare room in his house. I told him, you see. The day after I told you. He said it was my version of coming out. That I had nothing to be ashamed of. And that if Nathan comes anywhere near me, he'll get the entire gay population of Hebden Bridge to say they've slept with him on Facebook.'

She said it with a smile on her face. I had a feeling Nathan wouldn't find it so amusing, though.

'I'm going to report it to the police too,' she continued. 'I borrowed Simon's mobile and took photos of the bruises. He's saving them for me, until I'm ready.'

'Good for you,' I said. 'I can give you the number of a specialist domestic violence officer at Calderdale. It's important you get the support and protection you need.'

'Nathan won't hurt me,' said Catherine. 'Not once I've gone. There'll be no point. He'll have lost control. It's like spinning a plate. Once you've lost it, you can never really get it back. You have to start again with a new one.'

'Well, hopefully, you reporting it will help to stop that happening,' I said.

She nodded.

It suited her, her newfound strength. She had grown into it very well. Probably because it had been there all along underneath. She had, like many people, simply never realised.

'Right, I guess that's it, then,' she said. 'For our sessions, I mean. We've been a spectacular failure, really, haven't we? I mean, your job's supposed to be keeping people together, isn't it?'

'Not if it's not the best thing for them,' I said. 'And certainly not if one person is violent towards the other one.'

'Well, as long as I'm not going to get you a black mark from your bosses.'

'Not at all. In fact, I'm prouder of how you've resolved things than of any other case I've had.'

'Good,' she said.

I got out one of my business cards and handed it to her. 'Ring me any time,' I said, 'if there's anything I can do to help you. Or simply if you want to talk. As a friend.'

'Thank you,' she said, taking it and slipping it into her handbag.

I noticed her nail varnish. It wasn't chipped at all today. It was a strong red colour. It suited her.

I phoned the police a few minutes after Catherine had gone. It was as if she had left some of her strength in the room with me. I dialled the number for non-emergencies, knowing full well that it wouldn't be anything even remotely approaching an emergency to them. It was only in my world that alarms were ringing.

It took a while for someone to answer.

'Hello,' I said. 'I'd like to report a missing person.'

'Just a minute,' said the voice on the other end of the line. 'I need to pull up the form.'

Barbara lived in a two-bedroom terrace on the edge of Todmorden, close to the Lancashire border. But not, as she put it, too close. She still didn't think of herself as a 'bottom-dweller', having spent her childhood on the tops above Walsden, but I was glad she did live on the valley bottom now. It had made things a little easier for her since Ken died. Easier to get about, at least.

The house appeared pretty much as it had been before he died. Not in the way that some people refuse to move their loved ones' things after they've gone, but in the sense that Ken had seemed so much a part of the structure of it that simply removing his walking stick and cap from the hall hadn't really done anything to remove the sense that he was still present.

I loved Barbara's house. The flagstone floor in the hall, the little mullioned windows. But most of all I loved the fact that it was part of Chris's past. A part of it which I could actually access, which allowed me to build up a picture of his life before I knew him. There were photos, for a start. An awful lot of them. Pictures of a baby about six months old with laughing eyes and dark hair. And later, a wiry boy with bruised knees and scuffed shoes – the results of too much time spent scrambling up the hillside, according to Barbara.

I knocked on the door and went in. She never locked it, no matter how many times Chris and I told her to do so. Always said that we were being daft and that 'There's nowt worth taking any rate'.

'Hello, Barbara, it's only me,' I called out.

'Hello, love,' she said, coming out of the front room. 'Everything all right?'

I smiled at her, unable to say anything in reply.

'I'll put kettle on, shall I?' she said.

I followed her into the kitchen, taking deep breaths as she filled the kettle and put it on to boil. There was no easy way to say it. And I wasn't going to insult her intelligence by repeating the 'big adventure' line.

'Josh left home yesterday morning,' I said.

She stared at me, the softness gone from her face. 'Whatever for?'

'Lydia came back,' I said. 'I'm afraid it all got rather horrible. A lot of things were said.'

'What sort of things?'

'She admitted she'd slept with Josh's friend Tom. She said she'd had no idea who he was. Tom didn't either, apparently, until he saw Josh's photo in her room afterwards.'

'Tom? The quiet lad with fair hair? I remember him from Josh's parties.'

'He works part-time in a bar in Hebden now,' I said.

'Don't make excuses for her, Alison. He's still a wee lad to me.'

I nodded. I understood what she was saying.

'I'm afraid that's not all of it, though,' I said. 'She came to apologise. She was drunk, of course. Chris came home while she was there and it all got a bit out of hand. She claimed that he wasn't Josh's father. That she'd had a one-night stand with some guy in a band.'

Barbara stared at me. The moistness in her eyes was no longer that which elderly ladies seem to collect for no obvious reason.

'She's lying.' Her voice was firm and steely.

'I think so too.'

'But Josh didn't?'

'I tried to reassure him. He was pretty shaken up, though. He wasn't really thinking straight. He left a note. I didn't find it until yesterday morning. He took clothes with him. And a rucksack.'

I noticed Barbara's hand on the top of the kitchen counter. Her fingers were shaking.

'You go and sit down,' I said. 'I'll bring the tea in.'

Barbara went without arguing. Her usually steady gait was looking decidedly shaky. I put two sugars in her tea, even though she usually only had one. And popped a custard cream from the biscuit barrel onto the saucer. I took them in to her. She was sitting in the armchair, staring at a photo of Josh sitting on Chris's lap when he was about four years old. She probably took it herself.

'You couldn't separate them,' said Barbara. 'I always used to say when Chris went up on the tops with Josh in one of those carrier things on his back that it looked like they were joined together.'

'I know. I think that's what has made it worse. How close they were.'

'Have you reported him missing?'

'Yes,' I said. 'They're going to put a description out, although they're a bit limited in what they can do. What with him being sixteen.'

'If any harm comes to him –'

'It won't. He's good at keeping out of trouble.'

Barbara looked at me. That wasn't what she meant. I knew that.

'Where's Chris?' Barbara asked, as if suddenly noticing his absence from the room.

'At work. He's going to pick Matilda up from school in a bit.'

'Is he talking at all?'

'Not really,' I said. 'Not to me, anyway.'

Barbara looked at me more intently.

'This is all my fault,' I said. 'I knew Josh was seeing Lydia again. He asked me not to tell Chris.'

She nodded slowly.

'I'm sorry,' I said. 'I know it was wrong. I was trying to keep them both happy.'

'It's not your fault,' she said.

'Try telling that to Chris.'

'I will do, when I see him. There's only one person to blame here. And we all know who that is.'

'I thought she'd changed. I really did.'

'You're too trusting, Alison. That's your trouble. She's nasty. Manipulative. I should never have let her get her claws into Chris in the first place. I always told him she were trouble. He wouldn't listen, see. Too taken in by her. Well, it's obvious what he were taken in by. That's the trouble with sons. They're weak when it comes to women. They stop using their heads.'

'He spent most of yesterday up on the moor,' I said. 'And today he's refusing to talk about it.'

'He's wounded, Alison. That's why he's lashing out at you. He's like an injured animal. If you get too close, he'll bite.'

'He'll come round, though, won't he?'

Barbara shrugged. 'I don't know. This is going to really hit him hard.'

I stared at Barbara. The tone of her voice was unnerving me. 'Lydia knows, you see,' said Barbara.

'Knows what?' I asked.

Barbara hesitated for a moment. 'Knows exactly how to hurt him.'

I nodded. Though I suspected that Lydia knew something far more than that. Something which Chris had never found it in himself to tell me.

From the Counselling Room

I know it sounds stupid if I say it were Christmas tree what did it, but it were last straw, you know? Every single thing I do is wrong, nothing is ever good enough for her, and I never say a word, I just take it.

So one morning she were out shopping and I thought I'd surprise her and put up Christmas tree, I spent ages making it look really nice, and when she comes home she takes one look at it and tuts and shakes her head. So I goes out to shed for a bit and when I come back in she's taken lights and tinsel and every single bauble off and has started doing it from scratch. And I asks her what she's doing, like, and she says I'd done it wrong. Like there's some bloody manual on it and only one way it can be done.

I took one of baubles off tree and stamped on it right in front of her. Told her it were in wrong place. I'm not proud of what I done, it were a nice bauble and that, but sometimes a man reaches end of his tether and I guess that bauble just happened to be in wrong place at wrong time.

PART THREE

PART THREE

21

The knock on the door was bang on time. Matilda rushed to get it before I had the chance to dry my hands on the tea towel. I hurried through to the hall to see Caitlin standing there, her sleeveless summer dress showing off her tan, her violin case under her arm.

'Hi,' I said, stepping forward to give her a hug and drag Matilda off her at the same time. 'It's so good to see you.'

She had insisted on keeping her promise. Said she wanted to do it. That there was no way she was going to let Josh's little sister down. I'd offered to bring Matilda to her house, thought it might be easier for her. But she'd said she wanted to come here. Even insisted on walking up the hill from the bus stop. I suspected she'd thought it would be cathartic. Although, looking at her face right now, it appeared that wasn't the case at all.

'And you,' she said, forcing a smile.

We'd kept in touch, of course. Emailing or texting every day at first and, more lately, weekly. She'd told me how her revision was going. Bits and pieces about stuff going on at school. But mostly just about how much she was missing Josh. How she thought about him all the time. Wondered where he was, what he was doing. How chuffed he must be that he'd managed to get out of doing his exams. She'd said it with a smiley face emoticon, clearly trying to do her bit to raise my spirits. But she'd still texted me a few minutes after sending it. Worried that I might have taken it the wrong way.

'Matilda, you go up and make sure your bedroom's tidy. And clear a proper space for Caitlin. She'll be up in a minute.'

Matilda nodded, for once not bothering to argue about the need to tidy her room, and bounded upstairs.

'How did your last exams go?' I asked.

'Pretty good, I think. I guess I'll just have to wait for August to find out for sure.'

I smiled and nodded. I remembered how long that wait had seemed when I was her age. It wouldn't really be a drag for her at all now. She had grown used to waiting. We all had.

'You're looking well, anyway,' I said.

'We went away at half term. My parents have got a place in Tuscany.'

'Sounds wonderful,' I said, suspecting Josh would have gone, had he still been here. That it would have been their first holiday together.

'Yeah,' she said, though I imagined it hadn't been much of a holiday for her.

'Can I get you a drink of anything before you start?' I asked.

'No, I'm fine, thanks. Honestly.'

'Let's go and see how she's doing, then.'

Caitlin followed me upstairs.

I started to walk past Josh's bedroom, then turned round, realising that Caitlin's footsteps had faltered. She was staring at the closed door. All the light had disappeared from her face.

'May I go in?' she asked.

'If you're sure,' I said.

She nodded.

I put my hand on the door knob and pushed it open for her, standing back to let her go inside. She stepped forward uncertainly, like a child who'd asked to go on a fairground ride but, now the request had been granted, was having second thoughts. I took her hand and walked in with her.

I could do it because I still went in most days. Opened the window, shut it again at night. Keeping things aired, that's what I told myself. Though really it was my way of keeping the memories alive.

Everything was just as he'd left it. I understood why people did that now. It was like Mrs Darling leaving the nursery window open. You never knew when they might come back, and you wanted everything to be just as it had been, almost as if no time had passed at all. I hadn't even washed the sheets on the bed. So I could still kid myself that I could smell him.

Caitlin's bottom lip started to tremble.

I squeezed her hand tighter. 'He will come back,' I said. 'And when he does, everything will be waiting ready for him.'

'It's the not knowing I can't handle,' she said, a solitary tear running down her face. 'Where he is or what he's doing. Whether he's even thinking about me.'

'That's the only thing I am sure of,' I said, 'that wherever he is, and whatever he's doing, he's thinking about you. And when he comes back, he's not going to come back because of me, or his dad, or even Matilda. He's going to come back because of you.'

I wiped the tears away from the corners of her eyes with my fingers.

'You can come here whenever you want,' I said. 'If you simply want to sit in here and feel close to him, that's fine. I do it all the time.'

'Maybe when I come to do Matilda's lessons,' she said, 'I could come a bit early or stay a little later.'

'Of course,' I said. 'Whatever helps.'

'Mummy, when are we going to start?' Matilda called from her bedroom.

Caitlin smiled.

'Are you sure you're up to doing this?' I asked.

'Yeah,' she replied. 'I want to. I really do.'

I nodded and squeezed her hand one last time before she left the room. I stayed sitting there a while longer. Heard the first tortured sounds emanate from Matilda's room, Caitlin's voice offering encouragement.

Josh would have been pissing himself laughing. And would have been very proud of them both at the same time.

Chris got home from work not long after Caitlin had left. He worked a lot of Saturdays these days. I wouldn't have minded if he'd been genuinely busy, but that didn't appear to be the case. I got the impression he was editing a lot of stuff on his Mac which could easily have been done at home. The phrase 'avoidance tactic' sprung to mind.

I couldn't say that, of course. I couldn't say anything to

him. When you make a mistake as monumental as the one I had made, the price you paid was that you were rendered impotent on any matter of concern over the next six months, maybe longer. He didn't even have to say it in so many words, he could simply look at me, a look which said, 'Remind me again why I should listen to your opinion?'

'Good day?' I asked as he unpacked his gear in the downstairs study.

I didn't mean 'good' as in normal people's definition of the word. We didn't have good days now, we hadn't done for three months. What I actually meant was, 'You look down. Did anything bad happen at work, or is it just your usual down?'

'Not really,' he said. 'The family from last week only ordered one photo. The group I did today were hard work, the kids kept messing around. And I've got very little booked in for next week.'

I nodded. Orders had been down for a while now. And bookings had fallen off a bit too. Our bank balance was looking far from healthy, although I knew better than to raise this with Chris.

'Matilda's had her violin lesson,' I said, thinking that changing the subject might be the best idea. 'Caitlin said she did really well.'

Chris nodded but said nothing. Even the mention of Caitlin's name was enough to bring down the shutters on his face.

'I'll make you a tea,' I said. 'The kettle's not long boiled.'

When I returned to the study with his mug a few minutes later, he was scrolling through some photos, presumably of the sitting earlier that day. I stood in the doorway behind him and watched as he pulled each one up in turn. They were sharp – Chris's photos were always sharp – but they were not quirky or charming. They were joyless, going-through-the-motions photos, taken by a joyless, going-through-the-motions photographer.

'Are these from today?' I asked as I put down his mug.

He nodded. 'Yeah.'

'Happy with them?'

I didn't say it to be nasty. I wanted to check whether he could see it himself, or whether he was too wrapped up in his own misery to notice.

'They're OK,' he replied, not taking his eyes off the screen.

'You always wanted to do better than OK,' I said.

'Look, the kids were being annoying. It wasn't easy.'

'Were they having fun?' I asked.

'I don't know.'

'Only you can't see it in these photos. You can't see any sense of fun or joy, like you usually can with your work.'

Chris turned to face me. 'Well, thanks, Ali. That's made me feel a whole lot better.'

'I'm not having a go, love. I'm just saying it's missing. And I totally understand why it's missing. But the parents of these kids won't, and maybe that's why orders are down.'

'So you're saying I'm a crap photographer now?'

'No, I'm saying you're hurting and I can see your hurt in your photos.'

'So what am I supposed to do about that exactly? Turn up for work in a clown outfit?'

'Come on, I'm trying to help. I want you to let me in, instead of shutting me out like this. I'm hurting too, you know.'

'Not as much as me, you're not.'

'Well, tell me, then. Tell me how you feel.'

'Why?' asked Chris. 'So you can try to make me better? So you can fix me like you fixed everything else?'

I hovered in the doorway for a moment, feeling the knife twist inside me. I heard a sound in the hallway. I poked my head outside and saw Matilda standing there, tears streaming down her face.

'You're arguing again,' she said. 'Why can't you both stop arguing?'

I crouched down and took hold of her, the words echoing inside. Her tears wet on my face. Merging into my own.

I almost felt bad for taking Bob's money. Like some prostitute who he kept turning up to see, simply to talk. I was aware that he wasn't getting his full entitlement. And that someone else might have been better qualified to help him.

But the fact was, Bob didn't have anyone else. The only male friends he had were either husbands of Jayne's friends or people he played golf with, and he clearly wasn't going to discuss his marriage with any of them.

I'd asked him, of course, whether he was sure he wanted to carry on seeing me now that Jayne was refusing to come. I asked him every month when he came to see me, and he always answered the same way. That if one of them was still trying to save their marriage it had to be better than neither of them.

On this particular occasion, I knew as soon as he walked in that things were bad. He didn't even go through the polite pretence of the cheerful greetings.

'Jayne's not good,' he said, sitting straight down and looking at me. 'She's not good at all.'

'What do you mean by that?'

'She's been to doctor. He's got her on these antidepressants. Don't agree with it myself, but she reckons it's the only way to cope.'

'Cope with what?'

'Cassie's pregnant.'

'I thought that would be a good thing?'

Bob shook his head. 'Jayne burst into tears the minute she told her. She pretended to Cassie that she were pleased for her – excited, like – but it didn't look that way to me.'

'I suppose it means Cassie won't be over any time soon.'

'Baby's due in February, so there's no way she'll be over for Christmas, is there?'

'But Jayne could go over, surely?'

'She says she doesn't want to. Not on her own.'

'I take it you still don't think you could fly there?'

Bob shook his head. 'Makes me stomach turn just thinking about it. I know that must sound daft to you.'

'It's not daft. Lots of people have phobias. You can get help for it, though. There are fear of flying courses you can go on, hypnotherapy, all sorts of things.'

'I couldn't do it here, with you, like?'

I smiled at Bob. 'Sorry,' I said. 'Not something I'm qualified for.'

He nodded and looked down.

I was touched, to be honest. To have won his trust so much.

'Have you got a computer or tablet?' I asked. 'You could

get Skype set up or something. She'd be able to see the baby onscreen then. It's not the same as holding it, I know, but it would be something.'

'Aye, maybe we could look into that.'

'Good. It might be a boost for Jayne. To feel that she's connected. That she can still see her first grandchild.'

'I'm quite chuffed myself,' he said. 'Becoming a grandad for first time. It's a big deal. Just a pity I can't really share excitement with Jayne.'

'If there's any way you can get her back here,' I said. 'Any way we can get her talking again.'

'I'll try,' said Bob. 'But I don't hold out much hope.'

From the Counselling Room

I only watched Strictly for the dresses, not that there was that much of them to look at, Come Dancing used to be so much nicer. Anyway, he would watch it with me, he'd always liked Brucie, you see. Which was fair enough, the man was a national treasure, wasn't he?

Only one evening we were watching it and I happened to glance at him, and he was practically salivating looking at that girl Ola, or whatever her name is, and I realised like a great lemon that he didn't watch it for Brucie at all. And I felt so silly about that and so sad because we don't, you know, do it any more, and we haven't for a long time, and I used to think that was because he was too old and he simply didn't want to. But, of course, it wasn't that at all, it was that he didn't find me attractive any more, me with my wrinkles and saggy bits.

22

Luke was on his own. It wasn't his turn to be on his own; I'd already seen him and Kelly individually, and we'd been back to joint visits for a while.

'Is everything OK?' I asked, as he came in.

Luke looked at the floor for a long time before answering. 'No. Not really.'

'Did Kelly not want to come?' I asked, seeing I was going to have to help him out here.

'No. It's not that,' he said. 'She's got an appointment. At hospital, like.'

'Oh. Nothing serious, I hope.'

He stared at the floor some more.

I let him take his time.

'She found a lump,' he said. 'In her, you know, breast.'

'Oh dear,' I said. 'And the GP's referred her to hospital?'

He nodded, swallowing hard as he did so.

'And that's where she is now, is it?'

Luke looked at his watch. 'Yeah, well, she will be in about half an hour.'

'Who's got the kids?' I asked. 'She hasn't got them with her?'

'No. Me mam's got them.'

I looked at him. He may have been twenty-six, but on occasion I swore he was still sixteen years old.

'So why are you here, Luke?'

'I have got the right day, haven't I?' he asked.

'Yes, you have. And you were here bang on time. But your wife's about to go for an appointment with a breast cancer specialist. Why on earth didn't you just call me to cancel?'

'I didn't want to mess you about, like,' he said.

I looked at him. My eyebrows raised expectantly.

'She wouldn't have wanted me with her, anyway,' he said.

'Did you ask her?'

'No.'

'Why not?'

He shuffled his feet, his trainers squeaking together as he did so. When he spoke, his voice was barely above a whisper.

'Because she might have said yes.'

I was thrown for a second. I didn't have him down as a bastard. I really didn't.

'You didn't want to be with her?'

'Of course I did,' he said. 'But I don't think it would have been, you know, a good idea.'

He swallowed hard again. Sat on the shaking fingers of his left hand. That was when I realised.

'You couldn't bear it, could you? If it was bad news, I mean.'

He shook his head. His eyes filled with tears.

'I think I'd crack up,' he said. 'I'd be a jibbering mess on floor. Guys are supposed to be strong at times like this, aren't they? I don't want her to see how weak I am.'

'You're not weak, Luke. You love her to bits, that's all. And right now she needs to know that. Hopefully it won't be bad news and, even if it is, the survival rates are really good these days. But whatever happens, she needs you with her.'

Luke sighed and held his head in his hands. 'I've been a right eejit, haven't I?'

'Yep. But the good news is, you've still got time to put things right.'

Luke looked at his watch. 'Do you think I'll get there in time?'

'You will if you get a move on. I don't often say this to clients, Luke, but will you please get the hell out of here?'

He scrambled to his feet before stopping suddenly. 'I haven't paid you.'

'You don't need to. This wasn't a counselling session, it was a kick up the arse. And they come free.'

He smiled. 'Thanks,' he said.

'Now go. And let me know how she gets on, OK?'

He nodded and ran out of the room.

I usually loved the countdown to the school holidays. The children demob happy, the chance for all of us to get away and spend some time together without the usual distractions at home. We always went away for the first week of the holidays. I couldn't understand those people who opted to save it for the end of August. There was something glorious about the children coming home from school, having everything packed and ready, throwing it all into the car and heading off, knowing we had the whole summer stretching ahead of us.

Except this year, of course. This year it felt like the most torturous prison sentence was about to begin. If it had been just me and Chris, we'd have cancelled it, I knew that. But neither of us had wanted to disappoint Matilda. And I was certainly keen to keep some semblance of normality in her life.

The worst part of it was that we had let Josh pick where we were going to stay, as it would probably have been his last holiday with us. And Josh being Josh, he'd managed to find an old lighthouse which had been converted into a holiday cottage sitting high above the harbour at Whitby. So it wasn't even as if we could try to forget about the missing member of our party; it was going to be in our face the whole time. We were going to be staying at Josh's perfect holiday hideaway. Only Josh wasn't going to be there.

'Have you got your camera?' I asked Chris, as we stood in the hallway surrounded by suitcases, waterproofs and boxes of food.

'No. I'm not bothering.'

I frowned. He might as well have been leaving behind a prosthetic leg, his camera was that much a part of him.

'You always bring the camera.'

'Yeah, well. Busman's holiday and all that.'

'But your photos capture such beautiful memories.'

He shrugged. I realised he didn't want to remember. He wanted to blot the whole thing from his mind. Wanted each second to unfold and be instantly gone.

'For Matilda's sake,' I said.

'I've got my mobile. I can take any pictures she wants on that.'

It wasn't the same, and he knew it. They were fun snaps, the modern-day equivalent of a Polaroid. You didn't frame those kinds of photos or stick them lovingly in photo albums.

'Please.' My eyes locked on to his for a second.

He sighed, disappeared back into the study and came out again with his camera bag.

'Thanks,' I said.

'I don't know how we're going to find the space to pack it,' he said. 'We always have too much stuff.'

'We can put it on the back seat, next to Matilda.'

I said it softly, knowing he hadn't thought it through. That Josh's absence would leave a Josh-sized space on the back seat of the car. Not to mention a sizeable hole in the boot where all his stuff usually went.

Chris closed his eyes for a second. I went to put my hand on his shoulder. But before it actually made contact, he turned, picked up the suitcase and carried it out to the car.

Matilda emerged from her bedroom carrying her Dora the Explorer pull-along trolley. She was a bit old for it now, I knew that. But she hadn't complained. And as the next step up appeared to be a One Direction trolley, I was relieved not to have to go there just yet.

She paused on the landing and glanced in the direction of Josh's room. I put down the bags I was holding and hurried upstairs.

'I know it's hard,' I said, taking her hand. 'But Josh wouldn't want him not being here to spoil things for you, would he?'

'Why hasn't he emailed?' she asked. 'Or texted, or something.'

I stroked her hair. Maybe it was time we told her the truth. But if we couldn't cope with it, I didn't think it fair to expect her to.

'I guess he's busy,' I said. 'It's not easy to keep in touch when you're travelling.'

'Is he in a foreign country?' Matilda asked.

'He could be. We don't know for sure.'

'Is he going to get in trouble when he gets back?'

'No, love,' I said. 'I think we'll all just be glad to see him.'

She nodded, seemingly satisfied with my answers.

At least for now.

It was early evening when we arrived. The sun was dipping slightly in the sky, positioning itself perfectly for its dramatic exit later on. The temperature had dropped a degree or two, which was welcome as none of us were any good in the heat. We weren't in the lighthouse itself but in one of the two lighthouse keepers' cottages which nestled alongside it at the bottom of a narrow lane, a matter of yards from the cliff edge.

'Wow!' said Matilda as Chris pulled up outside. 'Are we really staying here?'

'Yep,' I said. 'That one there,' pointing to the cottage on the right.

Matilda jumped out of the car and ran down onto the grassy bank which surrounded our cottage, twirling around with her arms outstretched like Julie Andrews in the opening sequence of *The Sound of Music*.

'It's brilliant!' she shouted, her long hair flying out behind her as she twirled. For a moment her enthusiasm was strong enough to cut through the ache inside me. I decided to get the things from the boot of the car while the mood was right. Anything to prolong her sense of excitement a little longer. Chris was still sitting in the driver's seat, seemingly unable, or unwilling, to move.

'Come on,' I said to him gently. 'It'll be OK.'

He looked at me without replying, opened the driver's door and got out. Matilda immediately ran over to him, took him by the hand and pulled him down to the garden wall, from where you could look out over the sea and the cliffs below.

I started getting the things out of the boot: the round wicker basket, the red and white checked tea towel, the rope and the large metal butcher's hook which I'd managed to find on eBay. Fortunately, Matilda was too engrossed in trying to spot dolphins to pay any attention to what I was doing until I was ready.

'Come on, then,' I yelled. 'The lighthouse keeper's tea is ready.'

Matilda spun round.

As she did so, I pushed the basket from the rim halfway up the lighthouse where I had tied the rope, and it slid on the hook all the way down to the balustrade on the decking area where I'd fastened the other end.

Matilda squealed and ran over to the basket, pulling off the tea towel to reveal the sandwiches, fruit and iced lighthouse biscuits beneath. She looked up at me, her smile threatening to disappear off the edge of the cliffs.

'Thank you,' she said. 'This is so brilliant. It's just like the book.'

I pulled out the rather dog-eared copy of *The Lighthouse Keeper's Lunch*, which I'd been hiding in my bag.

'And after we've eaten I'll read you the story,' I said.

I caught Chris's eye as I looked up. There was a time when he would have been smiling. When he would have said something along the lines of 'Once a librarian, always a librarian.' When he would have recounted a tale of one of the book events I'd organised which he'd brought Josh to at the library. He didn't do any of those things now, though.

'Look,' said Matilda, opening the book. 'It's still got Josh's name in it.' She held the book up to reveal the 'This Book Belongs To' bookplate on which Josh had written his name in spidery letters.

I nodded and managed to force out a smile for her.

Chris turned his back and looked straight out to sea. It may have been the coastal breeze making his eyes water. But somehow I doubted it.

By the third day it was becoming unbearable. I understood that he was finding it hard. I understood that entirely. I even understood why he was taking it out on me. What I could not understand was why he was pushing Matilda away too.

'Right, then,' I said, as we set off up the steps to Whitby Abbey from the harbour. 'We'll count as we go.'

Matilda glanced over her shoulder. Chris was lagging behind us, seemingly unwilling to be part of it. Or be part of this family.

'Come on, Daddy!' Matilda called. 'I'm going to beat you to the top.'

Chris quickened his pace for a moment but soon fell behind again. It wasn't that he couldn't keep up. He could have run up the steps before we'd made it to the halfway point. It appeared to be more a case of not wanting to risk having fun.

'Thirty-nine, forty,' Matilda counted out loud.

I turned around again. His eyes were fixed on the steps. His face was somewhere else entirely, though. And wherever he was, he certainly wasn't with us. I turned back and carried on. It didn't get any easier. Each step was harder than the last.

'One hundred and ninety-nine!' Matilda made it to the top first. She did a little jig of celebration in order to ram home the point. I laughed as I came up the last few steps, blowing much more than I would have liked.

'Come on, Daddy!' called Matilda. 'Even Mummy's beaten you.'

Chris climbed up the remaining steps. He wasn't out of breath at all. He had hung back through choice, I knew that. He may have been physically on this holiday but he was not here in spirit.

'Let's go and look at the Abbey, Matilda,' I said. 'We can find out all about its history.'

Matilda ran off towards the ruins.

I started after her, then turned to look at Chris, who hadn't moved. 'Are you coming?' I asked.

'No, it's OK. You two go ahead. I've seen it before.'

I stared at him. He wouldn't even make eye contact with me.

'Matilda hasn't, though,' I said, before walking away.

I shut the lounge door behind me. Putting Matilda to bed had taken longer than usual because she had begged me to read an extra chapter of her Mr Gum book and had then laughed herself very much awake. I glanced at the mug of tea on the table.

'Sorry. It's probably cold by now,' said Chris, looking up from his Mac. 'Do you want me to make another one?'

I shook my head, picked it up and took a sip. It was cold, but I drank it anyway.

I had a couple of options open to me. I could get my book out and sit in silence opposite Chris, as I had done for the past three nights. Or I could try to talk to him. Really talk to him, in an attempt to salvage what was left of the holiday.

'Where would you like to go tomorrow?' I asked.

'I don't mind. Wherever you think,' said Chris, not looking up from his screen.

'It's just that, you know, because it's our anniversary, I want it to be somewhere you'll actually enjoy.'

He did look up this time. 'What's that supposed to mean?'

'Just what I said. I want you to have a nice day. I want us all to have a nice day.'

'Look, I'm sorry if I'm not the life and soul of this holiday, OK?'

'Even if you don't want to make an effort on my behalf,' I said, 'you could do it for Matilda.'

'She's fine. She's having a great time.'

'No thanks to you.'

'What do you expect me to do?'

'I want you to act like you care. To take a bit of interest.'

'And that will make everything all right, will it?'

'No. But it will make her happier.'

Chris looked up at the ceiling. The flashing of the light outside could be seen through the curtains. As if we needed reminding of how rocky the terrain was.

'Look. Whitby isn't the easiest place for me to visit, OK?'

'What do you mean?'

'I used to come here with Lydia.'

'Why didn't you say?'

'Because Josh wanted to come here.'

We sat in silence for a moment.

'He will come back,' I said.

Chris shook his head. 'No. Not now.'

'Please don't give up hope, Chris.'

He stood up and pushed back his chair. 'What's the alternative? Live some deluded existence, like this lot?' he said, pointing to his computer screen. 'I don't think so.'

He left the room. I heard him go into the bathroom. I realised he was going straight to bed. I stood up, walked round to the other side of the coffee table and sat down in front of his screen. He'd been looking at the online forum on the Missing People website. I'd given him the login details after I'd registered Josh as missing. I had no idea he'd ever looked at the site, let alone read what other people in a similar situation were saying.

I scrolled down. Lots of people: mothers, wives, sons, girlfriends. All of them clinging on to the hope that their loved ones would come home. That they would see them again one day. Or, at the very least, that they were still alive.

I searched for Josh's details again. I wanted to see his face on the screen, the picture I'd sent them taken on our summer holiday last year. He smiled out at me. Not a care in the world. Having no idea of what was about to hit him. To hit all of us.

I wiped my eyes. 'Night, love,' I whispered. 'Thank you. It's a great place. You'd have loved it here.'

The next morning there was an envelope with my name on it waiting for me on the kitchen table. For a moment I thought it was a leaving note, that he'd gone too. Until I saw him through the window, staring out towards the sea. I opened the anniversary card. It was his usual, understated style. Nothing flashy. Just a small heart on the front underneath 'Happy Anniversary' in an elegant font. I looked at the heart closely. Just in case I could see the crack where it had broken.

From the Counselling Room

I went downstairs one morning and he'd made me toast, and he never makes toast, so I suppose I should have known, and he sat down on the breakfast stool opposite me and said, 'I've met someone else. It's serious. I'm going to come home early from work and pack up my stuff and I'll be gone by the time you come home. No hard feelings, eh?'

And I just sat there staring at him, wondering if he was for real. I mean, you live with someone for five years and then ditch her out of the blue like that and think there's going to be no hard feelings?

I'm thirty-five, well past my sell-by date. What are the chances now of me meeting someone else and having children with him? Pretty non-existent, I should have thought.

I should have slapped him around the face. Or, better still, taken him to court for time-wasting and taking away my chance to be a mum. You should be able to press charges for something like that, surely?

23

It was a different woman who was sitting in the coffee shop waiting for me. The same elegant, sophisticated exterior but shining through it an inner confidence which I hadn't seen before. Even her skin seemed to have relaxed.

She was wearing a short-sleeved dress.

I smiled at her. 'Hi, Catherine,' I said, 'you're looking really well.'

She stood up and kissed me on both cheeks.

'Thanks,' she said. 'I feel pretty good too.'

'Can I get you anything?' I asked.

'No, I'm fine, thanks,' she said, pointing to the coffee in front of her.

I ordered a pot of tea at the counter and sat down opposite her. 'So, how's it all going?' I asked. 'I feel like I've got so much to catch up on. When did you actually leave?'

'A few days after I last saw you. Once I'd made the decision, there didn't seem to be much point hanging around.'

'You just walked out?'

She nodded. 'It was surprisingly easy in the end. I came home from work early and packed my stuff, loaded it all into Simon's van outside. I was going to leave before Nathan got home, but I actually decided to wait. I wanted him to see me go. I didn't want there to be anything deceitful or underhand about it. Simon was in the van outside, in case there were any problems, but I told him there wouldn't be.'

'I take it Nathan had no idea?'

'None at all. He came in and he didn't even notice all my stuff was missing. I told him I had something to tell him. I think he thought I was going to say I'd changed my mind. About trying for a baby, I mean. When I told him I was leaving, he just stared at me. He couldn't seem to take it in. I was almost beginning to feel sorry for him. Then he had the audacity to ask why. That's when I knew, really knew, that I was doing the right thing.'

'Did he try to stop you?'

'No. I just walked. I didn't say another word. He didn't either.'

'And have you heard from him since?'

'No. Not a thing.' She looked down into her coffee.

'And what about the police?'

'I reported it to them the day after I left. I phoned the woman whose number you gave me. She was good. Really supportive. She didn't make me feel like it was my fault at all.'

'That's because it wasn't.'

'No,' she said. 'I'm slowly starting to believe it too.'

'Have they interviewed Nathan?'

'Yeah. Apparently, he denied everything at first. Claimed I'd made it all up because he'd chucked me out. And then they showed him the photos. He cracked then. Broke down and admitted the whole thing. So I'm not even going to have to go through a trial.'

'What a relief.'

'Yeah.' She looked down again as she said it.

'You're worried about him, aren't you?'

She nodded slowly. 'That must sound completely ridiculous to you.'

'No. Not really. He was a massive part of your life.'

'I don't actually wish anything bad on him, you see. I'm glad I got out. Very glad. And I know I had to report it to stop him doing it to another woman. But I can't see how he'll survive prison, if he does get sent down. I don't think he's strong enough.'

'Weird, isn't it?' I said. 'You were actually the strong one all along. You just didn't know it.'

'I guess so. I actually wonder sometimes whether deep down that was why he asked me to go to counselling. If he wanted to get found out. Maybe it was the only way he thought he could stop.'

'You're probably being overgenerous to him there.'

'Maybe. But in an odd way I won't actually mind if he doesn't get sent down. He's admitted it, that's all I ever wanted. Because if he accepts it happened, he might actually do something about it.'

I nodded. She'd come such a long way since first walking into my room.

'And is it working out, staying at Simon's?'

'Yeah, he's been lovely. He's always fussing over me. I mean, I will get a place of my own at some point, when I'm properly back on my feet. But for now it suits me just fine.'

I nodded. She seemed very calm, very assured. She'd been

down, down to a place a lot of people had never even experienced, and she'd hauled herself back up again.

'You should be so proud of what you've done,' I said.

She smiled at me. 'I am,' she replied. 'And I'm also very grateful to you for all your help. For picking me up off the floor, literally.'

'You're very welcome,' I said. 'But all I really did was hold a mirror up.'

'Sometimes,' said Catherine, 'that's all people need.'

'I'm nine years old!' shouted Matilda from her bedroom the next morning.

There was a pause of a few seconds before our door was flung open and she launched herself onto our bed.

'Happy birthday, sweetheart,' I said, giving her a hug.

She climbed over onto Chris.

He kissed her on the forehead. 'Happy birthday, love.' It was barely more than a whisper.

I realised we hadn't really been tested yet. Everybody said the same thing when you heard them interviewed. That it was the special family occasions when you really missed your loved ones who weren't there. We'd struggled enough on ordinary days. I had no idea how we were going to cope with today.

Matilda was looking at us both expectantly.

'Right, then.' I smiled. 'I suppose we'd better go downstairs and see if we've got any presents for nine-year-olds.'

Matilda was up and out of the room before either of us had moved an inch.

I turned to Chris. 'Look, I know it's going to be tough. But let's make a real effort for her today.'

He nodded but said nothing.

I got up, threw on my dressing gown and went downstairs. I'd got the presents sorted myself. I'd run through some suggestions with Chris, but as I'd got nothing more than a 'Whatever you think' in response I'd decided to go it alone. Not that buying presents for Matilda was difficult. It was simply that I'd have liked to have felt there was somebody else on board the parenting train with me when I pulled out of the station.

Matilda was sitting in the hallway going through the pile of cards which I'd left on the mat the night before. I knew that I was helping to perpetuate the myth that posties still delivered their mail at the crack of dawn, when actually it was more like two thirty in the afternoon, but I did it all the same.

She looked up at me. The smile had slipped off her face.

I realised she hadn't been counting the cards. She'd been doing the very same thing I'd done over the past few days every time I'd picked up the post.

'Where's Josh's card?' she asked.

'It doesn't look like he's had a chance to send one, love,' I said.

'Is it because he's in a different country?'

'Maybe,' I said.

'So it might just be late. It might still come next week?'

'Let's wait and see, eh?' I said.

I heard the creak of the stairs behind me as Chris followed me down.

'Josh's card might be a bit late,' Matilda announced to him.

Chris looked at me. I shrugged.

Matilda picked up the rest of the cards and carried them into the kitchen.

At the point when you agree to having nineteen children come to your house for a themed birthday party, it never seems like a bad idea. You find yourself saying things like, 'It's so nice to do it at home rather than a soulless soft-play centre,' or even, 'We'll make up party games and I'll tell stories, we won't even need to get an entertainer.' You tend to blot out the likelihood that your favourite rug will have Ribena spilt over it, one child will cry and another will be sick, and you will be up past midnight the night before making witch's hat cupcakes and witches' broomsticks out of Twiglets tied around breadsticks with liquorice strings.

And you certainly don't imagine that you will find it nigh on impossible to get through the day because your stepson will have gone missing, your husband blames you entirely and your marriage is in serious trouble.

What had seemed like a good idea in April now appeared to have turned into a ridiculous thing to put ourselves through, given the circumstances. Backing out wasn't an option, though. There was no way I was going to disappoint Matilda.

Chris came into the kitchen and picked up the piece of paper on the worktop next to where I was preparing the buttercream.

'What's this?' he asked.

'The to-do list. I need to get the rest of it done in the next hour before Debbie brings Matilda back.'

He scanned it and shook his head. 'Why do you always make things so hard for yourself?'

'You know why.'

'She'd be happy if you just let them run around the house and gave them a plate of jam sandwiches.'

'I don't think so. Not after the last few years.'

The Roald Dahl party thing had started on her fifth birthday. *Matilda* had been the first one – fittingly, of course, given that she'd been named after her. There'd been a book tower, story-telling and even a hammer-throwing competition. We'd done *Charlie and the Chocolate Factory* next, followed by *James and the Giant Peach* and *The BFG*. Chris had made a joke last year that there was no way he was going to get a gun licence and shoot pheasants for a *Danny the Champion of the World* party. I thought of mentioning it now but decided against it. I didn't think he'd find it amusing any more.

'Isn't it a bit much? Nobody else seems to go to all this trouble.'

I felt the mercury rising inside me. It seemed I could do no right these days.

'You used to love all this,' I said.

'I just think she's getting a bit old for it.'

'Josh had one on his tenth birthday. He loved it, said it was the best party ever.'

Chris looked up at the ceiling. I saw him swallow. Maybe I shouldn't have said it, but I was tired of walking on eggshells.

'Yeah,' he said. 'I remember.'

'What else do you remember?' I asked, putting down the wooden spoon and wiping a floury hand across my forehead.

'What do you mean?'

'About Josh. I'm wondering what you remember. Only you don't talk about him any more. It's like he never existed.'

'Yeah, well, he didn't, did he? Turned out he was somebody else's son.'

'Don't do this to yourself, Chris.'

'What's the alternative? Cling on to the hope that he's mine? What good would that do? He's not here, anyway.'

'He'll come back.'

'You've been saying that for over three months now.'

'It doesn't mean it's not going to happen.'

'It means it's less likely.'

'How do you know that?'

'It says so on the Missing People website. Ninety-one per cent of cases reported are closed within forty-eight hours.'

I stared at him. 'Why don't you talk to me about it?'

'I'm doing that now, aren't I?'

'Only because I brought it up. You make it very clear you don't want to talk about Josh, and yet you're going online reading up about stuff.'

'I'm entitled to do that, aren't I? What are you now, the internet police?'

'There's no need to be like that. I was trying to say that I want to talk about Josh with you. We should be going through this together, not taking it out on each other.'

'And what if I don't want to share what I'm going through?'

I shrugged. 'Well, it makes it hard for me. I want to support you, but you're not letting me.'

'Because, believe me, you don't want to know what's going on inside my head.'

'It's probably very similar to the stuff going on in mine.'

Chris shook his head. 'No. You have no idea what I'm dealing with.'

'So let me in, and I can find out.'

'What, and try to fix me like you try to fix everything else?'

'That's not fair, Chris.'

'No. I've lost a son. That's what's not fucking fair.' He turned and left the kitchen.

I stood there, trying to compose myself. Trying not to cry into the buttercream.

A few minutes later, I heard the front door bang shut behind him. It was becoming all too familiar. Being walked out on. I toyed with the idea of going after him, pleading with him to talk to me. But there were only so many times you could pick yourself up off the floor knowing you were going to be knocked straight back down again.

Besides, I had witches' hats to stick on cupcakes.

Chris still wasn't back when Barbara arrived. She'd insisted on coming by bus. Said we'd be far too busy with the preparations to pick her up. She'd never missed one of Matilda's parties. Or one of Josh's either, apparently. And, aside from her grand-mother credentials, she was a welcome guest due to being remarkably unflappable in the face of chaos and particularly good at making sandwiches.

Matilda, who was approaching the outer limits of excit-ability, rushed to throw her arms around her.

'We're doing *The Witches* and we've got broomsticks and frog juice and pretend mice. And Mummy's being the Grand High Witch.'

'That's lovely, dear,' said Barbara, in true grandmotherly fashion.

'And you can be the grandmother because there is one and then you won't even need to dress up because you just have to look old.'

Barbara smiled at Matilda. 'And what are you being?' she asked.

'A witch. A really mean one.'

'Well, isn't it about time you went and got your costume on, then? Your friends will be here soon.'

Matilda nodded and disappeared upstairs.

Barbara turned to me. 'Anything I can do, love?' she asked.

'Sandwiches, please,' I said. 'I haven't even started on the sandwiches.'

Barbara nodded and walked into the kitchen. She stopped when she saw that Chris wasn't there. 'Where is he?' she asked.

'He went out for a walk,' I replied.

Barbara looked hard at me. She knew him too well.

'He's finding it difficult,' I said. 'Very difficult indeed.'

'He'll be back soon,' said Barbara, patting me on my arm.

He wasn't, though. Matilda got dressed. I put the finishing touches to the witch's hat cupcakes and got changed, and he still wasn't back.

'Where's Daddy?' Matilda asked.

'He went for a walk. He'll be back soon,' I said, repeating Barbara's assurance.

Matilda looked about as convinced as I had been.

The doorbell rang. The first guest had arrived. I switched to super-efficient party-host mode. But, inside, the knot was getting tighter and tighter.

It was Debbie and Sophie, both of them dressed in their finest witches' regalia. Matilda and Sophie ran off together into the lounge.

'Love it,' Debbie said, admiring my costume. 'The wig suits you.'

'I'm just hoping no one pulls it off,' I said. 'Only I wasn't prepared to go the whole hog and shave off my hair as well.'

'You disappoint me,' said Debbie. 'So much for attention to detail. Anyway, where's Mr Stringer the hotel manager? I thought he was supposed to be welcoming guests?'

'He's not back yet.' I said.

'Where from?'

'Being out.'

Debbie looked at me and nodded. 'It's OK,' she said, rubbing my shoulder. 'I'm very happy to double as Mr Stringer if needed.'

'Thank you,' I said. 'I might have to give you the camera, actually. He was supposed to be taking the photos as well.'

'Sure,' said Debbie. 'They won't be as good as his, mind.'

'I know,' I replied. 'But they'll be a damn sight better than nothing.'

The rest of the guests started to arrive. The one good thing about being dressed as the Grand High Witch was that I had no choice but to carry on. It wasn't her husband who had gone AWOL, it was mine. So I cackled and screeched and did everything required of a Grand High Witch while all the time, inside me, the time bomb ticked away.

The children sat down to their witches' tea. He was still not back. They ploughed through sandwiches, taking three bites of each and then moving on to something more interesting. Crisps were demolished, pizzas disappeared no sooner than they were put on the table, the witch's hat cupcakes were admired and devoured in record time. They had eaten too fast. They weren't supposed to be at this point yet. Debbie glanced at me. I looked at Matilda's birthday cake sitting on the kitchen counter, a number nine sparkling candle stuck in the brim. Maybe just a few more minutes. Someone knocked a drink over. A couple of the children got down to go to the toilet. They were starting to get restless.

'After you've done the cake, I'll cut it up and wrap it in serviettes for you, love,' Barbara said. 'So you can get it into the party bags in time.'

She would have been good in the war, Barbara. There'd have been no need to tell her to calm down and carry on.

I looked again at the clock. Only ten minutes until the end of the party. The other parents would be coming back to pick their children up at any moment. I squeezed through to the far end of the table where Matilda was sitting.

'I'm going to do your cake now, love,' I said.

She looked at me, her eyes hot and teary. 'But Daddy's not back yet.'

'I know, love, but it's nearly going home time. Your friends' parents will be here in a minute.'

'I don't want to do the candles without Daddy.'

'Nor do I. But we've got no choice, sweetie.'

'No,' she said, her voice louder and shriller. 'I want to wait for Daddy.'

'We'll do them again when he gets back,' I said.

'But we can't, the cake will have gone. We're putting it in the party bags, you said so.'

'I'll make you another one, then.'

'It won't be the same.'

She was right. It wouldn't be the same. Not the same at all.

I walked back to the kitchen and picked up the matches. My fingers were shaking too much to be able to light one. Barbara took the box from me and did the honours. The candles sparked instantly into life. I picked up the cake board and walked back towards the table with it. Debbie started the singing. I joined in, my voice struggling not to break. I put the cake down in front of Matilda. The light from the candle lit up her face. Caught the first tear as it trickled down her cheek. A camera flashed behind me. I turned quickly but it was Debbie taking the photograph. Capturing the moment for posterity.

I could make another cake, light another candle, take another photo. But the one which had just been taken would always be Matilda's ninth birthday party. In my mind, at least.

Presumably I switched to automatic pilot. People do in those sorts of circumstances. Because the next thing I remember, when sensation started to return to me, was standing in the kitchen, surrounded by debris from the party, with Matilda and Sophie being the only children left.

'The cake?' I asked.

'In the party bags,' said Barbara. 'We ran out of black servi-ettes so we used a couple of white ones instead.'

I nodded and looked out of the window. A small, dark figure was visible in the distance, along the brow of the hill. He would dip down out of sight in a minute, before re-emerging at the track leading to our lane.

'Why don't I take Matilda back with me for a bit?' Debbie asked. 'Give you a chance to get yourself sorted.'

'Thanks,' I said. 'That would be a real help.'

Debbie went to gather Matilda and Sophie. She got them ready quickly, obviously aware of the need to get her away from the house before Chris arrived back. I gave Matilda a kiss. Her eyes were still rimmed with red.

'There's some birthday cake here for when you get home,' I said. 'We'll get cleared up and you can open your presents when you get back.'

'Will Daddy be home then?' she asked.

'Yes,' I said. 'He'll be here.'

She nodded uncertainly.

Debbie took her hand and hurried her out of the house and up towards the lane. I shut the door and went back through to the kitchen.

Barbara was scraping plates into the compost bin. 'I've made you both a cup of tea,' she said, pointing to the counter. 'I'm going to run the Hoover over the lounge before it all gets trodden in.'

I glanced up at the window. Chris had emerged over the hill. He would be here in a couple of minutes.

'I understand that you're angry, love,' said Barbara. 'I'm

angry with him too. But please don't be too hard on him. He loves you all very much.'

'Well, he's got a funny way of showing it,' I said.

Barbara left the room. A few moments later, I heard the Hoover start up, swiftly followed by the sound of the front door shutting. Chris walked into the kitchen. He still had his boots on. His face was pale.

'I've missed it, haven't I?' he said.

I nodded.

'I'm sorry,' he said. 'I walked and walked and walked and I simply lost track of time.'

'Bollocks,' I said.

Chris appeared taken aback. 'There's no need for that.'

'There's every need for it. You didn't lose track of time. You couldn't face the party so you made sure you weren't here. You put your misery above everyone else's.'

'That's not true.'

'I think you'll find it is. I'll show you the photo, shall I?' I said, picking up the camera. 'Matilda in tears with her birthday cake. That'll make a lovely one for the album, that will. Maybe we can put a caption on it. Pretend that they were tears of joy rather than mention that she was bawling her eyes out because her own father didn't show at her birthday party.'

'I'm sorry, OK?' said Chris.

The Hoover stopped. Chris appeared suddenly aware of other people in the house.

'It's your mum. She's been helping me. Or did you forget she was coming too?'

'Where's Tilda?' he asked. 'I'll go and talk to her.'

'You can't. She's at Debbie's. She needed some time out. We all did.'

'I'm sorry. I'll make it up to her.'

I shook my head. 'You can't, Chris. The moment's been and gone, but she'll remember it for the rest of her life. You weren't there when she needed you. When I needed you. I know you're hurting, we're all hurting, but if you're not careful, you're going to push away the only family you've got left.'

He stared at me. His eyes trying desperately not to let the truth in. Then he turned on his heel and walked out.

'You can't keep running away, Chris,' I called after him. 'At some point you've got to face up to things.'

The door slammed shut behind him. I sat down at the table and started to cry. A moment later, I felt Barbara's hand on my shoulder. I turned round and let her pull me close, hold me the way she held Matilda. The way she must have held Chris when he was little.

'I'm losing him,' I sobbed. 'I can't seem to break through. One of these days he won't come back, just like Josh.'

'Nonsense,' she said. 'He won't leave you. He worships you.'

'So why does he keep pushing me away? Why won't he talk to me? Why won't he share what he's going through?'

'Because it's coming from deep inside. A place he's never let you go to.'

'What do you mean?' I asked, looking up at her.

Barbara's eyes were wet with tears. She sighed and shook her head. 'He didn't want you to know,' she said. 'He made me swear never to tell you. The only reason I'm going to tell you now is because I'm worried this thing with Josh is going to push him over the edge. And you're the only one who can help him.'

I nodded. The tone in her voice was scaring me. So was the idea that I didn't know my own husband.

Barbara sat down next to me and clenched her hands on the table. 'Chris isn't my birth son,' she said. 'He was adopted.'

I stared at her. Barbara wasn't who I thought she was. And nor was Chris.

'I had no idea.'

'No. He didn't want anyone to know.'

'Why? I mean, lots of people are adopted, it's nothing to be ashamed of.'

'Because of the circumstances,' said Barbara.

'What circumstances?'

She sighed. 'He were abandoned right after he were born. Someone found him wrapped up in a blanket outside a GP's surgery. It were a doctor's receptionist, called Christine. That's how he got his name.'

Our neatly potted family history exploded around me. Nothing was how I'd thought it was. Chris had no idea who he was. Where he had come from.

'What about his birth mother?'

'She were never traced,' said Barbara. 'We adopted him when he were six months old. He'd been with foster parents before that. We couldn't believe our luck, to be honest. We'd been trying for a baby for years. There were something wrong with me ovaries. Nowt they could do in them days.'

I nodded and squeezed Barbara's hand. My mind was rushing ahead. Piecing it all together.

'Lydia knew, didn't she?' I asked.

Barbara nodded. 'And yet she still did the same thing to Josh. That's how nasty she really is.'

'And when she told Chris that Josh wasn't his –'

'There's only so much someone can take, isn't there?'

'Jesus Christ,' I said, standing up. 'I'm going after him.'

'Thank you, love,' said Barbara. 'He so needs you right now.'

From the Counselling Room

I don't want to blame the baby for what's happened, but you can't get away from the fact that that's when the problems started. I had no idea I was going to feel like I did. I mean, nobody tells you, do they? Nobody says you're going to be blown out of the water like that by how much you love them and that every waking moment will be taken up with making sure the baby is OK.

Don't get me wrong, I tried. I put a Post-it note on the fridge telling me to remember to smile at Neil and one on the bathroom mirror to remind me to say something nice to him every day. Some days I'd forget all about him, you see. All that mattered was that she was OK. Maybe it was the sleep deprivation that was to blame. It certainly didn't help. I'd lie in bed at night, gripping the sheet with my fingers. I was always so tense because I knew that at any moment she'd wake up and that would be it for another couple of hours while I fed her and got her back down. And the thing that really did it was that he used to sleep through it. I mean, how is that even possible? It really used to piss me off and then, I suppose, there just came a point when I realised I didn't have any love left for him. I'd used it all up on the baby.

24

I ran across the field and started to climb the rocky track up the hill. He always went the same way. At least, I thought he did. He certainly seemed to come back from the same direction, anyway.

I thought of Hansel dropping a trail of white pebbles so he could find his way home. Only, in Chris's case, I was following a trail of hurt. Hurt so powerful I could almost smell it.

I blinked and shook my head but I couldn't get rid of it. The image of Chris as a baby, wrapped in a blanket, crying and alone. Somebody did that to him. The person who was supposed to love him most in the world. How could you ever recover from that? How could you ever see the world through anything but a prism of rejection?

I thought of my own mother, a woman who I barely ever saw, who was distant and removed from my life. She was little more than a woman I knew who happened to have given birth to me. But she had given birth to me, and she was my mother, and although she may have failed me in many ways, I knew who she was and where to find her if I needed to. Chris had never had that. Only the sense of abandonment. Of loss.

The afternoon was cooling slightly, and there was a clear

sky above me. I stumbled over a rock but quickly righted myself. The urge to get to him was overwhelming. Hurt compounding hurt. Layers upon layers of it squashed down and built up over the years. Then stamped on by me. Because I hadn't known. I hadn't understood. I hadn't been invited in.

I kept going. The terrain started to become more unfamiliar. It was a long time since I'd walked this far from home; Matilda would usually have complained that her legs were too tired by now. The sun had slipped behind a cloud. The breeze picked up as I climbed. Still no sign of him. He walked too fast. I wouldn't get to him, even at this half-run pace. The best I could hope for was to meet him on the way back. Supposing he did come back.

And then I saw him. The figure sitting on a rock on the next ridge along, staring out across the moors. I couldn't see his face but I knew it was him. He had his back to me, which was good. I was scared he would run off if he saw me coming. I slowed down a little, trying to get my breath back, to compose myself. To work out in my head what I was going to say.

But as I drew closer my pace quickened again. The need to get to him was too great. I stumbled as I neared him. He looked over his shoulder and saw me. For a split second I wondered if he might turn and run in the opposite direction. But he was tired of running, I could see it in his face. And I think he sensed that he didn't have to run any longer. Because I had run to him.

He stood up. I careered straight into him. Threw my arms around his body. Held him so tightly that I thought, at first, it was he who was gasping for breath. It wasn't, it was me. Gasping and sobbing and holding him to me.

'It's OK,' I said. 'I'm here now. I'm sorry. I had no idea.'

He looked down at me, frowning a little. 'Mum told you.'

I nodded. 'She had to. She was worried. She wanted someone to be there for you.'

His body started to shake.

I held him tighter still. 'It's OK,' I said, over and over again. 'Let it out. You can let it all out now.'

His tears mixed with mine. One soggy strand of hair stuck to another. We were joined. Reconnected. I breathed out. I let him cry for a long time, wanting to wring him like a sponge to squeeze every last tear out of him.

'I'm sorry I never told you,' he said, finally.

'I just wish I could have helped you.'

'I know. But I couldn't tell you. Not after what Lydia did.'

'What happened? The day she left you.'

He sat down on the rock. I sat next to him, holding his hand. Waiting for him to be ready.

'She hadn't been drinking. All the way through the pregnancy she hadn't touched a drop. And not after he was born either, because she was breastfeeding. She found it hard, I think. Not drinking. But not as hard as the responsibility of being a parent. Of not being able to take off when she wanted to. Go to a club, let her hair down. She missed work too. The people she used to be around, the whole scene.'

'Did she have post-natal depression?'

Chris shrugged. 'Maybe. I'd come home from work sometimes and she'd be sitting in the window, staring out into the blackness. It was almost like she was a caged animal. It didn't suit her, being cooped up at home with a baby. I guess she'd realised that. I tried to get her to go to the doctor, but she wouldn't. Said there wasn't a problem.

'The night before she left, when I'd come home, I could tell she'd been drinking. I had no proof. There was nothing to smell on her breath. It was probably vodka. But she had been drinking when she was supposed to be looking after our son.'

'Did you confront her?'

'Yeah. She denied it, of course. We had a massive row. She said I had no idea what it was like. That I ought to try looking after him. Said I was expecting her to turn into Mother fucking Teresa just because she'd had a baby . . .'

He paused.

I could hear Lydia saying it as well. See her finger jabbing into Chris's face. 'But she didn't threaten to leave or anything?'

'No. We actually had sex the next morning, before I went to work. It was how she made up, with sex. I had no idea it was how she said goodbye as well. I went to work. Had a pretty busy day, didn't really have time to think about it. And then I came home –'

He stopped.

I saw him swallow and shut his eyes for a second.

'How long was it before you realised?' I asked.

'Straight away. I knew pretty much straight away. Josh was crying. Really crying. I knew she wouldn't have left him screaming like that if she'd been in the house. She hated it when he cried. I ran through to the kitchen. We kept his cot in there, because it was the warmest room in the house. Josh was lying there screaming, his little fists flailing in the air. His face scrunched up and almost purple. I could hear it as I picked him up. The sound of my own crying too. Only, in my head, it was a baby's cry. The same as Josh's.' He looked down, brushed a tear away from the corner of his eye.

I rubbed my hand up and down his arm. 'How long had he been there?'

'I don't know. His nappy was sodden, I remember that. And he was obviously starving.'

'Did she leave a note?' I asked.

'Yeah. Said she wasn't cut out for motherhood, just as my birth mother hadn't been. And it would be better for Josh if, like me, he didn't remember his mother at all.'

'Jeez,' I said, shaking my head.

'Exactly. And you wondered why I flipped when she came back.'

'I'm sorry.'

'And then when she said Josh wasn't mine –'

'It was like his whole life had been a lie as well as yours.'

Chris turned to look at me. 'Yeah,' he said. 'It was.'

'Did you ever think of telling Josh? About your birth mother, I mean.'

'No,' he said. 'It wouldn't have been fair to Mum. She's my mother. And Josh's grandmother. And I didn't want him to think anything else.'

'When did she tell you?' I asked.

'When I was about eight or nine she told me that I was adopted. She made it sound like it was a very special thing. That they had chosen me to be their only child. I just accepted it. I guess you do when you're that age. But later, when I was a teenager, I started asking questions about my birth parents. That's when she told me. About me being abandoned.'

'And how did you take it?'

'Pretty badly. It's not an easy thing to hear. That the person who gave birth to you dumped you soon afterwards.'

'No one would do that lightly, though. She must have been really desperate.'

'I know. It doesn't make it any easier, though. I guess the only thing that did help was the fact that I'd been left at a doctor's surgery. Somewhere I was going to be found and looked after. You hear cases of babies being abandoned at rubbish tips. I can't imagine what that would do to you.'

'So where was the surgery?'

'Halifax. Illingworth, I think she said.'

'And you've never tried to find out any more?'

'There wasn't anything to find. Mum told me I was wrapped in a white blanket. There was no note. The police appealed for information but nobody ever came forward. End of story.'

'You could put an appeal in the paper to trace her. Or online. There must be websites for that sort of thing.'

'Why would I do that?'

'Because it might help you to deal with it all.'

Chris shook his head. 'No. I don't want to rake it all back up again. Some things are best left in the past.'

'Not if they affect your present.'

'Please don't start this again, Ali. You can't make this better, you know.'

'Well, someone's got to. Someone's got to put this family back together again. Look at us. In bits. All of us.'

'So what do you suggest?'

I hesitated before replying, guessing what his reaction would be. 'I think we should consider going for counselling.'

Chris rolled his eyes. 'That's your answer to everything, isn't it?'

'No, it's my answer when people are tearing each other apart. Not talking, not communicating. Unable to see a way forward.'

'We'll be fine.'

'What, even if Josh doesn't come back? We'll carry on like this, will we? You with your open wounds. Me always seeming to make everything worse. Matilda bawling her eyes out.'

Chris put his head down and sighed. 'I'm scared,' he said.

'Scared of what?'

'Of loving Matilda too much. In case I lose her, like I've lost everyone else I love.'

'You've still got me,' I said, looking away so he couldn't see my face.

'I didn't mean it like that.'

'Well, how did you mean it, then?'

'I know I'll always have you.'

'You make me sound like a congenital disease.'

Chris managed a half-smile. 'Maybe you could help us,' he said. 'Help put us back together again.'

I shook my head. 'No. You can't do it, not from the inside. I'm too close to it all to see clearly.'

'So what are you suggesting?'

'Relationship counselling. Not at my place. Somewhere else. With someone who doesn't know anything about us.'

Chris looked up at the sky. 'You do know that sounds like my idea of torture?'

'Yes, but what's the alternative? This is pretty much my idea of torture. We can't carry on like this, Chris. We've both got too much to lose.'

'It won't change things. It won't bring Josh back. It won't turn back the clock.'

'I know. And that's exactly why we need to do it. To find a way forward from where we are now.'

Chris sat for a while. 'I'll think about it,' he said eventually.

'Thank you,' I said. I glanced at my watch. 'We'd better be getting back. I said Matilda could open her presents when she got home.'

Chris nodded.

We both stood up. We walked back down the hill together.

Kelly and Luke came into my room. They were smiling. And holding hands.

'Hello,' I said, giving Kelly a hug. 'I'm so glad it was good news.'

'Me too,' she said. 'Turns out all the women in my family have had cysts. Me mam told me.'

'Your mum?'

'Yeah,' said Kelly. 'The doctors wanted to know about any family history of breast cancer. So I got in touch with her.'

'And?'

'I've been to see her,' Kelly said. 'And she's coming over to see the kids this weekend.'

'That's great,' I said.

'Yeah. She's said sorry and that. She was surprised, I think. That me and Luke are still together. That we've made a go of it, like.'

'See,' I said, turning to Luke. 'You've proved a lot of people wrong, you two.'

'Yeah,' he said. 'I guess we have.'

'Right,' I said as they sat down. 'We need to talk about where we go from here, then. How's the plan been going?'

'Yeah. Good,' said Kelly. 'We've been out together on a Friday night. Just the two of us. It were good, actually. We had a right laugh.'

'Great.'

'And Luke's mam said she'll have the twins one morning a week, so I've switched my hours at work so I get one evening off.'

'OK, so that's another positive. How are you feeling about the end of August, then? Is that still a date you feel you can work towards for Luke moving back in?'

Kelly looked at Luke. They smiled at each other.

'Actually,' said Luke, 'I've already moved back in.'

'Oh,' I said. 'When did this happen?'

'Pretty much after the hospital appointment,' said Luke. 'It's still hard work and all that, and I know it always will be. At least while the kids are little. But the thing with Kelly, it just made me realise what a lucky bastard I am.'

I nodded, unable to speak.

'I know we were supposed to be doing the plan,' said Kelly. 'And making all those changes and stuff. I'm sorry if we've messed your chart up and that.'

I looked down at the piece of paper in my hand. The spread-sheet with goals and objectives on it. Everything numbered and in date order.

'Do you know what?' I said. 'I've never been happier to do this.' I scrunched it up and threw it in the waste-paper basket.

They looked at each other. Kelly started to giggle.

'Sometimes,' I said. 'People don't actually need me. They just need to be reminded of why they got together in the first place.'

Kelly's lip started to tremble.

'Now go, before you get me started,' I said, smiling at them. 'I'll be here if you need me. I don't think you will, though.'

From the Counselling Room

I mean, I know it sounds stupid, but it wasn't just the cutting his toenails on the toilet lid and leaving them there thing. It was the fact that he had a fungal toenail infection as well.

25

Tania smiled and showed us into her room. A different room to the one where we'd had our initial assessment. I'd told Chris it would be easier second time around. Although I suspected that wouldn't be true.

Tania was stunning. Long, auburn hair. And one of those rare women who had a great fringe and actually knew it. She also had an hourglass figure the like of which you only usually saw in black and white films. And perfectly applied lipstick to boot. I wasn't sure it was wise, becoming a counsellor, if you looked like that. There was clearly a danger that your male clients would sit there wishing their partner looked half as good while your female ones would feel distinctly inadequate. I awarded myself a brownie point for being of the common cardigan-wearing, mousey-haired variety of counsellor. It must surely put my clients more at ease.

'So,' said Tania, 'I've had a look through Polly's notes. You said you felt there were several issues from your past which were impacting upon your relationship. And that your son leaving home had brought things to a head.'

'Josh is Chris's son,' I said. 'He's my stepson.'

'Yes, of course, I'm sorry,' she said, before turning to Chris.

'He's the son from your relationship with your former partner, Lydia, is that right?'

'Yes,' said Chris. 'At least, I thought he was. She says I'm not his father.'

'Right. And that, understandably, has caused a lot of upset.'

'You could say that,' said Chris.

It came out worse than he meant it, I was sure. But I was also aware that we had reached a tipping point. It could go one of two ways. Either Chris would defect to the cynical camp and make this extremely hard for everyone, or Tania could say something to bring him back in. Make him feel like this was not a waste of time.

'Have you got any reason to believe that she's telling the truth about that?'

'No. Only that she said it.'

'And you brought him up single-handedly from the age of six months old?'

'Yeah.'

'You were there when he was teething? Had his first tantrum? Threw up all over your best shirt? Fell off his bike? Called you up to his bedroom for the hundredth time to say he couldn't get to sleep?'

'Yeah,' said Chris.

'Then are you OK if I refer to him as your son? I think it's going to make it easier all round.'

Chris nodded. A hint of a smile on his face. I smiled at her too. Because I knew now that we had a chance.

'And Chris, I understand that this has been even more

difficult for you because you were abandoned as a baby by your birth mother.'

'That's right,' he said, looking down.

'And Alison, you've only recently discovered this?'

'Yeah.'

'So we've got two very hurt people here who have been through an incredibly difficult time. We're going to need to go there,' said Tania, 'we're going to need to go to some pretty difficult places, and I appreciate it's not going to be easy. I need to know that you both understand that and are willing to go ahead. To trust that I will see you through it safely.'

'Yes,' I said.

I looked at Chris. Waited for what seemed a long time before he finally nodded his head.

'Thank you,' said Tania. 'We're not going to go there today, though. Today I want to talk to you about how you met. How you first got together. I like to start with happy stories.'

I smiled at her. And forgave her for looking so bloody good.

'Alison,' she said, 'tell me about the first time you met Chris.'

I hesitated. It seemed such a long time ago now. We were such different people back then. There was no question that I couldn't remember, though. I remembered every tiny detail.

'It was at a *Charlie and the Chocolate Factory* event I'd organised at Halifax Library,' I said. 'Chris brought Josh, who was nearly six at the time. He was dressed as Willy Wonka. Josh, I mean, not Chris.'

I glanced across at Chris. He was watching, listening. Remembering, like me.

'And you got talking?'

'To Josh mainly. I was asking about his favourite Roald Dahl word, "whipple-scrumptious", it was, the same as mine.'

'And what about you, Chris?' asked Tania.

'Me? I thought she was barking. She hasn't told you what she was dressed as yet.'

Tania looked at me inquiringly.

'An Oompa-Loompa,' I said. 'I mean, you couldn't really be dressed as anything else, could you?'

'So you two got together despite the fact that, the first time he met you, you were dressed as an Oompa-Loompa?'

'Yes,' I said. 'Although I like to think it was because of it, not despite.'

I looked at Chris. He was smiling. Smiling like I hadn't seen for a long time.

'So how did you get to see him again?' asked Tania.

'He kept coming to events at the library that summer. Well, Josh kept coming and Chris kind of tagged along.'

'We were her groupies,' said Chris. 'Josh adored her, right from the start.'

'And that must have been a big plus for you.'

'Yeah, it was.'

I looked down at my feet. Wishing that he'd added something more to that. Something about what he felt about me.

'And so you asked her out in the end?'

'No. Josh did,' said Chris. 'He invited her to his party. He said he wanted a *Charlie and the Chocolate Factory* one. And she had to be there because I didn't know how to make chocolates and I couldn't do a good Grandma Josephine or Grandma Georgina voice.'

I smiled. Remembering the invitation which he'd brought to the library.

'And what about you, Alison?' asked Tania. 'What were your impressions of Chris at this point?'

'Intriguing,' I said. 'I found him very intriguing. He wasn't like anyone else I'd ever met. He was sort of dark and mysterious and I wanted to know more about him. Scratch beneath the surface.'

'So how did it move up to another level? How did it become a relationship?'

'It just sort of grew, I guess,' said Chris. 'We were seeing so much of each other with Josh that I simply got used to her being around. And at some point I realised that we'd started seeing each other without Josh around.'

Tania looked at me. I said nothing. Looked down at my hands.

'No big "boom, boom" thing going on with the heart, then, Chris?'

Chris appeared a little taken aback.

'Because I have to admit,' said Tania, 'if I was Alison, sitting here listening to that, I'd be feeling a little bit deflated about that description. It's hardly "Our eyes met across a crowded room" stuff, is it?'

'No, but that stuff's not real, anyway. That only happens in daft Hollywood movies and those books she reads.'

'What do you like reading, Alison?'

'Women's fiction, anything really, from *Jane Eyre* to Cecilia Ahern.'

'There you are,' said Tania. 'She's a romantic.'

'Yeah, and that's fine in the pages of a book,' said Chris, 'but it's not real life, is it? No one really stops dead in their tracks when they see someone for the first time.'

'You must have done, when you met Lydia,' I said.

Chris stared at me. He didn't appear to know what to say. Tania gave him plenty of time to deny it before stepping in.

'Why do you say that, Alison?' asked Tania.

'Because she's stunning,' I said. 'She's the sort of woman who could cause a multiple pile-up simply by walking down the street.'

Tania turned to Chris. Still he said nothing.

'I think what Alison is getting at,' she said, 'is that there was clearly a strong physical attraction between you and Lydia.'

Chris shrugged.

'Please just admit it,' I said. 'It's nothing to be embarrassed about.'

'OK, so there was. That's what it's all about when you're young, isn't it?'

'And people aren't physically attracted to each other when they get older?' asked Tania.

'Sure,' said Chris, 'but it's different, isn't it? You're looking for other things too.'

'Such as?'

Chris shrugged. 'Reliability.'

I raised my eyebrows. 'You can get that in a Ford Focus,' I said.

Chris managed a smile.

'A sense of humour?' suggested Tania.

'Yeah, of course.'

'OK, so you fell in love with this lady because she seemed reliable and had a good sense of humour?'

'Well, it was a bit more than that, obviously.'

'So tell me about it. Tell me what made you fall in love with her.'

Chris pulled a face. He'd never liked being put on the spot like this. I looked down at my hands, unsure if he was actually going to continue.

'She was very caring,' he said.

'So are nurses,' replied Tania.

Chris gave her a look. But he was smiling as he did so.

'OK, she was fun, huge fun. She didn't take herself at all seriously and was happy to look ridiculous if it made someone else smile. She had an infinite amount of enthusiasm, about books, children, everything really. Whatever she did, she gave it her absolute all. She was incredibly determined and would never give up, even on people like me who could be grumpy old sods at times. And when she walked into a room she absolutely lit it up, better than a fucking Christmas tree. Because when she smiled it just, you know, it got you right here,' he said, thumping his fist on his chest. 'And yet she had absolutely no idea how gorgeous she was. She didn't use it, the way some women do, she was completely oblivious to the effect she had on people. But she made people want to be with her. Not just at that moment but for the rest of their lives –'

He stopped abruptly, apparently as surprised at what had just come out of his mouth as I was. He looked at me. I could barely see his expression through the tears which had gathered in my eyes. But I smiled at him none the less.

'Thank you,' said Tania. 'I think someone in here really needed to hear that.'

'What did you think?' I asked, when we got in the car afterwards.

'It was OK,' said Chris. 'Better than I thought. I liked her.'

'Yeah,' I said. 'Me too.'

'Bit unconventional, isn't she?'

'You could say that.'

'It works, though.'

'Yeah. Look, about what you said –'

'Oh, don't worry,' he said, 'I didn't mean a word of it.'

I looked across at him. He managed to keep his face straight for a long time before he started laughing.

'Bastard,' I said with a smile.

'Come on,' he replied. 'Let's go home.'

From the Counselling Room

I found out what the memorable name he uses for his bank details is. It's 'Kylie'. WTF?

26

'So how's it going?' asked Debbie, as we walked back after dropping the girls off at a summer holiday playscheme in the village on Friday morning.

'Not bad,' I said. 'Better than I thought, actually. I mean, he's talking. He is at least talking. It sometimes takes Tania to give him a good kick to get him there, but he's getting better.'

'Good on him,' said Debbie. 'Dean found it really hard when we went.'

'You went for counselling?'

'Yeah. After the miscarriage. He wouldn't talk about it. I was in bits. I really thought we were going to split up at one point.'

'You never told me.'

'It's not the sort of thing you drop into conversation, is it? Oh, by the way, me and Dean nearly broke up once.'

'No. I guess not. Well, I'm glad it worked for you, anyway.'

'It didn't, really.'

'What do you mean?'

'It was pretty depressing, to tell you the truth. I'd sit there crying for most of the session and Dean couldn't seem to bring himself to say anything, which made me even madder at him. And then we had these horrible silences all the way home in the car.'

'So it didn't help at all?'

'No. She was well-meaning and that, the counsellor. But we both started dreading the sessions. They just seemed to make us more miserable. We stopped going in the end.'

'So how did things get better?'

'Time, I guess. And then me getting pregnant with Ben. Dean couldn't have been more supportive during the pregnancy. He couldn't do enough for me; looked after me when I was throwing up, massaged my feet when they were swollen, the whole works.'

'Did you tell anyone about the counselling? At the time, I mean.'

Debbie shook her head. 'No. We didn't want people to know we were struggling.'

'That's what all my clients say if I ask them. Daft, isn't it? Half the population keeping their relationship problems quiet because they think they're the only ones who've got them.'

'We're British, what do you expect?' smiled Debbie.

'I suppose you're right.'

'Have you told anyone? Apart from me, I mean.'

'Only Barbara.'

'What did she say?'

'She was glad, really glad. She just wants things to work out for us.'

'You must have the loveliest mother-in-law going.'

'I know. She's more of a mum than mine ever was. That's why it's so weird to think that she's not actually his mum.'

'Do you reckon his birth mum still thinks about him?'

'Yeah,' I said. 'You wouldn't forget, would you? Not ever. She's probably haunted by it.'

'She might have other children now,' said Debbie.

'Yeah, but I bet she still misses him. I bet she still thinks about him every single day.'

Chris was packing his camera bag. He'd already told me he didn't have any bookings at the studio. Which, for August, was pretty much unheard of.

'Where are you off to?' I asked.

'It's nice light. Thought I'd go up on the tops, get some stock stuff.'

I nodded. He must have had a lot of stock stuff by now.

'Why don't you take Matilda?'

'You know why, she'll probably start complaining when we're halfway up there.'

'I mean, to do photos of her. Somewhere nice. Outdoors.'

Chris hesitated, clearly unsure. 'I could do, I guess.'

'I was looking through the album, we haven't got any nice pictures of her in the past year. All those lovely ones we've got when she was little, and then this big gap.'

Chris shrugged. 'It's been a tough year.'

'I know. I wasn't having a go. But maybe we should make a bit more of an effort to make it fun for her. Perhaps she could take one of her puppets?'

'I'll give it a go, if she's up for it.'

'She'll be up for it. Go and ask her.'

I wanted him to do it himself. Matilda had a very forgiving nature but she hadn't forgotten her party, I knew that.

Chris went into the lounge where Matilda was watching *Scooby-Doo*. She came running out a few moments later, a big smile on her face.

'Daddy's taking me to his secret place on the moors. And I can take one of my puppets, as long as I try not to get it dirty.'

'Fantastic!' I said. 'You'll have a great time.'

She nodded and disappeared upstairs to get a puppet.

'Well, she certainly seems up for it,' I said.

'Yeah. Thanks.'

'If you can just have her back by midday. Caitlin's coming for her violin lesson at one.'

Chris nodded. He still hadn't seen Caitlin since she'd started coming round. I was pretty sure why. Matilda ran back downstairs brandishing the puppet which Lydia had bought her.

'I'm going to take Amy,' she said.

I looked at Chris, waiting for him to say something. He pursed his lips but said nothing.

I helped Matilda tie the laces on her walking boots. 'Right, off you go then,' I said, kissing her on the top of her head. 'And make sure Amy behaves for Daddy, OK?'

She smiled and skipped out of the door.

'Thanks,' I said to Chris.

He nodded.

'Take as much time as you need,' I said to Caitlin. 'Matilda's still finishing her lunch.'

It had become part of the routine now. Caitlin always came

five or ten minutes early and spent the time sitting in Josh's room. Mostly I left her on her own, but today I sensed she didn't want to be. So I hovered in the doorway for a moment.

'I've told him,' she said. 'That I come here and do this. I want him to know I haven't forgotten.'

She emailed Josh virtually every day, from what she'd told me. She'd never had a reply, of course, but she was convinced that he read them. Or if he wasn't able to at the moment, that he would do one day.

'He'll like that,' I said. 'Knowing that you're close to him.'

I wasn't going to insult her by saying that she didn't have to do this. That maybe she'd be better off trying to forget him instead of immersing herself in his memory. She loved him and this was her way of honouring that love. And who was I, or anyone else, to say that it wasn't the right way of coping or dealing with this situation? It was her way. That was all that mattered.

I went downstairs after Matilda and Caitlin had got started and popped my head round the study door to see if Chris wanted a coffee. There was a photo up on his screen of a girl crouching behind a rock, one arm up in the air inside a puppet who looked uncannily like her. The wind was whipping her hair across her face, and she appeared to be howling with laughter. He had captured not just Matilda but the essence of Matilda.

'I love it,' I said, barely able to speak. 'I absolutely love it.'

Chris turned round. There was pride in his eyes. And a glimmer of hope.

'Thanks,' he said. 'I've got loads more like this. She had a ball up there, she really did. And the light was gorgeous and there was just this fantastic sense of being out in the elements. Of it all being so natural.'

'This is what you should be doing,' I said. 'Not stuck in a studio, which you don't want to be in, and the kids don't want to be there.'

'You think so?'

'I know so. People would pay good money for this, Chris. It's like you've captured her spirit in a bottle. It's incredibly precious. And it's art, it's what you want to do.'

Chris nodded. 'You're right,' he said. 'I can't remember when I've enjoyed doing a portrait so much. And it wasn't just because it was Tilda. I've got loads of ideas of places I could shoot. And I could offer them some really nice canvas prints and black and white prints and everything.'

'There you are, then. Go for it. Make it your thing.'

'Yeah,' he said. 'I think I will. Thank you.'

'Don't be daft.'

'No, I mean it. Thanks.' He got up and kissed me ever so lightly on the lips.

I smiled at him and went out to make the coffee.

It was my turn. I knew that. I understood how these things worked. Chris had talked about his childhood the previous session. Or rather, Tania had coaxed him into letting go of snippets of information. Building up a picture. Of one side of the story, at least.

I sat upright in my chair, wishing I was in hers. That it was me asking the questions, soliciting information, allowing couples the space to reflect.

'So, Alison,' she said, turning to me, 'tell me about your parents.'

I nodded. I could see Chris looking at me out of the corner of his eye. I realised, perhaps for the first time, how little I had discussed it with him too. Maybe he wasn't the only one who'd played things close to his chest. It was hard to know where to start. I opted for the easy bit.

'My mum was a nurse and my dad was a train driver. I guess they ticked those boxes on the "What do you want to do when you grow up?" list and never changed their minds.'

Tania smiled at me. 'And what was their relationship like?'

'They argued a lot. They were both really busy at work, they kind of juggled shifts to look after me, so they weren't actually home together that much. But when they were, they argued.'

'What about?'

'Mostly Dad not doing the things Mum had asked him to do while she was at work. He was pretty rubbish at helping out around the house. I used to follow him around, tidying up and putting things away, so it didn't cause another row.'

'So you saw it as your job to smooth things over?'

I shrugged. 'Damage limitation, I guess.'

'And when they did argue, what did you do?'

'I went to my bedroom. Read books. It was my way of escaping, of blocking everything out.'

'Were you worried they might split up?'

I nodded and found myself swallowing, rather than managing to get the words out.

'Take all the time you need,' said Tania.

I glanced at Chris. His eyes were fixed on my face, his eyes reflecting the hurt in mine.

'I worried about it all the time,' I said. 'And then, when I was fourteen, they sat me down and said they were splitting up, which kind of validated all the worrying. Dad moved into a flat and I only got to see him at weekends. I really missed him. He was much warmer than my mum. She wasn't really like a mum at all.'

'And how long did that last?'

'Until I was fifteen, when Mum got offered a job as a ward sister at a hospital in Portsmouth. Maybe she did it on purpose, because she knew I wasn't happy. I mean, you don't just apply for a job hundreds of miles away without thinking through the consequences, do you? Anyway, she moved down there. So Dad sold the flat and came back to live in our house with me.'

'And how often did you see your mum?'

'Once a month, at first. She'd come up and stay with a friend for the weekend. But it soon got to the point where we only saw each other a few times a year.'

'And did that bother you?'

'Not really, because we didn't seem to have anything to say to each other even then.'

'And your relationship with your parents now?' asked Tania.

I looked down at my hands. 'My dad died three years ago,' I said. 'Heart attack. I haven't seen my mum for years.'

'I'm sorry,' said Tania.

I shrugged. 'Not everyone lives happily ever after, do they?'

'And then Chris came along and gave you a chance to do just that.'

'Yeah.' I glanced over at him.

He managed a hint of a smile.

'It must have been hard, though,' said Tania. 'Making that commitment after what you'd been through. Especially when Chris already had a son. You were taking on a lot.'

'I loved him. It was as simple as that. Anyway, Josh was a delight to have around.'

'You took Lydia on as well.'

'No. She was long gone.'

'Physically, yes, but emotionally?'

'I don't know what you mean,' I said.

Tania looked at me in a way which suggested she didn't believe the assertion any more than I did.

'Sometimes it's harder taking on the absence of someone and the emotional baggage they've left behind, than the person themselves.'

'I didn't think of it like that. Not at the time.'

She nodded again and turned to Chris. 'Why did you ask Alison to move into the house you'd once shared with Lydia?'

'It was where we were living.'

'Did you think about how hard that would be for Alison? Not only was she taking on your son, she was moving into the house you'd lived in with his mother.'

'She was happy to do it,' said Chris. 'I asked her. She said it would be best not to uproot Josh.'

'I understand that,' said Tania. 'And it's admirable that she put him first. But sometimes we put others first at our own cost, and sometimes it's too high a price to pay. Maybe Alison's still paying that price today.'

'What do you mean?' asked Chris.

'I mean that Alison has spent a long time living in Lydia's shadow, physically and emotionally. Perhaps it's time you helped her step out into the light.'

'And you think moving house would do that?'

'It might do.'

'It's not as if there's anything of hers left there.'

'When people have their houses exorcised there's nothing visible, is there? It's a feeling they're trying to get rid of. An atmosphere.'

'You're saying she haunts us now?' said Chris, raising an eyebrow.

'I'm saying her presence hangs very heavily over you both.'

'So how do you propose we get rid of it?'

'You exorcise her from you lives. And that starts with admitting your feelings for her.'

'The only feelings I have for her are negative ones.'

'And what about before?' asked Tania.

Chris hesitated before replying. 'I wasn't still in love with her when Alison moved in, if that's what you're asking.'

'But you had loved her, hadn't you?'

Chris nodded.

'I need to hear it, Chris.'

'Why?'

'Because I think Alison needs to hear it. Because I think she's lived with that silently hanging over her for long enough.'

Chris looked at me.

I blinked hard and fiddled with the button on my cardigan.

'Yes, I loved Lydia,' said Chris. 'I loved her more than I'd ever loved anyone and she hurt me so badly that I didn't think I could ever love again.'

I stared at the wall opposite and tried to stop my bottom lip from quivering.

'But you did, though, didn't you?' said Tania.

'Yes. Because I found someone who was so much better than her that she blew Lydia out of the water.'

'He's talking about you, Alison,' said Tania.

I looked at her and nodded.

'And now you have to believe it,' she said.

'I know.'

'And the reason you don't is because you've spent the last eleven years comparing yourself with her. It's not easy for a woman to compete with an ex, is it?'

'I wasn't competing with her.'

'Only because you didn't think you were even in the same league. And it turns out you were right. Though not in the way you thought.'

I managed a watery smile. Chris reached over and squeezed my hand.

'Chocolates and flowers on the way home,' Tania told him. 'The biggest and best you can find. She deserves nothing less.'

From the Counselling Room

We go to Bognor Regis every year on holiday, have done since we were married. I mean, don't get me wrong, I like Bognor Regis, but sometimes you can't help thinking it would be nice to go somewhere else for a change.

So one year I suggested Eastbourne. He gave me a look like I'd lost my mind and asked if they did day trips to Bognor Regis from there.

27

It was something Josh had once said which made me think of it. He'd told me that Lydia didn't do breakfast. She was one of those people who couldn't stomach anything before ten thirty in the morning. To be honest, I wasn't sure if she even got up before ten thirty most mornings, people working in the music industry probably didn't. She did brunch instead. Coffee and a croissant or something chocolatey. I could only conclude that she had one of those metabolisms which sucked up calories and blew them out into the atmosphere, where they were inhaled by people like me walking past unsuspectingly.

And despite the proliferation of cafes in Hebden Bridge, there was one blindingly obvious place to start. The cafe in the record shop on Market Street. A proper independent record shop. One that, admittedly, had racks of CDs now, but which still managed to smell of the vinyl that had once lined the walls.

Lydia had taken Josh there loads of times. I think it was the only cafe they ever went to. Josh had come back the first time telling me he'd had a hot chocolate which, according to the menu, was 'richer than Pink Floyd, smoother than George Benson and more luxurious than Sade'. I'd even impressed him a little by digging out a Sade album to prove that I had not only heard of her but had the LP to prove it.

I hesitated outside the door, aware that I was effectively stalking her and also that I had no idea what I was going to say if I did find her. I knew I had to do it, though. I couldn't put it off any longer.

I walked in and smiled an acknowledgement at the waist-coated man with long, grey-streaked hair at the counter at the far end, aware that I probably didn't look like one of his usual clients. No doubt he had already written me off as a cafe-only customer. I ordered a hot chocolate, as Josh must have done on numerous occasions, and opted for a small table for two near the counter, rather than one of the stools facing out of the window towards the street.

A song was playing which I didn't recognise. Something suitably edgy and alternative. I imagined Josh poking fun at me for not knowing who it was. Lydia would know it, of course. Lydia knew all those sorts of things.

I sat for a long time. Sipping the hot chocolate, wondering whether Josh used to sit at this table when he came here with her, unsure quite how long it was acceptable to make one hot chocolate last.

A steady trickle of people came in, some for a coffee, others to browse the CDs, several simply to have a chat with the guy at the counter. That was when I realised he probably knew Josh, by sight if not by name. And that he would definitely know Lydia. They had probably shared many stories together. Tales of who she'd met and what she'd got up to. She would have shown him the signed guitar, I was sure of it, before she gave it to Josh.

I looked at my watch. It had been almost an hour. Maybe she'd left Hebden. Done a runner at the same time as Josh. Too distraught over what she'd done to be able to face him again. Or maybe she was with him. Maybe he had forgiven her and they were together somewhere now. London, perhaps, hanging out with her friends in the music business. She might have pulled in a favour or two to get him a job.

It was no good. I was going to have to ask. It was crazy to waste time sitting here if she wasn't even still around. I stood up, pushed my chair back and wandered up to the counter. I decided not to even make a pretence of browsing the CDs.

The guy behind the counter looked up.

'Thanks,' I said. 'My stepson was right, you do a great hot chocolate.'

He nodded his thanks, seemingly still a bit wary.

'He used to come here with his mum,' I continued. 'She was one of your regulars. Long dark hair, works in the music business. Lydia, her name is.'

The man's face flickered into life as if he'd just tuned into a radio station that was worth listening to. 'Still is one of my regulars,' he said. 'She's usually here by now as well. She's got her name on that stool,' he said, pointing to the counter nearest him. 'Reckons our espressos are the best cure for a hangover, and she has a fair few of those.'

I nodded and smiled, as if I found that as endearing as he clearly did.

'And she's usually in most days?' I asked.

'Yep. Think Wednesdays might be her laundry day, mind. She's usually a bit later. Comes in while her wash is doing.'

I nodded. I didn't want to sit back down now. It would make it too obvious. 'Right. Well, thanks again,' I said, turning to leave.

'Who shall I say was asking after her?'

I hesitated before turning back. 'Don't worry, thanks. I'll catch up with her myself.'

He nodded.

I left the shop. He'd made it easy for me. There was only one launderette in town. I walked over the bridge and turned left, my pumps soundless on the cobbles, like a cat silently stalking its prey. I stopped at the door of the launderette. She was in there. I could see her through the window, cramming the last of some clothes into a machine. It was a dark wash, of course. I couldn't imagine Lydia doing whites. Part of me felt uneasy. That it was somehow wrong to be doing this here, when my prey was most vulnerable, innocently brandishing her smalls. There was nothing innocent about Lydia, though. I knew that already.

I opened the door. I don't know why Lydia looked round. It's not as if you would expect someone to come looking for you in a launderette. I wondered if the guy from the record shop had phoned her. Warned her someone had been asking questions. She stared at me. I half expected her to put her hands up in the air. To wave a pillowcase in surrender. There was no white flag, though. Just a steely glare.

I walked a few paces closer to her. The woman who had caused so much grief. So much pain. I wanted to hate her. I also wanted to hurt her. I couldn't do either, though. Because I was Alison. The woman who fixed things. Tried to make them better.

'Hi,' I said.

She eyed me warily, a box of washing powder in one hand. 'What are you doing here?' she asked.

'I wanted to see you,' I said. 'I wondered if you knew where Josh was?'

A slight frown creased her brow. I knew instantly that she didn't. If you were going to try to fake surprise, you would do it much better than that.

'Why should I know where he is?' she asked.

'He ran away,' I said. 'The morning after you came round.'

She stared at me, the frown increasing. 'You've not heard from him?'

I shook my head. The washing powder was shaking in her hand. I walked up and took it from her. Placed it on top of the machine. Her hand shook even more now that it was empty.

'I thought he might have been in touch,' I said.

She went on staring. I noticed for the first time how rough she looked. Her hair was lank and needed washing. Her face gaunt. Her eyes heavily made up, as ever, but heavier still with shadows.

'Is that everything?' I asked, pointing towards the machine. She nodded.

I picked up the powder and poured some into the dispenser tray. Shut it, turned the knob to forty degrees and pulled it out. The machine whirred into action. The water started hissing in, spitting venom at the dirt. Laughing as it smothered it.

'Is there somewhere we can go to talk?' I asked, hoping she wouldn't say the cafe.

She nodded. 'My place,' she said. 'You'd better come back to my place.'

We didn't speak on the walk there. It was as if we were both saving it up, keeping the words in our heads until we found some walls for them to bounce back off. She only lived a few streets away. There were kids playing in the road outside. Kicking a ball about in what appeared to be a concerted effort to disprove the theory that children didn't do that any more.

She stopped outside a battered blue wooden door and fumbled in her pocket for the key. Her hand was still shaking as she turned it in the lock. I followed her inside, into a gloomy hallway. The whole place was going to be gloomy. She was on the wrong side of the valley to catch the light.

'It's through there,' she said, pointing to another door at the end of the hall.

The room beyond was pretty unremarkable in the way that rented flats are. Cream-painted walls, a rug on the wooden floor which may have been her own and a worn green sofa with a throw over it beneath the window. A hallway ran off it to three further wooden doors, one of which would have been the room where she'd slept with Tom.

'Do you mind?' asked Lydia, holding up a packet of cigarettes which had been lying on the table.

I shook my head. I did mind, but I was in her flat. These were her rules.

She lit it, took a long, slow drag and looked at me. 'Did he take his stuff with him?' she asked.

'About half of his clothes, and various bits and pieces in his rucksack.'

'Passport?'

'Yeah. We've got no way of knowing if he's used it, of course.'

'Are the cops not looking for him?'

'We registered him as missing with them. But at the end of the day he's sixteen, and he left of his own accord. His details are on their database, but they haven't got the resources to do anything more than that.'

Lydia blew out. 'Fucking hell,' she said.

'I take it he hasn't been in touch, then.'

'Nothing since I came round. I texted him and called all that night and the next day. It just went to voicemail.'

'I know,' I said. 'Me too.'

It was weird to think about it. Both of us pulling from different directions. Both of us reaching the same message. Hearing the same Josh.

'I just thought he hated me. Wanted nothing more to do with me. I can't say I blamed him.'

'He was hurt, that was all. The people we love hurt us the most.'

'I didn't know he was Josh's friend,' she said. 'I would never have done it otherwise.'

'Why did you do it, anyway?'

'It's like you said. I'm a sad, lonely woman who knows she's past her prime. I screwed up on the only man I ever truly loved and I walked out on my own son. And you wonder why I hate myself? Why I'm left picking up any scraps of love or lust that are thrown my way?'

She walked across to the window and took another drag on the cigarette.

'Why did you leave?' I asked. 'When he was a baby.'

'Because I knew I wasn't good enough. I loved him, I loved him to bits. That's why it scared me so much, when I started drinking again.'

'Chris said you might have had post-natal depression.'

Lydia shrugged. 'It's no excuse, is it? Not for what I did.'

'It's not an excuse, but it explains it.'

'Being drunk in charge of a baby? I don't think so.'

'You needed help. Professional help.'

Lydia rolled her eyes. 'You don't let up, do you? Thinking you lot are the answer to everything.'

'I'm not saying that. I'm saying that a lot of new mums find it hard, incredibly hard, to adjust to being responsible for this tiny person.'

'I bet you didn't.'

I looked down. 'I did, actually. I didn't change a nappy for the first two weeks after Matilda was born. I wasn't capable. I was a wreck. Matilda wasn't latching on properly, so I couldn't feed her at first. I felt such a failure. How was I going to be able to look after her if I couldn't manage that most basic of things?'

Lydia stared at me. 'You didn't walk out on her, though, did you?'

'No, because I had Chris to support me. To show me how to do everything, because he'd been there before with you and Josh and he knew what he was doing. He even helped me with the feeding, got me to hold her in a different position. He probably remembered how you did it. Though he didn't tell me that, of course.'

Lydia sat down on the wooden chair next to the table. She traced her fingernail along the grain in the wood. 'I envy you, you know.'

'Me?'

'That day, when I turned up at your house. You looked like such a perfect family. You, all warm and radiant, your beautiful little girl, Chris doing his protective "They're mine, so fuck off and don't come anywhere near them" routine. You had what I could never have. You had a happy family. Because you were a good mum. You were what I could never be. Why I had to go.'

I sighed and went to sit down on the chair opposite her. 'It's ridiculous, isn't it?' I said.

'What is?'

'I've spent eleven years trying and failing to compete with you.'

'Why would you do that?'

'Because he loved you so much. It was there, in the house, etched into the bloody stonework. How much he loved you. And when I first moved in, every time I entered a room I imagined him being there with you. Unable to take his eyes off your face, stroking your hair, making love with you.'

'He never wanted me. I used to kid myself he did, but he didn't. Not really.'

'He did,' I said. 'He loved you more than he'd ever loved anyone in his life. He told me so.'

'When?'

'Last week. During our counselling session.'

'You're going for counselling?'

'Yeah. Things haven't been good between us since, well, you know. He's taken it all pretty badly. It's brought up a lot of stuff that he's never dealt with.'

She turned to look at me. 'He's told you, hasn't he?'

I nodded. 'Barbara told me, actually. Last month. She was worried about him.'

Lydia stubbed her cigarette out in the overflowing ashtray on the table and shut her eyes. 'I didn't do it on purpose. Leaving Josh wrapped up like that when I went. I didn't want him to be cold, that was all. It was only after I left that I realised what it might look like. That he would think I did it to get at him.'

'Why didn't you tell him you were leaving? You could have saved him coming back and finding Josh like that.'

'I didn't know I was leaving until after he'd gone to work. And once I'd made my mind up, I was determined to do it. If I'd called Chris to tell him, or taken Josh to him at work, he would have tried to stop me going and he would probably have succeeded.

'It was the hardest thing I've ever done, walking out on Josh. And I couldn't let him stop me doing it, because it was the right thing for Josh.'

'Why do you think that?'

'Jesus, he's bloody amazing. He's the best teenager I've ever met. He's funny, he's sharp and he's incredibly caring, and that's down to you and Chris, isn't it? That's the only reason I can live with myself. Because I know I did the right thing.'

'So you were basically putting him up for adoption, for a new mother?'

'Yeah. Chris took his time, as it turned out, but he got there in the end.'

I shook my head. 'So why did you come back?'

'Because I wanted to see that for myself. And I wanted him to know that I wasn't the demon he probably thought I was.'

'Chris never bad-mouthed you. Not that I know of, anyway. He gave Josh a box of memories of you. Things he'd kept over the years. A photo of you with him when he was a baby.'

Lydia turned to look out of the window, not realising I could see the reflection of her tears in the glass. 'I've been such a cow,' she said.

'No, you haven't.'

'Stop being so fucking nice, will you?' she screamed. 'I don't deserve it. I fucking lied to him. To them both. And now look what's happened. Just when I think I can't screw up any worse than I have done . . .' Her voice trailed off.

I knew straight away. Something lifted inside me, the world lurched back into focus. 'Josh is Chris's son, isn't he?'

She bit her lip and nodded. 'I'm so sorry.'

'I never doubted it, but Chris did.'

'Because he never got it. How I couldn't even look at any other man apart from him, let alone cheat on him. I slept around before I met him, and I've slept around since, but I never messed around when I was with him. I was far too much in love with him to do that.'

She sat silently, her head bent over the table, the tears dripping onto the wood, her body shaking, as if awaiting its inevitable punishment.

'Well, hit me or something, for Christ's sake,' she said. 'Or, better still, go and get a kitchen knife. I'll do it myself, you haven't got to get your hands dirty. I'll even wipe the handle before I do it.'

'No,' I said. 'Because that won't help anyone, will it? Least of all Chris or Josh.'

'It will help me,' she said.

I got up and pulled one of those reusable shopping bags out of my handbag. 'Where's your booze?' I asked.

She frowned at me before pointing to the door. 'Kitchen cupboard. Top left.'

I went through to the kitchen, took two bottles of vodka and one of gin from the cupboard and put them in my bag. I opened the drawers until I found the one in which she kept the sharp knives, then wrapped them in a tea towel and put them in too before going back into the main room.

'Any tablets?' I asked. 'I'm going to go through your bathroom cabinet, anyway. So it's better that you tell me now.'

'Just painkillers,' she said. 'Bottom right.'

I went and got them from the bathroom, checking the other shelves just in case. I went back into the room with my haul. She stared up at me. The eyeliner and mascara had run and smudged across her face. She looked a mess.

'Purse?'

She pointed to her handbag.

I took it out and checked her bank card was inside too. 'You've got enough food to live on for a couple of days,' I said. 'So you won't be needing this. It's for your own good, OK? Come and see me when you run out of food. Have you got anyone nearby you can call?'

She shook her head.

I picked up the phone book on the table, opened it on the help pages and put it in front of her. 'There are numbers there of people who can help you,' I said. 'You need to get some help.'

She nodded.

I had no idea if she meant it, but I had done all I could. It was no longer up to me. I squeezed her shoulder before walking to the door and seeing myself out.

I walked back down the hill into town, the bottles clinking against each other. I felt as if there were two lifts inside my stomach and someone was playing a game, calling them to the top and bottom in turn.

I went straight there. I didn't want to leave it a moment longer to put him out of his misery. I pushed the door of the studio, heard the bell ring. The sound of feet coming slowly down the stairs.

He would think the worst, I knew he would.

'Everything's OK. I haven't heard anything.' I said it almost before his face appeared.

He stared at me.

I took a few steps towards him. 'Josh is yours,' I said. 'Lydia lied. I've just seen her. She never cheated on you. She never even thought about it.'

Chris screwed his eyes tight shut.

I dropped the bag on the floor and ran to put my arms around him.

Behind me, one of Lydia's bottles rolled across the room.

From the Counselling Room

We were having sex, and he stopped right in the middle of it and said, 'Oh, before I forget, Mum said would you mind picking up some HP sauce for her next time you're in Tesco?'

And he just went back to it. Like that was OK.

28

'It's getting near Josh's birthday,' said Matilda as she put on her school uniform on Friday morning.

She was right, of course. It had always been the thing which had got Josh over the disappointment of having to go back to school after the summer holidays, the reminder that this meant his birthday was approaching.

'Yes,' I said. 'It is . . .'

There was a pause. I wasn't sure whether she wanted me to fill the gap or whether I should leave it to her.

'Do you think he'll come back for his birthday?' she asked, stopping for a moment with her head halfway through her school sweatshirt.

'I don't know,' I said. 'I hope so.'

'I would,' she said, pulling it down over her head. 'If I was travelling around somewhere, I'd make sure I was back in time for my birthday. It would be really silly to miss it. I mean, you don't get another one for a year.'

I smiled and nodded. 'That's true.'

'What if he doesn't come back for it?' she asked.

I sat down on her bed. 'Then we'll just have to hope that, wherever he is, he's having a nice day.'

She looked at me, clearly dissatisfied with my answer. 'Well, it won't be nice if he's not here with us, will it?'

I reached for her hand and pulled her closer to me. 'You miss him, don't you?'

She nodded, her brown eyes bulging with sadness. 'I thought he was only going to be gone for a little while.'

'So did we, sweetheart.'

'Then why hasn't he come back? Is he mad at us? Is it because of his mum and all the shouting?'

I sighed. It was getting harder and harder to be economical with the truth around her.

'Josh has had a lot happen in the past year. I think he needs some time on his own to sort things out in his head.'

'What if he never sorts them out?'

'Let's just hope he does, eh, love?'

Matilda nodded.

I kissed her on the top of her head.

'Are we going to buy him birthday presents and cards, like we normally do?' she asked.

It was a good question, and one I wasn't prepared for. I was caught between not wanting to raise false hopes and the desire to carry on as normal. And due to the lack of a parenting book with a chapter entitled 'How to deal with birthdays if one of your children has run away', I was going to have to come down on one side or the other.

'I'm not sure. What do you think?'

'I think we should. I think he'd be disappointed if he came home on his birthday and we hadn't got him anything.'

'Yep, you're probably right. How about we go shopping tomorrow to get them?'

Matilda smiled and gave me a hug.

'But please remember, love, that if he's not home for his birthday, it's not a problem, we'll just save them for when he is, OK?'

Matilda nodded. The smile remained.

And I hoped that the pile of presents from missed birthdays and Christmases wouldn't get too big before that day came.

'So how are you feeling now?' Tania asked Chris at our next session, when we'd updated her on Lydia's confession.

I knew what she was getting at. It was almost as if he had been clinging on to the idea that Josh wasn't his son as a way of trying to lessen the impact of his disappearance.

'Relieved. Obviously massively relieved.'

'You really didn't think he was yours?'

'I don't know,' said Chris. 'Everything happened so quickly, it was hard to get my head around it. But the fact that Josh ran away seemed to cement it in my head. The idea that it was true.'

'Because you thought he believed it?'

'Yeah.'

'And now you know it's not true?'

Chris shrugged. 'It makes it harder, in a way. Because I can't pretend that he's not my son, my responsibility. It focuses everything on the fact that he's missing. Nothing else matters any more.'

'Your relationship matters,' said Tania.

'Yeah, of course,' said Chris, looking down at the floor.

'And how do you think it's been affected by Josh's disappearance?'

'Pretty badly, obviously. I just haven't been able to talk about it. I've wanted to, but it's been too painful. Too many things tied up with it.'

'But now you've talked to Alison about those things and now you know that you're Josh's father, do you think you'll find it easier? Do you think you could give it a try?'

Chris looked at me and then back to Tania. 'Yeah,' he said.

'Good. And what about you, Alison?' she asked. 'How have you felt during all of this?'

I hesitated before replying, not wanting to make Chris feel bad but knowing I needed to be honest too.

'Frozen out,' I said. 'Because he wouldn't talk to me. And because he blamed me, which is understandable, I know. I mean, it is all my fault.'

'Because you didn't tell Chris that Josh was seeing Lydia again, you mean?'

'Yeah.'

'Remind me why you did that, Alison.'

'Because I thought it would make things worse. Cause big rows.'

'You thought the arguments would start again?'

'Yeah.'

'And you've always hated arguments, haven't you? Always worried they'd cause your family to break up. Ever since you were a little girl.'

I nodded, trying to blink back the tears. Chris reached over and squeezed my hand.

'You get it now, don't you?' she asked Chris. He nodded.

'Now, obviously,' continued Tania, 'you can come back next week and we can do a big session on how we go about forgiving each other for being screwed up by what happened to us when we were younger. Or you two can have a couple of weeks off, sort it out yourselves and spend the money you save on doing something nice together.'

Chris gave her a sheepish grin. 'The latter, I think.'

'Glad to hear it. Now bugger off and be good to each other.'

Lydia arrived while Chris and Matilda were out. I'd arranged it that way when she'd texted me. She stood on the doorstep looking considerably better than the last time I'd seen her, although that wasn't hard.

'Come in a minute,' I said.

She stepped inside. I had a carrier bag of her things ready in the hall. I picked it up and passed it to her.

'Not these,' she said, picking out the drink bottles and handing them to me. 'I won't be needing these.'

I nodded and took them from her. 'I'm sorry,' I said. 'I realised afterwards I should have gone and got your washing for you.'

'Don't be daft,' she said. 'It was fine. They know me there. They kept it for me.'

I nodded.

Lydia looked down at the floor. 'I'm going away for a bit,' she said.

'Right.'

'To my brother's.'

'Oh. I didn't know you had one.'

'Yeah, he's ten years older than me. He lives in Cumbria. He's got a family and that. I'm going to have to be on my best behaviour.'

'Good,' I said. 'I don't mean about the behaviour. I mean, that you've got somewhere to go. Someone to support you.'

'He got out before my mum got really bad with her drinking. He knows, though. He knows all about it and what to do.'

I nodded. 'Is she still around, your mum?'

Lydia shrugged. 'I don't know, but she's no good to anyone even if she is.'

We were silent for a moment. Lydia avoiding eye contact.

'Well, good luck, then,' I said.

'Cheers. I'm not planning on coming back. Not until I get myself sorted, anyway. And maybe not even then. I think I need a clean break. I've emailed Josh, told him that Chris is his father. Apologised to him. Not that he'll ever forgive me, of course, but I thought he had the right to know.'

'Thank you,' I said.

She turned to go, then looked back. 'You will let me know, won't you? If you hear anything, I mean.'

I nodded.

'Thanks,' she said. 'He's very lucky to have a mum like you.'

It was nearly time for Bob. I'd miss him, when he finally decided to stop coming. He was like a faithful Labrador lying at your feet: dependable, reliable, easy to please. The ideal start to a Monday morning, really.

I poked my head round the door to invite him in. It wasn't Bob, though. It was Jayne. She looked different from the last time I'd seen her. Her face was bordering on gaunt. The shadows under her eyes were darker and deeper.

'Hello, Jayne,' I said.

'I hope you don't mind me coming,' she said. 'Bob said you wouldn't.'

'Of course I don't. It's lovely to see you. Please, come through.'

She picked up her handbag and walked past me into the room. She smelt of Yardley perfume and sadness. She took a seat, the handbag perched on her knees. Seemingly glad of the handles to hang on to.

'So, how are you?' I said.

'I won't beat about the bush,' she replied. 'There's no point, because Bob will have told you, anyway. I haven't been good and that's why I'm here.'

'He's been ever so concerned about you.'

'I know. He's a good man. I'm lucky to have him, really. Never thought I'd end up with someone like him.'

'Why not?'

'Too good for me, really. Way too good.'

I decided to let it go for now. 'Anyway, I hear congratulations are in order. Bob told me you're going to be a grandma.'

Jayne nodded. 'Yes, that's right. Cassie's due in February. February, of all months.' She fiddled with the handles of her bag. I wasn't sure what she was getting at.

'Bob said you'd been finding it difficult.'

She nodded again, still not making eye contact.

'That you weren't planning to go over for the birth.'

'No. I don't think I'd be much help, really. Don't want to get under her feet.'

We both knew that wasn't the real reason. I let her settle herself for a moment before continuing.

'I'm not going to put any pressure on you, Jayne, but I know you came here today for a reason and I want to spend as much time as I can helping you, rather than keeping up the pretence.'

Jayne looked up at me. I could see her hands were shaking.

'I want to tell you,' she said, 'but it's harder than I thought.'

'I understand. I assure you you'll feel better, though, once you've shared it.'

Jayne sat for a moment, twiddled with the handles, adjusted her glasses.

'If I went over for the birth,' she said. 'I would see that baby coming into the world, and I would have its tiny hand grip my finger and I would hold it and I would cuddle it and kiss it. But very soon, far too soon, I would have to leave it, say goodbye and come away. And I couldn't bear it. I couldn't bear to do that again.'

She opened her handbag and started rummaging around for a tissue. I took one from the box on the table and handed it to her. I pulled my chair up next to hers so I could sit holding her hand.

'Cassie wasn't your first child, was she?'

Jayne shook her head. A strangled noise, something between a whimper and a sob, came from inside her.

'Please tell me what happened, Jayne. I won't judge and I won't tell anyone outside this room, if you don't want me to, OK?'

She nodded. 'I were sixteen,' she said. 'Sweet sixteen, supposedly. I worked in an office. Doing a bit of typing and filing and that. I were a pretty little thing, everyone said. It were nice to have that said about you. I didn't let it go to my head, though. And I didn't do anything to give him the wrong idea. At least, I don't think I did.'

'Who was this, Jayne?'

'Robert, my sister's husband. They'd only been married a couple of years. They had a baby, Julie, she were called, after Julie Christie. Pretty little dot, she were too, I were right proud to be her auntie.

'I'd just babysat for them while they'd been to pictures. First time they'd been out together since the birth. Good as gold she were, just started crying a few minutes before they got back. I had a bottle ready so my sister took her straight upstairs to feed her and change her and that was when he did it. Forced himself on me, like.'

I felt Jayne's hand tighten her grip on mine.

'What did you do?'

'Nothing. I didn't really understand what were happening at first. And by the time I did, it were too late. I couldn't get a sound out, I were too shocked.'

'What happened afterwards?'

'He didn't say owt. Just zipped himself up and took me back home in his car. Told me that if I said a word to anyone, he'd tell them I'd come on to him. That I'd been asking for it.

I made a mess in his car, of course. Because, well, you know, it were first time and that. I crept indoors and went straight up to my room and took off my dress, put it in a bag with my undies. It all went in dustbin next morning.'

'You didn't tell anyone? Not even your mum?'

'No. I felt so ashamed. Like it must have been my fault. I didn't say a word. And then, of course, my period didn't come, or the one after. I didn't realise straight away. I mean, nobody talked about that sort of thing in those days, not around where we lived, anyway. But then I started feeling sick when I woke up every morning, and that were when I knew.'

'So what did you do?'

'Nothing. I didn't know what to do at first so I didn't say owt. But then I went downstairs for breakfast one morning and I were physically sick in kitchen, right in front of my mum. I had to tell her. I told her it were Robert and what happened. She said I were making it up, that I'd got myself in trouble and I were a dirty little girl and I'd have to get rid of it.

'I couldn't, mind. I couldn't bring myself to do it. She booked me into a clinic. Told my father we were going away for a couple of days, some sort of shopping trip. So the night before, I packed a few bits and pieces. And first thing in morning I crept out of the house and caught a bus down to train station. I got on a train to Leeds and when I got there the next train out were to Manchester, so I got on that. I panicked a bit when we got past Bradford, mind. I'd never been outside of Yorkshire before. So I got off at Halifax instead.'

I realised it was me holding Jayne's hand tighter this time.

Too tight. I loosened my grip slightly. All the time trying to remember how old Jayne had said she was.

'Where did you go?'

'I went straight to the council and got a flat. You could do, in those days. I got a job too, a few days later. Doing some secretarial work for an accountant. Nice chap, he was, must have been near retirement age.'

'And what about when you started to show?'

'He didn't say a word. Too much of a gentleman. I'm sure he didn't approve, but main thing was he didn't fire me. I told him I were going to stay with an auntie in Scarborough for the birth. He gave me an extra pound in my pay packet the week I left.'

'And then what?'

'I stayed in my flat and waited mostly. Kept myself to myself, as they say. There were one nosey woman, so I told her the same story. Just to stop people asking questions, like.'

'So you were on your own for the birth?'

Jayne nodded. 'When the time came, I put the radio on to cover up any noise I might make. It were the hardest bit, trying to keep quiet through it all. And then he came, just before midnight, just when I thought I wasn't going to be able to do it on my own.'

'A boy?' My voice was breaking slightly as I asked.

'Yes. I always thought it would be a boy. I remember picking him up off the bed, wrapping him in towel. I couldn't quite believe he were real. I sat there holding him until the placenta came out. That were more of a shock than the baby, to be honest. I cut the cord with my kitchen scissors and flushed it down toilet, didn't know what else to do with it. He were so good, though. I did a bottle for him, it were the only thing I'd got in ready, and he drank it and went to sleep in my arms. He didn't cry or owt. It were almost as if he knew. I just lay there with him, looking at his little face while he slept, too scared to sleep, just waiting for the sun to come up.'

'And then what?'

'I put a nappy on him. Wrapped him up in a blanket to keep him nice and warm. My case were all packed ready. I put the towels in a brown paper sack. I'd stripped the bed first so sheets didn't get spoilt. I were all paid up with my rent, so I just left key on kitchen table, put the sack in the dustbin on the way out and went.'

For a second I wasn't sure. Maybe I'd got it wrong.

'You left the baby there?'

'Oh no,' said Jayne. 'I wouldn't have done that. They'd have traced me, see. And he might not have been found for hours. No, I took him with me, like I'd planned. It wasn't easy, carrying him and the case. We didn't have those slings they have now in those days. I actually carried him in a shopping bag, so no one would see. He were fine, quite happy in there he were. And then, when I got there, I just popped him on doorstep, making sure he were under cover in case it started raining. And that were it. I couldn't stop, because they were going to be opening at eight thirty. So I just had to turn and walk away, crying my heart out as I went.'

She was crying again now. She dabbed at the corners of her eyes with the scrunched-up tissue in her other hand.

'Where did you leave him, Jayne?' I asked, barely able to get the words out.

'Outside a doctor's surgery,' she said.

I nodded and gulped. I couldn't hold the tears back, though. Not any longer.

'I walked straight to train station afterwards,' she said. 'Let the wind dry my eyes on the way. I got a single ticket to Leeds, thought I could lose myself there in the big city, see.'

'And how long ago was this?' I asked. Just to be sure, quite sure, about it.

'The fifteenth of February 1969. I've never forgotten. I couldn't if I wanted to. Not with him being a Valentine's baby. Every year it gets worse as soon as I see the cards in the shops.'

'That day you didn't come,' I said. 'When Bob said you'd locked yourself in the toilet.'

Jayne nodded. 'It were worse than ever this year, what with Cassie having gone too. I just couldn't bear it.

'I don't even have a photo of him to remember him by. The only thing I've got is this.' She opened her handbag and took out a tiny clear plastic case and handed it to me. 'He had all this lovely dark hair, see. I snipped a little bit off before I left the flat. It's all I've got left of him.'

I looked down at the case in my trembling hand. Inside was a lock of dark, curly hair.

Chris's hair.

From the Counselling Room

It happened on Christmas Eve.

I was doing Santa's sacks for the children, trying to be as quiet as I could. And he walked past the plate they'd left out for Santa and stopped and stared at me and asked why there was a biscuit instead of a mince pie. And I had to tell him that they'd sold out in Lidl and I didn't have time to go anywhere else.

He picked up the vegetable knife – the one I'd used to cut the carrot in two, because it was a big one and Maisie had been worried that Rudolph wouldn't have been able to manage it whole – and he stabbed me with it in the hand. The blood was oozing out everywhere, it looked like I'd been nailed to the cross, and I looked at him and I realised for the first time that I meant nothing to him, absolutely nothing. Not compared to a mince pie.

29

I sat in the car at the end of the morning's sessions, still trying to take it all in. I had found Chris's mother. Without even looking. I hadn't told her, of course. I would need to seek some professional supervision before working out what to do there. It wasn't something they tended to cover in general training, discovering that one of your clients was actually your mother-in-law. I'd checked her date of birth on the file as soon as she'd left. It all fitted. There was no room left for any doubt.

Jayne had gone home to tell Bob. Said she thought she could do it, now she'd told the story once. She'd made an appointment for them to come back later in the week. Which just left me, wondering if I should tell my husband.

We hadn't talked about whether he'd want to meet her if he could. There'd been no point. Until now, that was. I felt like a gatecrasher at a family gathering. It seemed so unfair, that I should get to meet her first, even if it was accidental. But I knew that, if I was going to tell him, there was one other person I should tell first.

And also, something I wanted to do. Something which I didn't think Barbara or Chris had ever done.

*

Barbara was in the garden when I got there. On her knees, digging with her trowel in amongst the rose bushes. She looked up and waved at me, her hands caked with earth. All I could think was that Jayne would never do that. Jayne was definitely a gardening gloves and hoe kind of person.

'Hello, love,' she said. 'This is a nice surprise. Everything OK?'

I'd become used to the question over the past few months. A coded way of asking if there was any news without having to state what the news might be about.

'Everything's fine,' I said. 'I could do with a cup of tea and a chat, though.'

Barbara nodded, put down her trowel and stood up.

I followed her into the house and waited until we were sitting in the front room, two cups of tea and a plate of rich tea biscuits on the table between us, before saying anything.

'There's a couple in their sixties I've been counselling for a while,' I said. 'They've both recently retired and their daughter's emigrated to Australia. The husband thought it was empty nest syndrome making his wife sad. Anyway, it turned out it wasn't that at all.'

Barbara nodded. She knew I didn't usually talk about my clients, but she clearly had no idea where this was going.

'The lady told me this morning that she'd got pregnant when she was sixteen. That she had the baby on her own in secret and left him outside a doctor's surgery. In Halifax.'

Barbara put her hand to her mouth.

'It's definitely her,' I said. 'The dates check out and everything. Chris was actually born on Valentine's Day, just before midnight. She didn't have a photo or anything but she did have a lock of his hair.'

'Good grief,' said Barbara. 'After all this time.'

I nodded. 'I know. It was quite a shock. I didn't tell her, obviously. And I haven't spoken to Chris yet, either.'

Barbara looked at me, uncertainty written across her face. 'Are you going to tell him?'

'I don't know. I think I should. There've been too many secrets in our family. But I didn't want to do it without speaking to you first.'

'It doesn't matter what I think.'

'Of course it does. You're his mother.'

'She's his mother.'

'No. She's just the woman who gave birth to him.'

Barbara gave a little smile. 'Well, for what it's worth, I think he has the right to know.'

I looked down at my hands. 'There is one other thing. Something which makes it more difficult.'

I saw her face tense, her hands clench in her lap. I wished I could find a nicer way to say it but there wasn't one.

'The lady, Jayne, her name is, she told me how she got pregnant. It was her brother-in-law. He raped her.'

Barbara's eyes screwed up tight. I went across and sat down on the carpet next to her, rubbing her arm. When she finally opened her eyes, a solitary tear ran down her cheek.

'I always wondered,' she said. 'I mean, I hoped it were just a lass who'd got into trouble with her boyfriend or summat. But I always knew it could be worse. Ken told me not to think about it. You can't help yourself, though.'

'I just don't know how Chris would take it,' I said. 'It's such a horrible thing to hear.'

'It is,' she said. 'But not knowing how you came into the world must be pretty horrible too.'

I nodded. 'You're right. I'll tell him tonight.'

Barbara looked at me. 'Give him a hug from me, love, will you? I know it's daft, but he's still my little boy.'

I watched Chris playing with Matilda after her bath. Some daft game of theirs which involved a towel monster and the dreaded comb. He was making an effort, a real effort, I knew that. Because the gaping hole inside didn't heal over like the one in an earlobe which no longer sported an earring. This one was raw. You could still cut yourself on the edges, it was so sharp. And however much you smiled on the outside, it didn't numb the pain within.

He still had a smile on his face when he came downstairs from reading to her.

'What?' I said.

'She was doing Miss Root's voice in *Demon Dentist*. Scary. Very scary.'

'You know the boy's dad dies at the end, don't you?'

'I thought you didn't skip ahead? You always used to say you hated people doing that.'

'I know. Sometimes you have to, though. So you can help someone else to prepare for what's to come.'

Chris sat down opposite me at the kitchen table. The smile had disappeared from his face.

'It's nothing about Josh,' I said, knowing what he was thinking. 'It's about you.'

He frowned at me.

'I need you to know that I didn't go digging for information. This isn't a case of me meddling or anything like that. It was pure chance, really. Although, I suppose, in my line of work the chances are slightly higher than they'd be for most people.'

'Are you going to tell me what you're talking about?' asked Chris.

'One of my clients shared a secret with me today. The thing that's been eating away at her for years. Only it turns out it's the same thing that's been eating away at you.'

Chris was frowning at me now.

I reached out and held his hand. 'She abandoned her baby when she was sixteen,' I said. 'Outside a doctor's surgery in Halifax. On February the fifteenth 1969.'

I left the words to penetrate for a moment.

Chris looked at me, his eyes locking on to mine as if he might plummet from view without them. 'So it's definitely her?'

'She told me the date. You were actually born on Valentine's Day, not the fifteenth. She even has a lock of your hair . . .' I paused and reached down to the floor for my bag. 'I also went to the library and found a copy of the *Courier*, from the day she left you. Just to make sure it all tied up. I've got it here, if you want to have a look.'

I took a photocopy out of my bag and held it out to him. He hesitated before taking it, turning it over and staring at the photo of the baby underneath the front-page headline: 'Shopping bag baby abandoned outside doctor's'.

Chris looked up at me. 'This is me.'

I nodded. 'I know. I cried when I saw it. I cried a lot.'

Chris read it before looking up again. 'Did she say what time she left me?'

'About half an hour before you were found. She knew what time they opened. She made sure you'd be safe.'

'Did you tell her? About me, I mean.'

'No. I wanted to talk to you first. I don't have to tell her anything, if you don't want me to.'

Chris blew out and shook his head. 'I don't know. It's such a massive thing. I don't know what to do. What if I don't like her?'

'You would. She's nothing like your mum, though.'

'What do you mean?'

'She goes to WI meetings, paints watercolours, has her hair done regularly. That sort of thing.'

Chris nodded slowly.

'She's about my height, I think. Average size. Wears glasses. It's hard to say if she looks like you. I'd never noticed it before, obviously. Maybe a bit, around the chin, but that might just be because I was looking for it.'

Chris sat for a while.

'Did she tell you everything? About why she did it, I mean.'

I nodded. 'She was incredibly brave. Her mother wanted her to have an abortion. She couldn't bear to let that happen. So she ran away from home to give birth to you.'

'At sixteen? Jeez,' said Chris.

'She hasn't seen her family since,' I said.

'Did she tell you how it happened?'

'Yeah. Although it wasn't an easy story for her to tell.'

'Was she . . . ?'

I nodded, helping him out. 'It was her sister's husband. One night when she'd been babysitting for them.'

Chris shut his eyes.

I squeezed his hand. 'I'm sorry,' I whispered.

I sat with him, still holding his hand for a long time before he spoke again.

'Did she tell anyone?'

'Only her mum, after she found out she was pregnant. She didn't believe her, though. Or maybe didn't want to believe her.'

Chris looked down at the table. 'Has she got a family of her own?'

'Yeah. They've got a daughter who lives in Australia. She's expecting a baby in February.'

Chris sat for a while longer.

'So what happens now?' he asked.

'That's up to you. She's coming to see me again on Thursday, once she's told her husband.'

'He doesn't know?'

'No. She was too embarrassed to tell him. Thought he'd think badly of her. That's why they've been having problems.'

Chris shook his head. 'Do you think she'd want to meet me?'

'Yeah. I'm pretty sure she would.'

'I don't know how Mum would feel about it.'

'She's fine with it,' I said. 'I already checked. I wasn't trying to interfere or anything, I just knew you'd ask. She's happy for you to do whatever you think is best.'

Chris blew out and looked up at the ceiling.

'Barbara will always be your mum, love. Nothing's going to change that.'

'I know. It's a weird thing, that's all. Deciding if you want to meet the woman who gave birth to you.'

'You don't have to make your mind up now,' I said. 'Sleep on it, if you like.'

'No. It's OK,' he said. 'I know. I think I've always known. I just never thought I'd get the chance.'

'Is that a yes?'

Chris nodded. 'As long as you're there too.'

'Don't worry,' I said. 'I will be.'

When Jayne came in on Thursday morning her eyes were brighter, her step lighter; she even managed what appeared to be a genuine smile.

Bob smiled too. In a way I'd never seen before.

'Lovely to see you both,' I said. 'Please, do sit down.'

They did as they were asked. Jayne placed her handbag firmly on the floor next to her.

'So, have you had a chance to discuss things since Monday?' I asked.

'Yes,' said Jayne. 'We have. Bob took it very well.'

She said it as if he'd had every right to be angry with her. Her whole demeanour still reeked of guilt. I wondered how many years it would take to get rid of that. If, indeed, she ever would. I turned to Bob. He had a pained expression on his face.

'How did you feel, Bob?'

'Angry. At him, for doing that to her. And for getting away with it. And sad that Jayne hadn't felt able to tell me before, instead of suffering in silence all these years.'

'You understand why she didn't, though? That it wasn't that she didn't trust you.'

'Oh aye. People didn't talk about this sort of thing in our day. Everything were swept under carpet. Can't say it did anyone much good, mind.'

'And now you do know, does it change anything?'

'I feel awful about what she's been through,' said Bob. 'But I suppose it's also a relief to know what were causing our problems. I understand it all now. And I know it's not me what's upset her.'

'He's a daft bugger,' Jayne said. 'He thought this were all about me not being happy with him.'

'Obviously a lot of feelings have come to the surface here, a lot of misunderstandings, and it will be good for you both to talk those through over the coming weeks. I need to tell you, though, that after having a discussion with my supervisor, I'm afraid I won't be able to continue as your counsellor after today.'

'Oh,' said Jayne, her face dropping for the first time that morning, 'that's a shame.'

'I know, and I'm really sorry about it, but there's a professional reason why it wouldn't be ethical for me to continue working with you.'

They both looked at me. It was a moment or two before I could get the words out.

'I know who your son is, Jayne,' I said.

She stared at me, her brow creased. 'You've traced him?'

'No. No, I didn't do anything at all. I didn't have to. I'd heard the same story, you see, but from the other side. From someone who'd been abandoned as a baby outside a doctor's surgery in Halifax.'

Jayne's mouth dropped open. 'One of your clients?'

I shook my head. 'No, it's not, actually. It's someone I know personally. If you don't want to hear any more, I completely understand. We can leave things there. A new counsellor will take over and support you through it all. You're only just starting to come to terms with what happened, and you may well feel that it would be too much to take things any further at this stage.'

'No,' said Jayne, her voice trembling. 'I want to know. I've always wanted to know. He's my son. I need to know that he's OK, that he's happy and healthy.'

'He is,' I said.

She shut her eyes for a second. I heard her long, deep outward breath.

'If you'd like to get in touch with him by letter, or meet up with him in person, it is possible to arrange that. And a colleague of mine will help to support you through it.'

'He wouldn't want to meet me, though, would he?' said Jayne. 'Not after what I did to him.'

'He does.'

She stared at me and shook her head. 'He's probably just saying that. People don't like to admit how they feel, do they? He probably hates me. I wouldn't blame him if he did.'

'He doesn't,' I said.

'How can you be so sure?'

I hesitated before replying, but I felt it would help Jayne to know.

'Because he's my husband.'

Jayne stared at me. Her eyes bulged wide. She put her hand to her mouth.

'I'm sorry it's come as such a shock,' I said. 'It was quite a shock for me too when you told me.'

'You're quite certain it's him?'

'Yes, the dates tie up and everything. Obviously, if you wanted to have DNA tests done, that could be arranged. Or you could do the whole thing through Social Services, get them to check their adoption records.'

She shook her head, still looking utterly bewildered. 'No,' she said. 'There's no need, is there? Not if you're certain.'

'I am.'

'So, you're my daughter-in-law?'

'Yes. That's why I can't continue being your counsellor, you see.'

'Well I'll be jiggered,' said Bob. 'I didn't see that one coming.'

I smiled at him. At both of them.

Jayne was the first to speak. 'What's his name?'

'Chris,' I said. 'Chris Bentley. The doctor's receptionist who found him was called Christine, that's why they chose it. On his original birth certificate he was given the surname of Illingworth, but the couple who adopted him changed it to their surname.'

'Are they still alive?' Jayne asked.

'His adoptive mother is. His adoptive father died several years ago. He had a very happy childhood with them and he's still close to his adoptive mother.'

Jayne turned to Bob, and a smile flickered onto her face. 'I've found him,' she said. 'I never thought it possible.'

Bob smiled and reached over to grasp her hand.

'Have you got a photograph?' she asked me. Her voice had a note of childlike excitement.

I reached for my bag. I had thought she might ask. I handed her a photograph of Chris and Matilda I'd taken on holiday the previous year.

A gasp caught in her throat, her hand trembled as she held it, and a moment later she was crying, properly crying. So much so that Bob took the photo from her and put it on the coffee table to stop it getting wet. We sat either side of her, holding a hand each, as if pumping forty-four years' worth of pain and suffering from her.

'He's still got his hair,' she sobbed, 'he's still got all that lovely dark hair.'

I nodded and smiled and brushed away my own tears.

'The little girl?' she asked.

'Your granddaughter, Matilda. She's nine.'

Jayne grasped hold of the rest of my arm. Her whole body was shaking. I put my arms around her. The woman who had given up everything to give birth to the man I loved.

'Thank you,' I whispered. 'Because if it wasn't for you, I wouldn't have either of them.'

'How will I explain to her why I abandoned her father?'

'You won't have to,' I said. 'We'll do that for you. And we'll tell her that giving up your child so they can have a better life is just about the most selfless thing you can do.'

Bob handed Jayne a tissue from the box on the table. She smiled at him and blew her nose. Took another and dabbed at her eyes. I decided not to tell her about Josh. Not yet, anyway. This was her moment of joy after so many years of hurt. I didn't want that tainted for her. There'd be plenty of time in the coming days and weeks to fill her in.

'So do I take it that you'd like to meet him?'

She bit her bottom lip and nodded. 'Yes,' she said. 'Yes, I would.'

From the Counselling Room

I found out he leaves comments on loads of pages on Facebook. Like the BBC Look North one. They'd posted a photo of their new weathergirl and he'd left a comment saying 'Probably would'. When I checked back, he'd done hundreds of them, any time someone posted a picture of a relatively attractive female. One of them was only fourteen, for fuck's sake.

So I packed my bags then and there. Left a note for him on the kitchen table. It said 'Probably wouldn't'.

30

'What are you thinking?' I asked Chris.

We were sitting in his car, which was parked outside our house. We hadn't gone anywhere yet. He hadn't even got as far as putting the key in the ignition. But already it seemed like a very long journey.

'What if I don't like her?'

'It's not obligatory to like her.'

'No, but usually guys who don't like their mothers are complete wankers.'

I smiled. 'Remember what Tania said? You might not feel anything at all for her. That would be perfectly normal.'

'It doesn't seem right, though. Feeling nothing for the woman who gave birth to you.'

He still hadn't used the 'M' word. Maybe he never would. It belonged very firmly to Barbara. I understood that, and I suspected Jayne would too. It was only Chris who seemed to feel bad about it.

'It really doesn't matter what you feel. What's important is that you're giving her the chance to meet you.'

'Yeah, I guess you're right,' said Chris. 'You usually bloody are.'

He was smiling as he said it. I smiled back.

'She's going to be overjoyed to see you. It's her moment, you don't have to do anything or feel anything, OK?'

He nodded. Pulled his seat belt across. Started the engine.

'Right then,' he said. 'Let's go.'

We'd agreed between us that the first meeting should be at Jayne and Bob's house. It needed to be somewhere private, and my counselling offices were too formal. Besides, I was off their case now. This was a personal thing.

They lived in Brighouse. The sort of neat 1930s semi-detached which I had been expecting. We pulled up behind their Rover on the tarmac drive. Chris took his seat belt off. Let go of a long sigh.

'It's going to be fine,' I said. 'Just be prepared for the fact that she'll probably be very emotional.'

He looked at me and nodded. We got out of the car and stood on the doorstep, Chris holding the bouquet of flowers he'd bought in town. He rang the bell. It started playing 'Greensleeves'.

Chris turned to me, unable to suppress a smile. 'Do you reckon there are gnomes in the back garden as well?' he whispered.

The door opened. Bob was standing there, his face running through the whole gamut of emotions, like some weird computer game where you have to click on the appropriate expression for the moment.

'Hi, Bob,' I said.

'Hello, Alison. And you must be Chris.' He offered his hand. Chris shook it. 'Pleased to meet you,' he said.

'I take it those aren't for me?' said Bob, pointing at the flowers. Chris managed a polite smile.

'Come in. Let me take your coats. She's in the lounge.'

I stepped inside. It felt as if we were waiting for an audience with the Queen. Jayne wasn't doing it to be grand or aloof, though. I suspected she was actually rooted to the spot through sheer terror.

We followed Bob into the lounge. Jayne was sitting in an armchair in the corner. She stood up. Her eyes locked on Chris. She bit her bottom lip and blinked furiously. I looked at Chris. Heard a stifled sound from inside. And a second later they were embracing in the middle of the room. I couldn't be sure who had moved first or how fast. But they were now locked together. Both crying, both holding on very tight.

I turned to Bob. Smiled at him through blurry eyes and squeezed his shoulder. He nodded in acknowledgement. We both knew this was their moment. We were merely onlookers. Although we also knew that our lives would be changed irrevocably by this.

It was a long time before anyone said anything. It was Jayne's voice which finally broke through the tears.

'I'm sorry,' she said to Chris, pulling away slightly and clasping his hands. 'I'm so sorry for what I did.'

He shook his head. 'Ali's told me what happened. You haven't got anything to apologise for.'

'Yes, I have,' she sobbed. 'It's unforgivable, what I did to you.'

'What, gave up everything just to give birth to me? I owe my life to you. That's pretty amazing in my book.'

'I couldn't look after you, not on my own,' said Jayne. 'I was worried that, if I'd kept you, they'd have come and taken you away from me. Taken you back to live with him and my sister. And I couldn't bear that, you see. Not after what he did to me.'

She took a tissue from the pocket in her blouse and wiped her eyes. The sixteen-year-old girl seemed so close to the surface that I could almost see her, peering anxiously out of Jayne's eyes.

'Thank you,' Chris said. 'You did the right thing. I was brought up by wonderful parents. I couldn't have been happier, really. And even when they told me about what had really happened, I didn't hate you. I have never hated you.'

Jayne started crying again. Or rather, started a fresh round of crying; she had never really stopped. Bob sat her down on the sofa. Chris sat on the other side of her. Jayne still had hold of his hand.

'Sorry,' she said. 'I'm not normally this emotional.'

'There's no need to apologise,' I said. 'This is massive. And it's all happened very quickly.'

'I never thought I'd see you again,' she said to Chris. 'I didn't even dare picture you in my head.'

'That's probably a bit of luck,' Chris said. 'You might have been disappointed.'

Bob chuckled. Jayne was perhaps going to take a bit longer to get used to her son's sense of humour.

'You look like my father,' she said. 'He had hair like yours.'

'So I don't look like –'

'No,' said Jayne quickly. 'Not at all.'

'Good,' Chris said. 'I was worried I might. And that it would upset you.'

'Nothing can upset me,' Jayne said. 'Not today.'

Chris smiled at her. 'Ali says your daughter's expecting.'

'Yes. In February. Everyone was saying it would be my first grandchild, yet all the time I knew that might not be true. Then, when I saw the photo of you and Matilda . . .'

Jayne's voice broke off again. I looked at Chris. We'd agreed we would tell her about Josh today. We didn't want to hide anything from her any longer.

'Matilda wasn't your first grandchild, actually,' said Chris.

Jayne looked across at him, the frown momentarily back on her face. I realised that she might be thinking we'd lost a baby or something.

'Chris has a son from a previous relationship,' I said quickly. 'His name's Josh.'

'Oh. How old is he?'

'He's sixteen.'

'So does he live with you or his mum?'

'He lives with us,' said Chris, 'only not at the moment.'

Jayne was still looking at him. As was Bob.

Chris fiddled with his watch strap before continuing. 'He ran away from home,' he said. 'About six months ago. His mum walked out on him when he was a baby and I brought him up on my own, but she came back last year and that led to a lot of problems. And then she told him I wasn't his father.'

'What an awful thing to say,' said Jayne.

'Yeah. He was gone the next morning. We've since found out that she was lying but, well, the damage had already been done.'

'So you've no idea where he is?'

'Not really,' said Chris. 'He could be anywhere.'

'And he hasn't been in touch at all?'

'No,' I said. 'He took his phone and his iPad with him. His girlfriend and I have been emailing and texting, but we've heard nothing back.'

'Does he know that it was a lie?' she asked.

'Yes, his mum even emailed him to apologise,' I said. 'Although, of course, we don't know if he's actually reading his emails.'

'Have you emailed him?' she said, turning to Chris. 'To tell him that he is your son, I mean.'

'No, not directly, everyone else got in first.'

'Well, I think you should,' said Jayne.

Chris raised his eyebrows, clearly taken aback by her directness.

'He needs to hear it from his father. He thought he wasn't yours. He's lost, you need to reclaim him.'

Chris looked down at his hands. 'Yes,' he said. 'I suppose I do.'

We stayed longer than I thought we would. Long enough for two rounds of tea and biscuits. Jayne had a biscuit barrel like Barbara's. It was strange, two people who were so different, who'd had such different lives, but who still shared the same taste in biscuit barrels.

When it was time to say our goodbyes – or rather, our 'au revoirs', as Jayne put it – she held Chris for a long time before she let him go.

She turned to me afterwards. 'The last time I said goodbye to him –' she began, before her voice broke.

'I know,' I said. 'But that's not going to happen again. We'll see you very soon. You can come to ours next. Meet Matilda, if you want.'

Jayne nodded. 'I'd like that,' she whispered. 'Thank you. And I hope you get Josh back soon.'

I nodded and kissed her softly on the cheek.

Bob shook my hand and then patted it gently. 'Thank you,' he said, 'for everything. You've made her one very happy lady.'

'Good,' I said. 'She deserves to be. And thank you for standing by her.'

'It's what you do, isn't it?' shrugged Bob.

'No, it's what you did,' I said. 'And not everyone would have done that.'

We got into the car, waved the obligatory number of times as we reversed down the drive, turned round and finally pulled away. I imagined Jayne standing there, tears rolling down her face. Bob holding her, patting her hand and seeing her safely back inside where he'd no doubt put the kettle on.

I glanced at Chris. He was staring straight ahead. His eyes still moist.

'You needn't have worried that you wouldn't feel anything, then.'

'No,' he said, shaking his head.

I spent a long time putting Matilda to bed that night. Lingering over the bedtime story, snuggling with her under the duvet, listening to her ramblings about what kind of frog Kermit might actually be.

She may have been our only child, but she'd never really been an only child because she had Josh. That was why we'd never had another one. There was no need, we already had two children. Only now, we didn't. Well, it didn't seem like it, anyway. Certainly not to Matilda.

'Where do you think he's sleeping?' she asked.

I knew better than to ask who she was talking about. I always understood who 'he' was referring to.

'He might have got himself a little flat,' I said.

'Don't they cost a lot of money?'

'He'd be renting it. I expect he's working.'

'Really?'

'Yeah, you need to work to be able to afford a roof over your head.'

'What if he hasn't found a job?'

'I don't know, love.'

'Will he be sleeping on a park bench like Mr Stink?'

'No, sweetheart. There are hostels for people who can't afford somewhere of their own.'

'What are hostels?'

'Big rooms where lots of people can sleep, maybe on bunk beds.'

'Urrgh. Who'd want to share a room with my smelly brother?'

I smiled at her, imagining how much Josh would be missing that kind of taunt.

'I'm sure he'll have made some friends,' I said.

Matilda nodded and twiddled a strand of hair. 'He won't have got a new girlfriend, though, will he?'

'No. Caitlin's his girlfriend. You like her, don't you?'

Matilda nodded. 'And I don't want my violin lessons to stop.'

Chris was sitting in his usual place at the kitchen table when I came down. It was a wonder Matilda hadn't drawn a picture of him yet with his head sticking out of the top of a Mac.

I glanced at the screen as I walked past. It wasn't the usual Missing People website, though. It was an email. One that started 'Dear Josh'.

Chris stood up. 'I'll make some coffee,' he said. 'Can you read it and tell me what you think?'

I nodded and sat down.

Dear Josh,

I'm sorry I haven't written before. Ali's so much better at it than I am that I tend to leave it to her. Or maybe that's just my excuse for being crap.

Anyway, something happened today to make me realise I should have done this a long time ago. I met my birth mother. Grandma and Grandad adopted me when I was a baby. They told me when I was Tilda's age. And later, when I was about thirteen, they told me why I was adopted. I was an abandoned baby. I was left outside a doctor's surgery after I was born. It's a pretty tough thing to find out and it screwed me up a bit when I was a teenager. Actually, it screwed me up a lot and not just when

I was a teenager. It probably explains a lot of things I've said and done that I shouldn't have, and a lot of things I haven't said and done that I should have. That's not an excuse. I'm just saying. But I am sorry I never told you or Ali. I'd told your mum about it and then she'd walked out on you as a baby. So I got it into my head that if I told anyone else, they'd walk out on me too.

Grandma finally told Ali about it when she was mad at me for missing Tilda's birthday party (I couldn't bear to be there because I was scared of losing her too). And Ali was brilliant, as she always is, and persuaded me to go to counselling with her. We'd been having problems because I blamed her for letting you see your mum, and I wouldn't talk to her about how I felt (yes, I know, 'Loser'). Anyway, not long after that, one of Ali's clients revealed that she had abandoned her baby outside a doctor's surgery in Halifax when she was sixteen. She'd run away from home to have me after she'd been raped by her brother-in-law. Which, again, is a pretty tough thing to hear.

So that was how I found her. Or rather, how Ali found her. Her name's Jayne. She's a nice lady (although she won't have heard of any of the bands you like, and I have a sneaking suspicion she votes Tory). And the first thing she did when I told her about you was ask if I'd written to let you know that you are my son.

So, here I am. I think your mum has already told you this, and I know Ali and Caitlin have told you too, but I'm going to say it now. I'm your father. I always have been and I always will be. And when your mum said that I wasn't, it was the scariest moment of my life. Because of all the people I couldn't bear to lose, you come top of the list. I still remember the day when I came home from work and found you alone and screaming in your cot and I knew at that moment that whatever I'd felt for you before was nothing to what I felt then, or what I would feel the next day or the one after that.

We've been through so much together since then. Somewhere deep inside I still knew I was your father, but when you left I realised that you weren't sure who you were any more. And because I know exactly how that feels, it hurt really bad and made me doubt myself.

I'm glad your mum set the record straight. But even if she'd been telling the truth the first time, it wouldn't have changed anything for me, least of all how much I love you.

It was pretty emotional to meet Jayne today, and I'm hugely grateful to her for sacrificing so much for me, but she's not my mum. Grandma is. It doesn't matter that she isn't my blood relative, in the same way that it wouldn't have mattered if you weren't my blood relative. Not to me, anyway.

But it turns out that you are my son, in every sense of the word. And the hole you have left in my life, in all of our lives, is so massive that even though we have pretended to go on with our lives, everything actually stopped the day you left and won't start again until you come home.

Tilda misses having a big brother to annoy, Ali misses having the piss taken out of her about her cardigans, and I miss being able to hang out playing guitar with my best buddy and pretend I'm a hell of a lot younger than I am. You have a grandma who can't bring herself to say your name because it hurts so much and a girlfriend (I truly have no idea how you managed to land such a bloody amazing girlfriend) who sits in your room every week to feel close to you when she comes to give your little sister a violin lesson. And now, you also have another grandma who, though she's never met you, has already started worrying about you.

When you're ready, Josh, your family is waiting for you.

Love,
Dad

I wiped the tears away and turned round to face Chris, who was standing in front of the Aga.

'Is it too long?' he asked.

'No,' I said. 'It's perfect.'

'Good. Then press "send" for me, please, before I chicken out.'

Tania smiled at us as we entered her room. She also raised her eyebrows slightly as Chris strode in and sat down, pulling up the sleeves of his jumper as he did so.

'So,' she said, 'how are we today?'

'We're good,' Chris said. 'We're fighting.'

'Not fighting each other, I hope?'

'No,' said Chris with a smile. 'I mean, I'm fighting. And I think I'm finally on the same team as Ali.'

'Well, I'm bloody glad to hear it,' she said. 'What brought this on?'

'A few home truths from Jayne, my birth mother.'

'You see,' said Tania, turning to me, 'we go to all this trouble with our training and qualifications when all they actually need is a kick up the arse from their mum.'

I smiled at her. Chris smiled too.

'I've emailed Josh,' he said. 'Told him everything. Particularly how screwed up I was with the whole identity thing.'

'Do you think he'll come home?'

'I don't know. That's up to him. But at least he knows I care now.'

'And what about your birth mother? Are you going to see her again?'

'Yeah, I am. We've invited her round for Josh's birthday.'

Tania raised an eyebrow.

'Matilda wanted to do it,' I said. 'We think it's important for her that we mark it, rather than pretending none of us are thinking about it.'

'Are you sure you're up to it?'

'Yeah,' said Chris. 'I mean, it'll be tough and everything, but I'm going to be there this time. I'm not going to leave Ali to deal with it on her own.'

Tania turned to look at me. 'Is that what you wanted to hear?'

I nodded.

'Good. And what about the two of you? What happens now?'

'We struggle on together,' I said, 'just like everyone else.'

'No happy-ever-after glitter dust?'

'No,' I said. 'Just a bit more talking. A bit more understanding.'

'A bit more sex, hopefully,' said Chris.

I smiled at him and shook my head.

'That's what I like to hear,' said Tania. 'Someone being embarrassingly honest in the counselling room. So what do you think is the best way forward now?'

'We go away and work at it,' said Chris. 'Ali knows someone I can go and see to talk through all my stuff.'

'And you're prepared to do that?'

'Yeah. We're going to start looking around at houses too. We're not going to put ours on the market just yet, we're not sure it's the right timing for Tilda, but maybe next year, when things have settled down a bit.'

'And do you promise to love and cherish this woman and tell her all the stuff that's going on inside your head, even when it's dark and scary?'

'I do,' said Chris.

'And do you promise to love and cherish this man and take your mind off everybody else's problems long enough to remind yourself what a top catch you are?'

'I do,' I said with a smile.

'Marvellous. I'm very happy to pronounce you in a better state now than when you first arrived. You may kiss your spouse.'

I turned to smile at Chris. He got up, walked over and kissed me on the lips right in front of Tania.

'Thank you both very much,' she said. 'If you do wish to come and see me again at any point, I'll be here for you. In the meantime, please bugger off so I can help the poor sods who are quaking in their boots in the waiting room out there, having no idea what they are letting themselves in for.'

Chris shook Tania's hand and thanked her warmly. I gave her a hug, unable to manage any words.

'Now go,' she said, shooing us away, 'before you make my mascara run.'

I followed Chris out of the door. The couple in the waiting room were younger than us. I recognised the expressions on their faces. I smiled at them as we walked past.

'She's good,' I said to them. 'A bit off the wall, but good. You're in very safe hands.'

From the Counselling Room

I'm not a food snob, not in the slightest, and it's not like I'm one of those people who won't ever eat processed food, but I asked her one day if she'd mind getting something a bit healthier for my sandwiches than Dairylea, and she said, 'Of course, love. I'll get some Dairylea Light.'

31

I woke up. The realisation of what day it was and who wasn't there to celebrate it crushed me the instant I opened my eyes. One year ago, I would never have imagined how an empty room in the house could make so much noise. But then, one year ago I didn't know a lot of things.

It was a bright morning outside. The sun was already forcing its way through the curtains. I turned to look at Chris. I hadn't realised until that point that he was awake too.

'Did you get any sleep?' I asked.

'Not much.'

'It doesn't feel right, does it? Without him.'

Chris shook his head. 'Do you think it ever will?'

'I don't know. I remember reading an interview with a woman whose son had been murdered. She said it was still the first thing she thought about when she woke up and the last thing she thought about at night. But that, in between, there were sometimes periods when she'd go for a few hours without thinking about it.'

'I know it sounds awful,' said Chris, 'but at least, if you know what's happened, you can mourn. This not knowing, it's horrible.'

'He would never have –'

'No, I know. I'm sure of that too. Well, as sure as I can be, anyway.'

'Where do you think he is?'

I'd never asked the question before. Nor had Chris, although I suspected he thought about it as much as I did.

'A big city somewhere, I guess. One that he can lose himself in.'

'That's what Jayne did,' I said. 'After she left you. She got on a train to Leeds.'

Chris was quiet. Maybe I shouldn't have mentioned it. I eased my body closer to his, wrapped my arm around his chest.

'It's weird, isn't it?' said Chris. 'That both of them ran away from home when they were sixteen. Both because of me.'

'Both because they loved you,' I said, rubbing my hand up and down his arm.

'I guess that's one way of looking at it.'

'It's the only way.'

Chris kissed me on the shoulder. 'Thank you,' he said.

'What for?'

'Being bloody brilliant and putting up with me.'

'You've been through an incredibly tough time.'

'Yeah, and so have you. But no one's been there for you, have they?'

'They are now, though,' I said. 'That's what matters.'

He kissed me again. On the lips this time. 'So how are we going to do this?'

'We're going to get up and deal with it together and simply get through the day the best we can.'

We were interrupted by the sound of Matilda bursting out of her bedroom. She didn't run straight into our room, as she usually did. It was another door that we heard opening and shutting first, before a small, forlorn face appeared in our room, looking much as it would do if Santa hadn't come in the night.

'Come here, sweetheart,' I said.

She climbed onto the bed and buried herself tightly between our bodies.

'Wherever he is,' I told her, 'he's thinking of us right now. And he knows that we love him very much.'

'So why isn't he here?' she sobbed.

'Maybe there's some place else he needs to be right now,' I said. 'But the important thing is that we're here for him. And we'll save his presents, just like we said.'

'Are we still going to have a party tea?' she asked.

'Yes, love.'

'And can we still eat his birthday cake?'

'Of course,' I said with a smile.

'We'll save one slice for Josh, though, won't we?'

I looked at Chris.

'Tell you what,' he said to Matilda, 'we'll save two. Because you know what he's like, nicking things off your plate.'

Matilda smiled through the tears.

It was the best we could hope for.

The one good thing about the post coming later these days was that it avoided the crushing disappointment of there not being many cards on the mat on the morning of your birthday. Or, in our case, of being confronted with greetings for someone who wasn't there before we'd even got down the stairs.

The emptiness of the house wasn't so easy to escape from, though. We put the radio on, Matilda chatted away as usual, I even made a cooked breakfast in the hope it would distract from the quietness. It didn't really work, though. Especially as Matilda mentioned how much Josh loved hash browns within a few minutes of sitting down.

We waited until after breakfast to tell her. Chris had been adamant that he would do it. I still wanted to be there, though. Not being sure how she would react.

'It's not just Grandma and Caitlin coming this afternoon,' said Chris. 'We've invited someone new for you to meet.'

'Who?' asked Matilda.

Chris looked at me. I nodded.

'Although Grandma brought me up, she didn't actually give birth to me,' Chris said. 'She and Grandad adopted me when I was a baby.'

Matilda frowned at him. 'Does that mean she's not my real grandma?'

'She is your grandma,' said Chris. 'And she's still my mum. But what it means is that you've got another grandma. Grandma Jayne.'

'Why haven't I ever met her before?'

'Because I've only just met her. She didn't know where I was, and I didn't know where she was. Only Mummy found her again.'

'Why did she have you adopted?'

'Because she couldn't look after me on her own, love. She

was very young and didn't have her family around to support her.'

'Why not?'

'Her family wasn't very nice, love. So she moved away. She's got her own family now.'

'Are they coming too?'

'Her husband Bob is. Her daughter lives in Australia.'

'Is Bob my grandad?'

'No, love. She met him after she had me,' Chris continued. 'He's not my dad.'

Matilda was starting to look confused. Which was hardly surprising, given the circumstances.

'They're lovely, sweetheart,' I said, 'and they'll make a great big fuss of you. You're very special to them, OK?'

She nodded. 'Is Grandma Jayne Josh's grandma too?'

'Yes,' I said.

'Good. I'll get to meet her first. Do you think she'll bring presents?'

Caitlin arrived first. It was odd seeing her without her violin. Difficult, too. Because nobody could pretend she was here for any other reason than for Josh's birthday.

'Hello, love,' I said, as she stepped into the hall.

I went to kiss her on the cheek but, before I could, she threw her arms around me and burst into tears. Chris took Matilda, who had been hovering behind me, into the kitchen and closed the door.

'I'm sorry,' she said when she eventually looked up. 'I was so determined not to do that.'

'It's OK. We've all had a go already this morning. It's your turn.'

She managed a hint of a smile.

'Do you want to go upstairs?'

She nodded, slipped her boots off and followed me silently up to Josh's bedroom. We sat on the end of his bed, Caitlin clutching the duvet with one hand.

'I've still got his T-shirt,' she said. 'The one you gave me. Sometimes I think I can still smell him on it, though maybe that's just my imagination.'

'It doesn't matter which it is,' I said. 'As long as you've got him in some small way.'

'I really hoped –'

'I know,' I said. 'I did too.'

'The thing is, if he hasn't come home for his birthday, what is he going to come home for?'

'For us. Probably for you, mainly.'

Caitlin shrugged and wiped her eyes.

'You know we'd understand –'

'Please don't,' she said. 'That's all I get from Mum.'

'She probably just wants you to be happy,' I said. 'You so deserve that.'

'I will be,' she said. 'When he comes home.'

Barbara looked old when she arrived. It was the first time it had really hit me, how much of a toll this had taken on her. She might still be the rock of the family. But the fact was, she was made of something soft. And she was crumbling underneath.

'Ooh, it's blowy out there today,' she said as she wiped her eyes.

She'd only come from Chris's car. I knew she didn't want me to say anything, though. I gave her a hug, feeling the slightness of her frame beneath her jacket.

'Are they here yet?' she asked.

'No, just Caitlin. Are you sure this is OK? It's a lot to ask, I know.'

'It's the right thing for Chris,' she said, squeezing my hand. 'So it's fine by me.'

She went through to the lounge. Matilda ran up and hugged her. Caitlin stood up and gave her a kiss. It was like a wartime scene. Different generations of women left at home, mourning the young men who were missing.

Barbara went to put her present with the pile of others, which were arranged in the corner, as if underneath an invisible birthday tree. Chris came in behind me. I squeezed his hand. It felt like someone should say something, read a poem, or reminisce about Josh's early years. No one said a word, though. Because we couldn't mourn. Only miss. And there weren't really words for that.

I went to put the kettle on. Barbara started chatting about the weather. Matilda showed Caitlin a drawing she had done at school. Life went on, the best it could. It was all we could do.

It was about ten minutes later that there was a knock on the front door. It was daft, really. We were all expecting someone, and yet I knew we were all thinking exactly the same thing. I looked out of the window. Jayne and Bob's car was parked further along the lane.

'They're here,' I said. Just to make it clear who it wasn't.

Matilda followed Chris and me into the hall. She was holding my hand rather more tightly than usual. Chris opened the door. Jayne and Bob stood there, looking for all the world as if they had stumbled on some kind of gingerbread house in the woods and wanted to see if it was actually real.

'Hello,' Chris said, 'good to see you again.' He kissed Jayne on the cheek.

She grabbed hold of his forearms and smiled a lot. She didn't seem to want to let go. And then she caught sight of Matilda and let out a gasp.

'Matilda,' I said, 'this is your Grandma Jayne.'

Matilda went forward of her own accord. Jayne bent down and put her arms around her. She shut her eyes and held her for a very long time. When she did open them again, they were wet with tears.

'Josh isn't here, but we're still having a party tea,' Matilda told her.

'Well, that sounds lovely. Is it OK if we join you?'

Matilda nodded.

'And this is Grandma Jayne's husband, Bob,' I said.

Bob stepped forward and shook her hand.

'I know you're not my real grandad,' said Matilda, 'but do you mind if I call you Grandad Bob? Because it's easier, and I haven't got any grandads at all.'

'That would be lovely,' Bob said.

I took their coats. I could see Jayne checking her face in the mirror.

'Barbara's really looking forward to meeting you,' I said to her.

She nodded. I wasn't sure if she was actually capable of speech yet.

Matilda led them through to the lounge.

Barbara stood up.

'Grandma, meet Grandma Jayne,' Matilda announced.

They looked at each other for a second, perhaps recognising the differences first before they both saw through them to the thing they shared.

Jayne stepped forward, and I could see her hands shaking. A moment or two later those same hands were around Barbara's back. Holding her, squeezing her tight.

I gestured to Caitlin to take Matilda out of the room. She nodded, took her hand and asked if she could go and have a look at her bedroom. They left the room. I wasn't sure what emotions would come out here, but I wanted to make sure they were free to say anything which needed to be said. I took hold of Chris's hand, struggling to imagine how weird this must be for him.

'Thank you,' Jayne said, in little more than a whisper. 'For looking after him for me.'

'He was your gift to us,' said Barbara. 'I should be thanking you.'

They looked at each other, smiled and hugged again.

'I used to dream he'd be looked after by someone like you,' Jayne said. 'That he'd grow up with two parents who would dote on him.'

'Oh, we doted on him all right,' said Barbara. 'Didn't spoil him, mind. That's not a nice thing to do to a child.'

'Well, he's turned out lovely,' said Jayne, turning to grasp Chris's hand. 'Absolutely lovely.'

Chris was pulled into a group hug.

I smiled at Bob. 'Tea or coffee for Jayne?' I whispered.

'Tea, please,' he said as he followed me through to the kitchen. 'She doesn't want Barbara to think she's trying to replace her,' he said.

'I know,' I replied, 'and she doesn't. She thinks it's good for Chris. And if it's good for Chris, then she's happy. She's like any mum, really.'

Bob nodded. 'I've booked flights to Australia,' he said. 'For February. For both of us.'

I turned and stared at him. 'But I thought –'

Bob shook his head. 'I went on one of those fear of flying courses you mentioned,' he said. 'I suppose I realised that, however scared I was, it couldn't compare with how scared Jayne must have been when she gave birth on her own like that.'

I gave him a little hug. 'That's brilliant. Well done you.'

'Daft thing was, I actually quite enjoyed it in the end, when we went up on our little flight.'

'Australia's a bit further than that, mind,' I said with a smile.

'Oh aye, but I'll have Jayne with me, won't I? And we'll be going to see our grandchild.'

'Have you told Cassie about Chris?'

'Yep. She's made up about it, having a brother and being an auntie and that. Says there's an open invitation to you all to come over.'

'That's lovely. We'll give her a chance to settle down with the baby first, though.'

'Yes. And maybe your Josh will be back by then.'

I smiled at him and nodded.

We went back through to the lounge. Barbara was showing Jayne the photo albums she'd brought full of snaps of Chris's childhood. They were taking it in turn to ooh and aahh over how curly his hair was. Chris was sitting at the end of the sofa squirming ever so slightly and looking about sixteen. I imagined what Josh would say, if he were here. How he'd rib him about it. Maybe that was what Chris was thinking too.

We had the party tea, as planned. No one mentioned that the guest of honour was missing, just as nobody mentioned the pile of unopened presents in the corner, but his absence hung over the whole proceedings.

'Can we do the cake now?' asked Matilda, when the last of the tea things had been cleared away.

I glanced at Chris.

He nodded.

I couldn't help thinking we should have rehearsed this. I had no idea how we were actually going to do it. I needn't have worried, though. Matilda was very clear. The cake was standing on the worktop. It was round and smothered in a chocolate ganache. I'd told Matilda that people stopped doing their age in candles when they reached seventeen. She'd looked at me dismissively and insisted on putting one on. A purple one. I lit it now and carried the cake back to the table. It was doubtful if so many breaking voices had ever sung 'Happy Birthday' at the same time.

Matilda looked up at me with a frown when we got to the end. I knew what she was wondering.

'You do it for him,' I said.

She shut her eyes and blew.

Caitlin shut her eyes at the same time. I didn't need to ask what either of them was wishing for.

Jayne and Bob left first, with hugs and kisses all round and an offer to have Matilda to visit very soon. We waved them off before shutting the door.

'What did you think?' I asked Matilda.

'I liked them,' she said. 'It means I've got more family, which is good, because it was feeling a bit small.'

She said it in the breezy, throwaway-comment style favoured by nine-year-olds. I tried very hard to take it like that.

Matilda dragged Caitlin back to the lounge for one last game of Connect Four before she went.

'Well, I thought she was very nice,' said Barbara. 'And him too.'

'Good,' said Chris. 'They weren't too BBC2 sitcom for you?'

Barbara gave him the kind of reproachful look only a mother can.

'I like her too,' said Chris. 'Just not as much as my real mum.'

I left them hugging in the hallway. I went upstairs, supposedly to go to the toilet. I didn't really need to go, though. I took a detour instead. Found myself standing in Josh's room. Breathing him in and breathing him out.

'Everyone's going now,' I whispered. 'They all send their love. It hasn't been easy but we've survived. I think we're going to be OK. Not brilliant but OK. And sometimes, you know, OK has to be enough.'

I lay there in the stillness some hours later. We'd gone to bed early, because it was easier than staying up. You would have thought that, having imagined it so many times, I wouldn't have trusted myself. But I knew as soon as I heard the key in the front door that, this time, it was for real.

In a moment, I would wake Chris, would leap out of bed and hurtle downstairs. Matilda would be woken by all the commotion and run down to give Josh the two slices of birthday cake we'd saved and insist he eat them and open his presents right that minute.

Later, I would phone Barbara and listen to her tears on the other end of the line. And I'd text Lydia – with Chris's blessing – and smile when I received the 'Thank you' text back.

Later still, I would drive Josh over to Caitlin's and sit sobbing in the car as they hugged each other to death on the doorstep.

All that was to come.

But for now, it was simply enough to know that he was home.

ACKNOWLEDGEMENTS

Huge thanks to the following people: my original editor Jo Dickinson who was with me all the way during the conception of this novel and the 'labour' of writing it, and my new editor Kathryn Taussig who made sure everything went smoothly at the tricky bit where it emerged kicking and screaming into the world at the end! Also to the whole team at Quercus for their hard work, energy and enthusiasm; my agent Anthony Goff for his expertise and advice and everyone at David Higham Associates; Relate (www.relate.org.uk) and Missing People (www.missingpeople.org.uk) for providing invaluable research information and who both do tremendous work; my fellow authors on Twitter for answering the odd weird question and being supportive, encouraging and thoroughly entertaining colleagues in our virtual writing room; my family and friends for their ongoing support and encouragement; my wonderful son Rohan for always wanting to know what was going to happen next and for all his ideas (you and Matilda really would be the best of friends!); and my husband Ian, who had no idea what he was letting himself in for when he invited me back to see his photographic portfolio twenty-three years ago (I never said living with a writer would be easy!).

And you, my readers, for buying my books, borrowing them from libraries, spreading the word and sending the emails, Facebook messages or tweets saying how much you enjoyed one of my books, which have kept me writing at 12.30 a.m. on numerous occasions!

If you'd like to get in touch, please contact me via:

www.lindagreenauthor.com

🐦 @lindagreenisms

f @AuthorLindaGreen

📷 @lindagreenbooks

Discover the heartbreaking and emotional story of two strangers who change each other's lives . . .

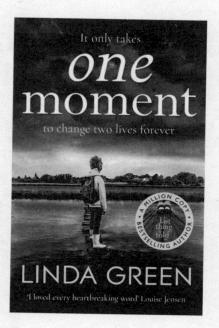

A BBC Radio 2 Book Club pick

Out now in paperback, eBook and audio

Quercus

Read the Richard & Judy bestselling novel
of long-hidden family secrets

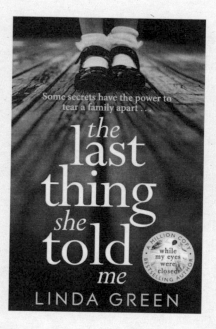

'A tale of love, loss and sacrifice with the cleverest twist'
Milly Johnson

Out now in paperback, eBook and audio

Quercus

**More nail-biting psychological drama
from Linda Green**

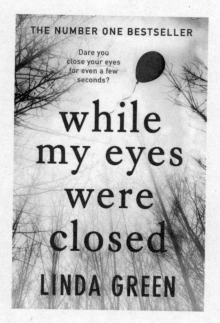

'Terrifyingly plausible'
Sunday Mirror

Out now in paperback, eBook and audio

Quercus

A heartbreaking story of love against all odds
from the No.1 bestselling author

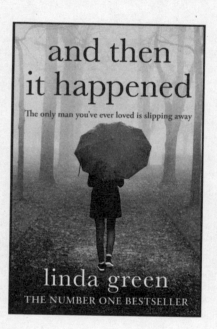

'Utterly riveting'
Closer

Out now in paperback, eBook and audio

Quercus

Discover more from the million-copy
bestselling author

LINDA GREEN

Visit
www.lindagreenauthor.com

for

Book extracts

*

Exclusive extra content

*

**And to subscribe to the mailing list for
exclusive book news and giveaways**

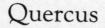

Quercus